Ella Grace _____, mother of five fur-_____te, read, cook the occasion_____vel when she can. She's thrilled to be writing a series based in her home state of Alabama.

Ella G_____ is the pen name for New York Times bestselling author Christy Reece, author of the sexy and suspenseful *Last Chance Rescue* series.

Praise for *The Last Chance Rescue* series:

'Sizzling romance and fraught suspense fill the pages as the novel races toward its intensely riveting conclusion' *Publishers Weekly, Starred Review*

'Romantic suspense has a major new star!' *Romantic Times*

'A passionate and vivacious thrill-ride! . . . I feel like I've been on an epic journey after finishing it . . . Exquisite' *Joyfully Reviewed*

'A very compelling romantic suspense. The romance is sensuous, and the story moves along at an excellent pace with a lot of drama and violence. The characters are distinctly drawn, and the pages are filled with intrigue and emotional intensity' *Romance Reviews Today*

'Steamy sex scenes, intense fighting scenes, the sensation of struggling to survive, edge-of-your-seat feelings, and finding your true self make this mind-blowing book a must read story!' *Coffee Time Romance & More*

'A heart-racing tale from start to finish . . . I loved every minute of it!' *The Romance Reader's Connection*

'[A] brilliantly plotted book. The love story, as always, is hot and emotive and balanced well with the exciting and well-crafted mystery. Her main characters are vulnerable yet strong, and even the villains are written with skillful and delicate brush strokes haunting your mind long after the book is done' *Fresh Fiction*

By Ella Grace

The Wildefire Series
Midnight Secrets
Midnight Lies

Midnight Secrets

ELLA GRACE

ETERNAL
ROMANCE

First published in the United States of America in 2013
by Ballantine Books, an imprint of The Random House Publishing Group,
a division of Random House, Inc.

First published in Great Britain in 2013
by ETERNAL ROMANCE,
an imprint of HEADLINE PUBLISHING GROUP

1

Cataloguing in Publication Data is available from the British Library

ISBN 978 0 7553 9532 3

Offset in Sabon by Avon DataSet Ltd, Bidford-on-Avon, Warwickshire

Printed and bound by CPI Group (UK) Ltd, Croydon, CR0 4YY

Headline's policy is to use papers that are natural, renewable and
recyclable products and made from wood grown in sustainable forests.
The logging and manufacturing processes are expected to conform
to the environmental regulations of the country of origin.

HEADLINE PUBLISHING GROUP
An Hachette UK Company
338 Euston Road
London NW1 3BH

www.eternalromancebooks.co.uk
www.headline.co.uk
www.hachette.co.uk

To Mae Blossom Reece,
my writing companion
and best friend for thirteen years.
Forever in my heart, angel.

Midnight Secrets

PROLOGUE

Beckett Wilde stumbled from his car and inhaled, taking fragrant honeysuckle-scented air deep into his lungs. Thunder rumbled like a far-off freight train. Brilliant streaks of jagged lightning lit up the ink-black sky. He took in another deep breath. Rain was coming. The drenching that had been threatening for days was finally on its way. And the humidity would be a thousand times worse. Summertime in Midnight was always hotter than a firecracker lit at both ends, but this year was breaking all sorts of records.

Wiping the sweat from his brow, Beckett shook his head to clear it and then narrowed his eyes to focus on the large structure in front of him. Hopefully by the time he made it inside, he wouldn't feel like he was going to throw up all that good Kentucky bourbon he'd just guzzled.

As he weaved toward the three-story mansion that had been his home since his birth, he cursed his lack of coordination. Time was when he'd been able to throw back a half dozen bourbons before he felt even the slightest difference. Tonight he'd begun to feel the effects after two. Damn, he was getting old.

Actually, it was probably his lack of drinking that

had created his low tolerance. With Maggie and the girls, he didn't feel the need to soften the edges of reality. They made getting up every morning something to look forward to—not dread.

The argument with Maggie at the country club had taken him off guard. Half the town had been there to witness their spat. By the time he got to Shorty's Bar a mile down the road, the other half knew about it, too. Damnable busybodies.

A few drinks in, he had begun to regret leaving her there like that. A wise man would've taken her home and had an adult conversation. Problem was, he and wisdom only had a passing acquaintance. Most times he did dumb stuff and Maggie would roll her eyes, shake her head, and forgive him. Being the handsome and charming only child of one of the oldest families in Alabama, Beckett got out of trouble about as easy as he got into it. Somehow Maggie loved him in spite of all that.

She had been in a tizzy even before they'd left the house. Their triplet daughters, Savannah, Samantha, and Sabrina, had left for summer camp this morning, and the girls had almost driven her crazy with their excitement and anxiety. Since Beckett had left for work early, he'd missed the brunt of their exuberant enthusiasm. He couldn't say he regretted that. He adored his young'uns, but three overexcited ten-year-olds and a frazzled, exasperated woman buzzing around the house in a frenzy was something he could handle for only a few minutes at a time.

Poor Maggie had been exhausted when he'd gotten home. He had hoped a night out at the country club would've put her in a better frame of mind. And it probably would have if he hadn't flirted with the new cocktail waitress. But those kinds of antics usually floated off his wife's back. She knew he wasn't serious. Hell yeah, he'd been a rabble-rouser and womanizer years ago, but once he'd fallen for Maggie, he'd given up those ways. Didn't mean he didn't like to charm the ladies. He was Southern, born and bred—stuff like that was ingrained in him.

The girls were gone. Even his daddy, who lived in the guesthouse out back, was in Mobile for the weekend. They were alone . . . that hadn't happened in a month of Sundays. Instead of drowning his troubles in bourbon, he should've taken advantage of this opportunity to woo his wife again. Didn't she know she was his life?

Cursing his selfishness, Beckett sped up, almost running the rest of the way to the side of the house, where he always entered.

The lights were off, but since it was going on midnight, Maggie had probably gone on to bed. He pushed open the door, giving little thought to why it wasn't locked. In Midnight, folks didn't have to lock their doors—one of the many advantages to living in a small town.

Beckett was in the middle of the kitchen when the first hint of something not being right hit him. It was too quiet. He told himself that the absence of his daughters just made the house feel different.

Assured that his uneasiness was unfounded, Beckett took another step, then froze. No, it was more than an empty house. The silence was eerily quiet, almost ominous. He shifted his gaze to the left and saw that the light above the kitchen island wasn't on. Since this was the only light in the house that was kept on at night, he began to wonder. Then he noticed that the fridge wasn't humming and the whir of all the ceiling fans on the first floor was absent and the reason for the silence hit him.

Hell, no wonder. The electricity was out—it was nothing more than that.

He dropped his keys on the counter. Though it was pitch dark, he knew every nook and cranny of this house. To the left of the counter was a small desk. Beckett opened the desk drawer and withdrew a flashlight. He clicked it on and pulled his cellphone from the clip at his belt. Maggie was probably asleep and didn't even know about the outage. If the power company couldn't come out till tomorrow, it was going to be a long, hot night.

As he punched in numbers, a sound in the next room stopped him. Lifting his head, he looked toward the entrance to the dining room. "Mags? How long's the power been out?"

No answer. Frowning, Beckett stepped forward. "Are you still mad at me? I'm sorry, honey, you know how I—"

Lightning flashed through the large bay window, casting light in the room and revealing a huddled body on the floor. Maggie!

Beckett rushed forward. "Maggie? Honey? What happened?" He fell to his knees beside her, barely noticing the warm wetness that seeped through the fabric of his pants.

Fear spiraled through him as he touched her face, which was soft and warm. His fingers went to her neck, feeling for a pulse. Nothing. Shock and denial screaming silently through him, Beckett reached for the cellphone he had dropped. An ambulance . . . he had to call an ambulance. Maggie was young and healthy—whatever had happened, they could save her. Dear Lord, he couldn't lose her . . . he couldn't!

"Don't do that."

Beckett whirled around. A man stood at the door.

Though it was dark, he had no trouble recognizing him—the man had been in his house many times over the years. "What did you do?" Beckett whispered hoarsely.

"I never meant this to happen."

Rage and disbelief shot through him. "You bastard!" Jumping to his feet, Beckett lunged toward the man he'd once called friend. A searing pain in the back of his head stopped him mid-flight. Stunned, Beckett crashed to the floor.

A deep, familiar voice rumbled above him. "Go turn the power back on. I've got another idea. This will work out better anyway."

Facedown on the hardwood floor, Beckett tried to move. The agony in his head intensified, stopping all movement. He closed his eyes and then opened them again when he heard voices. A small, insistent whisper in his pain-blurred mind told him to get up—that something had happened—but his brain wouldn't function properly. The pain was unbearable.

"What . . . happened?" Beckett mumbled, barely able to recognize the voice as his own.

Bright light flooded the room. Beckett blinked; finally able to raise his head slightly, he tried to focus. "What happened?" he asked again.

The deep voice above him answered, "You killed your wife . . . that's what happened."

"What?" Beckett whispered.

"Nobody's going to believe that," another familiar voice whispered.

"They'll believe what I tell them to believe."

Beckett knew he had to get up. Something was seriously wrong. Maggie . . . he had to get to Maggie. Dear Lord, what had they done to his Maggie? He tried to lift himself from the floor. Another pain seared the back of his head, more agonizing than before. Beckett's mouth opened to scream out with agony, rage, and betrayal . . . only a slight whimper emerged. Thick darkness blanketed his mind, cloaking him in its smothering, consuming embrace. Then nothing.

CHAPTER ONE

EIGHT YEARS LATER

"Savvy, have you seen my pearl necklace?"

"I think I saw it on your dresser yesterday," Savannah answered. A huff of exasperation followed. "My hair still won't lie down."

A soft snort of disgust and then, "I can't believe you two are acting so silly over some dumb dance."

Smiling, his arms crossed, Daniel Wilde sat patiently outside the bedrooms of his granddaughters and listened to their excited chatter. Tonight's dance was a special event for all of them—a benchmark moment they would all remember.

Savannah, shy and much too serious about most things, had surprised them all last month when she had firmly announced that she would be going to the dance. As it was her senior prom, she'd stated, it was a rite of passage for any teenager.

Her sister Samantha had been delighted to hear that news. Of course, there'd never been any question of whether Samantha would attend. The most popular girl in school, she had turned down at least a half dozen invitations before finally accepting a date from the star basketball player.

Their sister Sabrina, rebellious and sure to do the opposite of what people wanted or expected, had ada-mantly announced that she would most definitely not be going. Thankfully, and with much coercion from her sisters, she had changed her mind.

Uniquely individual, but in many ways so wonder-fully the same, the girls were the joy of his life. Dear Lord, how he loved them.

After Beckett's and Maggie's deaths, he had assumed responsibility for their care. Though the tragedy of his son's and daughter-in-law's deaths had made him want to lie down and die, too, he hadn't been able to wallow in his grief. Three devastated ten-year-old girls had needed him. Little did they know that they had probably saved his life.

Raising the girls hadn't been easy, but any sacrifices he'd made had been worthwhile. Other than the occa-sional advice he'd sought from some of his female rela-tives and friends, Daniel hadn't wanted or needed help. People had come out of the woodwork offering their assistance. A few had even offered to take one or two of the girls to raise as their own. Daniel had vehemently refused. Not just because he didn't want the sisters sep-arated or because they were his granddaughters. He'd had to do this for Maggie and Beckett. He'd failed them in so many ways. Taking care of their daughters was the very least he could do. And though he still grieved over the loss, he didn't regret one moment of raising these amazing young women.

Hearing the whispers and giggles go silent, Daniel called out, "You girls about ready? I want to get some pictures before your beaus get here."

Savannah came from Samantha's room. The girls' bedrooms all connected with one another—something their mother, Maggie, had insisted on when she learned she was having triplet daughters. She had said they would be one another's best friends. She had been right.

Though each girl, especially Samantha, had her own friends, the sisters were extremely close.

Daniel beamed at the demure but lovely picture Savannah made. "You look beautiful."

The uncertain expression changed to a glowing smile. "Thanks, Granddad. I'm glad you talked me into buying a new one instead of wearing last year's recital dress." Slender, graceful hands smoothed down the off-white satin. "I like it even better than I did when I tried it on at the store."

Before Daniel could speak, Samantha, a vision in ice blue, came through the doorway. "That off-white color looks great on you, Savvy."

Savannah threw her an appreciative grin. "Thanks for picking it out for me. I just wish I could do something with my hair."

"You need to stop trying to tame it. Let it go free."

"Or get it cut off, like I did."

Sabrina exited her bedroom and Daniel almost swallowed his tongue. The girls had gone shopping by themselves and this was his first look at their attire. Savannah and Samantha had chosen to wear elegant evening gowns. Samantha's off-the-shoulder dress was a bit more daring than Savannah's square-cut neckline with thin shoulder straps, but still respectable. The outfit Sabrina had opted for was neither elegant nor subtle. The only description he could come up with was "harem costume." In fact, the last time he'd seen this kind of costume was a rerun of *I Dream of Jeannie*. Though surely Barbara Eden hadn't worn combat boots.

"Sabrina Sage Wilde, what in the name of all that's good and righteous are you wearing?"

Everyone turned at the shrill voice behind them. Gibby Wilcox, Daniel's second cousin twice removed, had arrived. He had deliberately told her to come half an hour late. Gibby was a good-hearted woman but her nervous fluttering could wear thin at the best of times. He hadn't thought having her advise three teenaged girls on the proper attire for a prom was necessary. Now he wasn't sure he had made the right decision.

"I think she looks fabulous," Savannah defended.

Before Daniel could comment, Samantha nodded emphatically. "I agree. Very avant-garde."

Always one another's staunchest allies, as usual the sisters banded together. Daniel watched Sabrina's expression. The tilted chin spoke of defiance and the sparkle in her eyes told him she was waiting for him to tell her she couldn't go. He also recognized the vulnerability behind the bravado—an emotion she tried so desperately to hide from the rest of the world.

As the shock wore off, Daniel took a moment to reevaluate Sabrina's costume. Even with her midriff showing, the outfit was actually much less revealing than both her sisters'. Though demure, Savannah's gown hugged her slender figure like a second skin, and Samantha's gown, albeit decent, showed a bit more cleavage than he was truly comfortable with. Thankfully the wrap around her shoulders gave her more coverage. Sabrina was known as the "Wilde child" and had worked hard to earn the nickname. Yes, she had a different look, but that was to be expected. She thrived on being unique.

That settled in his mind, Daniel nodded. "I agree. She does look quite fetching."

"But, Daniel, surely you can't . . . I mean . . . she's a Wilde . . . I . . . ." Gibby shut off abruptly, her mouth opening and closing silently like a fish on dry land. A speechless Gibby was a sight to behold. Truth be told, he didn't think he'd ever seen that happen.

Unfortunately that didn't last long and she regained her composure quickly. "Well, at least make her wear decent shoes. Those look like something she found on the side of the road."

"Actually I found them at a Goodwill store in Mobile," Sabrina said. "They're very comfortable."

Daniel clapped his hands to get attention off Sabrina. "Now that everyone's ready, let's go out into the garden and take some pictures before your dates get here."

Giving him a look that told him he was going to get an earful once the girls were gone, Gibby rounded the girls up and herded them downstairs.

Daniel blew out a sigh as he followed behind them. No, raising three teenaged girls hadn't been easy, but it was the best and most honorable thing he'd ever done. He pushed aside the melancholy. Tonight was for his granddaughters. When the house was empty, he'd take the time to write his daily letter. How his wife, Camille, would have loved tonight's event. If life had been fair or just, the girls' mother and grandmother would have both been involved in readying them for this momentous occasion.

After his letter, he'd pour his one bourbon he was allowed each night and raise a glass to his beautiful daughter-in-law and handsome son, and once again apologize for not being wise or courageous enough to do what should have been done.

Alone at her table, Savannah tapped her foot in a nervous rhythm to the beat of the music as she watched the dancers on the floor. She felt out of place and uncomfortable, not an unusual occurrence. Social events always made her feel this way. Why had she thought her senior prom would be any different?

Out of the corner of her eye, she caught sight of her date, adding a new concern. That was his third swallow from a silver flask. She knew almost nothing about Billy Bartell. When he had asked her to the prom, she had been surprised but flattered. Having someone ask her out was unusual enough that it had given her a thrill of excitement. She had foolishly accepted, mostly because she had known no one else would ask her. She had hated the idea of going to the prom alone. Any other time she wouldn't have been so needy or desperate. Not dating regularly had never really bothered her. Focusing on her schoolwork and extracurricular activities took up most of her free time. But this was her senior prom—a watershed event, a dividing line between childhood and adulthood. After tonight, followed by graduation next week, she would no longer be a schoolgirl.

Now, as she watched her date take a fourth swallow of whatever was in the flask, Savannah was seriously regretting the decision.

Billy had seemed nice, kind of shy and awkward. He was new at school, arriving only a few months before graduation. Savannah had felt a sort of a kinship with him. She understood the feeling of aloneness and obscurity. She had felt that way for most of her life. No, she amended. She had felt that way after her parents' deaths. Murder-suicide was the stuff of TV news or fiction books, not a loving, secure family such as hers had been.

She'd once been a happy-go-lucky kid. But the summer it happened, everything changed. Life became somber and serious, and so had she.

Billy had seemed to share that air of seriousness. Savannah had felt no real zing with him, but that didn't concern her. She wasn't looking for zing. She had goals to achieve, and getting mixed up with any guy was not on her agenda until much later in life.

An image of the one boy she'd give serious thought to shoving aside her agenda for popped into her head. Slightly shaggy, golden-blond hair framed a handsome, intelligent face. His well-built, muscular body was at least six feet tall, and the confidence in his long-limbed swagger only added to his mystique. Completely out of her league and sphere of knowledge, Zach Tanner had secretly fascinated her from the moment she saw him. Not that he knew she existed. Having him notice her was only within the realm of her nighttime fantasies.

Zach was everything dreamy and sigh-worthy. She had first spotted him two years ago, when she'd been in town on an errand. He had been talking to Mr. Henson, the owner of Henson's Grocery. Actually they'd been arguing. Henson was shorter, but much broader and had the fierce look of an angry, snarling bulldog. Zach hadn't backed down. They'd almost been touching noses, their words heated and loud. Henson had been accusing Zach of something and he had been denying it. Unknown to either of them, Savannah had stood several feet away and watched the whole interlude. She had only caught bits and pieces of the argument because she'd been so fascinated by Zach. The way he'd stood, his shoulders so straight with an air of pride and self-assurance she could only imagine, fascinated her. He had seemed so mature . . . maybe even more so than Mr. Henson.

From that moment on, she had been on the lookout for him. Whenever she caught a glimpse of him, he always seemed preoccupied, as if he had a lot on his mind. Midnight was a small town and everybody knew one another. Being the kind of person who listened much more than she talked, she picked up more information than most adults thought she should know. Oddly, she didn't know all that much about Zach and his family. She knew he lived on the other side of town and that his mother, Francine Adams, was a divorcée. And though Savannah had heard more than a few whispers of "floozy" and "harlot" in relation to Francine, she knew little more than that. Zach had a brother named Josh who was two years younger than Savannah and played on the football team.

A heavy arm came over her shoulders, startling her. She twisted her head around to see an obviously drunk Billy Bartell sitting beside her, grinning. His face was flushed with color and beads of sweat rolled down his cheeks.

"Why don't we go to the car and make out?"

Her stomach roiling at the thought, Savannah shook her head. "I'm really enjoying listening to the band." Hoping the exercise would sober him up, she pushed away from him and jumped to her feet. "I love this song. Let's dance."

Billy grabbed her arm and pulled her back down. Alcohol-tainted breath covered her face, making her stomach turn even queasier. "Let's make our own music."

Breath held to avoid the alcohol stench, Savannah resisted the urge to roll her eyes at the cheesy comment. She tried to pull away from him, but he held tight. She tugged again. "Let me go."

"Not till I've had a taste of you."

Horrified, she stopped struggling to gape at him. "Excuse me?"

"Come on, Savannah. Everybody warned me you were the uptight one. But with sisters like Samantha and Sabrina, there's got to be more to you. Underneath that straitlaced, prissy air, I know there's a wild woman. Loosen up a little." Holding her with one hand, he reached into his jacket with the other and pulled out the silver flask. "Take a little sip and let's have some fun."

Not only had he insulted her, he had insulted her sisters, too. Torn between getting away from him and slapping him, Savannah took the flask he held out to her. She watched the triumphant grin disappear from his face as she poured the liquid onto the floor.

"Hey!" He grabbed her arm. "Stop that! That cost a lot of money."

More furious at her own poor judgment than she was

at the louse Billy had turned out to be, Savannah used both hands to push him away. "I'm leaving."

"You're not going anywhere, you ungrateful little bitch." He grabbed for her again but she managed to jump away in time.

"Back off, you jerk." Though she knew several eyes were on them, Savannah pushed her humiliation aside. Getting out of the room, away from Billy, was more important than her embarrassment.

Weaving in between tables, Savannah took rapid, determined steps, her eyes on her goal—the gym entrance. The temptation to run was strong but she resisted. She'd always done her best not to draw undue attention to herself; this would be no different. Blending into the background was something she was good at, and tonight she was glad for that. She hated the thought of people talking about her. There had been enough talk about the Wildes in her lifetime.

As she reached the door, she spotted one of Sammie's friends. A pleasant smile fixed on her face, Savannah said, "Hey, Megan, have you seen Samantha or Sabrina around?"

Megan pulled away from the guy she was plastered against. "Haven't seen Sabrina, but I think I saw Samantha and Toby going out to the parking lot a few minutes ago."

With a nod of thanks, Savannah headed outside. If she couldn't find either sister, she'd come back in and call her grandfather. How silly for her not to bring her cellphone with her. The sparkly little purse she'd been so excited about was only large enough for her lipstick, compact, and a small box of breath mints. She hadn't even considered that she might need a phone.

Calling her grandfather would be her last option, though. She and her sisters did their best to handle these kinds of problems on their own. Daniel Wilde was super protective of those he loved, and when it came to his granddaughters, he would move heaven and earth to keep them safe.

Her parents' deaths had occurred in early summer, and Savannah and her sisters had still been reeling with the grief when the new school year began. They had never anticipated the snide comments and cruel jokes of their classmates. Even at ten years old, Savannah had been mature enough to realize that most of the hurtful words were just being repeated from what kids had heard their parents say. That hadn't prevented the hurt.

At the beginning, she would tell her grandfather everything, but had soon stopped when she'd seen his reaction. Daniel Wilde had been livid. He'd confronted the principal, the teachers, and had even faced down a couple of parents. Not only had it been embarrassing for her, she had been worried about his health. His face would get purple with rage, and Savannah spent sleepless nights worrying that she would lose him, too.

She learned to keep her mouth shut. Whenever comments were made, she pretended she hadn't heard them. Eventually the kids stopped. By then, Savannah had become quiet and withdrawn. Getting lost in her studies or her favorite books was her way to cope.

No, calling her grandfather and telling him that Billy had been a skeevy creep would be her last resort.

Lost in thought, Savannah was in the middle of the overpacked parking lot when she realized that not only was her sister not around, coming out here by herself hadn't been the wisest decision she could have made. A group of boys, some dressed for the dance, some not, were leaning up against the cars, drinking and smoking. She turned to walk away and zeroed in on a new goal—getting away before any of them noticed her.

"Hey, Blondie, where you going in such a hurry?"

Not looking back to see if she knew who'd called out,

Savannah kept walking. Once again, she was tempted to run. This time she would have if her long dress and four-inch heels hadn't impeded her speed. She thought about taking a moment to stop and step out of her shoes, but the sound of rapid, heavy footsteps behind her kicked her heart rate into high gear and forced her into a running panic. A bulky body stepped out from the shadows and stood in front of her; Savannah jerked, her high-heeled feet skidding against the pavement to avoid a collision.

A wobbling, obviously drunk Clark Dayton stood before her. Sober, he was one of the most obnoxious guys she knew. Judging by the belligerent smirk on his flushed, round face, being intoxicated hadn't made him any nicer. After graduating last year, he had left Midnight for college. All three Wilde sisters had been glad to see him go. He had tried to date each of them, and when Savannah, the last one he asked, had turned him down, he had resorted to crude comments and behaving even more obnoxiously.

She stepped around him and said firmly, "I'm going back inside."

He grabbed her arm and whirled her around. Three other guys were standing behind him. She recognized Clark's cousin, Mason Hardy, but didn't know the other two. Savannah refused to panic. These jerks were just trying to scare her and admittedly doing an excellent job.

"Let me go." The words were a demand but she inwardly winced at how shaky and uncertain she sounded.

"I don't think so. It's about time you Wilde bitches learned a lesson. You ain't no better than anyone else."

"We never said we were. You—" She stopped abruptly. Getting into a verbal shouting match would accomplish nothing. She needed to get away and quick.

Her head twisted so she faced the school building, she

pretended she saw someone and called out, "Hey, guys, I'm over here!"

Clark twisted around, giving Savannah the opportunity to jump away from him and run. She took three steps forward before one of the boys she didn't know stood a few feet in front of her. He began walking toward her, leaving Savannah no choice but to back up. She slammed into an unmovable object—Clark Dayton. Beer-scented breath whispered in her ear, "We're going to have us some fun."

He backed away, leaving Savannah to turn slowly around and assess her situation—it wasn't good. She had somehow been corralled into a dark area of the parking lot. Four drunken young men surrounded her and there was no help in sight.

One of them thrust a bottle toward her. "Take a long, deep swallow . . . it'll get you in the mood."

Having no other choice, Savannah opened her mouth, took a deep breath, and screamed at the top of her lungs.

CHAPTER TWO

Zach Tanner rubbed his tired, gritty eyes and yawned widely as he steered his car toward home. A twelve-hour workday would've been bad enough, but he'd had to get up a couple of hours earlier this morning to study. Taking online college courses was a lifesaver since he couldn't afford to drive to the University of South Alabama campus every day, but it sure cut down on his sleeping time. The psychology test was at noon tomorrow and he was determined to ace it.

This was his last test for the quarter. The better he did on this exam, the better his record would look. It'd taken a lot of work to overcome his rep as a no-good kid. When he'd signed up for the army a couple of months back, he had been warned to keep his nose clean. Telling the recruiter he was following in his dad's footsteps had helped, but still the recruiter hadn't liked the black marks on Zach's records, no matter how unfounded they were. He had told him to keep a low profile in town and to stay out of trouble. Zach had done his best to comply. No way in hell was he going to jeopardize his chances. He'd dreamed too long and worked too hard to let anything get in the way. Come August, he was out of Midnight for good and on to a new life.

His family responsibilities were finally ending. After being the sole provider for more years than he liked to remember, he was finally free. His salvation had come by way of Leonard Easley, a widowed bank president from Pascagoula, Mississippi. He'd taken one look at Zach's mom and fallen head over heels. After all of Francine's machinations to find a man to take care of her, she'd ended up finding him on the side of the road when she'd run out of gas and Leonard had stopped to help.

It'd taken a few months before Zach was convinced that Leonard was really serious. His mother wasn't known for good judgment in her selection of men. Nor was she known for her self-control. If Leonard had wanted to, he could easily have kept a casual sexual relationship and Francine would have hung on for as long as she could. Instead, much to everyone's surprise, Leonard didn't want casual, he wanted forever.

The day after Leonard proposed, Zach had gone to the army recruiting office in Mobile and signed up. The U.S. Army was not only his ticket out of town, but also the chance to do something worthwhile. He had never known his dad; James Tanner had been killed in a brief conflict in Egypt when Zach was a baby. The stories his mother had told him made him want to be the kind of man his father had been—strong, courageous, and honorable.

He had a long way to go. Zach had been an outcast for most of his life. As the son of the town's "Jezebel," he had been called every vile name in the book. Also, being poor just seemed to piss some people off. Now it was time to prove that he had something inside of him. Something that didn't involve scraping, stealing, or wheeling and dealing just to survive.

His number one priority had always been his half brother, Josh. From the time his mother had walked in the door with the small blanket-wrapped bundle, Zach had felt responsible for him. His mother had reinforced those feelings when she'd placed the infant in four-year-old Zach's arms and said, "You're the big brother. You're supposed to watch out for him and protect him." And that's exactly what Zach had tried to do. When Eric Adams, Josh's father and Zach's stepfather, had walked out on the family, Zach's responsibilities as a big brother had taken on even more importance.

But now Josh was sixteen years old, a star football player who had an excellent chance of getting a football scholarship. With Leonard paying the family expenses, Josh would be taken care of until he was out on his own. That peace of mind had given Zach the permission to pursue his own dreams.

The cellphone in the console beside him blared out a loud ring. Zach glared at the thing. He didn't want to answer, even though he knew he would. He had resisted getting a cellphone because he knew he'd be on call 24/7, and he had been right. His mother thought nothing of calling him, no matter what time or for what reason.

Grabbing the phone before it could blare out another ring, he answered, "Hello?"

"Zachie honey, where are you?"

"I'm headed home, Mom."

"Well, what's taking so long? Your shift ended twenty minutes ago."

That was because he'd sat in his car for a full five minutes and just enjoyed the quiet. No one asking for anything, giving orders, or making demands. Solitude was a precious commodity.

Explaining that would do nothing but make her cry, so he said instead, "I'll be there in a few minutes."

"Leonard's already called to say good night, and Josh probably won't be home for hours. I'm lonesome."

Zach held his tongue.

"Could you stop and pick up some milk and cigarettes?"

"I thought you told Leonard you had quit smoking."

"That's only after we're married. Till then, what he
doesn't know won't hurt him."

So much for honesty in a relationship. "I'll stop for
milk. Not cigarettes."

"You're such a fuddy-duddy, Zach Tanner. I'm an
adult and your mama. You're supposed to mind me and
do what I tell you to do."

If only that were true. Zach had been nine years old
when his stepfather had up and left the family for another woman. That day, in between sobs of despair and
curses at her husband, his mother had announced that
Zach was now the man of the house. From that moment
on, his life had not been his own. Francine had de-
pended upon him for everything.

Zach had recognized early that resenting her demands
or control over his life accomplished nothing. His little
brother needed to eat. Zach had become an expert on
bargain shopping. The monthly swap meet on the outskirts of town became his hunting ground. Paying pen-
nies for dented or unlabeled cans of food or a quarter
for day-old bread at the bakery thrift store had sus-
tained them. When even those hadn't been available or
money had been scarce, he had resorted to various other
avenues of obtaining food, some legal, some not. He'd
learned early that pride or fear couldn't get in the way
of survival.

Social Services had been a constant visitor in their
home for a while. Zach had learned to lie about their
circumstances. His mother had told him horror stories
of what could happen if the family was split up. No
matter how hard his life got or what he had to do, the
thought of never seeing his little brother again wasn't

something Zach could accept. Eventually they had stopped checking on them.

"Zach, you still there?"

He shook himself out of his stupor. "Yeah, I'll stop for milk. Anything else?" Before she could say it, he added, "Besides cigarettes?"

"That's it. Don't be long, okay?"

"I'll be there as soon as I can." Zach ended the call and blew out a tired sigh.

Despite his happiness that the well-to-do Leonard was serious about marrying Francine, Zach had felt honor-bound to have a long talk with him—he couldn't allow the man to go into the marriage uninformed. Though Francine had good qualities, her number one priority would always be herself. Having Leonard know that fact up front would prevent any unpleasant surprises down the line—such as him leaving the way Zach's stepfather had.

Much to his surprise, Leonard held no illusions about his future wife. He told Zach that he had been a widower for over five years and missed being married. He had enough money to support Francine and her needs. Her lack of maturity charmed him instead of turning him off. Having her depend upon him for everything was exactly what he was looking for.

Deciding that the man did indeed know what he was getting into, Zach had given his approval. He just hoped Leonard could handle being a full-time caretaker for the rest of his life.

Though he loved her, Zach held no illusions about his mother. When she hadn't been dating, searching for a new husband, or trying to steal someone else's husband, she had been miserable. She had told him once that having a man in her life gave her purpose.

Instead of turning right onto Beach View Drive to go home, Zach made a left onto Grant Road. The conve-

nience store was only a couple of blocks away. Hopefully he could get into bed before midnight, since he
wanted to get up early for a couple more hours of study
time. Glancing over at the high school on the right, he
wondered about all the cars and then remembered that
this was senior prom night.

How could he have forgotten the prom? Josh was
there. Though his little brother wasn't a senior, one of
the senior girls had asked him to take her. Josh, being
Josh, had refused. The kid did everything he could not
to incur any added expenses. Zach wasn't having it and
had insisted that he go. He hadn't been able to go to his
own prom, not that he would've wanted to go, but choos-
ing not to go was a hell of lot different than not being
able to afford to go. Zach was determined his little
brother get all the advantages he hadn't had. That included proms, dances, dates, and all the other things
most teenagers took for granted.

Zach took a sweeping glance at the full parking lot
but didn't see the car Josh was driving—a baby blue
Lexus—Leonard's gift to Francine on the day of his
proposal. Maybe he'd parked on the other side. As Zach
drove by, his headlights swooped across the far end of
the parking lot and he caught a movement out of the
corner of his eye. Blinking to clear his sight, he saw
what looked like four guys standing in a circle. Though
they were in a dark area, away from the streetlight,
their menacing stance and total focus told him they
were surrounding someone. Some poor kid was about
to get an ass-whupping.

He told himself he was too tired to intervene. Early
on, before he'd learned a few hard-earned lessons, he'd
been the recipient of several of those beatings. They
weren't fun but they'd toughened him up. Besides, the
army recruiter had told him to stay away from anything
that could cause him trouble. One more blight on his

record and his dreams of being in the service would be toast.

A few yards later, Zach slowed to a standstill. How many times had he wished for someone to come rescue him or help him out? No one ever had. Was this guy wishing for the same thing?

The badass reputation Zach had worked hard to earn could now deter even the toughest asshole from bothering him. Maybe just by showing up, he could scare the little shits away and help a kid out.

Mentally shrugging, Zach made a quick U-turn and headed for the entrance to the parking lot. Whether he could just make verbal threats or he'd have to knock a few heads together no longer mattered. The closer he came to the menacing circle, the more imperative it seemed for him to put a halt to whatever was about to happen.

Not bothering to park, Zach stopped within a couple of yards of the group and turned his lights on bright. Four young men, two dressed in tuxedoes and two in casual clothes, whipped their heads around and glared. Oh yeah, he'd definitely interrupted their good time.

Zach opened the car door and got out slowly. "You guys having a party or what?"

"What the hell do you want, low-life Tanner?"

Hearing one of the many nicknames he'd been called much of his life barely penetrated his consciousness. A gap between two of the guys showed him exactly what the fine young men of Midnight were about to do. A teenaged girl stood in their midst, shivering and trembling like a candle about to be extinguished. Her wide-eyed, terrified expression revealed her helplessness. Rage like he'd never known before zoomed through his body, spiking his adrenaline and giving him a much-needed boost of energy.

Striding toward them, letting them know he was now

the predator and they the prey, Zach asked with a soft, growling fury, "What the hell do you guys think you're doing?"

"We're just having a little fun."

That came from one of the tuxedoed pricks, the quiver in his voice an indication that he was suddenly having second thoughts.

"This ain't none of your business, Tanner," Clark Dayton snarled. "This is private school property and you ain't in school no more."

Zach cocked his head. "Correct me if I'm wrong, Dayton, but didn't you graduate last year? Though by the sound of your speech, holding you back a few years might have been wise."

With a vicious curse, Dayton lunged toward him. Zach had plenty of time to step out of his way and let the jerk land on his face. The guy was not only drunk, he moved like a lumbering ox. But avoiding the collision never entered Zach's mind. Dayton slammed into him, apparently trying to knock him off his feet. Laughing at the piss-poor assault, Zach caught the idiot's whiskered chin in a clean uppercut. Dayton's mouth snapped shut with the satisfying crunching sound of breaking teeth.

Not even glancing at the now semiconscious Dayton, moaning and wallowing around on the pavement, Zach focused on the three remaining. "Anybody else want to give it a shot? Come on."

The two in tuxedoes backed away, one mumbling about not wanting any trouble. The remaining guy looked down at Dayton and then back at Zach. "You're going to pay for that."

"Bring it," Zach offered softly.

A clicking sound gave Zach a second's warning before a knife was jabbed toward his face. Jerking back, Zach threw out a kick and knocked the knife out of the guy's hand. The guy barely had a chance to know he'd lost his weapon before Zach was on him, taking them both to the pavement. The breath had been knocked out of his opponent, giving Zach the opportunity to pin him down by holding both of his arms above his head. Then, very deliberately, he positioned his knee over the guy's groin and pressed down . . . hard. Whatever breath the idiot had regained was expelled in a squealing sob.

"Next time you think about raping a girl, remember this, asshole."

"Get off me . . . please."

Taking his time, Zach got to his feet. Consumed with holding his privates and rolling around on the pavement, the guy never looked at Zach again.

Finally able to face the young woman he'd just saved, for the first time he realized her identity. Savannah Wilde. "You okay?"

Instead of nodding her head, answering yes, or hell, even running away, she did something that stunned him. With a sobbing "Oh, Zach, thank you," she launched herself toward him. Zach had no choice but to open his arms to catch her.

Wrapping her arms around his neck, she held on tight.

Zach forced himself to hold her loosely, because, for whatever insane reason, he instinctively wanted to hold her tighter and feel her body pressed up against his. His mind scrambled for a noble excuse. It was a reflex from the adrenaline rush, not because she felt so damn good or because no one had ever looked at him as if he was something special.

Whatever the reason, they had to leave. She needed to get to safety and he needed to get the hell out of here before the police showed up. No matter that he had saved one of the Wilde sisters from a gang rape or even worse, Police Chief Harlan Mosby would gladly haul his ass into jail. When it came to Zach, Mosby acted first and asked questions later.

Pushing her away slightly, he said, "You okay?"

"Yes, thank you," she answered softly.

"You have a car?"

"No." She glanced toward the school building and then back at him. "Would it be too much out of your way to take me home?"

The question stunned him almost as much as her jumping into his arms. Good girls, rich or poor, did not get into the car with Zach Tanner. Few parents wanted to see their daughters take up with the town's bad boy, especially one with no money or prospects.

She had to know who he was—she'd called him Zach. He knew little to nothing about the Wilde sisters, but he had heard that Savannah was "the brainy one." So far, she wasn't impressing him with her smarts.

"I don't think me taking you home is a good idea. Who'd you come with?"

She glanced nervously toward the school. "My date."

"Then what the hell are you doing out here?"

"He's inside getting drunk. I was looking for my sister."

The idiocy of some guys amazed him. While his date was in the parking lot close to getting raped, he was inside boozing it up. Figuring they had mere seconds before someone either called the cops or one of the guys on the pavement got up the courage to take him on again, Zach took Savannah's hand and pulled her to his car. "Let's get out of here."

Savannah sank into the car seat, her relief so great she could barely catch her breath. She had no doubt what Clark Dayton and his friends had wanted to do. And Zach Tanner had been the one to save her.

The driver's-side door squeaked open and Zach slid into the seat beside her. The heartbeat that had been slowing down sped right back up. She had never been this close to him before; he was even more handsome than she had thought.

"You live on Wildfire Lane, right?"

Too breathless to speak, she nodded.

The car shot forward. Out of the corner of her eye, she saw Clark leaning against a car. As they passed by him, he yelled out something and raised his hand, extending his middle finger in an obscene gesture.

Zach acted as though he didn't exist, but shot her a warning look. "Dayton won't forget this. You need to be on the lookout for him for a while."

"I don't plan to ever be in a position where I see him again."

"You're living in the same town . . . might be hard to avoid him."

She didn't bother to point out that she and Zach had lived in the same town and this was the first time they'd encountered each other. Instead she told him news that no one but her family knew. "I'm leaving for college in a few months."

"Oh yeah, where you going?"

"Vanderbilt University in Nashville."

A smile spread over his face and Savannah had to hold her breath to keep from gasping. She'd never seen such a transformation. Before, he'd been handsome but grim-looking. His smile changed him into just short of beautiful.

"Good for you. That's a great school. What are you going to study?"

"Law. I'm going to be a criminal defense attorney."

Zach nodded his approval as he turned in to the drive in front of her house. Savannah couldn't believe they were already here. It felt as though she'd just gotten into the car.

"Might want to mention this incident to your grand-daddy, just to be on the safe side."

She nodded absently, biting her lip in indecision. While she'd been in the midst of those hideous boys, a thought had flashed through her mind of how safe and staid her life had become. She was eighteen years old and had never done anything remotely exciting or risky. Here was her chance to do something different, be someone different. Her mind whispered, *Take a chance!* For some reason, she felt changed, as if her life had been altered. She didn't want to go back to the same boring Savannah. Taking that chance, Savannah blurted out her thoughts: "Would you like to come in and meet Granddad? I'm sure he'd like to thank you for basically saving my life."

Zach snorted and shook his head. "You really are an innocent, aren't you? Your granddaddy would probably lock you up until it's time for you to leave for college if he saw you with me."

She didn't bother to ask him why he felt that way. She knew what the gossips said about him. Having been the victim of many of those same gossips, she knew better than to believe their lies. What they said didn't faze her. Nor would it her grandfather.

"Granddad isn't one to believe the gossips. He said you have to look beneath the surface to get the true measure of a person."

Instead of arguing with her, he gave her another sweet smile. "Your grandfather sounds like a good man." He glanced at his watch. "But I need to get going."

Of course he did. He'd probably had a date tonight and was heading home. Or maybe he was just now going out. Since he was older, he didn't have to worry about curfews and stuff like that.

"Would you come for breakfast in the morning?"

Though he didn't move a muscle, she could tell she had startled him. His words confirmed the thought. "Excuse me?"

"Come for breakfast in the morning. We sit down at eight. It's really informal. . . . I know my granddad would be very excited to meet you." Before he could answer and give her the rejection she expected, she added, "Please, don't say no."

He opened his mouth and she was sure that was exactly what he would do, but instead he said, "I'll see what I can do."

Letting it go at that, she opened the car door and then looked at him again. "Thank you for saving my life."

"Just be careful from now on. Okay?"

"I will." And before her newfound courage deserted her, she leaned over and quickly kissed his cheek, loving the tingling feel of his five-o'clock shadow against her mouth. "You're my hero."

Before he could say anything or she could do anything crazier, Savannah jumped out of the car and raced toward the house.

CHAPTER THREE

Barely eight hours later, calling himself seven kinds of a fool, Zach stood on the front porch of the Wilde mansion. He had no good reason for being here and sure as hell didn't belong here.

In his whole life, he'd never had anyone refer to him as a hero. He'd been sneered at, laughed at. Had people call him everything from bastard and sleaze to the town slut's son. Had even seen people cross the street to avoid him. The very idea that even for a moment someone as pure and sweet as Savannah Wilde could consider him a hero amazed him. The temptation of experiencing that feeling again was hard to resist.

Of course, the moment Daniel Wilde, Savannah's grandfather, saw him, he'd be told to leave. His stomach grumbled and he shrugged philosophically. If nothing else, maybe they'd give him a biscuit or something before they kicked him out.

That might be humiliating for some, but Zach had long ago gotten over being prideful. Taking care of his family for so many years had made pride a useless emotion and one he couldn't afford. It'd been a while since he'd had to steal food or depend upon the kindness of others. Once he'd found a few folks willing to give him a chance to earn some money, he had stopped stealing. And though he could still go to the food pantries at some of the churches and get free groceries, he had stopped that, too. Food hadn't been as plentiful once he had started paying for it, but it had tasted a damn sight better than stolen food or charity.

And now that Leonard had come into their lives, there was plenty of money for groceries, but Zach would never allow himself to forget the gnawing ache of hunger. He was still as frugal as ever, but instead of spending all of his earnings on the necessities, he saved as much as he could.

Braced for rejection, Zach pressed the doorbell and waited to be told to go home. Seconds later, Savannah opened the door, and her brilliant smile of welcome was like a blast of bright sunshine after a long, dark night. Her long, wavy hair was pulled back by some kind of barrette, and she was wearing a pale pink sleeveless dress covered in butterflies.

"You came!"

She seemed so pleased to see him, Zach took a step forward before he remembered he hadn't been invited inside. Stopping abruptly, he cleared his throat and said, "I only came to make sure you were okay."

Yeah, okay, that was lame. But he figured giving her an out would save both of them the embarrassment when Daniel Wilde ordered him to leave.

Instead of accepting his words, she grabbed his arm and pulled him inside. "Nonsense. Granddad's so excited to meet you. Breakfast is ready. Hope you're hungry." She tugged on his arm again. "Come on."

Zach barely heard the door close behind him as he gazed around in awe. Never in his life had he seen anything so grand or clean. The closest thing was when he was a kid, he'd gone on a school trip to tour the governor's mansion in Montgomery. That had been larger, but this, in his opinion, was nicer.

The floor was polished mahogany, so shiny he could

see his reflection. The walls, a light lemony color, were covered with framed art and all sorts of family photos. A giant curved staircase seemingly miles away from the entrance spiraled up to the second floor. A balcony overlooked the first floor. The mansion appeared big on the outside but he hadn't imagined how immense it really was. Long past believing that anything could intimidate or impress him, Zach felt rooted to the floor and speechless. The gulf between his upbringing and Savannah Wilde's was like night and day, beans and apple butter . . . heaven and hell.

"Come into the morning room. That's where we have Saturday breakfast. Sammie and Bri are excited to meet you, too."

Barely comprehending that his feet were moving, Zach followed slowly behind Savannah, more intimidated with each step he took. Every room they went through reinforced the fact that he didn't belong here. He was about to come up with another excuse to leave when she led him to a large sunny room with a table laden with the best-smelling and most delicious-looking food he could ever imagine. What amazed him even more were the three smiling faces of the people surrounding the table.

Daniel Wilde came toward him, his hand outstretched. "Welcome, Zach. I can't begin to tell you how grateful we are for what you did for Savannah last night." Tears glistened in the older man's blue eyes.

"I was glad to help out, sir."

Mr. Wilde turned slightly and gestured behind him. "I'd like to introduce Samantha and Sabrina, Savannah's sisters."

Though Zach had never officially met either girl, he'd seen them around. He knew Savannah and her sisters were triplets, and though they looked almost identical, he thought Savannah was by far the most beautiful of the three.

"Come sit down," Savannah urged.

Zach watched as she pulled a chair out for him at the head of the table. Feeling more uncomfortable and awkward than he'd ever felt in his life, Zach lumbered over to the chair and sat down. Then, realizing that everyone was still standing, he sprang to his feet again, his face and entire body heating up in embarrassment.

When everyone was finally seated, Zach fell back into his chair and stared at the overflowing platters on the table: eggs, both fried and scrambled, bacon, country ham, pancakes, biscuits, gravy—sawmill and redeye—grits, and hash browns. Two glass pitchers, one holding orange juice and the other milk, stood beside a carafe of steaming coffee. The room was silent, as if everyone was waiting for him to say something. Before he could come up with anything, a gigantic and eager rumble of his stomach broke the quiet.

"We really didn't know what kind of food you liked, so we each made our specialty." Savannah paused and then added, "I made the biscuits and both gravies."

"It looks really good."

As if his approval was what they had been waiting for, platters of food began to be passed. Zach took a modest amount from each one and soon had an overloaded plate. When the last platter was finally passed, Daniel Wilde said, "Let's give thanks."

Everyone at the table bowed their head. Nerves and his grumbling stomach kept him from hearing much of the prayer, but when his name was mentioned, Zach's ears perked up. Savannah's grandfather thanked God for Zach being there to save her and for coming to breakfast. Had anyone ever prayed for him before? He didn't think so. It felt odd but he couldn't say he hated the feeling.

After a chorus of "Amen," Zach opened his eyes and watched as everyone began to eat. Deciding he'd been given the green light, he wasted no more time and dug into the best meal he'd had in his life.

Savannah had the hardest time concentrating on her own plate of food. She had never seen anyone eat the way Zach did. He attacked and demolished. Knowing that it would embarrass him if she stared, she forced herself to only glance at him every so often so it wouldn't look so obvious.

She still couldn't believe he'd actually come. Last night when she had issued the invitation, the expression in his eyes and his noncommittal reply made her almost positive he wouldn't. Not that it had stopped her grandfather from insisting that they make a meal fit for a king. After she had told him what happened and what Zach did for her, he'd been ready to go over to Zach's house and thank him in person. Knowing that Zach probably wouldn't want that, she had persuaded him to wait till morning to see if he would show.

Once they'd heard the truth, her sisters had been just as eager to thank him. Sammie and Bri had arrived home last night with a completely different story of what had happened. Rumors had been running rampant that a drunken Zach Tanner had shown up at the prom and had beaten up two boys in the parking lot. There had been no mention of how Zach had rescued her or what Clark Dayton and his friends had tried to do.

Savannah had been appalled at how the low-life rednecks had twisted the truth, making Zach into a villain instead of the hero she knew him to be. Thank heavens her grandfather had been wise enough to realize something else. It hadn't occurred to her that Zach could get into trouble. Why would it? He'd saved her life! Daniel

Wilde was smart in the ways of how this town worked, so instead of going to Zach's house to thank him, he had gotten into his car and made the short trip to the police station. And had arrived in the nick of time.

Granddad had said that Chief Mosby had been hell-bent on arresting Zach. It had taken over an hour to convince Mosby, plus a phone call to Savannah to corroborate the story, before he had agreed to not pursue the matter. Just the thought of what could have happened if her grandfather hadn't intervened chilled Savannah to the bone.

Though she wished Clark Dayton and his drunken friends could be arrested, Savannah knew that wasn't going to happen. There was no doubt in her mind what they had intended to do . . . when she closed her eyes, she could still see the evil intent on their faces. However, other than grabbing her arm once, they had never touched her. She could prove nothing.

"I heard rumors that you're going into the army, son. Is that true?"

Savannah jerked her head around at her grandfather's words. Zach was joining the army? Leaving town? When?

She watched as he swallowed a mouthful of food and then said, "Yes, sir, I leave for basic training in a couple of months."

"Service to your country is a fine and noble endeavor. You're a brave young man."

His face flushing, Zach mumbled, "Thank you, sir" and dipped his head down to his food again.

Pushing aside that disturbing news for the time being, Savannah searched for a safe conversation topic that would put Zach at ease. The way he kept his head down and barely looked at anyone, it was obvious he was uncomfortable. Since she knew so little about him other than all the rumors she'd heard, it was hard to come up with something. However, she did know a little bit about his half brother, Josh.

"Your brother is a good football player."

The statement came out of left field and was as lame a conversation starter as she'd ever given. Even her sisters were giving her wide-eyed stares as if she'd lost her mind. She knew almost nothing about football and had declared on more than one occasion that she would never understand why everyone in Alabama was so consumed with such a barbaric-looking sport. However, she did know that Josh was a football star in school, so she had taken a chance.

Expecting Zach to either ignore the comment or give her the same astonished look as her sisters, she was thrilled it had the opposite effect. That same smile she'd experienced only briefly last night brightened his too-solemn features. "He's amazing. College recruiters are already talking about him. I'd love to see him get a football scholarship to Alabama."

That was the longest speech she'd ever heard from him. Eager to seize on what appeared to be a topic of interest for him, she asked, "Did you play football in school, too?"

As soon as the words were out of her mouth, she wanted to withdraw the question. Of course he hadn't played sports in school. If her brain had been working at all, she would have remembered that.

His smile dimmed only slightly as he answered, "Nah, I was never any good at it."

Most likely it wasn't his lack of skills that had kept him from playing, but the responsibilities he'd taken on after school. She had heard that he'd had several part-time jobs while he had been in school. While other kids got to participate in extracurricular activities, he was working to help support his family. For the first time ever, Savannah was embarrassed by her family's wealth.

Her studies and the occasional chores at home were the only real responsibilities she'd ever had. She'd certainly never had to do anything to support her family.

Other than the clink of silverware, there was silence in the room again. Savannah took a bite of something from her plate and then shot her grandfather a pleading look.

With an imperceptible nod, her grandfather said, "You're a Bama fan, Zach?"

"Yes, sir." He grinned and added, "Roll Tide all the way."

"I really thought they'd pull off another national championship last season."

Savannah listened as her grandfather and Zach talked easily about players and statistics as if they'd known each other for years. Even Sammie and Bri piped in with their own observations and opinions. Savannah felt ignorant, a feeling she hated. She who buried her face in a book sometimes from morning till night knew nothing about the one subject Zach seemed the most interested in. As a bookworm who read anything and everything she could get her hands on, that was unsettling. Oh, she knew there were touchdowns, fumbles, and tackles, but was totally in the dark on the rules and procedures of the game.

Vowing to remedy her lack of knowledge, she listened intently as the discussion went from last season's schedule to the upcoming games this fall. And while she learned, she watched Zach. No longer ill at ease, he was leaning back into his chair, lively interest on his face.

So engrossed in watching him, she was startled when he stood and said, "Well, thank you for a delicious breakfast, but I have an appointment to get to."

Savannah jumped to her feet, almost toppling over the chair behind her. "I'll walk you out."

She was aware of three sets of eyes staring at them as

they walked out of the morning room. She couldn't have made it more obvious that she was awestruck and enthralled with their guest. But her sisters and grand-father knew her better than anyone. Hopefully her fas-cination wasn't as apparent to Zach as it was to her family.

They reached the front door and Zach turned to face her, that solemn, sincere expression back on his face. "Watch out for Dayton. He'll be pissed . . . I mean angry about what happened and might try to take it out on you."

"I will. You be careful, too."

He shrugged and opened the door. "Always am."

"Want to come back for supper tonight?" She winced, fearing he would see straight through that invitation. He did, but not the way she'd feared.

"You don't owe me anything, Savannah. Okay?"

She inhaled a shallow breath to steady her courage and answered with the truth, "Yes, I do, but that's not why I asked you to supper." Swallowing hard, she took the biggest chance of her life. "I'd like to see you again."

His expression softened. "Why?"

Because I've had a crush on you from the moment I saw you. Because I find you fascinating. Because I've never felt like this about anyone before.

She couldn't say any of those things, so she shrugged and gave him a bland but truthful answer. "I'd like to get to know you better."

Eyes the color of a stormy winter's sky stared hard as if trying to see beneath her words to an ulterior motive. She understood that he probably didn't trust a lot of people. That was something they had in common. Sa-vannah withstood his scrutiny and waited.

"I can't come to supper tonight."

Though she wasn't surprised at his refusal, disap-pointment swamped her. Before she could come up with a brave smile and another innocuous reply, he stunned her with an invitation of his own. "I'm working a concert in Mobile tonight. It's just a setup and teardown of equipment for a rock band called Stand and Deliver. They're pretty good. If you'd like to come."

"I'd love to." She didn't even worry about sounding too eager. This moment was too monumental to hide her excitement.

"I'll pick you up at five o'clock."

She barely nodded before he turned away and jogged to his car. Savannah stayed at the door long after his car disappeared from sight. Maybe it was her imagination or wishful thinking, but she could swear she saw a flash of attraction in his eyes. Could it be possible?

Closing the door, she turned and leaned against it. Zach had asked her out . . . he must find her somewhat appealing. Then the thought hit her. She had a date to go to a concert—something she'd never done before.

This called for major assistance from two people who were in the know. Samantha knew fashion. Sabrina loved rock music. She took off at a run toward the morning room. "Sammie! Bri! I need your help."

CHAPTER FOUR

Sitting beside Zach, Savannah watched his hands on the steering wheel. He drove with an ease and calm competency that defied explanation. Though she knew he was twenty, only two years older than she was, he possessed a steadiness that made him seem years older. He just seemed so strong and solid . . . and absolutely fascinating.

She caught herself chewing on her lower lip and stopped abruptly. The nervous habit was something she had developed after her parents' deaths. It had taken her years to quit, but when anxious, she often relapsed. And oh boy, was she nervous. Before Zach had arrived, she had felt reasonably ready for her date. Now she swore she had forgotten everything she'd learned over the last eight hours.

Her entire day had been devoted to preparing for tonight. While Sammie had chosen her outfit, fixed her hair and makeup, and given her a manicure and pedicure, along with the dos and don'ts of dating etiquette, Bri had coached her on various "manly" subjects she could discuss with Zach. An hour before her date, she had put a stop to it and asked to be alone. A mishmash of information had swirled around in her head with tornadic fury, her scalp felt sore from all of the tugging and straightening Sammie had done to control her wild locks, and the blouse both her sisters had insisted she wear revealed much more cleavage than she was truly comfortable showing. Now here she sat, exhausted and tongue-tied—not an impressive beginning for their first date.

"You sure you want to go tonight?"

Oh great, now he was wondering if she was having second thoughts. *Think of something, Savannah!* She swallowed past a bone-dry mouth and said, "I'm absolutely sure." Forcing herself to continue, she ventured, "Do you know someone in the band?"

Zach shook his head. "I have a friend of sorts in Mobile. Whenever something like this comes up, he gives me a call. I've been doing it for a couple of years now. Not a lot of thinking to do. Just some heavy work." He glanced over at her. "We'll find a good spot for you to watch. I've heard the band before. They're pretty good."

"Is rock your favorite kind of music?"

"Not really. I don't really have a favorite. I like all kinds. What about you?"

Before tonight, she would have said classical, but that was only because she hadn't bothered to listen to anything else. Experimenting with new stuff wasn't something she did often. She suddenly realized that just in the short amount of time she had known Zach, she had taken more chances than she had in the last eight years. Her parents' deaths had stopped any spontaneity she might have once possessed.

She answered bravely, "I'm open to just about any kind of music."

"Then you'll like Stand and Deliver. They're a mixture of rock, jazz, blues, and country."

Savannah nodded but was now at a loss on how to take the conversation further. Fortunately Zach was better skilled at small talk than she was, and much to her delight, asked the one question that opened up a conversational mecca for her. "I'm in the middle of reading Salinger's *Catcher in the Rye*. Have you read it?"

Three hours later Zach glanced over at Savannah and couldn't help but laugh. Music blasted like kegs of dynamite through gigantic speakers. Kids shouted, screamed, and sang at the top of their lungs with the band— everyone was pumped up on adrenaline. With the exception of the beautiful blond angel asleep in the corner.

Having worked these concerts often enough to know that the music sometimes gave him a headache, he always brought along earplugs. He had pocketed an extra pair for Savannah just in case. He was glad he had.

Over cheeseburgers and fries at the DQ close by the auditorium, he had listened as she expounded on her knowledge of rock music and football. He'd felt as if she were reciting every iota of information she had ever learned or heard. Zach had sat across from her and, despite every internal warning telling him he was a lunatic, had become entranced. Everything about her enchanted him—from her sweet smile to her fluttery mannerisms when she was nervous. Her clear green eyes held an innocence and loveliness he could barely fathom. She was like a beautiful butterfly, impossible to capture but mesmerizing.

They had arrived two hours before the concert was to start. The heaviest equipment had already been unloaded, but it was up to Zach and others to connect the electrical equipment and conduct basic sound checks. Instead of staying in the comfortable chair he'd pointed her to, Savannah had chosen to follow him around and ask questions, seemingly intrigued with everything. He patiently answered each question, both amused and charmed that she was so interested.

When the band started playing, she had seemed so

excited about the concert, he had half expected her to be front and center in the audience, dancing and whooping it up with the other teenagers. But he was beginning to see that Savannah Wilde wasn't like anyone else he'd ever known. She went to the chair he'd shown her to before and sat enrapt, as if it was the first time she had ever experienced anything like this. Half an hour into the performance, that had changed. That was when he began to notice her wincing with each clang of the drums or a particularly loud bellow from the lead singer. When he'd offered her the plugs, he wondered if pride would keep her from accepting the gift—she was trying so hard to show him she was having a good time. Thankfully her need for silence won.

He had left her in the chair to go to the other side of the stage to handle a sound problem. When he came back, the last thing he had expected was to find her leaning back in the chair with her arms crossed and her eyes closed. At first, he thought she was just resting, but he'd gently touched her shoulder and she hadn't moved.

The band would be insulted by her lack of attention, but Zach realized it made him like her all the more. As if he needed another reason.

As the band wound down with their final number of the night, Zach approached the sleeping beauty. The teardown wouldn't take all that long . . . maybe half an hour; however, he'd be out of sight of Savannah. No way would he leave her asleep and vulnerable. This concert was tame compared to some Zach had worked, but there were always one or two yahoos who drank too much and became convinced they were God's gift to women.

Touching her lightly on the shoulder, he ignored the tenderness he felt at how innocent and beautiful she looked. He shook her gently and watched her eyelashes flutter as she woke. Slowly opening her eyes, she looked up at him sleepily and slightly confused. Then, as she became aware, a sweet smile of welcome appeared. Zach's heart flipped over. Without conscious thought, he dropped to his knees before her. Lowering his head, he took her mouth . . . hotly, tenderly, his tongue swept against her lips. When she opened for him, Zach groaned against her mouth, losing himself in a taste he'd never known and feelings he had never imagined.

As he sank into the kiss, she wrapped her arms around his shoulders and pulled him closer. Any sanity he'd managed to maintain instantly vanished. His hands at her waist found their way under her blouse, and his fingers caressed skin soft as a rose petal. Zach forgot where he was, who he was . . . and most important, who the beautiful girl in his arms was.

When he felt her pull away slightly, it was all he could do not to still her movements and continue devouring the sweetest mouth he'd ever kissed. Instead he loosened his hold, almost wincing as his fingers trailed down her soft skin and withdrew from under her blouse.

Moist and swollen, her lips looked luscious and exactly as they'd tasted. Forcing himself not to go back for another delicious nibble, Zach raised his gaze to meet her eyes. Desire still pounded but healthy doses of guilt and recrimination were seeping into his consciousness, reminding him where they were and who they were. Expecting to see anger or, at the very least, shame in her eyes, he was stunned to see them gleaming like brilliant stars.

Groaning, Zach pulled away completely and stood. "I've got to get to work. You'll be safe here. Okay?"

She nodded, the soft glow of want and approval on her face more than he could fathom. Did she not know who the hell he was?

Zach turned abruptly away, not sure who he was angrier with, himself or Savannah.

* * *

Breathless, her heart thudding against her chest, Savannah watched Zach's long strides take him swiftly away from her. If she didn't count Tubby Thompson, who in the fourth grade chased her down on a dare from his friends and smacked his lips up against hers, she'd just had her very first kiss. The magazine articles that claimed first kisses were awkward, sloppy, or not good didn't know Zach Tanner. She couldn't imagine a more perfect kiss.

The absence of the noise she had successfully drowned out with Zach's earplugs told her the concert was over. She stood to stretch her stiff limbs and then realized belatedly why she hadn't known it was over. Holy crap, she'd fallen asleep. She had tried so hard to pretend she loved the music, and for half an hour or so, she thought she'd done a pretty convincing job. Then her head had begun to pound in rhythm with every drumbeat. When Zach had offered her the earplugs, she had almost refused. Silly, she knew, but she hated to think he'd been kind enough to invite her and she was wanting to drown out the music within the first hour. Thankfully, before she could refuse, she had noticed he wore them, too.

They had done too good of a job. Though she'd still heard the music, it was much less painful to her sensitive hearing. She never anticipated that she'd fall asleep, though. Zach probably thought she was the most boring date ever. Sammie and Bri were going to howl their heads off with laughter when she told them.

Savannah walked around the backstage area, listening to the back-and-forth between the men as they proceeded to take apart the equipment. Zach was on the other end of the stage, but every so often she'd feel his eyes on her. She shivered, remembering his mouth on hers, the heat in his gray eyes that made them gleam like a winter fire.

"Who's the blond chick with the great ass?"

The guy was several yards away and her back was to him, but since she was the only girl around, she knew he was referring to her. She also recognized the voice as belonging to Stand and Deliver's lead singer.

"She's with me."

Savannah whirled around, startled by the harsh tone that hardly sounded like Zach's voice.

"Introduce us."

Even from where she stood, she could hear the arrogance in the guy's voice. She tensed, wondering how Zach would handle the request. She didn't want to meet this man, but if Zach refused, would that keep him from getting jobs like this in the future?

"No." If possible, Zach's voice was even harder.

Savannah started toward them. What was the harm in having Zach introduce her? The last thing she wanted to do was cause him problems. Before she could take more than two steps, Zach had her firmly by the elbow. "Let's go."

"But, Zach, I don't mind—"

"I do."

Not giving her a chance to say anything else, he grabbed her purse and ushered her toward the door. In seconds, they were outside.

Confused by his attitude, she frowned up at him. "What's wrong?"

"I shouldn't have brought you here."

"But why?"

"I'd forgotten how rowdy these things can get."

Savannah raised her brows. Rowdy? If things had been any calmer, she might have fallen asleep again.

"You don't have to protect me from everyone, you know. I'm not helpless."

He didn't speak as he opened the car door for her. Savannah settled into her seat and watched him cross in front of the car. The thunderous expression on his face made her suddenly uncertain. He had seemed like such a gentleman. Had she misjudged him? Why was he acting so annoyed?

The driver's-side door opened and Savannah prepared herself to deal with his unexpected anger. Zach slid in beside her and stared out the windshield for several seconds. She opened her mouth, not sure what she was going to say, but then he turned toward her. Savannah lost her breath. That smile was back.

"I overreacted, didn't I?"

Her tense muscles loosened in relief. "Maybe a little."

"Sorry. I didn't know what to expect, so I got you out of there before anything could happen."

Zach was a protector, there was no other word for it. And if not for the extremely hot kiss earlier, he'd almost treated her as a sister . . . a family member. Then it hit her. Zach watched over those he cared about. A thrill of excitement zoomed through her, causing her to shiver. Zach cared about her!

"You cold?"

She shook her head and looked out into the night, grappling with her newfound discovery. Questions crowded into her mind. Why did he have such a rough reputation? One so bad that he had almost been arrested last night without any real proof of wrongdoing. She had heard unkind rumors about him and his family most of her life, but somehow Josh had escaped the talk. Yet, from what she could tell, Zach was more honorable than most any guy she knew. Even her grandfather believed in him.

Unable to hold back her question, inappropriate as it was, Savannah approached it gingerly. She definitely didn't want to offend him, but there had to be some kind of rational explanation for all the bad talk she'd heard. "Can I ask you a question?"

"Sure."

She swallowed past the discomfort of speaking to him about anything so personal. "Why do you have such a bad reputation when you're not a bad guy at all?"

He was silent for so long, she was sure she had made a mistake and offended him. Just as she was getting ready to issue an apology, he spoke almost absentmindedly, as if he was still thinking about her question. "I think a lot of people are all too willing to believe the worst of someone rather than form an opinion for themselves."

The look he shot her held a sadness and sorrow she never expected. "Don't believe everything you hear. Even if all evidence points to one answer, be brave enough to learn the truth for yourself."

Feeling as though she'd just gotten a philosophy lesson from a very wise man, Savannah turned away, lost in thought. Little did she know that Zach's advice was more than just wise words; someday it would make all the difference in the world to her.

CHAPTER FIVE

"Surely you're not going out tonight?"

In the midst of shining his shoes, Zach stopped briefly to look up. His mother was leaning against the door-jamb, a glass of white wine in one hand, a cigarette in the other. Her honey-blond hair was pulled on top of her head in an artless, messy style that somehow made her look much younger than her forty-two years.

Francine had always had a fragile, delicate air about her, and Zach knew she worked hard to foster that image. She had often reminded her sons that her beauty was her best asset.

"You going with that Wilde girl again?"

His mother had made it more than clear that she didn't approve of her son dating one of the wealthiest girls in Midnight. It had been a stupid hope that he could keep the news of his relationship with Savannah a secret from her. Francine rarely socialized with anyone in town, but news could travel like lightning in Midnight, and somehow, even without friends, she found out.

"This is your last night in town for a long time. I would've thought you'd want to stay home."

She left out the additional words "with me," but they were implied. He hated to admit it, because it was so downright freaky, but every time she brought up Savannah's name, he could swear she sounded jealous. The thought turned his stomach.

He'd already said goodbye to Josh, who was away at football camp. Leonard was out of town on a business trip. Zach knew that if he stayed home, it would be the way it had been since he was a kid. His mother would drink too much, talk about the days when she was the prettiest girl in Alabama, and lament that life wasn't fair. Zach had had his fill long ago.

This was his last night . . . his final night with Savannah, at least for a very long time. No way would he miss spending this time with her. He still hadn't even figured out how the hell he was going to say goodbye.

"Come on, Zachie. I'll order a pizza and we'll spend it together just like old times."

Zach shook his head. "I can't, Mom. Besides, Leonard's coming home tonight, so you won't be alone for long."

"That's not the point. Dammit, this is your last night in town. You'd think you'd want to spend it with your family."

Straightening to his full height, Zach fought the urge to tell her the truth. That getting away from her was the thing he was looking forward to the most. Knowing that would crush her, he instead went with a safe answer. "I'll get up early in the morning and fix us a big breakfast before I leave. How's that sound?"

She took another drag off her cigarette and then pursed her lips in a pout. "You know there's no future with that girl, don't you?"

Again he refused to get into an argument that no one would win. Especially since he wasn't so sure she wasn't right. He still couldn't believe he'd let himself get involved with Savannah. She had so many goals and dreams for her future. Would he be holding her back by trying to maintain a relationship that probably had little hope for survival? He would be gone for months; she would soon be leaving for college. They were going to be hundreds, maybe thousands of miles apart. Was there a reason to even hope for a future with her? His heart, which had taken over his thinking when it came to Savannah, whispered a resounding *Yes!* The last few weeks, being in her life, getting to know her and her family, had been the happiest time of his life.

An argument with his mother wasn't something he wanted to get into tonight. Especially when Savannah was waiting for him to pick her up. Grabbing his keys from the dresser next to his bed, Zach headed toward the door. He stopped briefly and dropped a kiss on Francine's forehead. "Don't drink so much you have a hangover in the morning. Okay?"

"Like anyone really cares what happens to me."

Any kind of rational conversation was out of the question when she was in one of her self-pitying moods. Without uttering another word, Zach walked out the door.

As he drove across town toward the Wilde mansion, dread, thick and dark, permeated his thoughts. The irony of the situation hadn't escaped him. He'd worked so hard on being able to get out of Midnight. Leaving his family had been his only worry, but with Leonard to take care of them, he had known they'd be okay. That had been his only concern. But now there was a new one.

Despite his reputation and lack of prospects, Zach had dated more than his share of women. Once he grew taller and started filling out, his monetary shortcomings had been less of a deterrent. But there had never been anyone like Savannah Wilde—unspoiled, without an ounce of pretension or artifice, and unbelievably sweet.

Once they'd gotten over their awkwardness, their relationship had advanced at an unbelievable pace. Learning that she had studied football books in an effort to have something to talk to him about touched him like nothing else. He couldn't remember anyone ever making the effort to do something like that for him. When he had told her to stop reading and he would teach her all she needed to know, he'd laughed at her obvious relief.

Though he had worked every day, he spent every evening with Savannah and sometimes her family. He still didn't have a lot of money, so most of the things they did were either cheap or free. Sometimes they would sit for hours and talk about everything or nothing. There were only two topics of conversation they studiously avoided. Savannah didn't like to talk about her father and what he had done. And Zach avoided talking about his mother. Other than that, nothing was off-limits. She'd told him he'd taught her to appreciate sports. Little did she know that she had taught him to appreciate life.

A few weeks ago, if anyone had told him he'd fall for one of the Wilde sisters, he would've laughed his ass off. Now he wasn't sure if he'd ever laugh again.

"Maybe he'll ask you to go with him," Sammie said.

Turning from the mirror where she'd been trying to tame her wild blond locks, Savannah faced her sisters. Sammie sat on the bed, in the midst of the three dresses, two skirts, and three blouses Savannah had tried on and tossed aside for one reason or the other. Bri sat in the middle of the floor, surrounded by the seven pairs of shoes she had changed her mind about.

Since she had been dating Zach, it had become a ritual that her sisters helped her get ready each evening.

But tonight was unlike any others and nerves and panic were close to overwhelming her. This would be her last night with Zach in who knew how long.

"Lots of girls follow their boyfriends to basic training. You could stay in a hotel or maybe get a temporary apartment close by. I'm sure we could get Granddad to go along with it."

As the romantic in the family, Sammie thought love conquered all. How her sister could believe such a thing after what happened with their parents was anyone's guess.

Savannah shook her head and turned back to the mirror. "He's going to be too busy training to have me trailing along after him. Besides, I've got to go to Nashville and find an apartment soon. Our plans were in place long before we met."

"But that was before you fell in love," Sammie argued.

Her image blurred as Savannah's eyes misted with tears. That was true. She had made her plans for her future before she knew she would love Zach forever. But he had never said he loved her. The hot looks and heart-stopping kisses they'd shared might mean nothing to him. They hadn't even gone all the way. They'd gotten close several times but Zach was the one holding back. Maybe that was why they hadn't had sex: he didn't love her and just didn't want her that way.

A derisive snort had her turning around again. Savannah recognized that sound. It was one of Bri's favorite ways to express her disgust.

"What?" Savannah asked.

"Why wait to see if he's going to ask you to go with him? Tell him you're coming with him and that's that."

Bri could do that. If she didn't like something, she either fought like the dickens to get it changed or she pretended she didn't care.

Not for the first time, Savannah wished she could be

a combination of both her sisters. Sammie was optimistic and cheerful, believing all things worked out, no matter what. Bri was a rebel and a fighter. When Savannah compared herself to her sisters, she always came up short. She was the cautious, practical one. Always weighing all of her options and overthinking everything. Maybe if she were more optimistic like Sammie or forceful like Bri, things would be different.

This wasn't the end. Even though she and Zach were headed in different directions, they had promised to call and email each other daily. When Zach got his first leave, he would come to Nashville to see her. This wasn't the end . . . it wasn't.

Knowing they were eyeing her anxiously, she pasted on a brave smile. "Millions of couples have long-distance relationships. There's no reason we can't."

She pretended she didn't see the doubtful look they shot each other. She had plenty of doubts herself without adding to them. Her trust issues weren't Zach's fault. Other than her grandfather, her sisters, and Aunt Gibby, she had trusted almost no one since that awful summer's night when her parents died. Until Zach. But she was aware her trust wasn't unconditional and was somewhat tenuous. She still wasn't sure of him or his feelings for her.

Pushing aside her worries for the time being, she whirled around. "How do I look?"

"Beautiful," Sammie answered.

"Your hair looks great, too," Bri said. "I'm glad you finally started wearing it loose like that."

Savannah self-consciously touched the unrestrained locks. Though she liked to keep her hair long, she'd always felt self-conscious about its wildness. Not calling attention to herself meant dressing as conservatively as possible, including the way she wore her hair. Long and golden with a natural curl that often had a mind of its own, her hair definitely drew looks. Subduing it with a barrette or ponytail had been her habit. That had changed the first time Zach had seen her hair loose. She'd been running late for their date and hadn't had time to secure it. When his eyes lit up and he'd remarked how pretty it was, she'd worn it unbound from then on.

Her fingers smoothed down the short peach sundress. "What about this dress . . . you don't think it's too revealing?"

"Absolutely not," Sammie said.

Frowning, Bri stood in front of her. "Why are you so nervous?" She gasped and added, "You're going to have sex tonight."

"What?" both Savannah and Sammie shrieked.

"Where on earth did you get that idea?" She was already nervous but Bri's question had sent her nerves zooming into panic mode. With this being their last night together for a long while, would Zach have those kinds of expectations? Did she?

"You just seemed so nervous, I thought that might be the reason." Bri shrugged and added, "Besides, it's about time one of us did it so we could talk about it."

A snort and roll of her eyes was Sammie's response. Savannah didn't answer, her mind still on the thought. She loved Zach. And despite the uncertainty of the future, she knew he cared deeply for her. Was it time to take their relationship to that level?

Their make-out sessions had gotten steamier and more frustrating. Zach hadn't pressured her to take it further, though. Was he just waiting for her to give him the green light? She could usually talk to him about almost anything. Should she talk to him about this?

An overloud, explosive sigh drew her attention back to her sisters. She glanced at Bri, who'd issued the disgusted sound. "What's wrong?"

"There you go overanalyzing and overthinking. If it

happens, it happens. There's no reason to get into a tizzy."

"Easy for you to say," Sammie said before Savannah could answer. "You're not dating anyone right now, so you don't know how tempting it can be."

"I may not be dating anyone, but I've been tempted. I just made up my mind that until I find a guy who really gets me, he's not getting me." Her eyes softened when they settled on Savannah. "Zach gets you, Savvy."

The hard lump of emotion that had been lurking in her chest all day traveled upward and clogged her throat. Bri was right. She had always felt like the odd one out. Boring, staid, and much too traditional. But instead of that turning Zach off, he seemed to really like her that way. Zach did "get" her.

Unable to speak coherently, she nodded and took one last glance in the mirror. Wide green eyes looked back at her with hope and despair in their depths. And in that instant, she knew she wanted her last night with Zach to be one they'd both remember for the rest of their lives. Did she have the courage to set that into motion?

"You look really pretty tonight."

A smile lit up her face. "Thanks. Sammie and Bri helped me pick out this dress."

Standing in line at the Five Star Cinema in downtown Midnight wasn't exactly the night Zach had planned. He stared unseeingly at the movie marquis as he argued with himself. Yeah, this was the right thing to do, but oh hell, he didn't want to be here.

What he had planned was dinner at one of the nicer restaurants in town and then some alone time at Dogwood Lake, their favorite make-out spot. The instant Savannah had opened the door, those plans had changed.

He should be used to her beauty by now, but tonight there was something more. Something almost luminous about her. Maybe it was because he wouldn't see her for several months, maybe it was his own imagination torturing him because he couldn't have what he wanted. Whatever the reason, he had known that making out with her tonight wasn't a good idea.

With only one theater within fifty miles, the Five Star was usually a happening place. On a Friday night in late July, it was the busiest place in town. They were lucky to have gotten tickets. He knew most everyone in line and had seen several people stare and whisper. Knowing that his and Savannah's relationship was the subject of gossip bothered him for only one reason. He didn't want Savannah hurt.

When they had started dating, he had warned her that his reputation would hurt hers. She had been sweetly indignant, saying that if people disapproved, their ignorance and lack of breeding were showing.

While he appreciated the sentiment, he went out of his way to not draw attention to them. Still, he knew the gossips relished the idea of the poor, bad boy of Midnight dating one of the beautiful and wealthy Wilde sisters.

Trying to concentrate on anything other than how beautiful she looked, Zach turned his gaze back to the movie marquis. It didn't matter; his mind's eye had a great memory. Smooth delicate skin, the color of summer peaches, glowed as if she had an inner light. Her hair . . . Zach swallowed and shifted uncomfortably as his body reacted. The first time he saw her hair loose like that, he'd been awestruck. Falling in cascading waves almost to the middle of her back, the color a mixture of dark gold and light blond, her hair had inspired more hot dreams than he'd ever had in his life.

The dress she wore tonight might be modest by most

girls' standards—he'd seen a lot more revealing ones. But there was just something about Savannah. Everything she wore, even if it was just a pair of jeans, hugged the curves of her beautiful body. Sometimes Zach had the hardest time not just staring at her. What he liked most was she had no idea just how appealing she was.

Keeping his hands off her had become increasingly difficult. Savannah had never said, but he knew she was a virgin. She had been bluntly honest that she had dated very little. Their kisses had become more and more intense, and every night he went home aching for her.

"You sure you want to see this movie?"

Jerked out of his lustful thoughts, he glanced down at her. "Why?"

"You keep glaring at the marquis like you're mad at it."

"It's just hard to concentrate with you looking so pretty."

The delight on her face caused an immediate reaction throughout his body. Hell, what was he doing standing in line for a movie he didn't want to see when this was their last night together for a long time? They would be in a theater, surrounded by droves of people, where he couldn't hold her, touch her, kiss her, taste her. Was he crazy or what?

A slender hand touched his arm in a soft caress he felt to his soul. Her smile, still a little shy and incredibly sweet, curved her luscious mouth. "Can I ask you a question? And be completely honest with me, okay?"

Zach nodded. "Absolutely."

"Would you mind if we didn't see the movie? I really just wanted to spend the evening with you . . . alone."

Needing no other encouragement, Zach grabbed her hand and pulled her out of the line. "Let's go."

As they turned to head back to his car, Zach spotted Daryl Yancey and his wife standing in line for tickets.

Zach had worked construction with Daryl; he knew the family struggled for every penny. With four kids, it was probably a rarity for the couple to be able to afford a night out.

He left Savannah briefly and handed the tickets to Daryl, with the vague excuse of just remembering they had other plans. Finally feeling the night was going in the right direction, he said, "How about dinner at Mickey's Steakhouse?"

Sunshine couldn't be any brighter than the smile she flashed him. "Sounds great. I'm starved."

CHAPTER
SIX

Zach drove down the bumpy graveled road to Dogwood Lake. In hindsight, going to a movie before dinner had been a dumbass move. He'd always prided himself on being levelheaded, slow to panic, but the moment he'd seen Savannah tonight, his mind and his libido had gone into an adrenaline overdrive. His first and only concern had been to get her to a safe place with lots of people around. Now, though she was no less desirable or beautiful than she'd been earlier, he had himself under control. Protecting Savannah was his number one priority—he would do nothing to screw that up.

The dinner at Mickey's had been a good choice. Medium priced, plenty of privacy, and the food was great. Savannah had probably had much better, but one of the many things he liked about her was her adaptability. Because of his budget, their dates had consisted of mostly hot dogs and hamburgers at the fast-food places on the outskirts of town or Captain Jimmy's Seafood Emporium out on the bypass. Not once had Savannah ever acted disappointed. Another thing he liked about her was her appetite. She made no bones about the fact that she liked to eat. Most of the girls Zach had dated acted as if a french fry would ruin their life.

Tonight was a special occasion, so the meal had been

pricier than usual. He'd been saving up for weeks—not only for the meal, but also for what was inside the jewelry box burning a hole in his pocket. He didn't know how he was going to approach the subject. Pretty words weren't exactly his forte. Savannah deserved them and a hell of a lot more.

Relieved to see that their favorite spot, a grassy clearing beneath several giant willows, was unoccupied, Zach pulled to a stop and shifted into park. It was already after nine o'clock and Savannah's curfew was midnight. Time with her was rapidly clicking away.

As had become their routine, he pulled a blanket from the backseat and got out. Savannah usually waited for him to open the door for her, but tonight, as if she was just as eager to be in his arms as he was to hold her, she jumped out of the car before he could get around to her.

They spread the blanket onto the soft grass, took off their shoes, and sat down. The full moon cast a shimmering golden path of light on the lake. The wide-open expanse of the velvet black sky was lit with what seemed a billion brilliant stars. Water gently lapping at the bank and frogs and crickets competing in a nighttime chorus were the only sounds. The night felt surreal and intense, as if they were the only two people on the planet.

Savannah snuggled against him and Zach wrapped his arm around her, holding her close. His face buried in the sexy mass of gorgeous hair, he inhaled deeply, taking in her fresh, unique fragrance, committing her scent to memory.

Her soft voice broke into the stillness. "Sometimes I think this is the most beautiful place on the planet, and then I think that it's only that way because you're here."

Chest tight with emotions and feelings he could barely comprehend much less communicate, he whispered into her hair, "I feel the same way. You make everything more beautiful."

"What am I going to do without you?"

Zach lifted his head and shifted around so he could look down at her. "It's only going to be a few months before we see each other. We'll call, text, or email daily. It'll be like we're still together . . . except for this." His mouth lowered to hers, covering it gently, thoroughly, devouring the sweetness he dreamed about nightly. She groaned and opened to him, allowing him entrance into the most luscious mouth that had ever existed.

Before he knew it, they were lying on the blanket and the gentleness disappeared, replaced by a heated, all-consuming passion. Savannah wrapped a long silken leg around his hip. Zach was more than aware that all he had to do was move a couple of scraps of clothing and he could be inside her. His hands glided up her leg, glorying in the satin softness of her inner thigh. He froze and shut his eyes tight. Denying himself what he wanted more than anything at this moment was one of the hardest things he'd ever done.

Breath shuddering, he rose up on his elbow and gently pushed her leg off him.

"What's wrong?"

Unwilling to admit how tempted he'd been or how close he'd come to forgetting about his promise to protect her, he shook his head. "Nothing. Just want to look at you."

Beneath the moonlight, her luminescent skin glowed ever brighter. "My hair's probably a mess."

Weaving his fingers in the wild tresses, he growled, "Your hair is sexy as hell."

A brilliant smile was followed quickly by a nervous biting of her mouth. "Would it be terribly selfish of me to ask you to come to breakfast in the morning? We'll make you something extra special."

She had no idea how much he would love to say yes. Spending extra time with her was incredibly tempting.

But he couldn't. He had made a promise to his mother that he would have breakfast with her. And though he had issues with Francine, Zach prided himself on keeping his promises.

"I wish I could but I promised to have breakfast with my mother. I'll still stop by on the way out of town. Okay?"

"I understand. I know she's going to miss you."

Zach nodded but stayed silent. Discussing his mother was taboo anyway. Talking about her tonight of all nights was impossible.

Reading his silence correctly, Savannah changed the subject. "I'll fix you a lunch that you can take with you so you don't have to eat at a fast-food place. Maybe you can find a roadside park on the way."

He had to smile. Savannah was always trying to make sure he ate well. Zach searched for the right way to convey how much he appreciated that and what she meant to him. Words failed him but he trudged forward. "These last few weeks have been a lot of fun." Bland and insipid words. As soon as they left his lips, he wanted to yank them back. They were an understatement of mammoth proportions. From the moment he'd met her, Savannah had treated him as if he was something special. And in all his years, he'd never laughed so hard or felt so good. Nor had he ever cared for anyone so much.

She tilted her head to look up at him, and her lips trembled for a second before she put on the smile he knew he'd dream about for the rest of his life. "I'm going to miss you so much but I'm so proud of you. I know your dad would be, too."

Though they rarely talked family stuff, he'd explained to her why he had joined the army. About his dad, his service and sacrifice. And in return, she'd told him about her mother. What a fine and beautiful person she was. It had often struck him as odd that they were from completely different backgrounds but had so many similarities. Maybe that was one of the reasons they fit so well together.

He swallowed hard and heard himself say, "You've got a lot of big stuff ahead of you, too. College and law school. I know your mom would be happy about your choices."

"I think she might be very surprised. Up until it happened, I never even paid that much attention in school—she was always encouraging me to study more."

She always referred to her mother's murder as "it." Never able to say those words.

"I've no doubt she would be proud of you and what you've become," he told her.

"I hope so." Her fingers traced his face as if trying to commit it to memory. "What am I going to do without you? You always make me feel better about everything."

"You'll be so busy, you'll probably forget about me in a few weeks."

Deep down he knew that was one of his biggest fears. They had this unbelievable connection now but what would happen when they were far apart for months at a time? Would she meet someone else? What if she wanted to date other guys?

"If you wanted to date other guys, I'd understand."

She froze in his arms. "Are you breaking up with me?"

Ah hell, he'd planned to tell her how much she meant to him and instead made her think he wanted to end things with her. "Of course not. I just don't want to hold you back if that's something you wanted to do."

Green eyes searched his face, questioning and vulnerable. To prevent himself from saying more stupid things, he pulled her back into his arms and lowered his mouth to cover hers. She tasted like butterscotch and vanilla, both flavors from the dessert sundae they'd shared ear-

lier. The memory of her taste would be with him until
he died.

With a sweet moan of surrender, she sank into his
arms. Seeking soft, firm flesh, his hands slid beneath
her dress and traveled up her silken thigh. Because of
the restrictions he put on himself, he kept his caresses
on the outside of her thighs. Though his fingers ached to
delve between her legs and plunge into the sweetness he
fantasized about nightly, he couldn't allow himself to
go further. He had made a silent vow not to coerce her
into having sex. No matter that every part of his body
throbbed with need and an aching desire, he intended
to keep that promise.

"Zach," she whispered against his lips.

"Yeah?"

"Make love to me."

Oh hell. Everything, including breath and heart,
stilled at her words. Grappling with his conscience,
Zach searched for the right thing to say. He knew what
he wanted to say, but his wants were way down on the
list. Savannah and her needs came first. "Are you sure
you're not just saying that because this is our last night
together?"

"Of course that's one of the reasons, but not the biggest. I want you, Zach. There's never been anyone like
you in my life, and whatever the future holds for us, I
want you to be my first time."

Zach searched for the self-discipline, the iron will
he'd held over himself. The aching need to be inside her,
loving her, thrusting deep into her sweetness . . . He
shuddered out a long breath and grabbed onto the best
argument he had for denying them both. "I don't have
any protection with me, Savannah. As much as I want
you, we can't risk—"

Taking his hand, she dropped an unmistakable foil-wrapped packet into his palm. "I bought these at a drugstore in Mobile a couple of weeks ago."

All available blood rushed south; sanity vanished, reason disappeared. Pulling her back into his arms, Zach went at her lips like a starving man, plunging his tongue inside again and again. As her tongue met and tangled with his, a growling groan developed in his chest. Only by sheer will alone did he keep from climbing on top of her, ripping away her underwear, and burying himself deep. The knowledge of how hot and tight she would be almost made him forget everything but his needs and just how much he wanted her.

A minuscule amount of sanity returning temporarily, he rasped against her mouth, "If at any point you want me to stop, you say the words and I will. Okay?"

Barely waiting for her whispered "Yes," Zach gently pushed her until she lay before him. In all his life, he'd never seen anything more beautiful. Moonlight shone softly on Savannah's face; her amazing eyes glimmered with need; her soft, slightly swollen lips beckoned.

Determined that she would know only tenderness and beauty for her first time, Zach came over her and began to slowly and gently make love to her. The small part of his brain that was still working told him that his life would never be the same again.

Reaching to unzip his pants, his hand instead hit a bulge that had nothing to do with desire and everything to do with honor—the jewelry box. Reason returned with painful, glaring clarity. He had claimed that his number one priority was protecting Savannah. Where was that protection now? Taking her on the ground like she didn't matter to him, when she meant everything?

Blowing out a long, pain-filled sigh, Zach sat up and then drew Savannah up to sit beside him.

"What's wrong?"

"This isn't the right time."

"What do you mean?"

He hated the quiver in her voice. Hurting her feelings was the very last thing he wanted. He took her hand and held it in both of his. "When we make love—and I promise you that we will—I want it to be in a comfortable bed, not on a cold, hard ground or with a curfew hanging over our heads. You're too special for anything else."

"But, Zach, I—"

Before he lost all of his nerve, he dipped his hand into his pocket again and pulled out the ring box. "I have something for you."

Savannah's breath caught in her lungs and her heart clenched. She knew she would remember this moment always. Zach's hand trembled slightly as he opened the box and revealed a small silver ring. The band had intricate weaving as if it were branches or limbs, in the middle was a rose, and at the center of the flower was a small, sparkling diamond. It was the most beautiful, exquisite thing Savannah had ever seen.

"Oh, Zach . . ." Tentatively and reverently, her finger traced the design of the band.

"It's a promise ring, Savannah." She heard him swallow hard and then he continued, "My promise to you." He swallowed again. "That I'm yours forever."

Never had she imagined anything more beautiful. "It's perfect . . . the most beautiful ring in the world."

"Will you wear it?"

"Of course."

She watched in anticipation as he pulled it from the box, took her hand, and slid the ring on. A perfect fit.

Zach cleared his throat. "With me going away, I wanted to make sure you understand how important you are to me."

The tears started falling before she could even try to prevent them. His sweet words and the ring were beyond wonderful. She wanted so much to savor this moment, but now all she could think of was that after tomorrow he would be gone. Electronic communication couldn't replace the arms that held her so tenderly or the mouth that kissed her so thoroughly.

"Hey," Zach said softly, "I didn't mean to make you cry."

Embarrassed by her lack of control, Savannah shook her head. "This is all so wonderful. You're so wonderful." She swallowed past the emotion clogging her throat. "I'm going to miss you so much."

"I'll miss you, too, but once I get leave, I'll come see you. Okay?"

Unable to speak coherently, she drew him toward her and let her lips show him what was in her heart. This was forever, they were forever.

Savannah put everything she had into the kiss, wanting Zach to always remember this moment. He had given her his promise with a ring and Savannah gave hers with this kiss. From now until the day she died, she was his.

But she wanted to give him more . . . everything. Renewed desire washed over her; passion swamped her, need consumed her. "Zach . . . please," she whispered softly. "I want this night to be even more perfect. Make love to me."

"Savannah . . . I . . ."

Taking the chance he wouldn't reject her, she caressed the hard length beneath his jeans.

He surged into her hand as he cursed beneath his breath. "Are you sure?"

"One hundred percent sure," she whispered.

A tortured-sounding groan came from deep within Zach's chest. Getting to his knees, he pulled her to hers and said roughly, "Raise your arms."

When she complied, he lifted her dress over her head.

Savannah watched his eyes as they roamed over her body. She saw heat and desire but she also saw adoration. Taking his hands, she placed them on her breasts. He made quick work of unsnapping the peach-colored demi-bra, allowing it to drop to the blanket.

Covering her breasts with his hands, he whispered, "You're beautiful, Savannah."

Never had she felt more beautiful or desirable. Everything within her wanted to speed Zach up, but he seemed to want to savor every inch of her breasts before he moved on. Heat zoomed through her as he paid homage to each nipple with his fingers, hands, and then his mouth.

Savannah held his head, weaving her hands in his hair. She wanted this; she wanted more. She wanted all he had to give. "Zach, love me."

Pushing her gently down onto the blanket, Zach hooked his fingers into her panties and pulled them down her legs. Savannah lay before him completely nude, feeling vulnerable and exposed. His eyes glittered down at her, and for the first time, she felt nervous.

"Aren't you going to take your clothes off, too?"

The smile he gave her was unlike any she'd ever seen on his face—wicked and sexy. "Give me two seconds." He went to his feet and barely had those words left his mouth before he was stripped bare, too.

Savannah lost her breath. Having seen his chest and bare legs when they'd gone swimming, she had known he was magnificent. All of him together, including the long, thick part of him she'd only felt beneath his clothes, was more than she had anticipated. Tentatively she touched his penis, marveling in wonder at the heat, length, and the hard silk of him.

He groaned and grabbed her wrist. Then, lowering himself over her, Zach took both of her hands and held them over her head. "It'll be best if you don't touch me for a few minutes. Okay?"

Willing to do anything he wanted, she nodded. At her acceptance, Savannah heard him whisper what sounded like a curse and a prayer and then, with all the gentleness she had come to expect from this man, he began to caress her as if she were the finest, most precious thing in the world.

Savannah forgot everything—past, present, and future no longer existed. Her only awareness was of Zach's hands, his mouth, and his soft whispered words of praise. And then, finally, when she was gasping and panting for more, she felt the long, hard length of him at her entrance. With one, slow gliding surge, he slid inside. Arms wrapped tightly around him, Savannah gave herself to her hero, the man of her dreams. No matter what they faced in the future, she knew that she was Zach's. And he was hers. This was forever. Nothing could tear them apart.

CHAPTER SEVEN

**TEN YEARS LATER
PRESENT DAY
NASHVILLE, TENNESSEE**

"Has the jury reached a verdict?" Judge Henry Houseman asked the group of twelve men and women to his left.

The jury foreman, her expression carefully blank to give no indication of the result, answered solemnly, "We have, your honor."

As the court clerk took the jury's decision from the foreman's hand and handed it to the judge, Assistant District Attorney Savannah Wilde stood behind the prosecutor's table, still and stiff. Though she had been through this process dozens of times, that moment of not knowing always twisted every muscle in her body into intricate knots of tension. She always found herself asking the same questions. Had she proven the case? Had she done everything she could to bring justice to the victim? Was this scumbag going to be set free like too many others had been?

His craggy face characteristically expressionless, Judge Houseman silently read the verdict. The anxiety throughout the room was like a living, palpable entity as the tension increased to a fever pitch. The entire audience held a collective breath, waiting.

The judge nodded at the foreman, who then read, "We the jury find the defendant Donny Lee Grimes guilty of murder in the first degree."

Breaths were expelled, some with anger, most with relief. Savannah fought the urge to shout, "Hallelujah!" Exhausted she might be, but the long days and nights she had worked this case had paid off. The murdering son of a bitch was going away, hopefully for a lifetime.

As the judge finished his instructions and set the date for sentencing, she glanced over at her boss, District Attorney Reid Garrison. Though his expression remained impassive, triumph gleamed in his eyes and the tension lines around his mouth had eased. They had needed this win. Not only because Donny Lee Grimes was a murdering creep who'd taken the life of a young father and husband, but because their record lately had been dismal. Watching murderers and rapists walk out the door due to technicalities or the prosecutors' inability to prove their case was not only gut-wrenching but reflected badly on the entire office. The mayor had chewed out Reid so many times lately, Savannah was surprised he still had an ass.

And the ass chewing he got from his superiors he gladly turned around and gave to his own people. Savannah had been on the receiving end much more than she cared to remember.

But all of that could be set aside today. This was a good day for justice. Donny Lee's connections hadn't saved him. The X-Kings, the gang he'd once been a prominent member of, had apparently cut him loose. Only a few veiled threats had been made against her— prompting an increase in her security—but nothing she hadn't been through before. Whatever influence Donny Lee once had with them was obviously gone.

The instant the judge stood and stepped down from behind the bench, Savannah allowed her tense muscles to finally relax. Exhausted, she dropped into the chair behind her and released a giant relieved whoosh of air. One more scumbag off the streets. One more victim's family had been given a slight amount of peace.

She ignored the weakness in her knees and the shakiness of her limbs. Having lived with the feeling for the last few weeks, she knew full well what it meant. She was on her final reserves. This was her last case for two weeks. Fourteen days of doing nothing more taxing than ordering takeout and turning pages of novels. She was about to take the first lengthy but very well deserved vacation of her career.

The sound of a ruckus caught her attention. Her head jerked up, too late. A large male body flew across the table toward her. A glimpse of Donny Lee's pockmarked face, red with fury, was all she saw before his two-hundred-pound body slammed into hers. Breath left her with stunning suddenness and Savannah crashed to the floor.

From a distance, she heard curses, screams, and shouts roar through the room. The disgusting man on top of her grunted almost unintelligible words of warning in her ear. Though dazed, Savannah wasn't too incapacitated to lift her knee and jam it directly into Donny Lee's groin.

Howls and curses almost split her eardrum. Donny Lee was lifted off her and Savannah could at last breathe. She sat up and leaned against the railing behind her, shaking her head to clear it.

The worried and furious face of her boss appeared above her. "You okay?"

"I'm fine," she answered, holding out her hand for him to help her up.

Eyeing her carefully, he pulled her to her feet. The

lines around his mouth and eyes had deepened. "We'll charge the bastard with assault."

Savannah breathed shakily as she flexed all moveable body parts, assuring herself that nothing was broken. The ache in her shoulders and back told her that she was going to be moving slowly and carefully for the next couple of days. Those fourteen days of doing absolutely nothing were going to be even more welcome.

As Donny Lee was hauled out of the room, shouting obscenities and threats to the room at large, Savannah kept a careful eye on him. He'd gotten away once; she wasn't betting on him not being able to do it again. She'd be ready this time. When the door closed behind him, she allowed herself to slump against the railing for support.

"You sure you don't need to go to the doctor?" Reid asked.

Savannah shook her head. "I'm fine. Just going to be sore for a few days."

"That bastard say something to you?"

"Nothing new. That it wasn't over . . . that they were coming for me." The silence after her statement had her gazing up at her boss. "What's wrong?"

"Maybe you need to extend your vacation till after sentencing."

A trill of fear swept through her. Not work for two months? She would go crazy. "I had to work my ass off just to take these two weeks. There's no way I can afford more—there are too many cases for the ADAs already."

"We'll make do. I'd rather have you alive and able to come back to work."

"Reid, seriously. Donny Lee was blowing smoke. Besides, I have police protection, I'll be fine."

He shook his head. "That police protection will be going away in a day or so." The stern, determined look that all his ADAs hated crossed his face. "I could order you."

A huff of exasperation caused the pain in her back to increase. Dammit, she wished she'd kneed Donny Lee even harder.

Reid continued his argument. "Just because we believe the X-Kings cut Donny Lee loose doesn't mean he doesn't have some old friends who wouldn't mind coming after you as a favor. As of now, you're off—two months minimum."

"I can't—"

Reid added, "Of course, I can't pay you full salary."

Though money wasn't scarce for her and he knew it, that wasn't the issue. "I'll hire a bodyguard. There's no reason for—"

He snorted. "Hell, Savannah, you'd think I was sending you to jail. Get out of town; get some sun. Go visit your sisters or take a long cruise. You've been working nonstop for more than three years without a break. You've got more vacation time built up than I do."

That was an exaggeration but he was right. Other than the one-weekend-a-month visit with her sisters, she hadn't taken any time off in years. And she wouldn't have taken these two weeks she had planned if it wasn't for the fact that she was just so damn tired.

But two months? An image of the Wilde mansion, empty and lonely, popped into her head. With two months to spare, no matter how much she dreaded the event, she had no excuses.

Her grandfather had passed away over two years ago. Other than the quick trip back to Midnight for his funeral, she hadn't allowed herself to think about what needed to be done. And neither had her sisters. Without her grandfather's larger-than-life presence, going back home had been too painful to face. As much as she hated the thought of returning to a place that held so many bad memories, it was going to have to be done at some point.

Her sisters wouldn't be able to spare the time. Samantha was a homicide detective in Atlanta and Sabrina was a private investigator in Tallahassee. Their caseloads were too heavy to take that much time off. Would she ever have a better opportunity to pack up their belongings and put the house on the market?

"You're not going to argue anymore?" Reid's voice indicated he was a bit disappointed.

Laughing, she shook her head. "Nope. I think you're right. I'll head back to the office and brief everyone. Then I'm off . . ." She swallowed hard. "For two months." A twinge of panic shot through her as she said those words. Work was her life, her panacea. Could she function that long without it?

Of course she could. She was going to be busy, just a different kind of busy.

Reid pulled his cellphone from his pocket, punched a key, and then held it to his ear. "I'll make sure you've got security until you leave."

Savannah nodded. Once she was out of town, they could all breathe a little easier. By the time she came back, Donny Lee would be in prison and any threats should be worthless. And she would be rested and relaxed. She would also have accomplished an important task that should have been handled two years ago.

Gathering her case file and notes, she shoved them into her briefcase. This definitely wasn't her idea of a vacation. Not only would she be dealing with the volatile emotions of saying goodbye to her grandfather one last time, she would again become immersed in the memories of her parents' deaths. Murder-suicide sounded so clinical and cold, but when it happened to the ones you loved most in the world, there was nothing clinical about it. Even eighteen years later, her stomach still twisted in grief as she remembered those dark days.

Her mind veered away from the other issue she had diligently forced herself not to think about since she had heard the news. Midnight had a new chief of police. No doubt she would be running into him. Seeing Zach Tanner after all these years wasn't something she even wanted to contemplate. What do you say to your first love? The first and only man who'd ever broken your heart? The one man you'd given your total trust to only to have it thrown back in your face? And the only man who, at the mere thought of him, could still cause shivers of arousal to strum through your body?

The best thing she could do was stay out of his way. She and Zach had nothing to say to each other. That ship had sailed a long time ago. And all of the hurt and sorrow from that time was just another dark moment in her life that she had put behind her.

As she made her way slowly out of the courtroom, a painful and humiliating thought flitted through her mind. Just because she remembered everything, down to the smallest detail of their short romance, didn't mean that Zach did. All the promises he'd made, including the last, most important one, had been lies. So what made her think he remembered her at all?

MIDNIGHT, ALABAMA

Police Chief Zach Tanner wasn't having a good day. It'd started too damn early. Getting a call in the middle of the night that Mr. Dickens's cattle were roaming free wasn't exactly murder and mayhem, but it was something he'd had to handle. By the time they'd been rounded up and Mr. Dickens had once again promised to get his fence repaired, it was long past dawn. Going home and grabbing a couple of hours' sleep hadn't been feasible. Now, five cups of coffee later, he was looking at the graffitied wall of Henson's Grocery, one of the oldest stores in Midnight. Other than the misspellings, Zach couldn't help but think that it actually looked better this way. Old man Henson had put off painting for years, but thanks to some idiots with nothing better to do, it looked like the old store was finally going to get a face-lift.

"What're you aiming to do about it, Chief?"

The sarcastic tone of his last word bounced off Zach with no impact. He and old man Henson had a past, and no matter how many years went by, neither of them would ever forget it. Which was just damn fine with Zach. Torturing the old bastard with his presence was, in its own way, a reward in itself.

Still, as chief of police, it was his duty to serve and protect even holier-than-thou useless pricks like Henson. Problem was, with only three deputies in a town of fourteen hundred people, Zach had learned early that certain issues couldn't get as much attention as he would have liked. But this type of vandalism would continue until either the culprits were caught or they found something else to occupy their time.

"I'll put one of my deputies on it, but be warned, there's not a lot of evidence here. Might want to reconsider those security cameras we talked about."

Brown tobacco juice splattered, landing barely three inches from Zach's boot. Henson wiped his tobacco-filled mouth with his sleeve and snarled, "Chief Mosby would've made this his number one priority."

That was because Mosby hadn't been above taking a few under-the-table bribes to help him choose his priorities. Henson had made it more than clear that he expected to be able to continue that service. At first Zach had laughed in his face, amazed at the asshole's audacity. That'd pissed the old man off but good. Then, when Zach had turned him down with the not-so-subtle warning that bribing an officer of the law was illegal, the man had been furious. Since then, Henson's hostility had become even more blatant.

Letting the man rile him wasn't worth Zach's time or energy. "I'll have Deputy Odom come by in a few minutes." With that, Zach turned away, ignoring Henson's mutterings.

He and Henson had never been on good terms. He hadn't known for a long time why that was and could have lived quite happily without ever knowing. Zach had just assumed that poor people pissed the man off. Of course, it hadn't helped that a teenaged Zach had been caught twice stealing food. The fact that it'd been from the dumpster in the back of the grocery store hadn't mattered to Henson. Until the trash collectors came by, that "gal-derned garbage in those dumpsters was rightfully his and nobody had a right to touch it."

He slid into his police cruiser, cranked the engine, and headed back to his office. The pile of paperwork on his desk wasn't something he was looking forward to, but it had to be done. When he'd agreed to become police chief, he'd made a commitment to do the best job he could.

Coming back to Midnight was only supposed to be a temporary thing for Zach. After two tours in Iraq and one in Afghanistan, he'd left the army with no real clear idea of what he wanted other than peace and solitude. He'd taken the time to finish up his degree and then had returned home with one specific goal in mind: sell the old house for what he could get out of it and then leave all the memories behind.

His mother had signed the house over to him when she and Leonard moved from Midnight. With Josh gone from home, too, and no one looking out for the upkeep, he had figured it would be in bad shape and he had been right. But something remarkable happened. In the midst of scraping, painting, and refurbishing the small, ramshackle house where he'd grown up, Zach had somehow found what he was looking for—a home.

Staying in Midnight made absolutely no sense other than the feeling that this was where he belonged. He had been treated like garbage by many of the good citizens of Midnight, so maybe it was his own twisted sense of humor that made him stay. Or maybe it was self-punishment for the sins he had committed. Most likely it was to piss certain people off. Whatever the reason, Zach was here to stay.

Finding a job hadn't been as big of a problem as he'd anticipated. Once his house was done to his satisfaction, he'd had a half dozen people approach him about doing work on their homes. Within a matter of months, he had a small business going with three employees and more job requests than he could accept. Though many folks still remembered the poor skinny kid that was always in trouble, Zach had no real problems until Henson's grocery store had been broken into. And who had Chief Mosby come to question? None other than Zach Tanner, former juvenile delinquent and still number one on Henson's shit list.

Zach had been torn between slamming his fist into Harlan Mosby's face and busting out laughing. He'd done neither . . . just quietly cooperated. Two days later, the punks had been caught.

There'd been no apology from Mosby or Henson; Zach hadn't expected one. However, Mosby's attitude had made him wonder just how soon he'd be called in to answer questions on another crime. It'd taken exactly a week. When Mosby had no idea of a suspect, Zach became his go-to guy. Though he was usually slow to rile, a fed-up and pissed-off Zach wasn't something most people wanted to tangle with. Ones who did lived to regret it. A very public confrontation had taken place in the middle of city hall. The results had been mixed. Many people had enjoyed watching a snarling Zach give Mosby his comeuppance. A few wanted to run Zach out of town. But Zach had gotten his desired result—the chief off his back.

Six months later, Mosby was calling it quits because of poor health and Midnight was in the market for a new police chief. The only person to step up for the job was Deputy Clark Dayton, a man who appeared poised to follow in Mosby's crooked footsteps. Time hadn't improved Dayton. He was still the same jerk he'd been in high school. At the urging of a few newfound friends, Zach had agreed to interview for the position. Much to everyone's surprise, including his own, he'd gotten the job.

Odd how he felt so at home in a place that held so many bad memories.

As if it had a mind of its own, the patrol car turned onto Wildefire Lane—something it did at least twice a day. Early on, he had told himself it was because he was the police chief and therefore it was his duty to keep an eye on vacant properties that might invite vandalism and theft. Empty homes were prime targets for all sorts of crimes. But he had long stopped trying to convince himself of something he knew wasn't true, especially since this had become a ritual long before he became police chief. No, he drove by the grand mansion for one reason only. Midnight held bad memories except for two magical months. And the woman who owned the house on Wildefire Lane had been the reason for that magic.

Ten years had passed since he'd seen her; held her in his arms, tasted her lips, heard her laughter, basked in her smile. She had gone on to fulfill her dreams. He had told her she would and he was glad to know that he'd been right. They'd been two kids who'd found what they needed at the time. Then life had interrupted in all its realistic and dirty glory.

As he came to the long drive leading to the mansion, Zach stopped the car. Even though it had stood empty since Daniel Wilde passed on, the residence was kept in perfect condition. Caretakers came weekly to mow the lawn, and a cleaning service dusted the furniture twice a week. He'd heard that fresh flowers were added to vases twice a week, too. With this place being the location of one of the most famous murder-suicides in Alabama in the twentieth century, gossip was rife about every aspect of the mansion. Some had even whispered that the ghost of Maggie Wilde still roamed the halls, calling out for her daughters. A few had claimed seeing a blond woman in white standing on the second-floor portico. Southerners did love a good ghost story.

The mansion was the traditional plantation-style home. Giant white columns, three on each side of the long, narrow porch, were so large and sturdy-looking, they appeared to be holding up the entire structure. White rocking chairs gave off the appearance of restful indolence, and blood-red roses creeping up the trellises splashed vivid color against the stark white background of the brick. Moss-draped giant elms and oaks hovered protectively over magnolia, mimosa, and weeping willow trees. In late spring and early summer, the scent of the flowering trees, along with the thick fragrance from the wild honeysuckle in the woods behind the mansion, was almost overwhelming in its sweetness.

A few people still came by on their way to Gulf Shores or Biloxi to take pictures and gawk at one of the most famous mansions in Mobile County. When Zach looked at the massive picturesque structure, he saw something else. In his mind's eye, he envisioned wavy, honey-gold hair that covered slender, delicate shoulders, eyes the color of new spring grass, and a smile like the first hint of summer after a bitter cold winter. And beneath that beauty, a genuinely sweet and kind spirit. Falling for Savannah had been so damn easy. Even ten years later, not a day went by that he didn't think about her. And not a day went by that he didn't curse himself for what he'd done to her.

The radio sputtered and the dispatcher, Hazel Adkins, croaked in her smoker's voice, "Chief, you coming back to the office anytime soon?"

Zach shook off his memories and grabbed the radio mic. "Headed that way right now. What's up?"

"Got a call from Reid Garrison, district attorney up in Nashville, Tennessee. Said he needed to talk to you real soon. Sounded kind of urgent-like."

Zach's heart stuttered. Savannah worked in the DA's office in Nashville. Did this have anything to do with her? He mentally shook his head. No. There was no reason the DA would even know about his past relationship with one of his prosecutors. This was probably about a case. Maybe some criminal was headed their way.

"Give me the number and I'll call him back right now."

While Hazel rattled off the number, in a small part of Zach's mind, temptation warred with his good sense. Should he ask about Savannah? As he pounded the number into his cellphone, he knew temptation would win out. Besides, finding out how she was doing was normal. They'd grown up in the same town. In fact, it'd be damn strange if he didn't mention her. Right?

Five minutes later, Zach ended the call and dropped the phone on the seat beside him. There'd been no need to ask about Savannah. The call had been all about her. Not only was she coming home, the DA wanted him to be aware of some threats that'd been made against her.

Zach checked the rearview mirror and then stepped

on the gas pedal, his mind whirring with myriad thoughts. He'd known that by coming back here to live, he'd see her again. The mansion was prime real estate and even in this economy would bring a pretty penny. He'd figured that she and her sisters would return someday and put the place on the market. Now that the day had finally arrived, Zach zeroed in on two major thoughts: It had almost killed him to let her go the first time. How the hell was he going to watch her come back to Midnight for only a short time and not try to convince her to stay forever?

And just how much did she hate him for breaking her heart?

CHAPTER EIGHT

Savannah flexed her fingers, wincing at their stiffness. The closer she came to Midnight, the tighter her grip on the steering wheel had become. She was still on 65 South, at least two hours from her destination. At this rate, there would be handprint indentations in the leather by the time she drove into the city limits.

Usually when she made a decision, she was determined to see it through. This time was different. Facing the morass of memories was so much easier in theory than in real life. Midnight was the place of her worst nightmare. Where her childhood had begun and ended much too soon. It was the place where her vulnerable, romantic heart had bloomed with overwhelming love and then was shattered beyond recognition. Years had gone by before she'd felt the slightest mend to her damaged heart. And very soon she would be seeing the man who had caused that devastation.

But she couldn't keep putting off the inevitable. Her granddad would have wanted them to get this over with and get on with their lives. She and her sisters had gone back for the funeral, of course. Daniel Wilde was one of the kindest, most generous men God had ever put on this earth. His kindness had thankfully included making all the plans and arrangements for his funeral. Though he had passed away unexpectedly, when she and her sisters had arrived home, expecting to have to make numerous decisions, they had discovered they needed to do nothing but mourn their loss and accept condolences.

Losing their granddad had left Savannah and her sisters too devastated to even contemplate selling the Wilde house. They had arranged to continue with the same cleaning and lawn service with the knowledge that at some point, one of them would have to return to do what was necessary. Savannah, ever the practical one, had mentioned this several times during their monthly get-togethers. She understood their reasons for putting it off—she had delayed also. Putting the house up for sale was the final goodbye.

She had called both Sammie and Bri to tell them she was going back, but they'd both been out. She wanted to make sure they were okay with her decisions about the sale. Granddad had made Savannah the executrix of his estate, but all three sisters had equal inheritance.

The cellphone she'd dropped on the front passenger seat rang. Knowing it was one of her sisters, she pressed the answer button on her steering wheel and said, "Hey."

"What the hell happened?"

Surprised at the worry in Sammie's voice, she asked, "What do you mean?"

"I just saw photos of you being attacked. Why didn't you tell me? Are you okay?"

"Photos? Where?"

"*The Tennessean.*"

Crap. She should have realized Nashville newspapers would've printed a story and photos if they had them. "I'm sorry, Sammie. I left you a message."

"Yeah, that you were taking some time off to go back home and get the house ready for sale. You never mentioned you were attacked."

Savannah shrugged and then winced. Dammit, her back still hurt. "It was no big deal."

Sammie's exasperated snort came through loud and clear. "Only you would say that, Savvy." Her voice softened. "But you're really okay?"

"I'm fine. Just a couple of bruises, nothing more." She took a breath and asked, "So, what do you think about me going down there?"

"Well, it's way past time for us to do something."

The hesitancy in her sister's voice wasn't lost on her. "I hear a 'but' in there."

"Are you really ready to see him again?"

Savannah didn't have to question who the "him" was. There were no secrets between the sisters. They had been by her side at every devastating moment.

"I honestly don't know if I'll ever be ready. I just know this needs to be done and I can't be a coward forever."

"Savannah Rose Wilde, you stop right there. There's not a cowardly bone in your body."

She disagreed but knew there was no point in arguing. Her sisters had always been her staunchest allies and defenders. They saw her as the innocent party but she knew the truth. There had been only one innocent in the entire ordeal.

"I just wish I could break away and be with you. You shouldn't have to do this alone."

"I'll be fine. Two months is more than enough time to get everything done. And seeing Zach won't be that bad. I mean . . . it's not like I still love him or anything."

Sammie's soft snort of doubt was something Savannah chose to ignore. She didn't still love Zach—she was sure of it. Well, almost sure of it.

"He probably barely remembers me."

"You know better than that."

Did she? She had loved Zach with a youthful, starry-eyed passion. And for months, without the slightest encouragement from him, she had held on to a useless, pathetic hope. Sure that he would come back; sure that there was a reasonable explanation for his desertion. When acceptance finally settled in, that hope had shattered into a million tiny pieces, along with her heart. And for a while, her life.

"Maybe I can sneak into town, do what I need to do and not see him."

"Ten minutes after you hit town, the gossips will have spread the news of your homecoming to every corner of Midnight."

Yes, she did know that, but a girl could dream.

"By the bye," Sammie said, "how on earth did you manage two whole months of vacation?"

"It's not exactly vacation. I was just going to take a couple of weeks and putter around the apartment. But then a creep I prosecuted and put away issued a couple of threats. Reid thought it'd be a good idea for me to get out of town until after his sentencing."

"I knew there was more to this story. Dammit, what did he say?"

"Nothing that hasn't been said before. It was an empty threat. He's got no clout left with his gang members, but Reid decided to be on the safe side. So since I had to take time off, I figured I might as well go back and deal with this."

"Yeah, as opposed to taking a trip to the Bahamas or a long cruise."

"It needs to be done."

Sammie sighed. "I know, I know. I just wish . . ."

"Hey, I'll be fine. Okay?"

"You know you only have to call me and I'll come."

"I know that and I love you for it. Maybe you and Bri can come down for our monthly meet."

"Good idea. I'll give her a call and see what she says. Have you talked to her?"

"Not yet. Had to leave her a voice-mail message, too."

"Check your email when you can. She sent both of us a note this morning. She's on a new project. Hush-hush. Said we probably won't hear from her for a few days."

The worry in Sammie's voice mirrored Savannah's thoughts. Even though the sisters were triplets, with only a few minutes between their ages, both she and Sammie had always looked at Bri as the one who needed to be shielded the most. To outsiders, that might seem odd, since Bri was a self-defense expert who could kick the ass of someone twice her size without breaking a sweat. But her family knew her inside and out. Beneath the tough façade she showed the world, Bri was a vulnerable, gentle-hearted woman who could be hurt too easily.

Five years ago, that tough façade had been all but destroyed. Bri had been engaged to a man they had all believed was perfect for her. Only weeks before they were to marry, disaster had struck. And then, after that disaster, total heartbreak and betrayal. Though Bri never talked about that time, Savannah knew she still reeled from the disillusionment.

Given her penchant for getting into trouble, Bri's career choice as a private investigator had always worried the family. After what happened, they became even more concerned. She had a reckless air that hadn't existed before. Thankfully, in the last couple of years, she seemed to have calmed down and now had an excellent reputation as an investigator.

"Did Bri give you any details of her case?"

"Of course not. You know Bri."

"What about you?" Savannah asked. "Anything big going on?"

"SOS . . . same old stuff. Got called in on a triple

homicide yesterday. Haven't slept in almost twenty-four hours."

Hearing that, Savannah was doubly glad she hadn't asked for Sammie's help. "Got any suspects?"

"Yeah, unfortunately . . . looks like the teenaged son did his entire family."

Savannah sighed her sadness. How did some lives get so screwed up? "That's awful. Is he in custody?"

"Will be as soon as we find him," Sammie promised grimly.

The Wilde sisters' career choices were an obvious testament to the impact of what had happened with their parents. No matter how much time passed, that legacy would remain with them always.

"Things still good with Quinn?"

"Oh yes." Her sister's sigh of contentment came through the phone line loud and clear.

Savannah smiled at the sound. Sammie had always had the easier time with relationships. She dated frequently but had never formed any lasting attachments. Then, at last month's get-together, much to their surprise, she had announced she had finally found "the one."

"I'm glad things are going well. Are we going to get to meet him soon?"

"If he can spare a couple of days, I might bring him with me when I come home for a visit."

"Excellent. I can't wait to meet the gorgeous doctor." An exit sign indicating several service stations caught Savannah's attention. "Listen, I'm about to get off the interstate and get some gas."

"Okay. Be sure to let me know if there's anything I need to do."

"Will do. Love you."

Savannah took the exit and pulled into a gas station. As she pumped gas, a large sign advertising a little mom-and-pop restaurant a couple of miles away tempted her.

Problem was, she wasn't hungry. The enticement came not from wanting to eat but from procrastination. For someone who prided herself on not putting things off, this particular event was much too long in the making. Determination forced her to finish filling the tank, get back in her car, and keep going.

Now set on getting the trip over with as quickly as possible, Savannah clicked on her CD player, hoping the diversion would take her mind off what lay ahead. Weird, but every song that played worked against her. Themes of lost love and old acquaintances and melodic warnings of "you can't go home again" bombarded her. If she were a believer in signs, she'd definitely turn back around.

A quick glance up at the sky made her wince. Even the clouds looked ominous. When she'd left Nashville, the sky had been a piercingly clear azure blue, but now, wicked, thunderous clouds obscured the sun. There should be more than an hour of daylight left, but it had gotten so dark, it seemed much later than the 6:30 P.M. on her dashboard clock.

She shook her head, undeterred. She was going back, come hail or high water. And from the look of the sky, both were possible.

MIDNIGHT, ALABAMA

She was coming home today. Zach had done his best to forget that knowledge and go about his normal routine. Of course, he would keep an eye on her, but only because that was his job. He had taken an oath to protect every citizen of Midnight, including one who was only here temporarily and would drive him out of his ever-loving mind while she was here. He would do what he was paid to do and nothing more.

Staying clear of her should be no problem. She was here to pack up the family's belongings and put the Wilde house on the market, not gallivant around town. And he had his hands full, including another vandalism. This was the fourth one in the last two weeks and he was getting damn tired of them. Once again, there'd been no clues, no witnesses. Nothing but badly misspelled words and a few satanic symbols that a five-year-old could have drawn better.

"Who do you think is doing this, Chief?"

Zach glanced over his shoulder at his deputy, Clark Dayton. He and Clark had never been easy around each other. Even before the incident with Savannah, some might have called them enemies, though Zach never could figure out what he had done back then to piss off the guy. The Daytons had been on the lower end of Midnight's society, but compared to Zach's family, they had been upper-crust wealthy. At that time in his life, to Zach, if a person had regular meals and clothes without holes, he was doing damn good. Back in those days, Clark had carried a giant chip on his shoulder and had delighted in pointing out the differences between his family and anyone poorer. He had often been Dayton's prime target. Zach hadn't cared. The man's opinion hadn't mattered then or now. He had ignored him, which somehow seemed to infuriate the guy even more. Then one night, everything had changed and Clark had done something that couldn't be ignored.

Savannah had been at the wrong place at the wrong time, Clark had been way past drunk, and Zach's life had changed forever.

"Guess that means you've got no suspects?"

Zach mentally shook his head. What the hell was he doing daydreaming about Savannah? "None yet, but they'll screw up eventually and we'll find them."

Clark scratched his neatly trimmed beard in an absentminded fashion Zach had become familiar with. It was usually followed by a hypothesis and then a conclusion. Clark had had a year and a half of college before he'd dropped out. Somehow, in that short amount of time, the man became a self-avowed philosopher and psychologist. Zach braced himself for one of his theories.

"I'm suspecting it's that new family that's moved into the Hogans' old house. They've got two teenaged boys that look just about right for this kind of thing." Another slow beard scratch and then he added, "I'm thinking I need to have a chat with them."

Zach's eyes narrowed. "What do you mean, they look just about right?"

Beefy shoulders barely shifted in a lazy shrug. "One of the boys has a wild look behind his eyes. Just don't look right. I don't like it."

His eyebrow lifted questioningly, Zach waited to see if Clark had any legitimate reason for his suspicions, other than he just didn't like the way the kid looked.

"I got an intuition about people. Can size up troublemakers. Both them boys have trouble written all over their faces."

Reminding himself that despite Dayton's somewhat ridiculous hypotheses, he was known to be a competent deputy, Zach said patiently, "We're not going to go harassing people without any solid evidence just because you don't like the way they look."

Clark's beard barely concealed the sneer on his thick lips. "Your attitude of 'let's just wait and see what happens' sure don't seem to be working."

Zach couldn't argue. They had no suspects. This damaged building, like the others, had no security cameras, and other than the defacement itself, the evidence was minimal. A cigarette butt and tire tracks weren't exactly road maps to the culprit. Last night had been a full moon; even without security lights, someone should have seen something. Hell, it was almost impossible to take a piss in this town without everyone knowing about it. How were these pricks getting away with it?

He turned his back to Clark and eyed the crime scene again. As graffiti went, it was distinctly unimaginative and colorless. Wouldn't take more than a couple of coats of paint to cover it up, which seemed kind of odd. If the perps wanted to really cause some trouble, they could have done much worse. Burn the place down or even bust some windows. This kind of vandalism didn't interrupt business. All it did was cause lots of talk and a hell of a lot of work for the police department. It also caused speculation on the competency of the new police chief. A light bulb went off in Zach's head and he cursed himself for not realizing it before.

"So if you don't want to consider the boys of that new family, you got any ideas at all?"

Zach did, but sure as hell wouldn't be sharing them with this man. He shrugged. "I'll think on it. In the meantime, why don't you finish up the reports on that brush fire that got out of control on Saturday?"

Dayton's mouth twisted, blatant resentment igniting in his eyes. The man hated taking orders from someone who'd once knocked the hell out of him. When Zach had taken the job, he'd met individually with every employee and offered each one an opportunity to leave. No one had taken the offer, including Clark. And though he hadn't wanted the man as his deputy, Zach had no cause to fire him. Yet.

Zach held Clark's gaze and waited for the deputy to mouth off. Apparently seeing the wisdom in keeping his thoughts to himself this time, he turned with a huff and stomped away.

Once he was gone, Zach walked around the property once more and let the idea solidify in his head. If the culprits were kids, wouldn't they do more damage or at least perform some act that left more of a mark? The way it was now, the only harm done was to the insurance company that had to pay the claim, and to the police department's reputation because they had no suspects.

Before Zach could pursue that line of thought any further, his radio squawked, "Chief, you there?"

"Yeah, go head."

"We got some trouble going on at Gertie's Wash and Wait."

"What kind of trouble?"

"Somebody set off fireworks in the dryers. Gertie says it sounds like a war zone. Minnie Dixon's in hysterics."

Zach dragged a weary hand down his face and jumped into his car. Hell yeah, it was definitely a full moon.

CHAPTER NINE

Dusk was falling as Savannah entered downtown Midnight. It was summertime, which meant shopkeepers stayed open an hour later than during the winter months. Since it was going on eight o'clock, blinds were being drawn, door locks were clicking, and Open signs were being switched to Closed. Her timing couldn't have been worse.

If she had wanted to avoid the attention her arrival would create, she shouldn't have driven through town till at least an hour later, when it would be shut down with the exception of gas stations and restaurants. She could see glimpses of curious faces peeking through those closed blinds. Of course everyone already knew she was coming. Within minutes of her notifying the housekeeping service and asking them to deliver some fresh food and staples to the kitchen, dozens of people had known of her impending arrival. Within an hour, no doubt everyone had known. News traveled faster than a runaway zipper in this town . . . there were few secrets in Midnight. And since the whole town knew, that meant Zach knew, too.

Breath came from her in small spurts and her heart thudded heavily against her chest—almost like a panic attack. Ten years had passed. She was a different person now. The confidence and strength she had lacked back then she now possessed in abundance. And though she knew little to nothing about the adult Zach, she had heard he'd seen active battle. War changed a person. Sometimes it brought out the best, other times the worst. How had it changed him?

As usual, when she allowed herself to think about Zach, she wondered how their lives would have been different if he had kept his promise. Would it have changed things? Would they still be together, or would he have eventually broken her heart anyway? Had he thought he was doing the kind thing by going cold turkey? Who knows, maybe he had been right. She would never know. Maybe he wouldn't have been the strong, emotional rock she had needed back then.

Breath shuddered through her. Three more blocks and she'd be on Wildefire Lane. So far, she had recognized no one. Hopefully her luck would hold. A good night's sleep would give her the energy boost to face whatever came her way tomorrow.

The instant she made a left onto Magnolia Avenue, she knew she had made a mistake. Not only were two patrol cars and an ambulance blocking her way, a crowd of twenty or more stood in the middle of the road. All eyes were focused on Gertie's Wash and Wait, a business that had been there as long as she could remember.

Knowing if she didn't turn around soon, she'd be stuck in the crowd of onlookers, Savannah made a quick swoop into a parking space with the intent of making a U-turn. Halfway into the turn, her foot unconsciously slammed on the brake, jerking the car to a stop. A tall, broad-shouldered man with thick sandy-blond hair was stalking out of the laundromat. The shock of seeing Zach again was so great, Savannah barely registered the fact that he had a woman in his arms.

* * *

Zach cursed softly and creatively. Of all the times for Savannah to arrive. Lindsay Milan had been trying to get his attention ever since he'd come back to town. When she'd collapsed into his arms at the sound of a firecracker going off, it was as close as he'd ever been to touching her. The woman was twice divorced and was working hard to find number three. He had avoided her advances thus far, but when she had crumpled against him, he'd had no choice but to catch her. He'd almost believed she had fainted until he saw the small triumphant smile curving her mouth. Though he was tempted to set her down immediately, he'd decided to carry her outside first. Now he wished he had followed his first instinct, especially since Lindsay's thin arms gripped his neck so tight, she was almost strangling him.

Lowering the woman's feet to the sidewalk outside the laundromat, Zach did his best to let her go. Lindsay wasn't having it. Her hold on his neck still tight, she leaned forward as if to kiss him. Zach jerked back, pulling at the fingers she had wrapped around his neck. The kiss she had intended for his mouth landed with a thud against his chest.

Exasperated, Zach grabbed Lindsay's shoulder and pushed her away.

"Get your hands off her."

Aw hell. Bad enough to have this woman throw herself at him every time he turned around, but to make matters worse, she was Clark Dayton's sister.

Zach turned to face Dayton. "She passed out. You need to get her to a doctor."

"That true, Lindsay?"

"I just felt dizzy for a minute. I'm fine." She grimaced a strained smile up at Zach. "Zach was just being kind."

Clark issued a sound between a grunt and a growl. "Let's go home, girl." His large, thick-fingered hand wrapped around his sister's thin arm and flexed. A brief wince of pain flickered across Lindsay's face.

Remembering some rumors of abuse from years ago, Zach eyed the two speculatively. Was this the reason she threw herself at any available man? She'd come back to live with her father and brother after her second divorce. Being an adult living back at home wasn't fun. Coupled with having an overbearing, possibly abusive brother, it would be hell.

"I think it'd be a good idea for someone at the hospital to take a look at you," Zach said.

Dayton pulled at his sister's arm again. "She said she was fine."

"Nevertheless, I think it would be a good idea."

Catching the eye of an EMT, Zach jerked his head toward Lindsay. "Mrs. Milan needs some medical attention."

Before Dayton could grumble another protest, Zach said, "Take the patrol car and follow behind the ambulance."

The EMT led Lindsay toward the ambulance; Dayton gave Zach another cold look and then clomped after them.

Zach turned and addressed the small crowd of onlookers. "Show's over, folks."

"But what happened, Chief?" a male voice called out.

"Somebody thought it'd be a good idea to throw some fireworks in the clothes dryers."

Their curiosity satisfied, most everyone turned away. A few stragglers moved several yards up the sidewalk. Finally the path was clear. A royal-blue Mustang convertible sat in the middle of the road, and behind the wheel was Savannah Wilde, staring at him. The light was dimming but he could make out her features. Her hair was still long . . . looked like it was pulled back, away from her face, in that prim, neat style she used to favor.

The familiar gut punch, one he hadn't felt since he'd last seen her, kicked him like a mule, almost taking his breath. Their eyes locked briefly, but Zach didn't move. He'd wait. Go over and talk to her later, let her know he'd be keeping an eye out for her, per her boss's request. Having their first conversation in ten years in front of nosey and gossiping townspeople wasn't a good idea.

He acknowledged her presence with a jerk of his head and turned away. He still had work to do here.

Savannah pressed on the gas pedal and shot forward, wincing as she narrowly missed hitting a group of people. Great. Not only had she stared at Zach like a drooling idiot, she had almost injured five or so of the town's citizens.

"Way to avoid getting noticed, Savannah," she muttered.

Zach had seen her—their eyes had made contact. And she'd gotten nothing from him other than a grim nod. She released a long shaky breath. Well, what had she expected? For him to run toward her with arms outstretched, declaring his love, along with an apology and an explanation? No, of course not. There was nothing he could say or do to change the past. Still, whether she wanted to admit it or not, his cool, barely there acknowledgment stung.

She didn't spare a glance at the giant fountain in the middle of the town square—which used to be one of her favorite places in Midnight. Designed to look like a mimosa tree in full bloom, it had limbs that sprayed glistening water from tiny holes, making them look like mimosa petals. At night it was even more spectacular, with lights making the petals appear pink. When she lived here, it was rare for her to come to town and not stop to throw a penny into the fountain and make a wish. When they were dating, she and Zach would sometimes sit on a bench beside the fountain and talk for hours. Maybe that was the reason she couldn't stand to look at it.

At last, she turned onto Wildefire Lane. Pulling into the drive, Savannah shifted into park and stared blankly ahead. That brief encounter with Zach had cracked the calm, impenetrable façade she'd worked so hard to develop for the last 450 miles. Now she felt open and exposed . . . vulnerable.

Her sigh weary, she opened the car door. Then, purse in one hand, keys in the other, she pulled herself from the car and stood in place, stretching her back and neck. Diversionary tactics. She was shoring herself up. When she'd been hundreds of miles away, it had been much easier to convince herself she was prepared for this upcoming emotional roller coaster. Now that she was here, the stark truth smacked her in the face. Memories emerged, denting and penetrating her ever-present defense shield.

The porch lights glowed brightly; they were set to automatically come on at dusk. Timers inside the mansion turned lights on and off at different times during the evening. The giant house looked warm, inviting, classically beautiful . . . and filled with love. At one time, that's exactly what it had been—or so she had thought.

Memories, uninvited but inevitable, flooded her mind. She and her sisters had been at camp when it had happened. Their grandfather had arrived to break the news and bring them home. She still remembered her surprise and then immediate anxiety at seeing him there. Instantly she had known something was wrong. How Daniel Wilde had been able to hold it together still amazed her. Not only had he been grieving for the loss of his son and daughter-in-law, but he had to deal with the knowledge that his son was a murderer. He'd had to put his grief on hold to be there for his granddaughters.

Eighteen years ago, she and her sisters had left home excited, happy, and secure ten-year-olds; their only concern was having a good time. One day later, they had returned traumatized and devastated, their whole world crashing around them.

Shaking herself from the unhelpful introspection, Savannah pulled the small overnight bag from the trunk. She'd take her larger suitcase out tomorrow, when she had more energy. The minute she slid the key into the lock and turned the knob, more memories swamped her. Grim determination kept her feet moving forward.

She threw her keys on the table beside the door, briefly noting that the lilies in the vase were fresh. Twice a week, a local florist placed lilies, her grandmother's favorite flower, throughout the house. It was something her grandmother Camille Wilde had adopted when she was newly married. Her husband, Daniel, had kept that tradition even after she died. Neither Savannah nor her sisters had the heart to discontinue the custom.

She walked across the shiny hardwood floor and then up the winding mahogany staircase, smiling faintly at the memory of sliding down the banister and bruising her bottom when she had landed abruptly halfway across the foyer. She quickly squelched the other part of that memory. The one where her father had laughingly picked her up and hugged her hard until she stopped crying.

When she got to the top of the stairs, she turned around on the landing and peered down into the grand old house. The expected desolation didn't come. This was a beautiful home and deserved to have a family love it the way she and her family once had. Despite the difficult days ahead of her, she was suddenly glad she had come home. This was the final step in putting the past behind her. After seeing Zach's reaction, it was obvious he'd done that, too.

The ringing of the doorbell had her running down the stairs again. She had hoped to have one night alone before the inevitable visiting began. Of course, maybe if she had been able to sneak in without being seen, that could have happened.

Shrugging resignedly, Savannah opened the door. The polite smile of welcome froze on her face as she stared at her visitor.

Zach stood on the porch, feeling like the awkward, gangly kid he'd once been. Maybe he should have waited until morning, given her a chance to rest. He'd told himself he just wanted to get this over with. He would explain that her boss had called and advised him of the threats against her. That he'd be on the lookout for anyone new or suspicious-looking. That he was here to help her if she needed it. Yes, those were the reasons he'd told himself he was here, and up until now, he had almost believed them. The instant the door opened and she stood before him, Zach knew all of those reasons were lies and excuses. How could she possibly be more beautiful than before?

Surprise flared in her eyes but she quickly recovered and gave him the blandest stare he could imagine. If he hadn't seen the quick flash of emotion, he'd almost guess she didn't recognize him.

"Hello, Savannah."

"Zach." She gave a nod of acknowledgment and maintained her hold on the door.

"Can I come in?"

Her grip on the door tightened noticeably. She wasn't

even going to bother to pretend she didn't want him there.

"I really don't feel up to company right now."

It'd been a long time since Zach had felt inferior. After an upbringing that no one in their right mind could call pleasant or normal, he'd worked hard at recognizing that wealth had nothing to do with the quality of a person. Funny thing was, Savannah was the first person to help him realize that. Even though their backgrounds couldn't have been more different, she and her family had always treated him as an equal. And she had always treated him as if he was something special.

Until now.

"This is official business, not a social visit. It's about the X-Kings and the threats against you."

Her eyes narrowed and a frown of both confusion and suspicion appeared. At least she was giving him something besides that cool composure. Before he could appreciate the change, the bland expression returned. "How do you know about that?"

"Your boss called me." Tired of waiting for an invitation that was apparently not going to come, Zach put his hand on the door and pushed it open. "This won't take long." He stepped inside, giving her the choice of either staying put and being within inches of him or backing away. And damn him for being disappointed that she backed away.

Her arms crossed in front of her, she now stood at least three feet away, leaving no doubt that she didn't want to be anywhere close to him. "I don't see that it's any of your concern. It was a pointless threat made by an idiot."

"It's my concern because you're in my town now. All residents, whether they're permanent or not, have a right to protection. You're no different."

Ice replaced the bland expression that'd been irritating him. "Believe me, I'm more than aware of that, Zach."

The words stung but the coldness hurt even more. "Then we need to talk about your safety."

"There's nothing to talk about. This house has an excellent security system and I have a handgun that I'm quite proficient with. There's nothing you can do for me that I can't do for myself."

"That's good . . . I'm glad you're trained. I'll still keep an eye out. Make sure you're safe until you leave."

Her lips, full and naked of anything but her natural pink color, trembled slightly before they stretched into the most fake smile she'd ever given him. "That's very solicitous of you." She started toward the front door. "I'll be sure to let you know if anything comes up."

"That's it?" Zach blew out a sigh. "Hell, Savannah, you act like we're strangers."

"We are strangers, Zach. It's been ten years. We're different people. Very different." She opened the door. "Good night."

She was right. They weren't the same people. So why the hell was his gut twisted with disappointment? Had he really expected anything else? Maybe he was lucky she didn't use her gun to force him out of the house. Did he deserve anything less?

Shrugging off the odd, inappropriate feelings of hurt, Zach gave her a curt nod and went through the door. He heard it close behind him and then the locks clicked. Yeah, that sounded about right.

CHAPTER TEN

Savannah leaned back against the closed door, imagining Zach on the other side, just standing there. For the first time in years, he was within touching distance. Not that it mattered. He might as well be as far from her as the sun was from the moon. Much more separated them than mere distance.

When at last she heard him move away, she slid bonelessly to the floor with a resounding thud. That had gone about as badly as it could have. The only things she hadn't done were cry or throw something at him. She hadn't expected to see him this soon. After the cool nod in town, she figured they'd run into each other in a few days. By then, she would have built up her defenses and been nonchalant about the whole thing. She would have exchanged pleasantries with him and acted like a mature, rational, and sophisticated woman greeting an old acquaintance. But now, there was no way he didn't know that she had never forgotten or forgiven him.

Her boss was too thorough; she should have realized Reid would notify the local law about the threats. Of course, he didn't know that the local law was once the love of her life. Not that it would have made a difference. The welfare of his employees was more important than matters of the heart.

She only wished she'd handled their first meeting better. She could turn on or off any kind of emotion when she was trying a case—be passionate or icy cold with little effort. But she had never been able to fake anything with Zach. So much in her personality had changed, yet apparently that one thing had remained consistent. And now, she had to figure out how to regroup. Show him that she truly felt nothing for him, nor did she hold a grudge.

Maybe it would have helped if he'd become unattractive. Why couldn't his thick blond hair have thinned out and become straggly? Or that strong jawline gone saggy and jowly? At the very least, a stomach paunch or stooped shoulders to lessen his appeal. None of that had happened. If anything, maturity had only improved Zach Tanner. At twenty, he had been tall and on the slim side, with ash-blond hair and clear gray eyes. A thirty-year-old Zach was broad shouldered and muscular as if he lifted weights on a regular basis. The light golden streaks in his hair told her he spent a lot of time in the sun. That square jaw she'd once covered in kisses seemed as hard as granite, and those lips she'd once let devour her were sensuous, sexy, and so very male. Everything about him seemed bigger, bolder, and even more fascinating.

She sighed. Why oh why couldn't he have at least gotten a wart or two?

Sharp pounding on the door behind her jerked her from her thoughts. Had Zach come back? Savannah jumped to her feet, grateful that the strength had returned to her legs. She'd made the mistake earlier of not checking the peephole. This time she would check, and if it was Zach or anyone else she didn't want to talk to, she'd simply not answer.

Standing on her toes, she peeked and then wearily shook her head. No way could she not open the door.

No matter how tired or dispirited you were, you never turned away family. Shoulders straight, she braced herself and opened the door.

"Hey there, Aunt Gibby."

"Land sakes, Savannah Rose, why'd it take you so long?"

Before Savannah could respond, the woman was pulling her forward for a hard, quick one-armed hug. Aunt Gibby didn't do anything slow, including hugging.

Savannah never even considered offering the excuse of being too tired for company. Not that the statement would stop Gibby. The older woman strode into the house with the confident air of one who knew she was always welcome. In one hand, she held a casserole—that had most likely been in the freezer since the millennium— and in the other hand, a jug of sweet tea.

Savannah followed the elderly woman into the kitchen, searching for a way to shorten the visit without hurting her feelings. She was coming up blank.

Aunt Gibby, who had been part of the Wilde sisters' lives since their birth, was neither their aunt nor was her name Gibby. She was Granddad's second cousin twice removed and her real name was Lorna Jean Wilcox. She'd been Gibby for so long, very few people even knew her actual name. Everyone called her Gibby.

Her eyes round with a seemingly innocent curiosity, Gibby asked, "Was that Chief Tanner leaving?"

Savannah didn't bother to answer. One of the many things she had always appreciated about Gibby, especially in this instance, was that she rarely required a response, because she answered most of her questions herself.

"Of course it was." Gibby nodded knowingly. "You two probably had a lot to talk about. Not seeing each other for all these years. Didn't look like you visited long, since he just finished taking care of that nonsense at Gertie's. I swan, I don't know what this world's coming to."

Savannah allowed the older woman's chatter to flow around her. Not having to answer was a blessing, since she was still reeling from her previous visitor. It didn't help to know that Zach might not even have come over at all if it hadn't been for her boss alerting him to the threats made against her. He'd come to tell her he would protect her, just as he would any citizen of Midnight— she was no different. How stupid to be hurt by something she already knew.

"And with the rash of crime we've had lately, I'm surprised he had time to visit at all."

Savannah tuned in at that comment. "Midnight has a crime spree?"

As if she realized she'd finally caught Savannah's attention, Gibby's expression grew livelier. "Well, mostly just vandalism so far, but there have been a couple of break-ins, too. I've heard more than one person say that Chief Tanner's job could be in jeopardy."

Silly, since she knew nothing about Zach anymore or his competency as a law enforcement officer, but she still felt the need to defend him. "Criticizing is a lot easier than being part of the solution. I'm sure Zach's doing everything he can to catch the people responsible. He needs the town's support, not their criticism."

Instantly she knew she'd said the wrong thing. Aunt Gibby's sherry-brown eyes were almost glowing as she exclaimed, "Bless your heart, honey, you still love him, don't you? Even though you were both so young and he broke your heart, I don't know how many times I told Esme and Beth-Anne that the love you two had was the forever kind that just don't die. I remember how you used to look at each other when you thought nobody was watching. It was just the sweetest thing."

Refusing to get into a discussion on her feelings for Zach, then or now, Savannah shook her head. "Law enforcement officials get a bum rap a lot of times. They're often overworked and underappreciated. It's nothing more than that."

Salt-and-pepper eyebrows arched over Gibby's twinkling eyes, the doubtful look saying she wasn't one bit convinced. Considering how weak and ineffectual her words sounded, Savannah wasn't convinced, either. She felt nothing for Zach, other than a lingering sense of disappointment. But that was only natural. She had trusted him and he'd let her down.

Her tired mind struggling to come up with a different subject, Savannah was surprised when Gibby did it for her. "So who's the young man you're seeing now?"

Savannah searched her memory for the name of the last man she had dated. Dan something or other. He'd been a friend of a friend—a blind date. They'd spent a boring evening together. Dan was in advertising and wanted to talk about their newest client, a large shoe manufacturer. He'd made the statement that because she was a woman, he was sure she would be interested in talking about shoes. Savannah had spent the evening hiding her yawns. Since they'd met at the restaurant, they'd ended their date the instant dessert was finished. She had never heard from him again, for which she was extremely grateful. But that had been over a year ago, and she hadn't dated anyone since.

She raised her gaze to answer and swallowed the vague, evasive reply she had planned to give. Gibby would have made an excellent attorney. The piercing, speculative look said she wouldn't settle for anything but the full truth. Suddenly wishing for anyone, including Zach, to knock on the door, Savannah scrambled for a satisfactory answer. One that would keep the woman from pursuing further questions. Telling her that she was too focused on her career to consider getting serious with anyone would only start the woman on an endless tirade of "You're not getting any younger," along with the ever-popular reference to her biological clock.

Just as Savannah opened her mouth, still not sure what she was going to say, the doorbell rang. Deciding someone up there really did like her, she jumped to her feet and dashed out of the kitchen. Anyone other than the devil himself would be invited in for a visit. She opened the door and quickly reversed that thought.

Savannah stared at Zach, who once again stood before her. She kept the door half-closed and put her polite mask back on. "Did you forget something?"

"Yeah." He handed her a small card. "Here's my cell-phone and home numbers. Call me if you hear or see anything suspicious."

"Couldn't I just dial 911?"

"Savannah, I'm not looking for an argument. I just—"

"Is that you, Zach?"

Before she could stop him, Zach pushed the door open and stuck his head inside. "Hi, Miss Gibby. How're you doing?"

"Just fine. In fact, Savannah and I were just about to sit down for a little supper of chicken almondine casse-role. My specialty. Why don't you come in and join us?"

Savannah kept her eyes focused on Zach, her glare telling him he'd better not accept, as she answered her aunt. "I'm sure Chief Tanner already has dinner plans. We wouldn't want to—"

"Actually I don't, and that sounds right up my alley. Thank you, Miss Gibby, I'd be pleased to join you."

Before she knew it, Zach was inside the house, walking beside the older woman as they headed into the kitchen. Savannah stood in the foyer, speechless. Zach stopped at the door to the kitchen and turned back. The grin he shot her brought back memories that she'd successfully squelched for years.

"You coming?"

She took a breath, straightened her shoulders, and headed toward the kitchen. She could do this. There were worse things than having a very brief meal with the handsome, sexy man who'd broken her heart. Odd that she couldn't think of any right now.

Zach sat at the kitchen table and eyed Savannah as she scurried around the room setting the dishes before them, pouring tea into glasses, and generally avoiding looking at him. She didn't want him here—that much was obvious. Her hostility bothered him but he couldn't blame her. What he had done was unforgivable. He had known that, though at the time it had made perfect sense.

"Chief, would you like lemon for your tea?" Gibby asked.

"Yes, ma'am. But you know you don't have to call me Chief, Miss Gibby. Zach'll do just fine."

The older woman blushed and giggled like a young girl. Zach hid a smile and glanced over at Savannah, who had just sat down to his left. The daggerlike looks she was throwing him made it clear she wasn't as easily charmed as her aunt.

"Any ideas on who's responsible for all these vandalisms the last few weeks?" Gibby asked.

His mouth loaded with the odd-tasting food, Zach swallowed hard and then took in a mouthful of iced tea to wash the taste away. "No, ma'am, not yet."

"That's a real shame."

He could think of a lot more colorful phrases for it.

"What kind of vandalisms?"

This was the first contribution Savannah had made to the conversation, and despite himself, his heart thudded at just hearing her voice.

"Mostly graffiti on buildings. This last episode of firecrackers in the dryers makes me wonder if they're going in a new direction."

"You think it's the same people?" Savannah asked.

"That's my theory. Low-level pranks. Minimum effort in each case. Just enough to cause havoc."

"Any suspects?"

He almost smiled at the rapid rate of Savannah's questions. She had a prosecutor's expression on her beautiful face. Damn, he'd love to see her in a courtroom.

"None yet," he answered. "Just a couple of theories."

His attention moved away from Savannah when Gibby clapped her hands together. Her eyes twinkling with excitement, she said, "I just had a brilliant idea. You and Savannah should talk about your theories and ideas. With both of you working on it together, you'd be able to—"

"Aunt Gibby, I'm here to ready the house for sale, not to assist in a police case. Besides," she continued, her gaze barely skimming his, "I'm sure Zach has all the help he needs without me interfering."

"Actually I'd be happy to get your take on it."

Surprise flickered and then was doused by alarm. For an instant, she'd looked terrified. What was that about? Hell, was she afraid to be around him?

With the expression of a satisfied fat tabby who'd just consumed a large rodent, Gibby said, "Excellent. I'm sure you'll find the culprit in no time." Before either he or Savannah could respond, she changed the subject.

"How's your mama gettin' along? Seems like a month of Sundays since we heard any news of her."

The beautiful woman to his left shifted, her interest apparent. No wonder. He hadn't been prone to sharing much about his family life back then. Not that discussing his mother had been necessary—her liaisons hadn't exactly been a secret. He ignored the small, insidious voice that reminded him that wasn't entirely true. There had been one he hadn't known about, and it'd ended up being the most important one of all.

"She's doing fine. She and Lenny are still living in Pascagoula."

"And that brother of yours? He still in the military?"

"Yes, ma'am." Zach didn't even bother to keep the pride out of his voice as he continued, "He completed his Navy SEAL training a couple of months ago."

"Josh is a Navy SEAL?" Savannah said. "I hadn't heard."

A grin split Zach's face, a usual occurrence when he was talking about his little brother. "I almost pounded him for not going army but he was on a set course."

Her beautiful mouth curved in a fleeting smile that was gone before he could appreciate it. "You're still very proud of him."

"The proudest. Kid turned out all right."

Gibby piped in, "Thanks to you, Zach Tanner."

Uncomfortable with the direction of the conversation, Zach turned his attention back to his meal. It might not be the tastiest he'd had in a while, but at least it kept him away from Savannah's too-penetrating gaze. Her eyes had lost their earlier animosity, which was a welcome change. If she wanted to talk about Josh, he had no problem. He could talk about his younger brother all day long. But when the conversation drifted toward himself, he'd just as soon not go there.

"Who's ready for dessert?" Gibby asked.

"I don't think I have anything to serve," Savannah answered. "I asked the service that's been cleaning the house to stock the kitchen with some staples, but I doubt that there's anything suitable for—"

"Nonsense, Savannah. Every self-respecting Southern woman stocks something for her man to satisfy his sweet tooth." The older woman sprang to her feet with the energy of someone forty years younger. As Zach watched in amusement and Savannah in apparent dismay, she opened the refrigerator, freezer, and pantry and then, not satisfied, began to open the cabinets. When she turned around, triumph on her plump, round face, she held a bag of Oreo cookies.

Zach jumped to his feet. "I'll get the milk."

Savannah slumped in her chair, realizing that she'd been speechless more in the last two hours than she had in the last ten years. Her kitchen had been taken over by lunatics. She glanced at Zach's almost-full plate and decided one mystery was solved. Poor guy couldn't take any more of the hideous casserole. Cookies and milk for dinner probably sounded like a reprieve from hell. She had managed only one small bite herself.

Aunt Gibby was one of the kindest, most loving people in the world, but she was also the worst cook. Had this been a fresh casserole, Savannah figured it would have been edible if not very good. From the taste of this one, it had been in the freezer for at least a couple of years, maybe more. Gibby was a self-proclaimed freezer queen, claiming that the appliance was the greatest invention since the automobile.

Hoping to save both herself and Zach from having to explain why they hadn't eaten their meal, Savannah went to her feet and grabbed their plates. "I'll just make room." She dashed to the sink and started rinsing the dishes, dumping the contents of both plates into the garbage disposal. When all evidence had disappeared, she turned to find Aunt Gibby and Zach sitting at the kitchen table with giant glasses of milk, both of them scraping the insides of their cookies with their teeth and thoroughly enjoying themselves.

An astonishing feeling of contentment swept over her—something she hadn't felt in a very long time. Blaming her giddiness on exhaustion, Savannah never-theless got into the spirit. "That's not right. Let me show you the proper way to eat an Oreo." She plopped down into her chair, grabbed the glass of milk Zach had poured for her and a cookie from the package, and then dunked. She quickly put the soggy cookie in her mouth and closed her eyes as the chocolate and cream melted on her tongue. "Delicious." She opened her eyes to find Zach staring at her, an odd expression on his face, al-most one of pain.

Mentally shaking her head at the odd thought, Savan-nah devoured four cookies and her glass of milk.

Aunt Gibby finished her milk and stood. "Well, I'd better get home or Oscar and Samson will think I've abandoned them."

"Oscar and Samson?" Savannah asked.

"That's right, you haven't met my new additions." Her eyes watered briefly. "When I lost Niblet two years ago this past spring, I figured it'd take two cats to re-place him. Oscar and Samson are brothers from the same litter and are both rapscallions. You'll have to come over and introduce yourself."

Savannah stood and started clearing the table. "I'll try to do that soon, but I have my work cut out for me here for a while." Placing the lid on the casserole dish, she held it out for Gibby to take.

"No, darling. You keep the casserole so you can have

something for lunch tomorrow. Just bring the dish back when you come for your visit."

The instant the older woman was out the door, the casserole would go down the drain. "Thank you, Aunt Gibby. You're always so thoughtful."

"That's what family's for. Your granddaddy knew that better than anyone."

As the three of them walked toward the front door, Savannah was glad to see that Zach had his keys in his hand. The shock of seeing him again was wearing off, leaving her feeling weak and drained.

"I'll walk you to your car, Miss Gibby," Zach said.

She patted his arm. "Thank you, dear boy." Her arms reached up and pulled Savannah toward her for a long, hard hug and a whisper of advice in her ear: "Don't let him get away from you this time. He's a keeper."

Before Savannah could even consider responding, Gibby went through the door, with Zach holding her arm. She turned before she got to the steps and said, "I expect you'll be busy this week, so I'll leave you to your packing. Pick me up for church Sunday at eight forty-five, though. And it's the monthly social after worship, so be sure to bring your mama's peach cobbler."

"Aunt Gibby, I'm only here for a short time and I have so much—"

"Nonsense. There's always time to worship the Lord and eat a good country meal. Get some sleep now. You're looking a bit peaked."

Zach gave her a searching glance and said, "It was good to see you again, Savannah. Call if you need me."

A slight nod seemed to be the safest response. Savannah waited until Zach and Aunt Gibby were down the steps and headed to the driveway before she closed the door. Leaning back against it again, she blew out a huge sigh. So much for wanting to fly under the radar. Not only would she be seeing most of the town on Sunday, there'd been a definite promise in Zach's eyes. He was going to want to talk.

Dwelling on that would get her nowhere. Savannah pushed away from the wall and went in to finish the few remaining dishes. Once that was done, she grabbed the overnight bag she'd dropped on the floor and made her way up the stairs. At the top of the landing, she veered left. With eight bedrooms on the second floor and an additional three on the third floor, she could have her pick. However, she automatically went to the room that had been hers the first eighteen years of her life.

She stopped at the door and took in the memories. Pale green walls with pink rosebuds—she'd picked out the wallpaper three days before her mother was killed. Her bed was a copy of a nineteenth-century cherry sleigh bed she'd seen in a magazine. Her grandfather had surprised her with it on her fifteenth birthday. Sammie and Bri had gotten new beds, too, but she'd always thought hers was the prettiest. To the left of the bed was a cherry and marble vanity where she'd sat for hours, most often trying to tame her hair. And hanging from the mirror were Mardi Gras beads she'd collected on her last celebration in Mobile.

So many wonderful memories, but so much heartache, too. Ten years of happy childhood had been destroyed in one brief, inexplicable act of violence. The betrayal she and her sisters had felt had overwhelmed them. Now, after eighteen years, her hurt had been replaced with sad acceptance and an intense bitterness toward her father. All the warm, wonderful memories she had of him had evaporated as if they'd never existed. Rarely did she even let herself think about him.

Savannah dropped her bag on the floor and headed out of the bedroom. The night after she lost her parents and every night until she left home, she had gone to her mother's sitting room and said good night. A silly tradition, but one she couldn't break. This house would soon belong to someone else and she'd no longer have the opportunity.

As she made her way to the other side of the house where her parents' rooms had been, she took a few seconds to glance at the photographs on the walls. If one took the time to view them all, the entire history of the Wildes was portrayed. Weddings, graduations, parties, holidays, and new babies covered the walls in a vast array of tradition and family unity.

Approaching the area where the most current photographs were displayed, Savannah let her eyes briefly whisk over the ones that included Beckett Wilde. Knowing the pain his granddaughters were going through, her grandfather had removed the ones of her father the day after her parents' funeral. He had replaced them after she and her sisters left home. A few of the pictures were of Beckett when he was much younger—a child, then a teen.

Her eyes swept over a family portrait they'd had taken the winter before their happy family had been destroyed. Anyone not knowing the events would assume they were looking at a loving, close-knit family, including a husband and father who adored his wife and children.

Unable to stop herself, her gaze moved to her father's high school senior portrait. Even with her prejudice, she couldn't deny that he had been an extremely handsome man. At just over six feet, with broad shoulders and strong arms, he had seemed larger than life to her; she'd thought he was the most beautiful man on the planet. His medium-brown slightly curly hair was longer in the picture than the way she remembered him. With a dazzling smile, twinkling blue eyes, and a deep, infectious laugh, he'd been able to charm almost everyone. Savannah stared deep into those eyes, looking for the killer that lurked behind them. If the eyes were a mirror to the soul, somehow he had been able to hide that spark of evil. All she saw was a seemingly uncomplicated, charming man with a hint of mischievousness. Nothing more.

Her eyes shifted to the portrait beside Beckett Wilde's. It was of Maggie, his beautiful wife, Savannah's mother. The photo showed a lovely woman with honey-blond hair and eyes the color of ripe clover; a gentle, teasing smile played around her full lips as if she were on the verge of laughter. And the first ten years of Savannah's life, that's what she remembered most—the laughter.

Turning away from the photographs and painful memories, she went to her mother's sitting room. Her grandfather had never changed anything about it. The room looked the same as it did the night Maggie Wilde was killed. Peaceful, serene, and filled with all the things she had loved and enjoyed. The sweater she'd been knitting as a Christmas gift for her husband lay on the arm of a chair. The book she'd been reading lay facedown on a side table. All the rooms in the mansion reflected Maggie Wilde in some way, but this room held the essence of who her mother had been: beauty, poise, laughter, and love—a beautiful, bright star that had been taken from her loved ones much too soon and in the most gruesome manner possible.

Savannah leaned against the doorjamb and whispered softly, "Good night, Mama. I miss you so much."

And, as she'd done when she was a kid and had been needing and wanting her mother with a deep abiding ache, she waited for a response. As before, silence was her only answer.

Turning away with a sigh, Savannah headed back to her bedroom. Today had taken its toll and exhaustion enveloped her like a thick, soggy blanket. A good night's sleep would bring perspective and a better outlook. Maybe she'd even figure out how she was going to avoid Zach while she was here. Because if tonight had proven anything at all, it was that the feelings he evoked in her were still as strong and volatile as ever. Which seemed ridiculous. What exactly did it take to destroy love?

CHAPTER ELEVEN

Depending upon the hour of the day, the clientele at Faye's Diner was a varying mix of what made up the town of Midnight. The majority of early morning breakfast diners were retirees and farmers. Professionals and shopkeepers came at lunchtime; teenagers and families at night.

Zach knew exactly what to expect when he walked into the diner at six o'clock the next morning. The fragrances of frying bacon and homemade biscuits were almost overwhelmed by the scent of the collard greens Faye was preparing for the midday meal. He made a mental note not to come back for lunch. He'd eaten his fill of greens when he was a kid. They'd been abundant and easy to stuff into his backpack when no one was looking.

Dishes clattering, the hum of low-key conversation, and the latest country hit playing on the old jukebox in the corner came together to create a homey if somewhat stereotypical small-town Southern restaurant. But this place was special. He'd been all over the world and he'd never eaten better or cheaper food than what he could get at Faye's.

Aware that the conversation had lulled seconds after he stepped foot in the door, Zach nodded at those who met his gaze but stayed focused on his goal—the counter where Faye stood, waiting to serve him the hottest, blackest coffee in all of Alabama. After the sleepless night he'd had, nothing else would do it for him.

No doubt everyone in the restaurant already knew that Savannah had returned home. The gossips could work faster than a chicken hawk in a henhouse. Zach didn't question how news traveled so quickly. He'd seen it happen hundreds of times before. Though the town had embraced technology as lovingly as any modern city, email, Facebook, and Twitter had yet to replace the telephone. Nor had they replaced Faye's Diner, Gertie's Wash and Wait, or Tillie's Hair Today. The juiciest tidbits could still be picked up while sipping coffee, waiting for your clothes to dry, or taking advantage of the newest special in Tillie's vast array of daily coiffure deals.

"Morning, Chief." Faye, middle-aged and as stern-looking as any four-star army general, wasn't much of a conversationalist, which was another reason he liked her.

He nodded as he sat down. "Let's do the special this morning."

In admirable synchronicity, she poured coffee with one hand, wiped the counter with the other, and yelled, "Special! Over easy!" over her shoulder.

He took a swallow of the blistering-hot liquid and finally began to feel close to halfway human. Should've known seeing Savannah would bring back the nightmares and all the ghosts of past regrets. For a man who'd always been one to make a decision and stick to his guns, his regret over his actions ten years ago ate at him daily. Last night, they had almost consumed him.

She had looked so much like the beautiful Savannah he had known, but he'd noticed some marked differences. At eighteen, Savannah had been slim with soft curves. The Savannah of today was slender almost to the point of thinness. Even more disturbing, there was a cool brittleness to her. He tried to tell himself that her job as a prosecutor had most likely impacted her personality. Dealing with criminals was bound to have a negative influence. His demons whispered something else. They told him his alienation and selfishness were the cause.

What he had done was unforgivable. So why the hell had he expected a different reception from her? All the tender emotions she'd once had for him had been devoured by hurt, disappointment, and anger, leaving bitterness in their wake. A voice inside him whispered that bitterness wasn't what he'd glimpsed in her eyes. Instead he had seen hurt and anger. Could they be healed? Could he make up for the sins of his past?

Before he could dwell on that tempting but improbable idea, Faye's special—fried eggs, bacon, grits, biscuits, sausage gravy, and a side of sliced tomatoes—slid in front of him. Hunkering down over his meal, Zach made sure his body language discouraged even the most thick-skinned person from trying to make conversation. Problem was, there was always one person who believed they were the exception. Today that person was Sarah Jane Riley.

Sliding onto the stool beside him, she spoke in a high, shrill voice, making sure everyone in the restaurant could hear. "Chief, heard you had dinner with Savannah Wilde last night."

Zach didn't even bother to lift his head; the massive amount of food in front of him held his total focus.

"Bet it was good to see her after all this time."

Again, Zach didn't acknowledge Sarah's attempt at conversation. Unfortunately the woman had a reputation of causing controversy in the hopes of creating something out of nothing.

"I even heard some folks say that your car was still there this morning."

Zach raised his eyes then. He'd stared down more than one prick in his lifetime. The fact that this one was a woman made no difference to him. His reputation of being slow to anger often made people believe they could say just about anything to him without consequences. And though he'd been known to take more than his share of abuse, having someone he cared about besmirched or hurt in any way was one thing he refused to tolerate.

The cold, hard stare, unblinking and unforgiving, pierced through Sarah's thick skin. Her eyes wide with surprise and not a little alarm, she jumped off the stool and backed away. "I . . . uh, I was only repeating what I heard."

"Then I suggest you call them the liars that they are." Zach kept his voice low and soft but there was no mistaking its lethal edge.

"Sure thing, Chief."

Sarah returned to her table, where several other women were seated; all had the same wide-eyed surprise on their faces.

Though no longer hungry, Zach made a point to return to his meal with the nonchalant air of one who doesn't give a damn. When his cellphone rang, he didn't bother to check the identity of the caller, relieved that he didn't have to continue the pretense of enjoying the meal.

"Chief, those vandals have struck again."

Recognizing the voice of one of his deputies, Bart Odom, Zach said, "Hold on."

Standing, he threw down enough money for his meal, plus a liberal tip for Faye. As he turned away from the counter, Sarah and her friends all seemed amazingly interested in their meals; not one of them lifted her head as he walked out the door. He knew better than to think this would stop their gossiping. They'd recover and return to their ways as soon as some other juicy tidbit caught their attention.

Out on the sidewalk, he walked to his car and said, "Okay. Where?"

"The high school."

Now, that was different. Was his theory wrong or was this an unrelated incident? "Don't guess there's any need of asking about witnesses."

"Nope. Nobody saw nothing."

"Okay. Get photos of the crime scene and canvass the neighborhood again. I—"

"I think you're gonna want to see this one for yourself."

He planned to when he had time, but something in Bart's tone seemed off. "Why?"

"You'll know when you see it."

About to suggest to his deputy that he stop being so dramatic and tell him the damn news, Zach held on to his patience and said, "Okay, write up the report and I'll check it out after—"

"I think you might want to come now, Chief."

Now even more curious, Zach jumped into his car. "Be there in five minutes."

Three minutes later, Zach grimly took in the new act of vandalism. The other graffiti had been random drawings and a few vulgarities. This had a distinct message. One he most definitely did not appreciate. In large, blood-red letters splashed on one side of the beige brick building was a warning: *Go Away Wilde Bitch.*

Barring the probability that the X-Kings gang had come all the way to Midnight to leave a written message for Savannah, he considered the other possibilities. Some jerk's idea of a joke? Savannah *was* the talk of the town right now. It could be meant for him—it was damn close to the area where he and Savannah had first met. And the man at the top of his suspect list had been present at that meeting. Or he could be reading too much into it and it was just a random act of stupidity.

Whatever the reason, Zach wasn't amused.

He shot Bart a hard look. "Take photos of the scene and rope off the area. I'll be back later."

Once in the car, he headed toward Wildefire Lane. His gut told him she wasn't in any danger, but until he saw or heard for sure, he wouldn't be able to concentrate. She wouldn't appreciate hearing from him again, but she'd have to get over it. Making sure she was safe was his priority.

As he drove, he made a quick call to Gibby Wilcox. Stupid to not have gotten Savannah's cellphone number last night, although he wasn't sure he would have been successful. Thankfully Gibby seemed preoccupied and provided Zach with the number without her usual chatter. He tapped out Savannah's number, quickly added it to his phone book, and then hit Call.

"Hello?"

"Savannah, it's Zach."

The soft little gasp that came through the phone line went straight to his groin. Hell, hardening at such an insignificant sound made him feel like a teenager, when anything and everything could turn him on. And that's the way it was with Savannah—just about anything and everything she did had turned him on.

"What do you want, Zach?"

The cool, hard tone doused the desire like an ice-cold shower. His tone matching hers, he said, "As we established last night, I'm checking to make sure you're safe."

"And as I told you last night, I don't need your protection."

"Whether you want it or not, you've got it. I'm assuming since you answered the phone, you're fine."

"How astute of you, Chief Tanner."

Zach slowed to a stop in front of the Wilde mansion.

Need warred with common sense. What he wanted to do was bust open the damn door, pull her into his arms, and devour that beautiful snarling mouth until she groaned with the same arousal running through him. Common sense told him to get his ass to the office and do his job.

"Call me if you need me." He ended the call before she could hurl another insult. Having accomplished his goal of assuring himself she was fine, he made a U-turn and headed to the police station. He had a pile of paperwork to wade through, but first and foremost, he was going to start making some inquiries. Did the pricks not realize that bringing Savannah into the equation upped the urgency quotient about a billion percent? No way in hell would he allow her to be threatened in any way.

Savannah pocketed the phone with a huge sigh, resisting the temptation to throw it across the room. Her anger wasn't with Zach, but herself. Why the hell couldn't she act like a mature person with him? Why was it she could be a cool, rational law professional who'd been known to intimidate even the most hardened criminal with an icy glare, but with Zach she was this too-emotional, slightly childish woman? Last night she'd done everything but stick her tongue out at him. And her response to his phone call had definitely been on the shrewish side.

After a restless night filled with nightmares and oddly erotic dreams about Zach, Savannah had woken just after sunrise with a slight headache and in an irritable mood. Her first order of business had been making coffee, in hopes of heading off her headache, and iced tea for later, since the temperature was supposed to be close to a hundred today. Then, because she'd still felt so listless, she spent a half hour taping boxes together for her grandfather's belongings. That had been the extent of her accomplishments. She might have two months to get everything done, but if she continued at this pace, she'd be here that long, plus some.

Taking a sip of her now-cold coffee, she grimaced and headed back to the kitchen. Maybe another pot of coffee and breakfast would help. She quickly prepared more coffee and was in the midst of toasting an English muffin when the doorbell rang.

She peeked out of the kitchen window and caught sight of the big silver Mercedes. Only one person in town drove a Mercedes. Putting her breakfast on hold, Savannah went to open the front door to Midnight's mayor, Lamont Kilgore, and his wife, Nesta, who was bearing a large platter of cinnamon rolls. Their kind faces wreathed in welcoming smiles, the Kilgores were the epitome of Southern warmth and friendliness.

Lamont grabbed her in a bear hug, then pulled away and turned her to his wife. "Doesn't she look as pretty as a daisy in springtime, Nesta?"

Nesta put down the platter and hauled Savannah into her arms, hugging her with the same enthusiasm. "Looks more and more like Maggie every time I see her."

It was hard to be in a bad mood with the older couple grinning at her as if she were the prodigal daughter. Granddad had always said the Kilgores could kill you with kindness. She never had figured out if he had meant that as a compliment or an insult.

She led them to the sitting room and then offered the coffee she'd just made. Nesta jumped up and said, "I'll get the coffee. You stay here and visit with Lamont."

And that's the way the entire visit went. Lamont asked questions and shared the goings-on in Midnight while his wife flitted in between the kitchen and sitting room. As Nesta refilled the coffee cups and served the still-warm rolls, she added tidbits here and there to aid Lamont. Savannah had always been impressed at how she seemed to know when to add what. Like a comedy skit, it was almost as if they practiced it at home before taking it out on the road.

Two hours later, she felt as if she knew all the minutiae of each person's life since she had left town.

"Lamont, I believe we're about to put poor Savannah to sleep."

Sitting up straighter in her chair, she shook her head. "No, I'm sorry. I just didn't sleep well last night."

Nesta leaned forward and patted her hand sympathetically. "So many memories here, both good and bad."

Unable to refute the accuracy of her statement, Savannah smiled and nodded.

"I heard that Chief Tanner stopped by last night," Lamont said.

Oddly, this was the first time Zach's name had been mentioned. It seemed as if they had talked about every resident of Midnight with the exception of the too-handsome chief of police.

"He just came by to—" She stopped herself. If she told them about the threats in Nashville, they'd just worry.

"To what, dear?" Nesta asked.

"To say hello. You know, old friends and all." She inwardly winced, sure they would see right through such a lame excuse.

Instead Lamont said, "I can't tell you how reassuring it is to have someone of Zach's caliber as our police chief."

"You're an admirer of Zach's?"

"Oh yes," Nesta answered for her husband. "He's finally brought integrity to an office that we both believe was corrupt. Our previous mayor, Lord rest his soul, seemed to think it was easier to keep Harlan Mosby as police chief than to look for a new one. When Lamont became mayor, one of his priorities was to find a good, decent man to be chief of police."

Lamont nodded. "We found that man in Zach Tanner."

Silly, but a huge lump of emotion welled inside Savannah's throat. She might have her issues with Zach, but to hear others talk about him in such glowing terms was a delight. For so long, he'd been the bad boy of Midnight, and now not only was he the police chief, but he'd also gained the town's respect.

"Zach is a fine and honorable man." As she said the words, she realized she actually meant them. How good it felt to say something nice about the man for a change. She'd spent way too many years either ignoring his existence or hating him. In her heart, she had always known that Zach had the kind of character most people could only dream about.

"Being a war hero certainly helped him get the job."

"Zach's a war hero?"

Lamont nodded, eager to share all he knew. For the next half hour, Savannah was glued to her seat as he related what he knew about Zach's time in the military. Not allowing herself to find out anything about him for the last ten years had left her with a hunger to know as much as possible.

"My heavens, Lamont, we've got to be going if we're going to get to the dentist's office at eleven."

In a flurry of movements, both Nesta and Lamont hugged her again and practically ran toward the door. Savannah followed behind them. The Kilgores were known to be sticklers for being on time.

They were driving away when Nesta stuck her head out the window and said, "Forgot to tell you. Come for dinner . . ." She looked back at her husband and said something, then turned back to Savannah. "Thursday night. Lamont's getting a fancy new grill."

Before she could answer yes or no, the car roared away. About to close the door, she caught her breath as two more cars appeared in her driveway. She'd been spotted. No way could she pretend not to be home. Huffing out a sigh, she watched as two women she had gone to school with got out of their cars, both waving at her as if they were the oldest of friends. Which was curious, since they'd barely acknowledged her existence back then. No doubt about it, visiting time in Midnight had definitely started.

CHAPTER TWELVE

Two hours later, Savannah locked the door and closed the plantation blinds on the first floor. She had sat through depositions involving gruesome crimes that had been more pleasant than the visit she'd just had with Sylvia Johnston and Carrie Long. Within five minutes of their arrival, she had realized they were here for only one reason—to determine if she had come back to Midnight for Zach.

Not that they'd asked her outright if she was still interested in her old boyfriend. She almost wished they had, since that might have shortened their visit. Instead they talked around the subject.

Pride or just plain stubbornness had kept her from revealing any of her thoughts about Zach. Sylvia and Carrie's frustration had been obvious. Savannah had ruthlessly used their frustration against them, and she now knew much more about Zach. When the women had left, they'd looked suitably confused, realizing they'd learned nothing new from Savannah.

That was it for today. She was through entertaining. With the blinds pulled, anyone who stopped by would assume she wasn't at home. She'd been up for hours and all she had to show for it was a stomach roiling from too many sweets, a throbbing headache, and way more information than she'd ever wanted on the citizens of

Midnight. With the exception of what she'd learned about Zach.

He was a war hero. That didn't surprise Savannah. How many times had she marveled at how protective and caring he was when they were dating? Zach was a born protector. It was completely in keeping with his personality to have saved lives while he was in the service. That was one of the biggest reasons she had held on to hope for so long. No way would he leave her like that. He was too good, too honorable . . . too caring. Savannah pushed aside that old familiar pain.

As mayor, Lamont had information about the new police chief that others might not know. He'd said Zach didn't like to talk about his experience in the army but that he had been an Army Ranger and had both a Bronze Star and a Purple Heart.

A Purple Heart. That meant that Zach had been wounded. That knowledge hurt much more than Savannah wanted it to.

And thanks to Sylvia and Carrie, she had also learned that Chief Tanner was considered the best catch in town. Apparently every unmarried female between the ages of twenty and forty had set their sights on him.

As she walked up the stairway, Savannah rubbed her neck to relieve the tension of the morning. First aspirin and then work. Becoming entangled in the news and goings-on in Midnight was pointless, even if that included learning more about Zach. Not that she was that interested. She mentally rolled her eyes. Who was she kidding? Love him or hate him, Zach had always fascinated her. And the way it was going, every person she met was going to want to talk about him. Might as well soak up all she could. When she returned to Nashville, she'd have to go cold turkey.

After downing three aspirin tablets, Savannah headed into her grandfather's room. The instant she opened the door, the scents she always associated with her granddad—Lagerfeld cologne and pipe smoke—brought the memories back so vividly, she could almost imagine he was in the room with her.

She took a moment to walk around the room, touching a comb on his dresser, opening a music box that had been her grandmother's, picking up his favorite pipe that he always kept beside his bed.

He had stopped smoking cigarettes when her grandmother got sick. After she died, he'd developed a pipe-smoking habit. No, actually, come to think of it, he'd started smoking the pipe only after her parents' deaths. The stress of raising three granddaughters and losing his son and daughter-in-law had probably had a lot to do with that.

However stressful it had been for him, she couldn't imagine anyone doing a better job.

She gazed around the large room he'd once shared with her grandmother. Camille Wilde had passed away when Savannah was five. Though she barely remembered her, Daniel Wilde had done what he could to help his granddaughters realize what a phenomenal person his wife had been. One of the many reasons she'd admired her grandfather so much was how he had loved his wife. And despite the fact that he'd only been in his early fifties when she'd passed away, he had never remarried. As far as she knew, he'd never even dated again. She smiled as she remembered how she and her sisters had tried to come up with women he might be interested in so he wouldn't be alone. They'd played matchmaker for a couple of months until he had caught on and had gently explained that no one could replace Camille in his heart and he was perfectly content to stay single for the rest of his life.

She went to the bureau at the far end of the room. First she'd empty the drawers and then call the churches to see if they wanted his clothes. If not, she might have them shipped to a homeless shelter in Mobile. She opened the first drawer and was immediately swamped with the memory of her first piano recital. She hadn't wanted to take piano lessons. She had been eleven years old, and by then, all she had wanted to do was bury herself in her books—they were the only things that made sense to her in a world that had become so chaotic. Her grandfather had insisted she try, promising her if she didn't like it after the first month, she could quit. Six years later, she had still been taking piano. And despite her intense shyness, she had enjoyed playing in the school recitals.

Taking out the program of that first recital, she opened it to the first page and was surprised to see her grandfather had written a note beside her name. His handwriting was a bit scratchy but it looked something like *You would be so proud of her, son.*

She dropped the program and closed the drawer, vaguely disturbed by the words. They had rarely talked about her father after her parents' deaths. Any mention of his name usually ended up with her or one of her sisters crying. Her grandfather had respected their wishes and avoided bringing him up. Savannah suddenly felt guilty for that. Even though he had killed their mother and destroyed their happy family, Beckett had still been her grandfather's only child. How he must have grieved for him.

Unsettled by her thoughts, she turned away. Maybe the closets first. Then later, when she wasn't feeling so emotionally raw, she'd sort through his dresser and bureau for the more personal things. She crossed the room and opened the large walk-in closet. Suits, sweaters, jackets, shirts, and pants were all neatly hanging. Shoes, all with a military shine, gleamed at her from their shelf. Taking a deep breath, Savannah set to work.

Three hours later, she had reached the back of the closet and was almost at the end of her energy. Thankfully her grandfather hadn't been a clotheshorse or a pack rat, but still there'd been more clothes than she had anticipated. Seven boxes were now packed with a nice assortment of clothing that someone, somewhere, would be able to put to good use.

The doorbell had rung three times in as many hours. She was glad she had closed the blinds and not answered. Making social calls and knowing the ins and outs of one another's lives was part of the culture here. So different from a big city like Nashville, where one could go days or weeks without seeing a neighbor.

Her arms loaded with sweaters, Savannah turned. A tall, mountainous figure stood at the entrance to the closet. She squeaked out a small squeal and dropped the sweaters on her feet.

"Sorry. Didn't mean to frighten you. I rang the bell and knocked several times. When no one answered, I got concerned."

Hands on her hips, Savannah glared at Zach. "I wasn't answering the door because I have so much to do. And how the hell do you have a key to the house, anyway?"

Broad shoulders lifted in a shrug. "Your grandfather never changed his spare-key hiding spot. Can't believe that fake rock in the flower bed is still there."

She stepped around the pile of sweaters and held out her hand. "I'll take the key and put it away. I didn't realize it was still there."

Instead of handing the key to her, he looked down at the pile of clothes at her feet. "Need some help?"

Stooping down, she grabbed up the load of sweaters and marched toward the door. Zach thankfully backed away, allowing her out of the closet that was becoming more than a little claustrophobic.

She dumped the clothes on the bed and turned to face

him. Before she could ask why he was here, he whistled and said, "You've gotten a lot done already."

Her eyes shifted away from him and took in the scene. All of these boxes and only two small moments where she'd broken into tears. One had been caused by the half pack of Juicy Fruit gum she'd found in a jacket— her grandfather had rarely been without gum in his pocket and Juicy Fruit had been his favorite. The other time was when she'd found a cashmere scarf he'd carefully folded and put in a bottom drawer. The scarf had been a gift from her mother, given to him for Christmas . . . the last Christmas they'd all been together.

As she swallowed around another inconvenient lump, a thought suddenly occurred to her. "There are still lots of nice things here that aren't too outdated. I know Granddad would have been pleased if you took some of them. He was thinner but you guys were about the same height."

The instant she said the words, she regretted them. Zach had grown up incredibly poor. She had meant nothing by her offer other than wanting the clothes to go to someone her grandfather had liked. However, offering Zach used clothes was probably not the most diplomatic thing she could have done.

Thankfully he didn't seem to see it as an insult. "I appreciate that." He stepped toward the bed and pulled a navy cable-knit sweater from the pile.

Savannah smiled, not surprised to see him select that particular one. It had been her grandfather's Saturday morning sweater. In the short time they had dated, Zach had come for breakfast almost every Saturday. Granddad was always wearing that sweater . . . even during the summer months. Daniel Wilde had been a traditionalist; she had loved his predictability. He had provided the wonderful normalcy and security she and her sisters had so desperately needed.

"His Saturday morning sweater was one of his favorites."

He shot her a glance. "I'll wear it Saturday morning in his honor."

Emotions clutched at her heart. Before she could get all misty-eyed again, she said, "What are you doing here again?"

"I need to talk to you about something." Before she could ask what, he said, "I brought dinner."

She swallowed a laugh. He'd probably brought dinner to prevent her heating up more of Aunt Gibby's casserole. When she didn't respond immediately, he added, "It's from Captain Jimmy's."

Her heart and stomach leaped in glee. That had been one of their favorite places to eat when they were dating. It'd been cheap and good. "Gumbo and fried catfish?"

A smile she hadn't seen in ten years flashed over his face. "Hush puppies and slaw, too."

Savannah headed to the door. "I'll set the table and pour the tea."

Zach released a quiet, relieved sigh as he followed Savannah down the stairs. She had every right to demand he leave. Coming in uninvited hadn't exactly been his brightest idea, but ever since he'd seen the graffiti this morning, her safety had been a concern. The dinner was a cheap bribe. He knew if he could get her to open the door, the food was his magic key inside. He hadn't anticipated that she wouldn't answer the door. Alarm had zoomed through him that something had happened. Before he knew it, he was looking for the hidden key. Yesterday, she had told him she had a gun—he was damn lucky she hadn't shot him.

He had never been one to overreact, but with Savannah he'd often done so, and in extreme ways. Zach refused to question why after ten years nothing had changed.

The next hurdle would be getting her on board with his plan. Gibby's suggestion last night had given him the idea. Would Savannah see through it to his real reason—mainly just to be with her? He mentally shrugged. It was worth a shot.

Grabbing up the box of food he'd placed at the front door after he'd come into the house, he headed to the kitchen. Savannah had already filled their glasses with ice and was now placing plates and silverware on the kitchen table.

"I made fresh tea this morning. That okay with you? Or I have Coke, if you'd rather."

Shaking his head, he put the box of food on the table and began to unload. "Tea sounds good. It's been a hot one today."

She poured tea into the glasses. "I didn't even see the sun today."

"I passed by around noon and saw that Carrie and Sylvia were keeping you company."

"I guess you could call it that."

"You're exciting news to Midnight. Not every day a favorite daughter returns."

Her nose scrunched in a cute grimace. "We both know I was never a favorite of anyone's. But thanks all the same."

He disagreed. She'd been a favorite of his from the day he'd met her. But bringing that up would be sure to spoil the easy atmosphere they had going right now.

"I did learn something interesting from Sylvia and Carrie, though."

He took a bite of a crunchy hush puppy and swallowed. "What's that?"

"Apparently you're the number one catch in Midnight."

It was Zach's turn to grimace. "That's because ninety percent of the male population here is either married or over eighty."

She laughed and popped a piece of catfish into her mouth and then closed her eyes on a groan. "Oh my gosh, I'd forgotten how good this stuff is."

Mesmerized, Zach couldn't look away. She was just so damn beautiful and still didn't seem to be aware of her appeal. That had been one of the first things that had attracted him to her. Savannah had always been self-deprecating about her looks, saying that Samantha and Sabrina were the beautiful ones. And without a doubt her sisters were attractive, but compared to Savannah, they were poor imitations of the real thing.

"I've heard more gossip in the last twenty-four hours than I have in twenty years, most of it surrounding you."

He cleared his throat. "You know a lot of the gossip in this town is fabrication."

She tilted her head, her brows arching slightly. "So why'd you come back here? Ten years ago, you hated everything about this town and couldn't wait to leave it behind."

Zach didn't bother to tell her that her statement wasn't quite true. He hadn't hated everything. He took a long swallow of tea and shrugged. "At first, I had no intention of staying. My plan was to sell my house and go someplace as far from here as possible."

"What changed your mind?"

Another opportunity to delve into the past, and one he wasn't prepared to take right now. If they could keep up this easy back-and-forth for a little while longer, then maybe, at some point, he could open up the gnawing dark abyss that contained the truth. For now, he relished being able to speak to her without the open hostility she'd shown before. The less seedy side of why he had decided to make Midnight his home was his safest bet.

The chair creaked beneath him as he leaned back into it and stared over her head, remembering. "The town was the same but oddly different. The house needed a hell of a lot of work before I could even consider selling it. Concentrating on that project, doing business in the town, getting to know the people again as an adult . . ." He shrugged. "I don't know . . . it suddenly began to feel like home. For the most part, with the exception of a few, people treated me as an equal." He shrugged again. "Guess I got a different perspective of everything."

"But why police chief?"

"Chief Mosby's issues with me go way back. When I came back, it was about the same. Didn't matter that I was an adult with a fairly impressive military record. Every time there was a crime he couldn't immediately solve, I was called in as the prime suspect. Pissed me off. When I heard about his retirement, it got me to thinking. The law in this town has been suspect for years. I knew I could do a damn sight better. I took law enforcement courses in college and thought I might apply to the police academy in one of the larger cities one day. With a little urging from a few friends, I threw my hat into the ring. I think everyone was shocked when I was offered the job."

Light green eyes twinkled with gentle humor. "I still can't believe you're the law around here."

He grinned. "Just mind your manners and you'll be fine." His eyes narrowed. "What about you? I thought your big dream was to be a defense attorney. Why a prosecutor instead?"

"About the time I started law school, I changed my mind."

"Why's that?"

"There was a murder-suicide case in Nashville. Only the suicide didn't happen. The guy lived through his attempt and pled temporary insanity. Got off with a slap on the wrist and some counseling. I followed the case closely and was convinced that he had never intended to die. Temporary insanity had just been his out. Made me rethink what kind of career I wanted."

Didn't take a psychiatrist to interpret why she'd changed her mind. Understandably her parents' deaths had made a huge impact on her life.

"You like what you do?"

" 'Like' might be too strong of a word. When I win a case, I'm relieved, knowing justice has been served. When I lose, it bothers me more than what's probably healthy. But to know I'm doing some good by getting criminals off the street and bringing justice for the victims . . . yeah, that satisfies me in a way I didn't anticipate."

What would she say if he told her he had come to Nashville to see her? He wouldn't tell her that . . . at least not tonight. There would be too many questions. She would want to know everything. Before she left town, he would have no choice. This discussion had been delayed much too long. She hadn't wanted to listen to his excuses years ago. And even though they weren't any more substantial now, he needed to clear the air. Telling her wouldn't erase the pain for either of them, but she needed the truth. Hell, she deserved a whole lot more than that, but the truth was at least a start.

For now he would just concentrate on rebuilding her trust and then he would see where that led. Getting his hopes up that it would lead to forgiveness was one thing. That it could go further than that wasn't something he could even let himself consider. One step at a time was his only recourse. If forgiveness was all that she could give him, it was a hell of a lot more than he deserved.

CHAPTER THIRTEEN

Savannah took one last bite of catfish and then relaxed back into her chair, at peace for the first time today. She told herself it had nothing to do with the handsome man sitting across from her. She was tired and hungry and it had been much too long since she'd eaten the delicious but horrible-for-you food at Captain Jimmy's Seafood Emporium. Other than Faye's Diner, Captain Jimmy's was the oldest restaurant in Midnight. Her grandfather had rarely taken them there, but when she and Zach had been dating, they'd eaten at the restaurant at least once a week.

"So what were you wanting to talk to me about?" She tensed slightly as she asked the question. However, she was reasonably sure it wasn't about their past relationship—he wasn't acting like the discussion was going to be intense. If she was wrong, she'd cut him off immediately. What had happened was in the past. He had broken her heart and her trust—two things she didn't give lightly. She ignored the small whispering voice in her mind calling her a coward. She shushed it quickly. She didn't owe him a chance to explain . . . she didn't.

"Your aunt Gibby mentioned the rash of vandalisms. . . . I wanted to get your take. I was beginning to develop a theory and then something happened today that makes me even more certain of where my thoughts are headed."

"What happened?"

"Remember where we first met?"

She almost gawked at him. How could she forget? Zach had saved her from a possible gang rape. "Of course."

"There was a vandalism there last night, with a warning for you to leave."

"Why would anyone even care that I'm here, much less want me to leave?"

"I think it was meant for me."

"What? Why?"

"I believe the majority of the crimes are more about making me look bad and pissing me off than they are about defacing property. Summertime is usually a breeding ground for bad behavior by bored kids with too much time on their hands. That's what the graffiti is made to look like, but I'm not convinced. Conveniently, none of the businesses have security cameras. No one is ever around to see anyone suspicious. And you know damn well that very few things in Midnight aren't witnessed by at least one, if not more, persons. Every piece of property is owned by or closely associated with someone who was opposed to me being the police chief."

"So what's the endgame . . . their purpose? Do they want you to quit?"

"Quit. Leave." His broad shoulders shrugged. "I don't know. Either way, it's not going to work. I just need to figure out where they're going next and be there."

"Can I help?"

Zach nodded. "Thanks, I could really use your help." He grinned and added, "You're one of the only people I'm sure isn't guilty."

"So what do you want to do? How do we set them up?"

"First we need to come up with a list of possible suspects. That'll narrow down the locations that are apt to be hit. After that, we'll decide which locations are the most likely and set a trap."

"That'll work for me. I can work here all day, then help you at night."

Zach stayed silent. Now wasn't the time to tell her that no way in hell was she going to be in on setting the trap. Most of the suspects he had in mind would most likely never think to bring a weapon . . . just spray paint and maybe a few bricks. That didn't mean they wouldn't turn nasty if cornered. Putting Savannah in any kind of danger wasn't something he was willing to risk.

"Let's put our list together first."

Her chair scraped against the tiled floor. "Let me get some paper and a pen."

While she did that, Zach gathered up the remains of their dinner and put them back in the sack. He'd drop them at a dumpster on the way home. By the time she had returned, he'd put the dirty dishes in the dishwasher and started a pot of coffee.

"Wow, you're quick and domesticated."

Zach shrugged and pulled out a chair for her at the table. "You learn to be fast in the army."

"And the domestication?"

"That came from having a mother who wasn't. If I didn't do it, most times it didn't get done."

The silence that followed his statement was awkward. That had probably been the first time he'd openly criticized his mother. Wouldn't have happened with anyone else. Even though they never talked about his family issues, Zach had the tendency back then, and apparently he still had it, to tell Savannah things he wouldn't ordinarily share.

Instead of asking him more about his mother or going on to a different subject, she stunned him with her next words.

"I met your mother once. Did she ever tell you?"

"No. When?"

The shaky breath she took gave him barely a warning before she said, "When you didn't show up that morning, I went to your house."

Zach closed his eyes briefly. Hell no, Francine hadn't told him. Not that it surprised him. What pissed him off was not realizing that sooner. He should have known that's exactly what Savannah would have done. Hell, and he hadn't thought he could feel worse. No doubt his mother had gone out of her way to make Savannah feel as unwelcome as possible.

Aware that a response was expected, Zach opened his mouth; a dry croak was all he managed. Clearing his throat, he tried again, "She didn't tell me. What did she—"

She held up her hand to stop him. "No, wait . . . I'm sorry. I shouldn't have brought it up. I don't want to talk about that time. Okay?"

Her remote expression was telling. The hurt lingered, still festering. The wound between him and his mother had been closed, but the one with Savannah was still open and painful. Zach knew he couldn't take away the pain, but he would tell her the truth—all the nasty, ugly, dirty truth. Not yet, but soon.

Returning to their previous topic, Zach took the notepad and pen she put in front of him and started listing names. Tension filled the air.

Finally she broke the silence with "So who's your prime suspect for the vandalism?"

"One of my deputies."

"What?"

"Yeah. Tells you a lot about the kind of law that was running this town."

"Who's your deputy?"

"Clark Dayton."

Her eyes widened in obvious astonishment. "Clark is a deputy? I would've thought he'd be dead or in prison by now."

"If it weren't for Mosby, he might've been. He dropped out of college and came back here to live. Started working for Mosby not long after."

"Why did you keep him on?"

"I had no reason to get rid of him. He might've been an asshole back then, but they've been known to reform."

"If you're suspecting him, apparently he hasn't."

"I've had no real reason to complain till now. Other than having a shitty attitude sometimes, he's competent."

"So why do you suspect him?"

"I thought he seemed a little too smug yesterday when we were at one of the crime scenes. After I left here last night, I drove by Henson's house. Dayton's car was in the drive."

"You suspect Ralph Henson's in on it, too?"

Zach merely nodded at her question. Explaining why Henson would love to see him fail and leave town was a discussion for another day.

"Just because Clark and Henson see each other after work doesn't mean they're guilty."

"No, but my gut tells me I'm right. Now I just have to prove it."

She grabbed the notepad from him and said, "Who else?"

As Zach named a couple of other men who'd been vehemently opposed to him becoming police chief, he watched Savannah. Had he really thought he could see her again and be satisfied with just her forgiveness? Though having her offer that forgiveness would go a long way in easing his conscience, he was stupid for even considering that it would ever be enough. For ten years, he'd tortured himself with what might have been. Could he really let her go without doing everything he could to recapture what they had?

"Savannah, I—"

She looked up and Zach swallowed his words. The panicked expression on her face gave him his answer; her words confirmed the thought. "Zach . . . no. I can't."

With barely a pause, as if the moment never existed, Zach said, "The locations of the vandalisms are Henson's Grocery, Dale's Car Wash, Opal's Flower Shop, Max's Garage, and Gertie's Wash and Wait."

"And the school building," she added.

"Yeah. That's not consistent with the other properties, but the message was clear. They couldn't have said it more plainly than if they'd taken an ad out in the paper. It was meant to piss me off."

"And it did."

"Hell yeah."

"How do Dayton and Henson tie into these locations?"

"I spent a good part of the day checking courthouse records. Besides his grocery store, Henson is financially tied to the car wash, the flower shop, and the garage. Dayton's aunt is Gertrude Barnes of Gertie's Wash and Wait."

Savannah nodded. "Definitely suspicious."

He reached into his pocket and withdrew a sketch he'd drawn earlier of Midnight. Smoothing it out on the table, he used the pen to point at the likeliest locations for their next hit. "I figure these businesses, before they decide to do something more drastic."

Savannah went to her feet and peered over his shoulder. This was as close as he'd been to her in ten years.

Zach did his best to ignore her scent, delicately sweet and beautifully familiar. Closing his eyes briefly, he willed his aching body to settle down. He was damn lucky she let him get this close to her; no way would he jeopardize that by going after what his body demanded.

He pointed to a row of businesses on Cooper Street. "It took some digging, but I found three other businesses that Henson has monetary ties to: Green's Dry Cleaning and, on the other end of the street, Ava's Bakery." Pointing to another street, he said, "And Frank's Hardware over on Hartman Road."

"Green's has been there as long as I can remember, but Ava's is new."

"Yeah, Ava opened her doors only four months ago. The place stood empty for years and has been totally renovated. I doubt Henson would do anything to it. And Frank's does a brisk business. I don't see him harming it, either. The dry cleaners is another matter. It's in bad shape. Wouldn't be much of a loss."

"Shouldn't Henson be smart enough to realize if things keep happening to his properties, the insurance company is going to investigate thoroughly?"

"Not if he's able to hide his association. Henson's not listed anywhere as an owner."

"Then how do you know?"

"Let's just say that you can learn just about anything you want in Midnight if you ask the right people."

She laughed and Zach's chest tightened. There wasn't a more beautiful sound in the world than Savannah's laughter.

"So what's the plan? We stake out the places until we catch them in the act?"

"Not 'we' exactly."

Savannah raised her eyebrows. "I thought we were working on this together."

"We are. I just don't—"

"Do you have anyone else you can trust to help you watch?"

"No . . . but that's not the point."

"Why did you come to me if you don't want my help?"

Hell, he was beginning to feel like he was on the witness stand. "I wanted to talk it out with you."

"Fine, we've talked it out and now I'm going to help you catch them in the act. I can keep an eye on one of the businesses while you watch the other one. If I see anything suspicious, I'll let you know."

Before he could object again, she raised her hand to stop him and issued an ultimatum: "I'm helping. Deal with it."

Zach had his own ultimatum. "Before I agree, you have to swear you won't interfere. Your ass stays in the car, out of sight. Understand?"

"A lookout only, I promise. Now what's the game plan?"

Asking for her help had been a ruse to be with her, and she'd turned the tables on him. He should have known this would happen; Savannah had always been able to see straight to his soul.

Her eyes were gleaming with triumph, and a small smile tilted her lips upward. Zach gripped the table, desperate to feel the curve of her mouth beneath his. Hell, how was he supposed to work with her when all he could think about was getting her under him?

This had been a real bad idea.

CHAPTER FOURTEEN

Dinner with the mayor and his wife held more than one unexpected surprise. Savannah arrived at their home with a bouquet of flowers for Nesta and a first edition of *The Great Gatsby* for Lamont. She'd spent part of the day in her grandfather's library packing up books to donate to the local library. When she'd come across the book, she'd immediately thought of Lamont, who loved classic literature.

As soon as she had turned in to the drive, she'd realized that the small, intimate dinner party she had hoped for was something more. Five other cars were parked in the large driveway. Silly not to anticipate a larger crowd; the Kilgores were known for their entertaining. Fortunately she soon realized she knew everyone and there was no need for introductions. Even after all these years, meeting new people could be difficult for her. The shy, insecure Savannah still existed beneath the confident professional. The fact that they had all been friends with her parents made their attendance even more appropriate.

"Savannah, you remember Lisa and Richard Tatum, don't you?"

Turning away from chatting with Lamont, Savannah greeted the Tatums. Richard had gone to school with her father, and Lisa had been one of her mother's best friends. "Of course I do." She leaned forward and hugged the couple. "How are you?"

"Oh, you know us, not much changes here in Midnight. Lisa is still the best cook in town." He patted his round belly. "And I'm still her number one fan."

She laughed appropriately, took a sip of her chardonnay, and smiled her way through the conversation. Richard was the talker in the family, often answering for Lisa. Surprisingly his wife didn't seem to mind, often nodding her head in agreement as if that was what she had planned to say anyway. It would have driven Savannah crazy, but apparently it worked for them. Even now, Lisa was gazing up at her husband as if his words were golden.

Nesta was the kind of hostess Savannah loved. Just when the conversation seemed to be waning and she was about to start scrambling for a new topic, the older woman came to the rescue.

"Savannah, can I steal you away for a moment?"

Trying not to nod too eagerly, Savannah murmured something appropriate to the Tatums and followed Nesta to another couple—Doug and Paula Fisher. Both Doug and Paula had gone to school with her father. With the exception of the Kilgores, she had always felt closer to the Fishers than any other of her parents' friends.

Though the days following her parents' deaths were a blur of pain and confusion, she remembered how kind the Fishers had been. One particular memory stood out. On the day of the funerals, she had been trying to find some privacy from all the guests that had congregated at the Wilde house after the service. Instead of going to her bedroom, she had gone outside to escape to the guesthouse behind the mansion. Her grandfather had been living there but had moved his things into the mansion the day before. The house would be empty and she could find the privacy she sought.

On the path that led to the house, she had spotted Paula sitting by herself in the lush flower garden that had been Maggie Wilde's pride and joy. Paula's eyes had been focused on something in the distance, and Savannah had known immediately what she'd been gazing at—the giant oak tree where Beckett Wilde had been found hanging.

Savannah had continued on to her destination but the look of anguish on Paula's face had always made her feel a certain kinship with her—as if the older woman understood her devastation.

Savannah was in the middle of laughing at a story about one of the Fishers' grandsons when she heard a deep, familiar voice. Startled, she turned and did her best not to show a reaction. Had Zach known she was attending this dinner? Was it merely a coincidence that the Kilgores had invited all married couples, leaving her and Zach as the only singles attending? She glanced over at Nesta and had her answer. The woman's eyes were twinkling with delight. Savannah mentally shook her head. Heaven save her from well-meaning matchmakers. First Aunt Gibby and now Nesta.

Following Savannah's gaze, Paula said, "It's so good to see Chief Tanner in a social setting. Seems like every time we've seen him lately, he's been tied up with those vandalisms."

"I just don't understand why he can't figure out who's doing them," Richard said. "Seems like our tax dollars are being wasted if he can't do his job."

Savannah turned swiftly back to the couple. Her mouth opened to defend Zach, but then she swallowed her words. Both Richard and Paula were eyeing her in unashamed speculation. Well crap, them too?

More than a little frazzled, she turned back to Zach,

who appeared to be the only other surprised person in the room. Savannah couldn't decide if this was more of a conspiracy or an intervention. Either way, it wasn't going to work.

Nesta clapped her hands to get everyone's attention. "Thank you all again for coming. Lamont says the steaks are perfect. So let's all go in to dinner."

Savannah stepped back out of the way and watched the couples head into the massive dining room. She looked over at Zach, who had held back, too. The chagrined expression on his face told the tale, and his words confirmed her thoughts. "I think we've been set up."

Disarmed, she laughed and took the arm he held out to her. "Let's not disappoint them."

Zach couldn't believe how easily Savannah was taking to being set up. He figured she would accuse him of being in on it and was relieved she'd seen through the ruse. This wasn't the first time the people of Midnight had tried their matchmaking on him. It was, however, the first time he was pleased with their efforts. There was no one he'd rather spend the evening with than Savannah.

She looked beautiful. Her sleeveless lavender sweater showed her slender, toned arms and golden skin to perfection. And her skirt hit just below mid-thigh, revealing a delicious amount of her long, lean legs. He was pleased to see that the shadows beneath her eyes had disappeared and the tense set to her luscious mouth had eased. He also noted that she wore her hair loose and flowing the way he had always preferred it. Since she hadn't known he would be here, he wasn't stupid enough to think she wore it that way for him.

Zach pulled out one of the two empty chairs remaining at the table for her and then sat beside her. He could have sworn that just about everyone at the table grinned in approval at them.

"Chief Tanner?" Margie Atkins, Lamont's elderly aunt, interrupted Zach's musings. "Do you have any suggestions for getting Earline Barton to stop letting her dog Posey come over and use my yard as his own private toilet?"

It was often frustrating and sometimes weird, but he couldn't say being chief of police here was ever boring.

"Have you talked to her about it, Mrs. Atkins?"

"Several times. She just keeps saying that she'll have a talk with the dog. Now, I ask you, how's that going to help? I've got brown spots all over my yard where Posey has piddled. I know you're busy, what with the vandalisms and all, but I do think she'd do something if you talked to her."

The beautiful woman beside him issued a noise that sounded like a cross between a snort and a snicker. He shot a quick glance at Savannah, who had the look of an innocent lamb; the twinkling in her eyes belied the innocence. She was getting a kick out of his Posey-peeing dilemma. Deciding to turn the tables, he said, "Savannah's been studying law much longer than I have. Do you have a suggestion for Mrs. Atkins?"

Shooting him a "Touché" look, she surprised him and began to make some suggestions. As he watched her, he wondered about the kind of life she led in Nashville. She was obviously successful. The confidence she exuded was so different from ten years ago. The shyness he remembered seemed to be gone, and in its place was a woman sure of herself and her place in the world. He had loved the shy, sometimes awkward Savannah, but couldn't deny that the new, more confident Savannah was just as enticing.

Did she have someone significant in her life? Their

conversation last night had been all about the vandalisms. Things were too uneasy between them to share
personal information. Although if she had asked him
anything personal, he would have answered her questions. Even if she'd come out and bluntly asked him why
he had left town so abruptly ten years ago, he would
have spilled everything. But she hadn't asked. Maybe
she didn't want to know. He'd tried twice last night to
bring it up, and each time she'd shot him down. And
despite the civil conversations they'd had the last couple
of days, hurt and cool detachment lingered in her eyes.
She hadn't bothered to hide her animosity the first time
she saw him. Hell, maybe he was living in a fool's paradise. What if that's all they had left—hurt and anger?

Odd, but Savannah immediately detected a change in
Zach. Even without looking at him, she felt a tension in
him that hadn't been there seconds before. Chancing a
quick glance at his profile confirmed her thoughts. The
grim set of his mouth told her something had upset him.
What could it have been? From what she could tell, the
conversations around them had been innocuously pleasant.

"You okay?" she whispered softly.

"Yeah. Fine."

The terse reply was a surprise. She didn't know this
Zach. This was a harsher, more austere version of the
man she'd seen over the last few days. Not sure how to
handle him and the ridiculous shiver of arousal that this
new Zach gave her, she turned to the man seated to her
left. Kyle Ingram had been one of her father's friends.
Out of all the people at the party, she knew the least
about him and his wife, Noreen. While everyone else
had been a frequent visitor before and after her parents'
deaths, the Ingrams had been scarce.

Before she could come up with some bland comment about the weather, Kyle surprised her and said, "You look almost identical to your mama."

"Thank you, that's a lovely compliment."

"You know, I went out with Maggie when we were teenagers."

"You did?" Her mother had been from Mobile and had met her father in college. "So did you go to college with Mama and Daddy?"

His craggy face had always looked a little sad to her. Her question made him appear even more melancholy. "No, I knew your mama when she was growing up. Her family and mine were real close."

That was a surprise to Savannah. Other than knowing that her mother's parents had died in a car accident when Maggie was still in college, she knew little of her mother's side of the family.

Hearing about her mother like this was a special treat. "What was she like?"

A gentle albeit sad smile curved his mouth. "Delightful. She had such a sunny disposition and the most wonderful laugh."

He had been in love with her. The glaze of tears in his eyes and quiver of his mouth were a clear indication of his grief. Though she would have loved to chat about her mother more, since he had apparently known her well, Savannah hated to cause him more distress.

As she searched her mind for a different topic, Kyle continued, his eyes taking on a faraway look as if he were in a different time and place. "She was the most popular girl in school, you know. But you never would have guessed it. Not a vain bone in her body. She was a cheerleader, too. Did you know that?"

Yes, she had known that. She'd always believed that was one of the biggest reasons Sammie had pursued the same type of activities. Somehow she felt closer to her mother by trying to be exactly like her.

Savannah nodded. "I've seen pictures of her cheer-leading."

His expression went from the faraway look of before to something dreamy and not a little creepy. "Such a beautiful, talented girl."

Uncomfortable with the look of stark longing in Kyle's eyes, Savannah scrambled for something safer. "So if you grew up in Mobile, how did you end up here in Midnight?"

"He followed your mama here."

She'd been so intent on her conversation with Kyle, Savannah hadn't realized the woman across the table from them was listening intently also. Noreen Ingram had always made her uncomfortable. Sour and angry at the same time, the woman never seemed to have anything kind to say to anyone. No wonder poor Kyle always looked so sad.

Instead of responding to Noreen, Savannah kept her focus on Kyle. "I'm sure it was a comfort to Mama to have a friend from her hometown so close by."

Again, before Kyle could answer, Noreen snorted her disgust and said, "More like it drove her crazy. She had her very own stalker."

"Noreen . . . please." Kyle's voice was just above a whisper but the embarrassment and misery in his tone were easily detectable. Everyone at the table went silent.

"Mrs. Ingram, your roses are looking particularly beautiful this year."

Zach's comment to Noreen not only defused a vola-tile situation, it had an amazing effect on the woman. A smile of delight lifted the sour expression to one of al-most prettiness. Amazed at the transformation, Savan-nah stared at her and didn't realize for several seconds that Kyle had left the table and was rushing from the room. The glimpse she got of his face showed tears were streaming from his eyes.

Should she follow him? She didn't know Kyle that well but she hated to see anyone so obviously upset. Somehow she felt responsible for his distress. Torn, Savannah's quandary was solved when a large, callused hand covered hers under the table. Squeezing gently, Zach whispered, "He'll be fine. Don't worry." Then, as if he'd said nothing to Savannah, he continued to charm Noreen.

Grateful for Zach's diplomacy and ability to ease the tense atmosphere, Savannah whispered a quiet "Thank you" and tried to pull her hand away. Zach wasn't having it. Her heart in her throat, she shot a sideways glance at him. Nothing in his face revealed that they were holding hands. She tried once more to pull away. This time, though he didn't release her hand, she did notice a small smile curve his mouth.

Not wanting to attract attention, she stopped tugging. Everyone had gone back to their meal and their own conversations. Kyle returned; his apology that he'd had something in his eye brought comments about the allergy season but nothing more.

The rest of the meal passed in a blur. She knew she ate and even managed to answer when someone spoke to her, though she wasn't sure she made sense. Her concentration was shattered by the hand holding hers and by the large masculine thumb that caressed the inside of her palm in slow, erotic circles. She was stunned to realize that each time he completed a circle, she felt a corresponding and answering throb to her sex.

How the hell could one become aroused by a thumb in the middle of dinner surrounded by a tableful of chattering people? And who knew the palm of one's hand was an erogenous zone?

After a dessert of bananas Foster and coffee, everyone made their way back into the living room. Disturbed beyond bearing, Savannah sat quietly the rest of the evening, smiling and nodding but adding little to the conversation. As soon as the first guest got up to leave, she followed quickly behind them.

Offering her thanks to Lamont and Nesta, she zoomed out of the living room, toward the front door. Zach was on the other side of the room, but his gaze had caught and held hers before she could avoid him. There was no mistaking the message in his eyes.

Savannah practically ran from the house to her car. She started the engine and drove swiftly away, more disturbed than she'd been in years. Her thoughts were a mishmash of emotions and sensory overload, and her entire body felt flushed and unsettled, decidedly needy. The hand that Zach had held tingled as if he'd left an imprint.

She sighed shakily. If a subtle caress of his thumb could create this burning heat inside her, what was she going to do when he tried to do more? No use trying to deny . . . it would happen. The look in his eyes when she'd left had said it all. Zach not only wanted her, he intended to have her. Perhaps the scariest part of all was, she knew she wouldn't deny him.

CHAPTER FIFTEEN

Binoculars in one hand, walkie-talkie in the other, Zach kept a close eye on both the dry cleaners across from him and Savannah's car at the other end of the street. He wasn't expecting trouble. If Savannah saw anything at Ava's Bakery, she was to do nothing more than notify him on the walkie-talkie and then leave. That had been their agreement. And before they'd left her house, he'd made it clear there'd be hell to pay if she did anything else.

She had been unusually quiet all evening. He didn't have to ask himself why. Their brief interlude at the dinner party was still very much on his mind, too. He'd gone to bed, hard and aching, and had dreamed of kissing Savannah, devouring her sweetness and burying himself inside her. The next morning, he'd woken up even harder.

There had been no doubt she'd been turned on, too. Her breathing had been elevated and the rapid beat of her pulse when his thumb had passed caressingly over her wrist told him what she was feeling. And it was exactly what he wanted.

It was going to happen. As inevitable as the tide, he and Savannah would soon ease the desire building between them. Problem was, he owed her explanations before anything more happened. Would that destroy the need? Not for him, but would it for her?

Hell, he still didn't even know if she had someone significant in her life. Just because he saw the heat in her eyes didn't meant she wasn't committed to another man. Separation of feelings from sexual arousal was something he'd learned long ago. No one before or after Savannah had ever captured both his heart and his passion. Only with this one woman had he ever come close to complete fulfillment. And the longer she stayed in Midnight, the harder it was going to be to let her go.

If anyone had told her that she'd be helping Zach Tanner out less than a week after returning home, she would've said a few choice words about their sanity. Yet here she was, sitting in her car, keeping an eye on Ava's Bakery on the off chance that she could catch sight of someone vandalizing it.

But he had no one else to trust. She didn't know why she wanted to help him. Maybe because when they had talked at her house the other night, the pain she'd seen in his eyes was a reflection of her own hurt. Seeing Zach hurting in any way wasn't something she wanted. Way too afraid of the answer she'd get, she didn't question why she felt that way.

Zach was at the other end of the street, watching Green's Dry Cleaning. They were taking a chance the vandals wouldn't choose Frank's Hardware store two streets over. Savannah had suggested she keep watch on it, but that idea had been instantly shot down. When he got that hard look in his eyes, she knew not to argue.

This harsher, edgier Zach was difficult for her to come to terms with. The Zach she had known had been a gentle man through and through. Sometimes awkward and shy and always, always considerate of her feelings. Never would he have issued commands or given her steely-eyed looks. So why did a shiver of excitement zip up her spine whenever he did it now?

Savannah veered away from rationalizing the unexplainable. She took another sweeping glance with her binoculars and saw nothing out of the ordinary. Settling back against the soft leather of the seat, she took a sip of the strong black coffee she'd brought with her. Early in her career, she'd done some surveillance. "Boring" and "uncomfortable" were the only descriptions she could come up with. However, she was known for her patience, so boring though it was, she had usually gotten what she needed. The sooner the vandals were caught, the sooner she could get back to the real reason she'd come home.

Though she still had tons of work to do, she'd taken part of the day to meet with a real estate agent. Oddly, she'd gotten emotional a couple of times. She told herself she was ready to move on and say goodbye to the house forever, but now that the time was drawing near to do just that, it was harder than she'd thought it would be to let go.

One would think she would be anxious to get rid of the location where her mother was murdered and where, just a couple of yards from the back door, her father had hung himself. The place should be a morbid reminder of all the violence, heartache, and misery she and her family had endured. Instead, as she went from room to room, pointing out different aspects of the house to the agent, wonderful memories had come to her.

Christmastime had been a big deal for her mother. The house was always decorated to the nth degree, turning it from a beautiful old home into an enchanted wonderland. During the holidays, there had been parties galore, and she and her sisters always stayed up an hour past bedtime to be able to attend the festivities. And at every party she could remember, her mother and father had been front and center, seeming to adore each other. When had it all gone wrong?

The walkie-talkie beside her sputtered, startling Savannah from her memories. "Anything yet?" Zach asked.

They had chosen not to use cellphones since the light might attract attention. She pressed the talk button. "Nothing. What about you?"

"A couple of cars have passed by but nothing suspicious."

"It's only a little after two o'clock. Maybe they wait till later, when they're sure no one will be around."

"Maybe, but Dayton's working tomorrow. As lazy as he is, I don't see him staying up this late," Zach answered. "Let's give them a few more minutes and then call it a night. I'm sure you're exhausted and want to go to bed."

Had his voice deepened, gotten huskier, with those last words? Savannah told herself to ignore the flare of heat. When he'd come by this evening, she had wondered if they would discuss the incident that had occurred at the dinner party. She'd left the Kilgores' house in a state of arousal she hadn't felt in years . . . all because of a little hand-holding and thumb action. The hurt he'd dealt might still be there but so was the attraction and the need—things that only Zach had ever made her feel.

Savannah gave herself a mental shake. Okay, so she didn't hate him as she had once thought, but neither did she intend to feel anything warm toward him. He had broken her heart, abandoned her when she'd needed him the most. How could she just let that slide?

"Savannah, you there?"

"Yes . . . yes, I'm here." Remembering his comment, she added, "And I am tired."

"Everything okay?"

"Fine." She winced. Going from warm and friendly to cold bitch in mere seconds was sure to bring about more questions. With Zach, it had always been about extremes.

"Okay." Even with the distortion of his voice caused by the walkie-talkie, she detected the doubt in his tone.

Savannah dropped the walkie-talkie on the seat beside her and tried to tell herself she felt no guilt for being cool to Zach. They weren't friends and she was helping him out. That was all. In fact, she shouldn't even be here. She should—

The knock on her window caused her to jump a foot off her seat. Coffee splattered everywhere. Zach stood at the passenger door, peering in the window.

Savannah pressed a button to unlock the door. As soon as it opened, she said, "Dammit, Zach, you scared the crap out of me."

Instead of apologizing, Zach slid into the passenger seat and said, "I can't wait any longer."

"Wait for what?"

"For this." He pulled her toward him and put his mouth over hers.

Savannah ignored the dampness of the spilled coffee and the insistent voice telling her this wasn't a good idea. With a groan of surrender, she melted into his arms. This was exactly what she wanted, what she needed. He tasted so incredibly wonderful—coffee, mint, and Zach. Weaving her fingers through his hair, she pulled him closer, opened her mouth to him, and let him take control.

Zach knew he could be making a huge mistake, but right now, he couldn't think why. Ten-year-old memories and thousands of fantasies couldn't compare to the reality of her taste, as addictive as any drug. He could spend a lifetime with his lips on hers.

Expecting her to pull away any minute, Zach took advantage of the time he had left. His hands roamed over her body, seeking and relearning all the secret places, silken sweetness, and inner fire. His heart thudded and his chest squeezed tight when instead of pulling away as he had feared, Savannah relaxed into him, accepting and needing.

His groan a combination of relief and thankfulness, Zach put all he had into the kiss. Every fantasy, every wakeful night, and every regret he had endured was pouring out like a gushing faucet. It might not change anything, but in this moment of sweetness, if this was the only chance she gave him, he intended to have all the things he had denied himself for so long.

As her tongue met and tangled with his, their hands roamed over each other, exploring all the delicious places they used to touch to drive each other crazy. Zach's hands were beneath her blouse, finding the silky, soft skin he remembered. The firm flesh of her breasts was a welcome and beautiful weight against the palm of his hands.

Savannah's hands roamed under his shirt, caressing his stomach, then delving into his jeans to clutch his ass in a tight squeeze. Zach groaned again. Much more of this and they'd be in serious trouble. Savannah's little Mustang barely had enough room for him to sit, much less do all the things they wanted to do to each other.

Pulling away slightly, Zach whispered, "Let's get out of here."

She stared up at him. Though the car was dark, moonlight gave him enough light to see her expression. The passion slowly faded from her eyes, revealing a morass of emotions. Had he really thought she would fall into his arms and into his bed that easily and quickly?

"Savannah . . . I know we need to talk. I just—"

She shook her head and pressed her fingers against his mouth. "Let's go home, Zach."

This was beyond crazy. Sanity would return any minute, Savannah was almost sure of it. But the minute Zach's mouth touched hers, she had been lost. Every aching dream she'd had over the last decade couldn't compare to that one delicious but much-too-brief kiss.

He was following behind her in his car. Would he be cooled down by the time they arrived at the house? She knew she wouldn't. In fact, just thinking about that kiss kept her throbbing and wet. One touch from him and she would explode.

How irresponsibly she was acting wasn't something she was allowing herself to think about. If she allowed rational thought at all, she knew she would never go through with this. Regrets and recriminations would come tomorrow. Tonight was theirs.

She parked in the drive and was about to open the car door when it opened for her. Taking her hand, he said, "Do you want to talk first?"

Startled, she looked up at him. He was giving her an out. An opportunity for their long-overdue discussion to take place. Could she make love to him without knowing the truth? Her mind whispered *No*, but the rest of her body said something else. Whatever Zach's reasons were, he still wanted her. And stupid and foolish as she might feel tomorrow, she had wanted this for too long to back out now.

Taking chances had never been her thing. Impulsive and reckless were not her personality traits. But right now she wasn't the too-serious and boring assistant district attorney. She was Savannah Wilde reborn and was going to make love to the man she'd given her heart and trust to years ago. The fact that he had broken both couldn't matter right now.

"Let's talk after."

Still holding her hand, he pressed a kiss against her palm and released her. "Race you to the bedroom."

Like two teenagers, they ran to the house and entered through the side door, closest to the kitchen.

At the slam of the door, Zach slowed things down. Pressed up against the wall, Savannah watched as he moved in for another devouring kiss. This time, his mouth molded over hers, sipping and drawing deep groans of need from deep within her. Her only thought to get them skin-to-skin as soon as possible, one of her hands tugged at his shirt buttons while the other went for his zipper. Zach grabbed both of her wrists and, with one hand, held them above her head.

"What are you doing?" The breathless, needy voice barely sounded like her.

"I've waited too long to rush this." His mouth roamed over her face and neck as he murmured softly, "We're going to take it slow and easy and it's going to last all . . ." He punctuated the last words with a hot kiss to her mouth. "Night." And another deep kiss. "Long."

Heat almost consumed her as Zach moved from her mouth, down her neck. He stopped briefly to unbutton the front of her cotton shirt and then expertly flipped open the front clasp of her bra. Before she could appreciate the coolness of bared skin, his hot mouth was covering her breast, drawing a nipple deep into his mouth and sucking hard. Savannah's whimper of need joined in with Zach's groan as he moved to her other breast and set up the same delicious suction.

With him still holding her arms above her head, her only recourse was to press her lower body against him.

When the long, hard length of his penis settled against her mound in the perfect spot for maximum pleasure, she began a slow, steady rub against him. The throbbing in her sex flushed her entire being with a need she wanted to never end. At the same time, she wanted to end it immediately, to attain that seemingly insurmountable peak of exquisite bliss. As she reached for the glorious feeling she'd only ever felt with this man, the sound of a phone barely penetrated the roaring in her head.

She felt the change in him almost immediately. One moment he had been devouring and insatiable, the next he was pulling away. Though he was breathing heavier than normal, his eyes and expression changed in an instant from desire to almost expressionless. How could he turn it off so quickly?

As he grabbed the cellphone from his pocket, he let go of her arms. Savannah pulled away from the wall and wrapped her arms around herself. Feeling vulnerable and exposed, she turned away from him and looked out into the backyard.

Vile curses spewing in his mind, Zach answered the phone but kept his eyes on Savannah. Of all the fucking times for an interruption. He answered with a growling "Yeah?"

"Sorry to disturb you on your night off, Chief, but we got a situation over at Miller's Feed and Seed."

"What's the problem?"

"Looks like the vandals struck again, only this time there's a whole lot more damage than usual."

Shit. Miller's Feed and Seed was not on his list of probable locations. His theory of Henson's and Dayton's involvement just got a whole lot iffier.

"I'll be there in ten minutes."

Zach ended the call and looked over at the woman across the room. She didn't need to say the words; her body language spoke volumes. Severe regret had set in. Didn't matter that going to bed with her before getting the past out of the way had been a bad decision. He had never wanted to say to hell with doing the right thing more than he did right now. If that call hadn't come in, Savannah would be wrapped around him right now and he'd be deep inside her. At that thought, a new wave of arousal hit him hard.

Teeth gritted with the need to shove aside his responsibilities and go after what he'd wanted for so long, Zach said, "I'm sorry . . . I've got to go."

The quick and jerky nod of her head, along with the sight of her arms wrapped around her waist in obvious self-protection, hit him hard. He had hurt this woman in so many ways. If he was the good, decent man she had once called him, he'd turn around and walk out the door. Leave her alone to patch up the new wounds he'd caused. She deserved so much better than anything he could offer. So why the hell was he walking toward her, instead of away?

"Savannah," he whispered as he reached out for her. "I don't want to leave you. You know that. Right?"

"Just go, Zach. This was a mistake. If that phone call hadn't come, I would have eventually realized it. We can't go back to the way it was. There are too many problems. Too much has happened."

His reputation of being slow to anger vanished in an instant. "Like hell it was a mistake." He grabbed her shoulders and pulled her around to face him. "Yes, we need to talk, but listen and listen good." Ignoring the fact that her arms were still crossed, he plastered his body against hers, their foreheads touching, and said harshly, "We will finish this. We both want it. Before you leave town, we're going to have each other. Make no mistake about it." To emphasize the point, he ground his mouth against her hot, supple lips, taking comfort in the fact that not only did she not bite him, she opened her mouth and kissed him back.

Knowing if he didn't leave now, he wouldn't leave for hours, Zach dropped his arms and backed away. "Get some sleep. I'll stop by tomorrow."

Before she could tell him no or to go to hell, he turned and strode out of the room.

"What do you mean you kissed him?"

Savannah winced at the censure in her sister's voice. She had spent a sleepless night aching for something she knew she shouldn't want. At first light, she'd given up on sleeping. Every time she closed her eyes, she thought about him. Even alone in bed, Zach was there with her.

Knowing if she didn't talk to someone soon, she would explode, she'd grabbed her cellphone and called Sammie.

"Well, it was more he kissed me but I let him."

"Where?"

"In my car . . . and then in the kitchen."

"I mean on your person. Did he kiss you on the mouth?"

"Of course on the mouth, Sammie. He's not my uncle."

"No, he's the man who fucked you and left."

Savannah winced. This was more of a Bri reaction than a Sammie one. Sammie was the romantic of the family. That's why she had called her instead of Bri. If anyone would understand her feelings, it should be her. But she should have remembered that when it came to defending her sisters, Sammie could be as ferocious and protective as a mother bear.

Unable to argue with the truth, Savannah sighed and said, "I know that's how I should see him, but I don't."

"Did he at least explain why he did what he did?"

"He tried."

"And?"

"I stopped him."

"Holy hell, Savvy. Have you taken leave of your senses? If I'd known you'd react to him that way, I would have taken time off and handled the house myself."

Pride stiffened her spine. Okay, so she'd acted rashly, which was an unusual occurrence for her. That didn't mean she couldn't handle the situation. And despite the unpleasant lecture, talking to Sammie had helped. "I just needed to regain my perspective."

"Don't let him use you again, Savvy. Men will do that in a heartbeat, without blinking an eye."

Savannah sat up in bed. She'd been so focused on her own problems, she had paid little attention to the undercurrents of Sammie's comments. She swiftly reviewed her sister's remarks. The bitter words had sounded more like Bri's, with maybe a side order of some ultra-feminist man-hater's. They'd definitely not been characteristic of her usually sunny-side-up sister Samantha.

"What's wrong, Sammie?"

There was only the slightest hesitation before Sammie answered, "Nothing. I just don't want to see you get hurt again."

"Are you sure?"

"Absolutely. Now, other than the inappropriate kissing, tell me what else is happening in Midnight. You've been there almost a week, so I'm sure you've been apprised of all the goings-on."

Savannah allowed the change in subject, more than aware that her sister wanted to avoid her questions. As much as she wanted to pull the truth out of her and find out what or who had hurt Sammie, she trusted her sister. She would tell her when she was ready. That had been their pact since they were little girls. When one of them was hurting, the other two would be there for her no matter what.

Wanting to hear her sister laugh and get her mind off her worries for a while, Savannah weaved as much humor as possible in with the news she'd heard since she had returned home. Glad to hear Sammie's laughter, she settled back against her pillow with a relieved sigh.

"So how's the packing coming?"

"I've got most of Granddad's room packed up. I'm spending the next few days in the library. I'd forgotten what an extensive book collection he had."

"Okay, I'm calmer now. Let's get back to Zach."

"Oh, Sammie, I don't know. The moment I saw him . . . it was like the first time. He's even more beautiful than before and almost everyone here loves him."

"Including you?" Sammie said softly.

A swelling ache developed in her chest. No, she couldn't love him again. Not after everything she'd gone through . . . she just couldn't. Instead of denying it as she should, she said, "I don't know."

"If nothing else, Savvy, find out why he did what he did before you do anything crazy. Okay?"

Her sister was right. She'd almost fallen into bed with Zach before she knew what really happened ten years ago. That would have been beyond stupid.

"You're right and I will."

"I've got to get ready for work. Keep me updated. Okay?"

"Will do." Unable to let her worry for Sammie go, she added, "Call me if you need me. Okay? I can be there in just a couple of hours."

Her sister didn't ask what she meant, she simply said, "Thank you, Savvy. Love you."

"Love you, too."

Dropping the phone on the nightstand, Savannah rolled over in bed and pulled a pillow over her head. Hiding from her problems wasn't really her thing, but maybe, for just today, that's exactly what she would do.

CHAPTER SIXTEEN

Hands pressed against the wall of the shower, Zach let hot water gush over his head as the memories he had squashed for the past few hours returned full force. Savannah had been within seconds of climax. He had felt her pulsing against him, had heard the soft hitch in her breath—something he remembered from past experience. Just before she came, she would release the softest and sweetest little gasp. He could get hard just thinking about that small delicate sound.

He'd almost had what he had been longing and dreaming about for years. But with that one phone call, everything had come to a screeching halt. Not only had it been painful for both of them to stop, he knew full well they were going to have to start all over again. Just how long would it take to get back to that place? Who knew, but he wasn't going to stop until they both got what they wanted.

The hell of it was, the untimely interruption had been all for nothing. The vandals at Miller's Feed and Seed weren't the same people. Not only had they caused more damage than was typical of the other vandalisms, the idiots hadn't noticed the camera in the corner recording every move they made. Now two teenagers were locked up, their parents were furious, and Zach was no closer to catching the other idiots than he was before.

He hadn't slept but that wasn't an issue. As an Army Ranger, he'd gone for a couple of days or more without sleep. Didn't mean he would be in a good mood, though. Sleep deprivation combined with an unquenched thirst for Savannah just made him doubly pissed.

He turned off the shower and grabbed a towel. Drying off quickly, Zach was dressed and headed out the door in a matter of minutes. Going by to check on Savannah before he went to work was probably not a good idea. She was most likely still asleep. And if she wasn't, it meant she hadn't slept well. The reason she might have had difficulty sleeping was one of the reasons he wanted to see her. If he could clear the air as soon as possible, maybe he could regain some of the ground he'd lost last night when he'd walked out the door.

No, he wasn't stupid. He knew they had a lot more to get through than that one event. However, he did owe her an apology. If there was one thing the past had taught him, it was to own up to his mistakes. And he had one major one to make up to Savannah. Question was, would she let him?

After another hour of tossing and turning, sleeping only a few moments at a time, Savannah gave up. It was close to eight o'clock and all she had to show for it was a headache and a severely overheated body. Too bad she couldn't blame it on the hot temperature outside, but since the thermostat was set at a cool seventy-two degrees and she'd yet to step outside, she knew the weather wasn't the issue. Zach Tanner was the problem. Last night he had awakened feelings and emotions she had successfully squelched for years. And now they were back and had apparently brought along some risqué friends. Never had she had such erotic dreams.

Sitting at the kitchen table, Savannah sipped her second cup of coffee and tried not to stare at the wall Zach had pressed her up against last night. She'd been two seconds away from climaxing when his cellphone rang. She didn't blame him for answering the call and leaving. That was his job. No, she blamed herself for being in that position in the first place. How many times had she sworn that if she ever saw Zach Tanner again, she would tell him exactly what she thought of him? Instead she'd kissed him like there was no tomorrow and had almost gone to bed with him.

Savannah still remembered the bewilderment she had felt when he didn't show up that morning. She'd known he was having breakfast with his family, but he had promised to stop by before he left town at noon. At eleven-fifteen, after getting no answer to the numerous voice-mail messages she'd left him, she had swallowed her pride and gone to his house. His mother had greeted her at the door but hadn't invited her inside. She had said Zach had left early that morning. She'd told Savannah he wasn't coming back and that she should forget about ever seeing him again.

In shocked denial, Savannah had stood on the tiny, worn porch of Zach's house, shaking her head in disbelief. Only hours before, she had given him her heart and her body, and Zach had given her his promise. She had been wearing that promise on her finger. No way had the woman been telling the truth.

The hurt had been crushing but Savannah had refused to give up. One week went by and then another. Her grandfather had offered to contact him. Had even gone so far as obtaining the phone number where she would be able to leave a message for him. Savannah hadn't wanted to use it. Though the hope faded with each passing week, pride and hurt prevented her from making the call. Then came the day when she'd had no choice. She had made the call. Five calls in three days. He hadn't returned any of them.

On that last call, when she had hung up the phone, she had accepted it was over. Whatever had changed Zach's mind about them no longer mattered. She had locked the promise ring away and her heart as well.

If only that had been the end. She soon learned that there were different degrees of pain and heartache and they could come in stages. Some were like the tide: they came and then drifted away, leaving residue but no real destruction. Others came and stayed, became a part of who you were—as much a part of you as muscle, blood, and bone. That kind of pain changed you, developed you . . . could almost destroy you if you let it. She had almost let it.

The doorbell rang. Even with all the visitors over the last few days, she already knew it was Zach. He would want to know how she was, apologize for having to walk away. He might even expect that they could start up where they'd left off.

There was no point in denying the truth. Something deep within her still felt a strong connection and bond with Zach. And judging by his demeanor since her return, he felt something, too. Lust and nothing more? Who knew.

Feeling much older than her twenty-eight years, Savannah made her way toward the front door. If she ignored him, he wouldn't give up. Might as well face the tiger now.

She didn't know what to expect when she opened the door to Zach, but it wasn't a man holding a large bouquet of red roses and a tender look of apology that should melt any woman's heart. She wished she could say she was immune.

"I just wanted to drop by before I headed off to work. I'm sorry about last night."

Telling him it wouldn't happen again was the sensible and rational thing to say. Unfortunately, when it came to Zach, sensible and rational weren't part of her emotional vocabulary.

With a small smile, Savannah took the flowers he held out for her and sniffed them appreciatively. "Thank you, but that wasn't necessary. What happened on the call? Was it the same guys, you think?"

He shook his head. "Just two bored kids out for some kicks. Security cameras caught it all."

"So, when's our next stakeout?"

Though Zach was often hard to read, she saw relief in his eyes. And since she had seen through his ploy early on, she knew it wasn't because he really needed her help.

"How about next Tuesday night?"

"Works for me. See you then."

She went to close the door, but Zach placed his palm on the door, stopping her. "I know we need to talk . . . get everything out in the open."

Yes, they did. But not right now. With her lack of sleep, if they talked today, she'd go beyond the basket-case stage into full nuclear meltdown. Still, it had to be done. "How about tomorrow night?"

He shook his head. "I'm on duty Sunday and Monday night."

"Sounds like Tuesday would be best for that, too, then."

He looked as though he wanted to say something else, but finally nodded his head and stepped back.

Savannah whispered, "Thanks for the flowers," then closed the door.

Sunday morning in Midnight meant one of three things. One either went to the Baptist church on Harper's Drive,

the Methodist church on Beechum Road, or the nonde-
nominational church over on the bypass. As her granddad used to say, "Midnight is full of sinners. Come
Sunday morning, if you're not in church, you're going to
be the subject of the gossipers, so you might as well go
and cut down on their fun."

Her grandfather had been a regular at the Baptist
church, but Aunt Gibby was Methodist through and
through. After her parents died, Savannah and her sisters had alternated between the two churches. Gibby
had insisted that they needed the diversity of both de-
nominations, and Daniel hadn't argued.

Savannah closed the car door behind her aunt and
followed her into the large foyer. Returning to church
here felt familiar and comfortable. The minister was the
same one as when she was a kid, the pianist played the
same songs, and the song leader had the same nasal
tone she remembered from long ago.

Gibby liked to sit on the front pew. And Savannah
was treated to more than a few whispers and speculative stares as she walked beside her aunt. Even with a
job that was often in the public eye, she still didn't like
to call attention to herself. This wasn't the worst part,
though. That would come after the service. Years ago,
the leading members of the Methodist and Baptist
churches had made the decision to unite as one congre-
gation once a month for a Sunday social. When the non-
denominational church had started up about fifteen
years ago, they had wisely invited them to participate. It
was a tradition that everyone seemed to enjoy. Not only
did you get some of the best Southern cooking in Alabama, but you could also pick up the latest gossip you
might have missed. Though the subject of the gossipers
was often in attendance, their presence rarely stopped
the talk. You just had to lean closer to hear the juiciest
parts.

As the old familiar songs were sung, Savannah couldn't help but remember the many times she and her sisters had sat beside her parents on a Sunday morning just like this. Sunlight on the stained-glass windows gave them an almost ethereal glow, making the worship service seem even more reverent. Feeling an odd ease within her, she turned her attention to the service, hoping for comfort and solace for what she would soon face with Zach.

She was so immersed in the uplifting sermon, it wasn't until she stood at the end of the service to sing the closing song that she knew the identity of the person who had come in late and sat behind her. The deep baritone was unmistakable. Years ago, Zach had kept her entertained and in stitches as he parodied some of the popular rock songs on the radio. And though the song they sang now certainly wasn't a parody, Savannah had no trouble recognizing the deep masculine voice.

Tempted to turn around, she resisted the urge. Pretending he wasn't there was her best bet. She should have known Aunt Gibby wouldn't cooperate. The moment the service was over and they stepped into the aisle, Gibby exclaimed, "Chief Tanner, it's about time you graced us with a visit. I thought those Baptists had snared you for sure."

The too-infrequent smile lit up Zach's face. "Actually, I just go there to keep an eye on them. I figured y'all had it all together over here."

Gibby cackled. "You got that right." She winked at Savannah and grabbed her arm. "Let's get out of here as soon as possible so we can snag a good spot at the park."

Knowing many eyes were on her, Savannah gave Zach what she thought was a cool but pleasant smile of acknowledgment and then led Gibby down the aisle toward the entrance.

*   *   *

Zach blew out a ragged sigh as he watched Savannah walk away. The wariness was back and he cursed himself for letting that happen. He should have figured out a way to see her last night so they could have had the discussion that needed to take place. Now he felt as if he was starting at square one, right where he'd been the first day of her return.

"It's so nice to see you here, Chief. Are you going to the social?"

The sugary sweetness of Lindsay Milan's voice gave Zach chills. There was such a desperate neediness to her tone. When she grabbed his arm and tightened her fingernails into his skin, he had to grit his teeth not to jerk away.

His mind on the beautiful woman who had just left, Zach nodded an acknowledgment and pulled away gently. "Mrs. Milan."

Lindsay was having none of it. She held tight to his arm and asked the same question, only louder: "You going to the social, Chief?"

Something in her tone grabbed him. Pulling his thoughts away from Savannah, he took a moment to assess the woman still hanging on to his arm. Dark circles shadowed worried-looking eyes.

"Let's go, Lindsay."

The growling voice came from Carl Dayton, Lindsay and Clark's father. Zach had had few dealings with the older Dayton. He was a not-so-successful farmer whose wife had left him years ago. Rumor was that she had finally gotten up the courage to leave him after years of abuse. Was Lindsay getting the same treatment? There was no proof that anything like that was going on, and coming right out and asking would only cause problems. However, he couldn't ignore the possibility.

Well aware he might pay for this later, he turned back to Lindsay and said, "Actually, I am going to the social. Would you like to ride with me?"

Relief and something like gratitude gleamed in her expression. She nodded eagerly and held on to his arm tighter.

Carl gave a seemingly warning glare to Lindsay before he walked away.

"Thank you, Zach," she whispered.

"What's going on? Are you in trouble?"

"I—"

"Zach Tanner, as I live and breathe. I thought it'd take handcuffs and a gun to get you inside this church."

They both turned as Reverend Simmons practically shouted at him. Zach couldn't blame him. Not only had the man taken every opportunity to invite him to attend services, the minister was almost totally deaf. Shouting was the norm for him.

Grinning, Zach shook the man's hand and exchanged small talk. All the while, he kept a close eye on Lindsay. Something was definitely going on with her. When one of the parishioners interrupted them, Zach took the chance to walk away, Lindsay at his side.

More than aware of the whispers and sideways glances of those they passed, Zach made it outside without anyone else stopping him. He stopped abruptly when he saw Savannah in the parking lot with her aunt, helping her into the car. In that instant, she looked up and saw him. He watched as her eyes shifted to Lindsay, whose hand was still on his arm, then her face stilled and became expressionless.

For the first time in a long while, Zach felt helpless. Every time he made any kind of progress with her, something happened to diminish it.

With the knowledge that there was nothing he could do right now, he walked with Lindsay to his car. Knowing that others could still hear them, he waited until they were both in the car, then said, "Okay, what the hell's going on?"

Seeing Lindsay Milan's hand on Zach's arm as if she had a claim on him cut Savannah deep. She had believed he was sincere, that he still had feelings for her. Was she being a fool once again?

"You're not worried about that one, are you?"

Aunt Gibby's voice broke into her thoughts. Savannah hadn't even realized she was just sitting in the driver's seat, staring out the window. She started the engine and backed out of the parking lot. Thankfully, as was usual with Gibby, responding to her questions wasn't necessary.

"Sure, she's pretty. But honey, Zach hasn't looked at a woman since he got back in town. And now that you're home, he can't look at anybody else."

"Aunt Gibby, don't. That was over a long time ago."

"Oh, I know you both think it was, but when you're in love, it's never truly over."

Gibby had never married. Savannah didn't know much about her aunt's younger days, but the way she had made that statement made her think that Gibby knew all about lost love. Not wanting to pry, Savannah shook her head and said, "What we had wasn't real love."

As if she hadn't spoken, Gibby continued, "You know, your granddaddy wanted to hunt Zach down and skin him alive for breaking your heart."

She wasn't surprised. Her granddad had been up close and personal with her heartache. Had held her while she cried, been with her every step of the way. Even the peace-loving Daniel Wilde must have wanted to exact vengeance against the man who'd broken his granddaughter's heart and spirit.

"I think he even went to see Zach's mama."

"Really? When? He never told me."

As if she hadn't heard her, Gibby went on. "Course, when I asked him what happened, he got all secretive like he did on occasion. Hated when that happened."

"He never told you anything about the visit?"

"Nope, but he seemed to calm down after that." She glanced at her watch and said, "We'd better get going or all the good sittin' spots will be gone."

Savannah drove the short distance to the Midnight community park and pondered on Gibby's revelations. Her grandfather had never mentioned going to see Zach's mother. What had he learned that made him "calm down" about Zach?

Suddenly she was exasperated with herself. Why the hell did she still not know why he had left town without saying goodbye? Or why hadn't he contacted her until months later? She had been here a week and had seen Zach almost every day since her return. On one of those occasions, why hadn't she just asked him outright? Or let him talk instead of cutting him off? When had she become such a coward?

She discounted the opportunity she'd had years ago. When Zach had finally contacted her months later, she'd been emotionally raw. Too much had happened. She had deemed it too little, too late, and had refused to speak to him, just wanting to forget.

Learning the truth now wouldn't change the pain of the past, but she deserved to know. And Zach deserved an opportunity to explain.

Three long rows of picnic tables sat beneath giant oaks: four tables of casseroles, vegetables, and meats, two for tea, lemonade, and soda, and three tables filled with breads and desserts. It was a massive amount of food, but since the majority of the town's citizens would eat here today, Savannah knew that within an hour the tables would be almost bare.

After settling Gibby into a lawn chair beneath a shade tree, Savannah stepped around blankets and running children as she made her way to the tables. She was greeted by everyone she passed, with either a smile, a wave, or a "Welcome home, Savannah."

Deciding what to put on Gibby's plate was easy. She loved casseroles and, other than turnip greens and collards, hated anything remotely green. With a plate loaded with what she knew were her aunt's favorites, Savannah turned to the beverage table and almost ran over Zach.

"Whoa, that's a lot of food."

Unable to raise her head higher than his chest, she stretched her lips into a semblance of a smile and nodded. "Gibby's hungry."

A callused finger caressed the edge of her jaw and then settled on her chin to tilt her head up. "Can I see you later today?"

Despite the ninety-degree temperature, Savannah shivered. Zach's voice had gone low and intimate, as if they were the only two people in the world. She examined his handsome face, seeing honest sincerity and absolutely no secrets. Unwillingly her gaze shifted to the woman a few feet behind him, putting food on a plate. Lindsay Milan had obviously come to the picnic with him. Was he dating her? Was Zach low enough to ask her out while he was at an event with another woman?

Zach surprised her by reading her thoughts. "We're not dating."

She believed him. With the exception of that one significant time, Zach had never given her any cause to doubt his honor. However, she wanted to be clear on what she expected.

"I have questions I want answered."

"I'll give them to you. I promise."

He shouldn't have used those words. The last time he'd made a promise, her life had fallen apart.

And again, Zach read her perfectly. "Okay, bad choice of words. Give me a chance to explain, Savannah. Please."

"I thought you had to work."

"I do, but I take my dinner break at six."

"I'll see you then." Turning away, she grabbed a sweet tea from the table and strode rapidly to Gibby. Thinking that her aunt would complain about it taking so long, Savannah was relieved when she took the plate and said, "Thank you, sweetie, that looks wonderful. Now, you go off and get yours before it's all gone."

Though nerves were jumping in her stomach like manic crickets, she did as she was told. Again she stopped on the way to visit with those she hadn't seen since her grandfather's funeral. Answering questions about herself and her sisters took considerable time, so by the time she returned with her own plate, Gibby was holding court with several women surrounding her. Savannah didn't know all of them and felt comfortable sitting a little away from the group and halfway listening as she picked at her meal.

The talk she and Zach had put off for almost ten years would happen tonight. Would she be able to talk about everything? Was she ready? For self-protection, she hadn't allowed herself to think about that time in her life in years. Dwelling on what might have been, the grief, the pain . . . accomplished nothing.

"Savannah Rose, I do believe I'm ready to go home and take a nap."

Savannah stood and gathered up Gibby's belongings, along with the lawn chairs they'd brought with them. As she expected, Gibby didn't leave without visiting a half dozen people on the way to the car. Standing by her side, waiting, Savannah took in the scene. Men and women of all ages were sitting or standing in small groups, laughing, talking, and eating. Teenagers played softball in the small ball park, and yards away, older men threw horseshoes and played croquet. Young children played hide-and-seek, staying close by, where mothers and fathers could keep an eye on them.

It was a picturesque and almost poetic-looking scene. How many towns had Sunday socials anymore? Growing up in this kind of environment had made her take it for granted. Now, with new eyes, she could appreciate the sheer simplicity of small-town closeness. Yes, they gossiped and complained about one another, but they had something most big cities had lost. They had community.

Brown eyes twinkling, Aunt Gibby gave her a knowing smile. "Now, admit it. You had a good time today."

Savannah laughed. "It may not have been as agonizing as I thought it would be."

"Midnight isn't perfect but we have our good points."

Leaning over, she kissed Gibby's soft, wrinkled cheek. "And you're one of the best."

A blush colored the elderly woman's face to a rosy glow. "I miss having you girls close by."

A wave of guilt hit Savannah. After she left for college, her visits had been rare and short. Her sisters had visited much more often than she had. Returning to all the old memories and pain had been too difficult. Suddenly she wished she had been braver, less self-absorbed. Gibby had been a huge part of her life when she was growing up, and Savannah felt as though she had abandoned her.

"I'm sorry, Aunt Gibby. I'll try to come back more often. I promise."

She patted Savannah's hand. "Thank you, child. That would be wonderful. Now take me home so I can take my nap."

As they drove away, Savannah glanced up in the rearview mirror and swallowed a gasp. Kyle Ingram stood only a few feet away from the rear of her car. The look of longing in his eyes was a startling and uneasy reminder. Midnight might be much more pleasant than what she remembered, but the town had its share of oddities. Kyle was most likely just reminiscing about her mother, but the gleam of adoration she'd glimpsed in his eyes sent chills up her spine. She had seen too many unbalanced people in her career not to recognize the symptoms. There was something not quite right with Kyle Ingram.

CHAPTER SEVENTEEN

At six o'clock exactly, Zach was at Savannah's door. He'd thought about nothing all day but their upcoming discussion. Opening up the gnawing chasm of darkness after all these years of suppressing it was going to be bloody hard. Only for Savannah. How many times had Josh asked him what happened? Not even for his brother could he reveal what occurred that night. But for Savannah, he would. Not only because he owed her an explanation and apology but because . . . hell, because despite everything within him telling him he was a fool, he was still crazy about her.

Her smile of uncertainty when she opened the door was a reflection of his own doubts. Would this change everything between them? Or nothing at all? Would it put the past to rights or destroy this new and fragile beginning? How could he make her understand, when he sometimes had trouble justifying his actions even to himself?

"Hope you're hungry."

"I didn't expect to eat. You didn't have to go to the trouble of making a meal."

She shrugged and led him into the kitchen. "I know it's your dinner break, and I had to eat, too."

The nonchalant comment made it appear the meal would be something simple and quick. Nothing could have been further from the truth. The table held a delicious-looking meal of roast beef, mashed potatoes and gravy, green beans, fried okra, sliced tomatoes, and rolls. And on the counter, he spotted a pecan pie. Despite his nervousness, his stomach made an approving leap.

Unable to hide his surprise, he said, "You went to a lot of trouble."

She blushed and waved away his compliment. "I didn't feel like packing this afternoon, so I decided to play in the kitchen."

Never had he wanted to kiss her more. The shy smile and blush reminded him of when they'd first started dating. She'd been so sweet, so insecure, and so very unaware of her effect on him. Since she had returned, her mask of sophisticated coolness had covered the naïve, young beauty he'd fallen in love with. Just one glimpse of the girl he'd loved made his heart ache. She had been innocent and pure, and he'd screwed up massively.

Pushing aside the regret, he asked, "Anything I can do to help?"

"No, we're set. Have a seat and I'll pour the tea."

She placed the iced tea before him and then sat down across the table from him. "Hope you don't mind eating at the kitchen table. The dining room is too formal and the morning room is still too hot this time of day."

"I always enjoyed eating in this kitchen. Brings back lots of good memories."

It was an opening he expected her to take. Her smile was wistful. "We did have a lot of good times in here." The smile disappeared and, as expected, she went straight for the heart. "Why, Zach?"

The roast tasteless in his mouth, Zach swallowed and put his fork down. "When I left here that night, I had every intention of coming back the next day to say goodbye before I left."

She blew out a shaky breath, her relief apparent. It hurt that she had believed he had led her on. Had she thought that once they'd had sex, he'd gotten what he wanted and it was over? Had his promises not meant anything? Zach jerked himself out of his unwarranted hurt. He was the one who'd left without a word, the one who hadn't contacted her for months. He had no right to be hurt.

"When I left here, I remembered I'd promised to cook breakfast for my mom the next day. I knew she wouldn't have gone to the store. I could've gone across town to the mini-mart, but Henson had just started experimenting with staying open twenty-four hours. Most times I tried to stay away from that store because of our history. But I was cocky . . . told myself I was leaving town the next day and the bastard had no control over where I went and what I did."

He shook his head as the memories washed over him. "Not a day goes by that I don't wish I'd made a different decision."

TEN YEARS AGO

Zach parked in the almost empty parking lot and got out of the car. With any luck, he could avoid old man Henson, get the few things he needed, and be in bed by one. Tomorrow was going to be a busy and emotional day. If he'd been stronger, he would have said his final goodbye to Savannah a few minutes ago and not have to go through the gut-wrenching agony again. But tonight she had given him her body and her heart, and saying goodbye after something so phenomenal had been impossible. Unwise or not, seeing her one more time before he left wasn't something he could resist.

His mind on Savannah, Zach was in the store and gathering things before he realized it. Other than the checkout clerk up front, no one was around. He made his selections quickly. Arms loaded with breakfast items, he was halfway to the checkout when his perfect night went to shit.

"What are you doing here, boy? I told you never to come back to my store."

Sighing, Zach turned and faced the man. Might as well get it over with. "I'm just here for a few things. I'm not stealing. Just buying. Okay?" He turned back around and started toward the checkout.

Henson grabbed his shoulder and tried to pull him around. The old man was a big guy but no match for his youth and strength. Zach didn't budge and Henson had no choice but to let him go. Hoping he'd be able to get away without another confrontation, Zach just kept on going. No way in hell was he going to get into trouble his last night in town.

The kid at the checkout had obviously heard the altercation. His Adam's apple wobbled spasmodically as he nervously swallowed. Zach patiently waited as the kid carefully scanned each item. Old man Henson would be a bear to work for; the poor kid had probably been chewed out more than once. Finally he told Zach the amount he owed. Zach handed him the money, grabbed the bag, and walked out the door.

He was in the parking lot, counting himself lucky that nothing else had happened, when Henson growled from behind him, "I warned you not to come back."

Zach threw his groceries in the passenger's side and closed the door. "I'm gone after tomorrow. You don't ever have to see me again. That should make you happy."

Henson sneered. "Boy, the only thing that would make me happy would be if you'd never been born."

He'd always known Henson had it in for him, but Zach was stunned at the sheer loathing in the old man's eyes. "Why the hell do you hate me so much?"

"You ruined my life."

"And just how the hell did I do that?"

"I gave your mama money to get rid of your carcass. Instead of using it like she should have, she stayed in town and flaunted her pregnant belly all over Midnight."

Revulsion liked he'd never known filled Zach. No. No way in hell was this self-righteous son of a bitch his father. "You're full of shit, old man. My father was killed in the service."

"You're 'bout as dumb as you look," Henson sneered. "That's what she told everybody. Ask your mama how she got knocked up when James Tanner was halfway round the world. Your mama was like a bitch in heat when she didn't have a man around to satisfy her itch. She caught me in her trap."

Zach took a step forward until he was inches from Henson's face. His jaw clenched with fury, he bit out, "You're not my father. You got that, asshole?"

"Shit, boy, you think I'd come out and say something so disgusting? Your mama and me screwed around. She said she couldn't get pregnant. Was using protection. She lied . . . like all bitches do."

Zach had no words. The thought of this man's blood running in his veins was too vile to even contemplate. He stared hard at the man. Were there similarities? Henson's eyes were brown, not gray like Zach's. That meant nothing. He'd seen pictures of James Tanner, who'd had blue eyes. Zach knew he'd gotten his eye color from Francine.

Narrowing his gaze, he peered closer. Were their

cheekbones similar? Or the shape of their noses? Maybe, but there was nothing that stood out and said absolutely that Ralph Henson was his father, except for one thing—Henson's expression said he believed he was speaking the truth.

"How do you know Francine didn't get pregnant by someone else?"

A glint of arrogant pride entered Henson's eyes. " 'Cause I was on her day and night for a whole month. She didn't have the energy to spread her legs for anybody else."

Zach had no choice; he had to hit him. Slamming his fist into Ralph Henson's face was one of the most satisfying moments of his life. Standing over the bastard lying on the ground, Zach snarled, "You spew lies like that again and I'll make sure you live to regret it."

As a threat, it had been weak at best. But after what he had just learned, he was surprised he was able to form any coherent words at all.

Zach turned away from the piece of crap on the pavement. He had to see Francine immediately; he had to know the truth. The little voice inside him—the one that he hated because it never lied to him—said that he'd already heard the truth. Ralph Henson was his father.

His mind reeling, Zach never heard the noise behind him. Pain sliced into his head; he pitched forward and darkness followed.

He woke to pain. Harsh whispers and laughter echoed around him. The unmistakable smell of blood and the stench of something vile filled his nostrils. Every part of his body felt wrenched, bruised, battered, or broken. He tried to raise his head . . . knew he needed to get up. What the hell had happened? Agony split his side. He'd been around long enough to recognize a booted foot had just slammed into his kidney. He breathed through the pain and struggled to his knees. The headlights from several cars shone brightly in his eyes. He blinked, tried to get a clear picture of where he was. His vision was impaired . . . something warm and wet was running down his face, into his eyes. He saw three blurred figures; couldn't make out any faces. Henson and his friends? Fury trumped pain. Damned if they'd get away with this.

He got to his feet. Swaying unsteadily, he balled his hand into a fist and swung out blindly. He felt a small satisfaction when fist met flesh. Excruciating pain exploded in his jaw. Multiple fists slammed into him from every direction. Shielding his face with his left arm, Zach lashed out with his right arm. His knees wobbled, his feet unsteady. His brain occasionally registered that he'd scored a hit to something or someone. A hard blow slammed against the side of his head and he fell facefirst onto the ground. Someone jumped on top of him, began pummeling in earnest. Blessed unconsciousness descended once again and this time Zach welcomed the dark relief.

Minutes or hours later, he woke. The sky above him held a light pinkish tinge. It was almost dawn. Painfully he turned his head and tried to comprehend his surroundings. As far as the eye could see, there was only flat, open landscape—a cow pasture.

Hissing at the pain, he raised his head and that was when he realized he was not only naked, his entire body was covered in blood and cow manure. Every muscle and part of his body throbbed and ached. The agony it took to breathe told him his ribs were either cracked or severely bruised, his nose was busted, and he could barely see for the searing pain in his head.

Every breath brought a curse as he raised himself up, got to his knees, and then his feet. He had no idea where he was, but if he didn't get his ass in gear, he'd be walking home in broad daylight.

Finally standing, he swayed back and forth like a drunk, and only sheer determination kept him from falling. He took a second to get his bearings. Seeing the Midnight water tower in the distance, he determined where he was and the location of the road. Figuring he was at least two miles from his house, he stumbled forward. He'd make it home before he was seen or die trying. Several yards ahead of him, he spotted his wallet. Swallowing a groan, he leaned down and picked it up. Bastards had even taken his money, all thirteen dollars. But they'd left his license and that's all he cared about.

At last finding the road, he bellowed like a crazed man as he climbed the fence. Knowing his legs would never hold him, Zach dropped and landed on his ass. His body jarred and he again allowed himself the luxury of screaming at the pain.

Back on his feet, he dragged one foot in front of the other. And as he stumbled home, fury burned the pain and humiliation away. He had been treated like shit for most of his life in this town. And thanks to Ralph Henson, he now knew he came from shit.

It took him almost two hours to get home. He'd had to hide twice behind bushes when a couple of cars had driven past him. He pulled himself up to the porch and found the key under the doormat where his mother always left it. Cynically he wondered how many men in town knew about the key.

He opened the front door and all was quiet. His mother and Leonard were still in bed. His first priority was to get the stink of cow shit off his skin. Turning on the water as hot as he could stand it, Zach scrubbed every particle of his body until it was raw. The pain in his body was numbed by the fury still fueling him.

Once he felt reasonably clean, he brushed his teeth, drank down a gallon of water, and then, with painful slowness, dressed. Since he was already packed, he had only one other item on his agenda. Shoving open his mother's bedroom door, he felt a small amount of satisfaction when the noise startled her. She shot straight up from bed. Leonard lay beside her, still snoring. Apparently she had tired him out.

At first she smiled, as if thrilled he'd woken her. When he just stood and stared at her, she frowned and said, "What's wrong? Why are you looking at me like that? What happened to your face?"

"Who the fuck is my father?"

Even as he said the words, a small, still-decent part of him cringed. Never had he talked to a woman this way.

"What are you talking about, Zachie? You know who your daddy is. He was a war hero."

He cocked a brow. "Not a piece-of-shit asshole named Ralph Henson?"

The instant he said the name, Francine's expression revealed the truth. He turned and walked away. She caught him at the front door. "I'm sorry, baby. I had to lie to you. That bastard wanted me to get rid of you. I did it all for you."

Giving her one last glare of disgust, he walked out the door. Though he had intended to drive to Fort Benning, he didn't care about his car . . . he cared about nothing but getting away. He hitched a ride to the bus station and left Midnight and everything it stood for behind him. He refused to give thought to anything, including the innocent young girl he'd made promises to and whose heart would soon be broken.

And now she knew the truth. Savannah stared down at the now cold meal. Stupid to have spent so much time on dinner. She had known this wouldn't be a pleasant social event. Her stomach roiled. What an idiot she had been. Of course she had suspected something traumatic had happened. Zach leaving without saying goodbye had made no sense. But she had been so very hurt and then so very afraid.

She cleared her throat, struggling not to reveal the tears she desperately wanted to shed. "Why didn't you come to me, Zach? I would have taken care of you."

He shook his head. "I was hurt and humiliated, Savannah. I had only one priority and that was to get as far away as possible. Having you see me like that would have killed me."

Her eyes roaming over his face, she compared the Zach of today to the boy she had fallen in love with. The ruggedness was new, as were the lines around his mouth. His eyes probably told the biggest story. Years ago they had been a soft, beautiful gray. Now they were steely hard.

She remembered thinking when they were dating that a twenty-year-old Zach seemed so mature and manly. But he had been just a kid. A boy who'd been beaten and humiliated. One who'd learned the cruel truth about his parentage. Was it any wonder he'd left that night?

Swallowing past the sympathy she knew he wouldn't want, she said softly, "Did you go to basic training as you'd planned?"

"I tried to. Only I was so banged up, they took one look at me and put me in the hospital instead. Had some broken ribs, a bruised kidney, a concussion, and a broken nose."

Unable to not offer some kind of solace, Savannah reached across the table and touched his hand. "I'm sorry that happened to you."

His mouth twisted in a grimace. "And I'm sorry I did what I did."

Now that she knew the truth, the hardest question of all had to be asked. "Why did you wait so long to contact me?"

He pulled his hand away from hers and pushed his fingers through his hair. "I was out of it for almost a week. When I woke up and could think more clearly, I still couldn't talk to anyone about it. I knew you would have questions, and I didn't want to give you the answers. Then, the longer I waited, the easier it was to convince myself that you were better off without me. My mind was so screwed up. I wanted to be completely separated from my past." He swallowed hard and continued, "I'm so damn sorry."

She was, too, for more reasons than he knew.

"What made you change your mind and call me?"

"The army. The training I went through. I was reminded that a man is measured not by his parentage but by what's inside him. It no longer mattered that James Tanner hadn't been my biological father. The stories my mother told me about him made me realize that he was the kind of man I wanted to be. Ralph Henson was a sperm donor, nothing more." He shrugged and gave her a sad, twisted smile. "I guess I finally got my head out of my ass and realized how stupid I'd been."

Leaning forward, his eyes held hers. Savannah saw sorrow and sincerity but something more. Something she wasn't sure she was ready to explore.

"When you wouldn't talk to me, I didn't know what to think. At first, I figured you were angry and hurt, which you had every right to be. Then, when you kept rejecting my calls, not answering my emails, I wondered if you'd somehow heard about what happened."

Breath exploded from her in disbelief. "Surely you can't think the identity of your father mattered to me."

He shrugged. "I couldn't come up with another reason. I thought it was either that or maybe you'd heard what they did to me."

"How long did it take you to realize that none of that would have mattered?"

He smiled. "Only a few hours after I thought it." His mouth flatlined grimly. "I don't blame you for not taking my calls. You had every right to hate me."

"I didn't hate you. I—" But was that the truth? Perhaps a part of her had hated him. She now regretted not going to Fort Benning and demanding to see him. Her lack of assertiveness had cost her. Instead she had allowed herself to fade away again. And then she'd almost lost everything.

"You what?"

Savannah looked up, realizing he was waiting for her to finish her sentence. "I was just so very hurt."

Regret darkened his expression even more. "I know. I'm so sorry."

She waved away his apology. Not because it didn't mean anything but because he had apologized enough. She now knew the truth, and though so much of their lives might have been different if either of them had reacted another way, the real villains of this tragedy continued on as if nothing had happened.

"Why did you never press charges against Henson?"

"I had no proof it was him. Never saw any of them clearly. It was his word against mine and we both know my word meant nothing in this town."

"Then why come back here to live? Why would you—" She stopped abruptly. "Did you come back to exact some kind of revenge against Henson?"

"No, not consciously. I actually did intend to spruce up the old house, sell it, and get the hell out of here as soon as I could. Somehow, I got a different perspective."

Horrified, she asked, "About Henson?"

"Hell no. That'll never change. But the town in general just felt different."

She smiled, understanding. "And torturing Henson with your presence?"

He gave her a half smile. "Icing on the cake."

"So that's why you suspect he's in on the vandalisms?"

"Yeah, in fact, just got that confirmed today."

"Really? How?"

"Lindsay Milan."

Realization came, followed quickly by relief. "So that's why. . . ." She nodded. "She's Clark's sister."

"Yeah, she overheard a conversation between Clark and Henson."

It was unkind of her but Savannah couldn't help but wonder if one of Lindsay's reasons for coming forward was because of Zach. If it had been Chief Mosby, would she have told him?

"What did she hear?"

"The dry cleaners is their next target. I plan to be there, too."

"Won't Henson and Dayton know who fingered them? Everyone saw you together at the social today."

Zach grimaced. "She hasn't been shy about her interest in me, so most everyone will just assume I succumbed to her."

She wanted to ask him if he had but wouldn't. Lindsay was only a year older than Savannah and very attractive. Most men would be thrilled with the attention she threw Zach.

As if he recognized her need for reassurance, he added, "She's leaving town."

Ignoring the happy skip of her heart at that news, she said, "Can I help you at the dry cleaners?"

"No, I've got it covered. Thanks."

Her eyes dropped to the now unappetizing food on

her plate. There didn't seem to be anyplace to go with the conversation. Learning the truth should have, at the very least, put her mind at ease. She had convinced herself that because she had allowed Zach to make love to her, he'd no longer wanted or respected her. She was the one who'd asked him to make love to her, the one to bring condoms. Looking back on it now, that seemed silly. But at eighteen, insecure and brokenhearted, believing that was the reason had made perfect sense.

Knowing the truth didn't give her the relief she had expected. Immeasurable sadness filled her—not unlike the dark despair she had felt years ago. She had originally planned to tell him everything. Now she wasn't sure of anything. What purpose would it accomplish? Hadn't they both suffered enough?

As if he realized they had nothing else to say to each other, Zach stood. "I'm sorry you went to so much trouble for dinner and I ruined it."

Savannah stood, too. "It'll make good leftovers for tomorrow."

"I guess I'd better get back to work."

"I'll walk you out."

Like two strangers, they went to the door in silence. The distance between them was more than either of them could possibly breach. What they'd had years before was gone. It had been a brief, intense attraction that perhaps might have died naturally if given enough time. But that hadn't been allowed to happen. And now only empty space remained. Stupid, but she felt as if someone had died. She pushed down the knowledge that someone had.

Her hand went to the doorknob to open it, then she caught her breath when Zach's hand covered hers. Her eyes shot to his, questioning. Longing for something she was too afraid to even voice, she whispered, "Zach?"

"I'm so damn sorry, Savannah. For everything."

Unable to stop herself, Savannah went into his arms. Zach held her hard against him, his breath shuddering from his big body. Savannah savored the beauty and comfort of his embrace as bitterness and anger washed away. Long moments passed as they finally let go of the past.

She felt Zach's arms loosen, and with great reluctance, she dropped her arms and tried to step back. Zach wasn't having it. Pulling her hard against him, he covered her mouth in a searing, soul-deep kiss Savannah felt to the tips of her toes.

A sob caught in her throat as she poured out her longing into the kiss. When he pulled his mouth from hers, he was gratifyingly breathless. "I'll call you tomorrow."

Speechless and more hopeful than she'd been in years, Savannah nodded and watched him leave. After his car disappeared from view, she closed the door and leaned against it. Her fears that the only connection they had was in the past were unfounded. What exactly they did have, she didn't know. Overanalyzing when it came to matters of the heart had gotten her into trouble before. She vowed to let things go at their own pace.

As she headed back into the kitchen to clear up the wasted dinner, two major issues pounded against her vow of not worrying. In a few weeks, she would be returning to Nashville; Zach's job was here. Could she just walk away? Would it matter to Zach? Did their current attraction mean anything or was it just residual feelings from long ago?

The other issue was even more difficult to consider. However, no matter how difficult it was, she knew she had to come clean, too. She tried to push away the worry that it might destroy the fragile bond they were building. Whatever the outcome, Zach deserved the truth.

CHAPTER EIGHTEEN

"Hello."

Savannah's groggy, sleep-filled voice made him smile. Zach knew he'd woken her up. After all, it was only a little after five in the morning. The sun was just coming up and most sane people were still asleep. He'd return to his sanity tomorrow. Today he felt like a thousand-pound weight had been lifted from his shoulders. He'd finally shared the truth with Savannah and she hadn't slapped his face or told him to go to hell. He'd deserved both reactions. Having her forgiveness was much more than he could have dreamed of, but dammit, he wanted more. He wanted everything.

But all of that could wait until tomorrow. Today he wanted to play. And the only person he wanted to play with yawned into his ear and said, "Huh?"

"I said, do you want to go blackberry picking with me?"

"At night?"

Swallowing a chuckle, he explained, "It's almost dawn. The blackberries are ripe and the best time to pick them is in the morning before it gets too hot. Let's pick blackberries, have a picnic, make pies, and—"

"Whoa, wait a minute."

He tensed. Had he read her wrong last night? Holding his breath, he said, "What's wrong?"

"Separate buckets?"

Relieved, he chuckled. When they were dating, they had gone blackberry picking once but had only had one bucket. For every berry she had picked, he'd eaten three. They'd walked out of the woods with barely enough fruit for a tart, much less a pie. "Yes, separate buckets."

"I'll be ready in twenty minutes."

Zach grabbed his keys. "I'll bring coffee."

Exactly fifteen minutes later, Zach arrived on Savannah's doorstep. The instant she opened the door, he handed her a cup of steaming coffee, doused liberally with cream, just the way she liked it.

Her smile brighter than the sunshine coming up behind him, she accepted the cup and took an appreciative sip. "Hmm, perfect."

Zach ground his teeth and ignored his body's response. Only Savannah could make those kinds of noises sound erotic. He had no plans to do more than hold her hand and maybe steal a kiss or two. And as disappointed as his body was going to be, he refused to try to take their relationship any further yet. They had ten years to catch up on.

He examined her attire—jeans and a long-sleeved shirt. She was definitely dressed for the occasion. Amazing how sexy a woman could look in cotton. Her golden-blond hair was neatly fixed in a long braid, making her look more like the young woman he'd fallen for years ago than a sophisticated law professional. "You ready?"

"Yes. You have the buckets?"

He nodded. "And I picked up a dozen doughnuts on the way. They're in the car."

Her grin cheeky, she asked, "How many are left?"

She knew him too well. Laughing, he pulled her to the car. "Eight."

* * *

Lying back on a blanket that covered a soft bed of grass, Savannah dozed happily in the shade. In the distance, a whip-poor-will competed with a bobwhite for the loneliest-sounding song. A bumblebee buzzed close by, and if she held her breath and listened closely, she could hear the train that ran once a day through downtown Midnight. Savannah sighed her contentment. Supposedly Zach was somewhere fashioning what he called a sunbonnet for her. She couldn't wait to see his creation.

What a spectacularly wonderful day this had been. When he'd woken her at what her sister Bri would refer to as "the butt crack of dawn," she had been stunned. The last thing she expected to be doing today was picking blackberries and giggling like a teenager. But this was exactly what they'd both needed. Yesterday's sorrow and tomorrow's worry had been completely obliterated. Today was to be enjoyed and savored.

The blackberries, at least what was left of them, were nestled beneath the shadiest part of the tree. Though her stomach was filled with berries now, she looked forward to making a cobbler out of what remained.

"Okay, it's not as fashionable as I'd planned, but it should work."

She sat up and then swallowed her laughter. Zach had taken off his white T-shirt, cut it up to the neck, and then weaved sticks into it. Lopsided and quite ugly, the bonnet looked more like a sheik's headdress.

"Did you make that for me or for you?"

He grinned as he placed it on her head. "It's my new line of genderless attire."

Feeling silly and goofy, she stood and posed in several different positions. Before she realized what he was doing, Zach had pulled his cellphone from his pocket and was clicking pictures.

"You'd better not put these on the Internet. I'll never live it down in Nashville."

He took one more shot and then pocketed the phone. "These are for my private collection."

Though she knew she looked ridiculous with the T-shirt hat still on her head, she had to admit she did feel cooler. Scooting over, she made a place for Zach to sit on the blanket. As he lay beside her, it was all she could do not to lean over and kiss his smiling mouth. He had done nothing more intimate than hold her hand since he'd picked her up that morning. Though she longed for his kiss, she was loath to change the light-hearted atmosphere.

Lying beside him, she gazed up through the tree branches at the intensely azure-blue sky and blazing sun. A perfect summer day. And a great chance to get to know him again. "Did you like being in the army?"

"Don't think I can say I liked it, but I didn't hate it, either. Everything—the training, the friends I made, the places I went—all helped build me into the kind of person I wanted to be. I left Midnight a kid; the army made me a man."

"You saw a lot of combat, didn't you?"

"Yeah. More than I wanted. But there were days when we weren't being shot at or hunting down terrorists. Those weren't too bad."

"Lamont said you were awarded a Purple Heart." She rose up on an elbow to look at him. "You were injured?"

"Got some shrapnel in my right side and leg. I was lucky. So many weren't. So many never came home."

Breaking her pledge not to touch him, Savannah ran her hand down his arm in a comforting caress. "I'm glad you made it home."

Smiling, he rolled over and propped himself up on his elbow to face her. "Tell me about being an assistant district attorney. You want to be the DA someday?"

Two weeks ago her answer would have been a definitive "Of course." But right here, right now, she hesitated giving a definite answer to anything about the future.

"Maybe . . . I don't know. I like the challenge of what I do, and when we win, it's a great feeling."

"But?"

She shook her head. How could she articulate what she wasn't sure of herself? She only knew that, for whatever reason, she hadn't missed work the way she had thought she would. "That seems like a million miles away from the here and now. Let's talk about something else."

"Like what?"

"What's your plan to catch Henson and Dayton in the act?"

He shrugged. "I'll just be waiting for them. As soon as they enter, I'll walk in."

"Without backup?"

"Their weapons are spray paint and misspelled swearwords. I think I'll survive it."

Savannah sat up and glared at him. "You don't know that, Zach. Just because they only write bad graffiti doesn't mean they don't come armed."

"You're right. Point taken. But I'll be fine."

She wanted to argue more but could see she would get nowhere. When he changed the subject to something less controversial, she went along with it, but that didn't stop her from being concerned. Ralph Henson had almost beat Zach to death once before. If given the chance, would he try again or do something worse?

Damned if she would let that happen.

CHAPTER NINETEEN

The night was dark and moonless. The only light came from the lamppost at the end of the street. Zach stood beneath one of the giant moss-covered elm trees that lined many of the streets of downtown Midnight. He was across the road and three doors down from the dry cleaners. Wearing his old camo pants, a black T-shirt, and a black ball cap, he blended into the night. In the army, he'd earned the reputation of being able to disappear and reappear at will. If Henson hadn't been so old and Dayton so out of shape, he would've liked to go full army on them. He wouldn't. Scaring the shit out of them was one thing; giving them a heart attack wasn't exactly his plan.

According to Lindsay, her brother Clark and Ralph Henson would be hitting the building tonight. This morning, while the two Dayton men had been out of the house, Zach had loaded Lindsay's little Chevy with all of her belongings and watched her drive away.

When she had told him about overhearing the conversation between Clark and Henson, she had insinuated she wanted something other than money in exchange for the information. Though Zach wanted the information, he'd definitely not been interested in her payment method. Instead he'd taken the opportunity to encourage her to leave town and start out fresh somewhere else.

There was something about Lindsay that reminded him of his mother—a desperate neediness. But she had something his mother had never possessed—someone who believed she could do better. The stern talk he had given her might not have been what she had wanted, but once she realized he was serious, she had backed off and listened.

Now Lindsay was headed to Charleston, South Carolina, with two thousand dollars in her purse and an interview with one of his old army buddies who'd recently opened a gym. Learning that Lindsay had an accounting background gave him hope that she could get a job and start a new life. At the very least, maybe she could get away from the influence and abuse of her father and brother and learn to depend on herself.

He hadn't seen Savannah today. Though he'd been tempted to call her, he was allowing her some space. Yesterday had been about as perfect as he could have hoped for, but he didn't want to push her. When they'd been together before, with him going into the army and her going away to school, everything had been rushed, felt desperate. And though their time was once again limited, maturity had given him patience.

Mocking laughter echoed in his mind. Patience . . . hell. Last night he'd taken her home and left her at the door with a quick kiss on her cheek. And all he'd been able to think of since then was the regret he felt for not kissing that luscious mouth deeply, thoroughly. He knew if he got within ten feet of her today, patience would be nothing but a word. A desire and need that went well beyond his knowledge was building up inside him. Since that kiss in her kitchen the other night, he had been on a slow simmer. One spark of encouragement from her and he'd be on full burn.

Here he stood, only a few miles away from what he wanted most in the world but unable to claim it. Instead he was waiting for two idiots to show up and spray-paint a building just so they could feel powerful. If it hadn't been so damn aggravating, he'd say to hell with it and let them screw up their properties as much as they wanted. Problem was, if he didn't stop them, they'd either get him fired or might even try something more drastic. He'd put up with enough shit from Ralph Henson. Damned if the man would get the best of him again.

Savannah didn't approve of his plan. She'd made that clear yesterday. While he appreciated her concern, he wasn't worried. Yeah, they were breaking the law, but this was a personal attack against him. And he was going to handle it on his own, in his own way.

Zach wasn't the green kid he'd been before. He had been an Army Ranger, had killed more people than he liked to remember, and had saved lives. No, he wasn't Superman, but neither was he naïve. Savannah feared it was a setup; Zach knew better. It was two redneck jerks who thought they were too damn smart to get caught. Nothing more, nothing less.

A small light flickered across the street. Eyes narrowed, Zach peered closer. Yeah, someone was standing on the outside of the building. The light wavered shakily and then clicked off and on a couple of times. Either someone was having battery problems or the dumbasses were too stupid to know how to use a flashlight. He was going with the second theory.

Staying low, Zach crossed the street at a run. He stopped and hunkered down behind a large mailbox, waiting. No law said Henson couldn't enter his own building. Zach would have to catch the man in the act of spray-painting and then play it out.

He waited patiently, as he'd been trained. Soon they'd reveal themselves. Adrenaline pounded and he was distantly amused to realize that this was probably the most excitement he'd had on the job. Said a lot for sleepy little Southern towns.

"I'm getting damn tired of doing this stuff, Henson. It ain't done no good."

Zach recognized Clark Dayton's voice. When he wasn't trying to impress anyone, the guy really did sound like a country hick.

The sound of breaking glass was followed by Henson's gruff reply. "If this one doesn't get his ass fired, we'll do something that'll definitely catch everyone's attention. I promise. By this time next month, Tanner will be out of here. With your experience, the mayor and city council will have no choice but to appoint you as police chief."

So that was Dayton's incentive. Apparently he didn't realize that these crimes reflected on the entire police department, not just Zach. The mayor hadn't yet come out and expressed his disappointment in the department's lack of progress on the vandalism crimes, but he'd asked Zach about them frequently. Dayton might have more trouble than he anticipated getting Lamont and the city council on his side.

"Let's get this over with," Dayton answered. "I gotta be at work at seven in the morning."

Zach swallowed a laugh. Yeah, Clark would definitely arrive early at the police station, only not as an employee.

The men entered the building and closed the door behind them. Zach crept closer. While Henson held the flashlight, Dayton shook the can of spray paint and began to spray. Zach quietly walked in the door behind them. They were so intent on their tasks, neither of the men were aware of Zach's presence until he flipped on the light switch beside the door and said, "Don't worry about coming into work, Dayton. You're fired."

The men whirled. Zach couldn't stop the grin that

spread over his face. Their expressions were similar to two eight-year-old boys who'd been caught stealing candy. Both men sputtered, searching for an excuse. Henson recovered first. "I got every right to be here. I own this dry cleaners."

Though Zach knew that was true, he wasn't about to let the man off that easy. "I'm going to need to see proof of that."

"Courthouse has documents."

"Courthouse is closed right now. Looks like I'll just have to lock you two up until you can prove ownership."

"Now see here. I ain't going to jail for entering my own store."

"If you're the owner, why'd you break the window?"

"I . . ." Henson glanced over at Clark for help. Dayton was having his own issues. Sweat beaded on his brow and rolled down into the beard he was so fond of. Finally Henson came up with what he apparently thought was a good excuse. "I left my keys at home, so I had to break the window to reach through and unlock the door."

"And what's your reason for showing up here at one-thirty in the morning with a flashlight and a can of spray paint?"

"I'm redecorating."

This time Zach did laugh. "I always heard you were a cheap son of a bitch, but redecorating with a can of spray paint seems a little extreme." Zach glanced over at Dayton. "Clark, you got anything you'd like to add?"

"I . . ." He swallowed and said, "You're not fit to be police chief. It should be my job."

"The mayor and city council saw differently, since they appointed me chief and not you." Zach held up his handcuffs. "Now, let's get this over with nice and easy."

"Wait!" Henson snarled. "If you arrest me, you'll ruin my reputation."

"Should've thought of that before you decided to break the law."

Henson held out his hand as if to ward him off. "I'll tell . . . I'll tell everyone that secret."

Zach raised his brow in challenge. "What secret is that? That you and some of your redneck buddies beat the shit out of me ten years ago? Or the other one that you told only me?"

The older man's lips pursed so tight, they resembled a prune. He hadn't expected Zach to call his bluff.

Zach nodded. "Yeah. You go ahead and tell that one, Henson. I'm not the one who couldn't keep my pants zipped."

Apparently deciding that a night in jail was better than the entire town hearing that he was Zach's biological father, Henson's mouth remained tightly closed, his expression grim.

"Now turn around." The men turned around; Zach had them cuffed in seconds and then backed away. Taking the radio from his pocket, he called his on-duty deputy, Arthur Norton. "Artie, I'm over at Green's dry cleaners. Got a couple of overnight guests I need you to come by and pick up."

"I'm a couple of minutes away."

Zach switched off the radio and eyed the sad-looking idiots before him. "You have the right to remain silent . . ."

As he recited their Miranda rights, he found it interesting that while Henson's shoulders seemed to stiffen with each word, Dayton's became more slumped and dejected. They would be released later today with no charges. Zach wasn't looking to put either of them away. He had accomplished what he wanted. They'd been found out. Continuing their misadventures would be pointless. Just in case they didn't realize this, Zach issued a warning after he finished reciting their rights. "Listen and listen good. Tonight you need to give careful thought on where you think this should go. I'm giving you this one chance. Fuck with me again and I'll find every way possible to make sure you spend quality time behind bars and not just one measly night. Understand?"

Neither man answered but that was fine with him. They'd had their warning. And he was telling the truth.

Deputy Norton walked in the door. "I'm here, Chief. What's going on?"

"Henson and Dayton need a ride to jail. Lock them in separate cells. It'll give them privacy for some quality thinking time."

As the men walked toward the door, Zach followed behind Henson and spoke softly so only he could hear. "I'm sure glad I inherited my mother's smarts and not my father's, because it's pretty damn obvious he's a moron."

Henson's back only got stiffer and then he walked out the door. Zach gave a nod of satisfaction. Damned if he didn't feel quite pleased with the outcome. The vandalism would stop, Henson would back off, and Dayton was no longer his deputy. All in all, a good night's work.

Zach spent the next few minutes securing the building and covering the smashed window with some cardboard he found in the back. Locking the door behind him, he turned and then stopped suddenly when a slight scratching noise caught his ear. Seconds later he heard a soft, distinctly feminine sigh. What the hell?

Though he could deny it till doomsday, Zach already knew what he'd find when he rounded the building. Savannah stood against the wall, close to the back door. She was facing away from him, so he could walk up and grab her without any trouble. Before he took a step, he dropped his eyes to her hand. Hell, she had a gun in her hand. Never in his life had he wanted to spank a woman. This stunt might just change his mind.

A good scare would work just as well, and he went for a big one. With silent strides, he reached her in seconds. Wrapping both arms around her, he pulled her off her feet. She shrieked like a banshee and tried to kick backward.

"Quiet down, you little spitfire."

She continued to struggle, either not realizing or not caring that it was Zach who held her. He shook her to get her attention. "Dammit, Savannah, what the hell do you think you're doing?"

She froze. "Zach?" she whispered.

"Hell yeah. Who'd you think it was?"

"You scared the crap out of me."

"Good. I meant to. What the hell are you doing here?"

"I'm watching your ass."

"You're watching my ass? You didn't even know where my ass was until I walked up behind you."

Savannah gritted her teeth, more than aware that he was right. Okay, so it'd been a lame-brained thing to do. Ever since he'd told her he was coming out here alone, she couldn't stop thinking about it. He might trust Lindsay to have told him the truth; Savannah hadn't been that gullible. She didn't want Zach to be faced with what he'd gone through ten years ago. No way in hell was she going to allow him to be hurt again. The fact that he had handled the situation within minutes with barely a harsh word spoken was a bit humbling. Zach would no doubt get a kick out of teasing her.

"You handled that quite well."

"Thanks. It's my job."

She couldn't blame him for his cockiness. He was

probably feeling downright smug. "Since the excitement is over, I guess I'll go home."

"Not without me," he growled into her ear.

"What?" For the first time, she realized that she was still plastered against Zach's body and he was very aroused. Savannah shivered. He was holding her so tightly, she could feel every hard inch of him against her. Of all the times to get turned on, this wasn't one of them. Her body didn't seem to care that it wasn't appropriate, and apparently neither did Zach's. It was all she could do not to rub herself against him.

Breathing out a shaking gasp, she said, "What do you want?"

"You."

Just one word but she heard the longing. Her nipples peaked and a throbbing began between her legs. Yes, this was what she wanted, too. "Aren't you on duty?"

"No," he said bluntly. "Where's your car?"

"A block away."

"Mine's closer."

"Okay, let's go."

"In a minute. I need something first."

Before she could ask what, he whirled her around. Moving with lightning speed, he took the gun from her now limp hand and shoved it into the small of his back beneath his waistband. Then, pulling her forward, he slammed his mouth against hers. Heat flooded through her, drenching her entire being. Long-dormant thoughts and feelings she'd once believed dead sprouted and unfurled as need, want, desire, and a million other emotions overwhelmed her senses. Wrapping herself around Zach's big body, Savannah gave in to the intensity.

Apparently sensing her need, Zach pressed her against the wall of the building and built the fire. His hands roamed, one delving beneath her blouse, the other smoothing itself up her thigh, underneath her short skirt.

His fingers hooked into her panties and tugged. She heard a slight ripping sound, knew and didn't care that the delicate fabric was being shredded. When those long, hard fingers found her crease, they plunged deep into her wet heat. Savannah gasped out a "Yes" and tried to hold his fingers inside her by squeezing her thighs closed and riding him.

Zach's husky laughter thrummed through her senses, his gruff words of "Let go, Savannah" bringing her to climax in a shattering, explosive moment of ecstasy. As she spiraled down, he gave her soft words of praise and adoration, making her feel as though she'd given him a gift, instead of the other way around.

"You okay?" he rasped into her ear.

"Yes . . . for now." Feeling bold and powerful, she added, "But I want more . . . much more."

"Me too."

Pulling away from her completely, he said, "Come on."

Savannah took the hand he held out to her and allowed him to lead her to his car. The entire city of Midnight could be watching them right now and she wouldn't care. Maybe in a year, or a hundred, she'd be shocked and embarrassed that Zach Tanner had just given her the most delicious orgasm of her life against the wall of Green's Dry Cleaning. Right now that didn't matter. Her only concern was going home, letting him give her many more, and allowing her to do the same for him.

They were in his car and headed to her house before she realized it. Zach's urgency was patently obvious. Any other time she might have been amused that someone as controlled and stoic as this man was revealing that his control was almost gone. Nothing felt amusing, or even lighthearted. She glanced over at him; the tic in his jaw confirmed her thoughts. This was a man on edge . . . she wanted to be the one to send him over.

They made it to the house in record time. If she'd been concentrating on anything other than the heavy atmosphere of desire in the car, she would have noticed that they had broken several speed limits and traffic laws to get there in the fastest time possible.

Zach pulled into the drive and then to the back of the house. She appreciated his sensitivity in hiding his car. Visiting for a few hours was one thing. It caused talk but nothing else. Having his car seen overnight would be something else. Wedding rumors would be running rampant, along with other things she didn't even want to consider. This time with Zach was something she wanted to share with no one.

Savannah didn't wait for him to open the car door but pushed it open and came to meet him as he rounded the car. She held her hand out to him, and they practically ran to the back door. She opened the door, slammed it shut, and his mouth was back on hers.

Zach had never been this turned on or felt such urgency in his life. Savannah was right there with him. Within seconds they were ripping the clothes off each other. The mudroom wasn't exactly the most romantic location, but damned if he'd stop. When his hands met silk-smooth skin and he realized she was completely naked, Zach knew he could wait no longer. "I've got condoms in my pants." Which were unfortunately on the floor and he'd have to let her go to get to them. Something he didn't want to do.

"No. No condoms. I'm on the pill. We're fine." The words were said between gasps and moans.

"You're sure?"

Her hands closed around him, held him tight, and then rubbed his length up and down. He heard an "Uh-huh" and then he couldn't think any longer. Savannah was on her knees. Hot, moist breath was a warning and then her mouth closed around him. Zach held her face in his hands and watched as she took him deep and then withdrew, over and over. They had never done this before. She had kissed and caressed him there but nothing like this. How in the hell was he going to stop? The only thing he wanted to do was continue surging and retreating until nothing mattered except filling her mouth and letting go. Teeth gritted, he reminded himself that he'd been waiting for this moment forever, and pulled out.

The passion and want gleaming in her eyes almost made him reconsider. "What's wrong? Didn't you like that?"

"Oh hell yeah, I liked it . . . too much." He grasped her under her arms, pulling her to her feet. Kissing her softly, thoroughly, he tasted himself and almost came. "I want to be inside you when I come. We'll save the playing for later."

She nodded, the glassy look in her eyes telling him she was already concentrating on something else, namely his fingers that were plucking at her taut nipples. Zach leaned down and captured a peak with his mouth and sucked hard. A soft gasping squeal was his reward, then she held his head as he concentrated on each breast, giving each one equal treatment. When he lifted his head, he was gratified to see both nipples wet and gleaming, distended even more. Tempted to go back for another taste, he stopped when she said, "I want you inside me. Now."

He wanted that, too, but there was something he had to do first. Whirling her around, he pressed her against the wall and went to his knees.

"Hey, no fair," she said breathlessly.

"You said you wanted me inside you." He parted her legs and speared her with his tongue, thrusting deep.

Withdrawing, he growled, "This is me." He licked and thrust again. "Inside you."

Her hands went to his hair; apparently she'd decided not to argue. As he plunged, retreated, licked, and then thrust once more, the soft gasps and moans coming from above were the most beautiful sounds imaginable. Her fingers weaved through his hair as she undulated, riding his tongue, her moans growing louder. Zach thrust harder, deeper . . . Savannah's entire body tightened and then she came, throbbing sweetly against his mouth.

Unable to wait any longer, Zach went to his feet and grabbed her butt. Picking her up, he pressed her against the wall and then plunged deep, impaling her to the hilt.

"Wrap your legs around me," he muttered.

When she complied, he held her ass in his hands and began a quick rhythm of plunge and retreat that continued on and on. Every second he held on, he took as a gift. Savannah's eyes glittered up at him, the intensity of her expression one he'd remember even in his old age. And then she came . . . Zach knew he'd never seen anyone more beautiful or perfect. The next second, he couldn't think at all. Climax almost blowing his head off, he let out a growl of fulfillment that could probably be heard all over the house.

Still feeling the urgency, he gave them no time to recover. "Let's find a bed." Holding her trembling body tight against him, he said, "Think we can stay attached?"

She tightened her legs around him and whispered, "Let's try. Just don't let go."

"Never." With each step, he grew harder. They made it to the stairway but there was no hope of going up the stairs as aroused as he was. Turning so he could sit down, he plopped down to the first step, kept her legs tight around his waist, and growled, "Ride."

Looking both intrigued and excited, Savannah balanced on her knees and began a slow, steady ride. They kept their eyes focused and fixed on each other, and each plunge inside her caused ripples through both of them. Finally, as her moves became quicker and less co-ordinated and her breath started coming in rasps, Zach grabbed her hips and pushed her down until he was buried as deep as he could go. She came on a wail of ecstasy, and seconds later, Zach followed.

CHAPTER TWENTY

Savannah rolled over and looked down at the man sleeping beside her. They'd behaved like wild, untamed animals and every muscle in her body felt as fluid and liquid as if she'd been given an all-over body massage, inside and out. She smiled as she reflected that the description was quite apt.

Their one and only time years before hadn't prepared her for what had happened tonight. That long-ago time had been sweet, delicious, but wonderfully awkward. Tonight had been all heat, no awkwardness, and full of spectacular pleasure beyond her knowledge.

Her eyes roamed over Zach's broad shoulders and slightly furred chest. That was another major difference. His body looked so different from that of the man she'd known ten years ago. Though he had been muscular and well built before, now his arms and chest were massive. The tattoo of an eagle on his upper right arm was a new addition, as was the jagged scar on his side. Knowing the pain he must have felt brought tears to her eyes. This man, so different but somehow the same, continued to awe and fascinate her.

Lying back against the pillow again, she stretched luxuriously and was surprised to hear the rumble of her stomach. She shot a glance at the clock. Four in the morning seemed like an odd time to get up and eat, but she was suddenly ravenous. The thought of making breakfast and bringing it to Zach in bed had her feet on the floor before she could finish the thought.

"Where're you going?" The sleep-slurred growl sent tremors of arousal throughout her bloodstream.

"Thought I'd make breakfast."

"Time is it?"

She winced. "Four o'clock."

Grabbing her by the waist, he rolled over, taking her with him until she was under him. "And cooking breakfast is the only thing you could think to do this early?"

Her hand rubbed his scruffy face, loving the prickle of bristles against her fingertips. "You have another suggestion?"

He raised her leg, bent it slightly, and paused at her entrance. "Too sore?"

Yes, she was, but that didn't stop her from grabbing his butt and pushing him deep. As he surged in, she gasped at the fullness.

"Okay?"

"Oh yeah." Her body arched, accepting him, wanting him even deeper, to be as close to him as possible. How many nights had she dreamed of this? Eventually she had stopped fantasizing, stopped dreaming. And in many ways, stopped living.

Unable and unwilling to share those thoughts, Savannah showed him with her body just how okay she was. Arms and legs wrapped around him securely, she gave herself over to the delicious feelings only this man could create inside her. Soon she'd have to think about consequences and the future. But not now. Right now all she wanted was to feel and to appreciate. When climax came upon her, she closed her eyes and let the earth and its problems fall away. In the arms of her one and only lover, everything was perfection.

*   *   *

Zach rolled away from the panting, glistening woman. Never in a thousand years would he have thought she would be in his arms like this again. He knew he didn't deserve her easy forgiveness. There had been so few questions about his past, what he had done and where he had been. She had told him very little about herself, either. What was going on in that beautiful head of hers? A vague sense of uneasiness swept through him. Why *had* she gone so easily into his arms? What did this mean? Was she ready for something more? Should he talk about that? Ask her what she wanted?

He huffed out a frustrated breath. Hell, Savannah was the one who was supposed to overanalyze and over-think. Not that he was impulsive, but he usually went with his gut and faced the consequences when necessary. But now, with her warm breath still caressing him, the feel of her satin-soft body still moist and wet from his release, he wanted to know everything.

"Tell me about your life in Nashville."

"What?"

"We've not really talked about those kinds of things. Where do you live, an apartment or a house? You have any pets? What's your favorite restaurant?"

"Apartment. No pets. Don't have a favorite restaurant. I've already told you I like my job. There's not much more to say."

Vague uneasiness became full-fledged concern. She wasn't even being evasive. She was basically telling him her life in Nashville wasn't any of his business. "Savannah, where do you see this going?"

She sat up and grabbed the sheet to cover herself. Zach felt the hit to his chest. She was covering herself, the move an obvious one of self-protection. Maybe the forgiveness he thought she had given him wasn't real.

Maybe for her, last night's hot sex had been nothing more than that. A need had been quenched. But as for him, he knew he wanted more . . . a hell of a lot more.

"I'll make breakfast." She went to her feet, still holding the sheet to her body.

"Answer my question first," he said quietly.

She turned, and for the first time, he felt as though he didn't know her. Her face was still beautiful and so very familiar, but there was a blankness he wasn't used to seeing.

"I don't think we really need to talk about the future right now. This is all too new and it's too soon."

Zach rolled over and set his feet on the floor, his back to her. She was right. This was all too new and he didn't want to spoil what had been to him the most satisfying night of his life. Problem was, he wanted it to have meant just as much to her and it was obvious that it hadn't.

"I can't stay for breakfast."

She was silent. He turned to see her reaction and wasn't surprised that she had turned her back and was getting dressed. Why was he pushing her? Why couldn't he just let this play out and enjoy what they had right now? He had more than he ever thought he would have with her again. Why wasn't that enough? Questioning himself would do no good. With anyone else, he might have been able to take it one day at a time and just enjoy the fun. But nothing had ever been that simple with Savannah.

He looked around for his clothes and remembered they were still downstairs in the mudroom. He headed toward the door.

Savannah stopped him with a hand on his arm. "Let me at least make you some coffee."

"I'll get some at home."

"Zach, don't be angry."

"I'll have your car brought back. You got an extra set of keys?"

"Yes," she said softly. "But—"

He walked out the door. He told himself he didn't want her to call him back, but that was a lie. He didn't allow any kind of vulnerability in his life anymore, but with Savannah, he was open and exposed. And though he knew it was stupid to have expectations of more after what he had done to her, he couldn't help but be hurt at her rejection. They'd wasted so many years, and though it was stupid of him to expect to be able to just pick up where they'd left off, it was obvious they still had a strong attraction to each other. Why couldn't they build on it?

Zach nodded. Hell yeah, they could build on what they had. He was known for his patience. He'd just be persistent, wait her out. Seduce her. Show her how much she still meant to him. Show her that this time, it could last forever.

Zach grabbed his clothes and threw them on. Then, stooping down, he picked up Savannah's skirt and withdrew her car keys from the front pocket. By the time he got to his car, he had a plan. Savannah was wary, understandably. Instead of pressuring for more right now, he would sit back and woo her like she deserved. He could do things now that he couldn't do back then. Savannah might not know it but she had issued him a challenge and he had accepted it. She was about to get some major wooing from the man who'd lost his heart to her ten years ago and had never reclaimed it.

Savannah swallowed her now cold coffee, grimacing as the liquid hit her queasy stomach. She'd been sitting at the kitchen table since Zach left, unable to do anything but stare into space.

She had hurt him and she hated that. Now she wasn't sure how to proceed. Her heart just would not allow her to take her feelings any further than what had happened between them last night. The sex had been wonderful—the most satisfying night of her life. But sex was all she had to offer. Opening herself up to vulnerability like before wasn't something she could allow. Explaining her reasons without ripping open a vein and bleeding her heartache all over again was going to be difficult. But he wasn't going to just let this go . . . she'd seen the evidence in his eyes. And he deserved the truth; it was just a matter of how long it would take her to work up her courage to tell him.

Sighing her sadness, she finally stood and poured herself another cup of coffee. She was severely behind. Her grandfather's clothes were packed and ready to be picked up, but his library was taking longer than she'd anticipated. Her grandfather's interests had been extensive and the library director at the Midnight Public Library had been thrilled when Savannah had called and offered to donate his collection.

Problem was, she had no energy for or interest in packing anything right now.

Opening the back door, she stepped out onto the large bricked patio and inhaled the thick, warm air. A humid tropical paradise surrounded her. Her mother had designed and planted most of the flower garden. After her death, her grandfather had taken over, eventually becoming something of a gentleman gardener. Every conceivable exotic and tropical flower and plant surrounded the patio. The memories of the barbeques and impromptu picnics they'd shared here brought a smile to her face and an ease to her soul. She realized she hadn't taken any time to explore and enjoy her favorite places around the house and estate. Today she would do just that. Yes, being back home evoked some hideous memories, but the vast majority of them were wonderful.

Decision made, Savannah took the path to the guesthouse. After her grandfather had moved from the guesthouse back into the mansion, she and her sisters had taken over the small house as their meeting place. Whenever they had wanted complete privacy to talk "girl" stuff, the guesthouse had been their oasis. A place for privacy and a sanctuary.

She opened the front door and was immediately reminded of all the sister meetings they'd had here. Secrets had been shared, tears shed, and plans made.

The décor hadn't changed much since her grandfather had lived here. A new sofa here, a fresh coat of paint there. Built years after the Wilde house, the guesthouse looked from the outside like an exact replica of the mansion, just on a much smaller scale. But the inside had a completely different floor plan. A small living room and kitchen and two large bedrooms made up the first floor, an open loft took up the entire second floor, and the third floor held a smaller bedroom and an attic. The guesthouse was cozy and comfortable—a perfect hideaway.

Savannah took a few minutes to walk around the interior, picking up a framed photo of her and her sisters at the beach when they'd been barely old enough to walk. Some of the things here were castoffs from the mansion that one Wilde or the other no longer needed but couldn't bear to part with.

She wandered into a bedroom and stopped. Dozens of boxes she'd never seen before were stacked against one wall. She strode over to them, flipped the top off one of the boxes, and gasped. It was filled with letters. Withdrawing a stack, she dropped down onto the bed and read:

My dearest Camille, today I went to the library and checked out five of your favorite books.

She shuffled to another letter. The first line read:

Cammie, I had dinner with the Neelys tonight. Marvin still drinks too much.

Letters from her grandfather to her grandmother. Were all the boxes filled with them? Standing, she opened another box and found the same thing.

Touched beyond measure, Savannah sat on the bed again and flipped through more of the same. Every detail of her grandfather's life was written to the wife he lost years ago. From the looks of it, he wrote her every day.

How he must have missed her.

Getting to her feet, she suddenly noticed that dates and years were written on the sides of some of the boxes. She stacked and restacked, putting what she could in correct date order, and then began to read in earnest.

Two hours later, the sun was glaring full force through the blinds and she had only made it through half a box. So many letters . . . so many memories. They detailed her grandparents' romance, from the day they met through their courtship and too-short marriage. She didn't know what moved her most . . . that he had loved her from the moment he met her and chronicled that love with letters, or that even after her death, he had continued writing to her. The boxes to her left were dated long after her grandmother's death. One box was dated the year of his death.

She'd had no idea about the letters. She knew he had worked in his office each day for years. Somehow she had assumed it was related to family business. Now she knew many of those hours were spent in long conversations with her grandmother via these letters.

Opening up another box, Savannah picked up a letter that was apparently the first one written—the night a young Daniel Wilde had met his future bride, Camille Rose Harris.

My dear Camille, we met tonight at a party given by my good friend Carver Nelson. You were wearing a pink dress with white lace and I couldn't help but think that your name fit you to perfection. Your skin was like the cream color of a white rose, and the way you styled your golden hair reminded me of a beautiful camellia flower. The moment you smiled at me, my heart almost burst. When you accepted a dance, it was the happiest moment of my life.

Her grandfather had often shared stories of their courtship. He'd said that it was love at first sight. His letter bore that out. How would it feel to be so loved and adored that even after death, the love was as strong as ever?

She placed the lid on the box and opened another one. Many of the letters were short, some just one or two sentences. She pulled out a short one, and tears flooded her eyes as she realized it was written the day of her grandmother's funeral: *I said goodbye for the last time today. I looked upon your beautiful face, kissed your sweet lips. You're not there anymore, I know that. But you're still with me, my love, I know you are. We buried you in the cemetery beside your parents. I know you're in heaven with them now. I'm glad you're together but I'm so very lonely, my darling.*

Wiping the tears from her face, she opened another letter. This one was more upbeat, filled with news of the town and people they had known. Settling herself into an old rocker beside the window, she drew a box close to her and immersed herself once again in her grandfather's thoughts from so many years ago. She unfolded another letter and, as she checked the date, felt a chill sweep up her body. It was dated the day after her parents' deaths.

My dearest Camille, something dreadful has happened. Our son is gone and so is our dear, sweet Maggie. They say it was a murder-suicide. That Beckett killed Maggie in a fit of rage and then, out of guilt, took his own life. How is that possible? How could our beautiful son have committed such an atrocious act? Yes, he had issues with his temper when he was younger. And there was that sadness that often seemed to sweep over him, but that hadn't happened in years. Not since he met Maggie.

I was gone, out of town, visiting Austin and his family in Mobile. I was told there was a terrible argument at the country club. Opal, our cleaning lady, found Maggie's body and then the police chief found Beckett hanging from the old oak out back. My heart is bleeding . . . how could this have happened? And what about their sweet, precious children? What am I to do? I wish you were here with me. You would be my solace in this madness.

Swallowing the lump in her throat, Savannah refolded the letter. Part of her wanted to stop reading now; reliving those days was still too painful. But her grandfather had rarely talked about that time, understandably. Seeing his thoughts and feelings gave her not only a different perspective but also an odd sense of closure.

She opened up another letter, this one dated four days after her parents' funeral.

Cammie, I have come to the conclusion that it is all a lie. There is something devious and wrong in this town. I don't believe Beckett committed these awful deeds. After talking with several people at the country club, I believe this was a lie perpetrated by the real murderer. Someone killed Maggie and then killed Beckett, framing him for Maggie's death. I have no proof. I've gone to Chief Mosby with my suspicious and he laughed them off. When I told him I would never believe our

*son was capable of murder or suicide, I swear he threat-
ened me. Not in so many words, but his eyes took on a
gleam. He mentioned the girls, Savannah, Samantha,
and Sabrina. Told me I should concentrate on taking
care of them. That they should be my concern. He told
me their welfare was in my hands. Which, of course, it
is, but I don't believe that's what he meant.*

*I don't know what to do. The children are my life and
my responsibility. If I pursue this, will something happen to them? Or am I just using them as an excuse because I'm a coward? I wish you were here to tell me
what to do. How can I continue on, knowing that my
beloved son and daughter-in-law were murdered? Yet
how can I put their children at risk? Please, Cammie,
tell me what I should do.*

Barely aware of her surroundings, Savannah never
noticed that the letter fell from her hand to the floor.
Waves of shock and denial pounded through her. Never
in all these years had she heard it suggested that her father hadn't committed the murder. There had never
been any doubt that she'd ever heard of. Was this just
something her grandfather had come up with to help
him deal with his pain? What proof had he had? Other
than what he referred to as the vague threats by Mosby,
was there more? What had made him suspicious?

Frantic to know more, Savannah delved back into the
box. Each successive letter showed her grandfather's
tortured thoughts about what he should do, whom he
should discuss his suspicions with. It seemed he ended
up trusting no one because he wasn't sure who was involved. His friends in Mobile told him to drop it, and
even Aunt Gibby urged him to let it go, telling him he
was pursuing something that had no hope of a good
outcome. Finally it appeared he had accepted that nothing could be done and apparently went to his grave

wondering if he had allowed the murderer of his son and daughter-in-law to get away.

Savannah stood. Though stiff from sitting too long, she barely paid attention to her body as her mind raced with all she had learned and the multitude of questions she now had. Was this possible? Had the man she had despised for killing her mother and destroying their happy life been an innocent victim? Who would have done such a thing? And why?

She ran from the guesthouse as if demons chased her. Entering the main house, she grabbed her purse from the kitchen counter and then ran out the door. Thankfully Zach had kept his promise—her car was in the driveway, and a note lay on the seat: *Had Manny check your tires and oil. You were a little low on both.*

For the first time, she noticed that her car was much cleaner, inside and out. Not only had Zach had her tires and oil checked, he'd had her car detailed. The interior smelled fresh and citrusy and the deep blue exterior paint gleamed from its bath. A wave of emotion swept over her at the sheer sweetness of the act. He had left this morning hurt and angry. Instead of maintaining that anger, he'd done something incredibly thoughtful and kind.

She would call and thank him; maybe invite him for dinner. She didn't like how they'd left things.

That settled in her mind, Savannah started the car. Now she had only one thought. She had to see Aunt Gibby and find out what she knew. Had her father really been innocent? If so, who had murdered her parents?

CHAPTER
TWENTY-ONE

Zach was on the sidewalk talking to Mayor Kilgore when Savannah flew by in her Mustang. Hell, if he'd had his patrol car close by, he would've jumped in and run her down to issue a ticket. Where was she going in such an all-fired hurry?

"You two looked awfully chummy the other night. Nesta said she saw definite sparks."

Discussing his love life with Midnight's mayor wasn't something he planned to do. Lamont's bright eyes twinkled with questions he was apparently dying to ask. Zach shifted the conversation to something else he knew the mayor was concerned with. "I don't think we'll have any more vandalisms."

"Really? Does that mean you caught the culprits?"

As far as Zach was concerned, the incident last night was over and would stay private. He'd had another blunt talk with both Henson and Dayton.

Clark Dayton had been uncharacteristically meek, apologizing repeatedly. He confessed to every vandalism crime, including the message on the school wall about Savannah. When a furious Zach had gotten in his face and threatened bodily harm if he came within a mile of Savannah, Dayton had stuttered out another apology and promised he wouldn't. He'd even offered to paint over the words. The man seemed sincerely remorseful. Time would tell just how sorry the idiot was.

Henson, unfortunately, had been his same predictable self. Unrepentant, he had denied doing anything wrong and had threatened Zach with a lawsuit for harassment. As they'd walked out the door, Zach had issued one final warning. If another vandalism occurred, he was coming after both of them and would hold nothing back.

The arrests were known only to his department, and he wanted to keep it that way. His answer to Lamont's question was deliberately vague. "Let's just say I had a long discussion with some people who know some people. I don't think we'll see anything happen again."

"That's good, Zach. Real good. All that talk about you not being able to handle your job will die down now."

The mayor's words confirmed what he already knew. As lame and stupid as Henson's and Dayton's crimes had been, they'd been effective.

"I appreciate your support, Mayor."

"How about you and Savannah coming over to the house next week for dinner?"

Accepting social engagements without talking to Savannah wasn't something Zach felt comfortable doing yet. Though he hoped to hell they could get to that point someday. "I'll check and see if she's available. We'll let you or Nesta know as soon as possible."

With a nod and a hearty politician's slap on his back, Lamont was gone.

Zach eyed the road that Savannah had sped down, tempted to find her and ask her what was going on. Instead he forced himself to head back to his office. He had paperwork to finish up, a new deputy to hire, and plans for wooing one skittish assistant DA.

*   *   *

Visiting Aunt Gibby was never as simple as it sounded. First there were the social niceties to get out of the way. Even though Savannah had just seen her aunt a few days ago, the older woman went through the ritual of asking about Savannah's health and her sisters' health and a long discussion on whether or not it was going to be as hot this summer as it was the year before. When Gibby asked about her progress on the house, Savannah, at last, felt she could bring up the subject of the letters.

"Oh yes, I know your grandfather was a great letter writer. Why, I think I still have some letters he sent me from years ago."

"Did you know he wrote to my grandmother even after she died?"

Sadness dulled Gibby's eyes. "That doesn't surprise me. Daniel missed Camille so very much."

"I read some this morning that I found surprising."

Gibby poured herself another cup of tea. "What's that, dear?"

"He said he didn't believe that Daddy killed Mama or that he committed suicide. He believed they were both murdered."

The nervous clatter of the teacup before it crashed to the floor told Savannah she'd definitely hit a nerve.

Savannah grabbed a napkin and went to her knees to dry the spill and pick up the shattered china pieces. She glanced up at Gibby, whose face had gone sheet white. "You think that, too, don't you?"

Gibby's gaze dropped; her fluttering, nervous fingers wiped at the moisture on the table. "I didn't say any such thing."

Savannah took her seat again. "Then say something, Gibby. Please . . . tell me what you know."

Gibby slumped back into her chair, and her eyes went unfocused as she remembered. "We were all stunned. There'd never been any indication that Beckett would do anything like that. When he was younger, he had a temper, but we hadn't seen any indication of that since Maggie came into his life. She just seemed to calm him." She smiled sadly and added, "You know, like she was his center, and as long as he could concentrate on her, nothing else mattered. When you girls came along, I've never seen a happier man in all my born days.

"Anyway, I wasn't at the country club when he and your mama had their argument. I heard about it, of course. Esther Lovell called me right after it happened." She waved her hand in her fluttering way. "You know she was always the biggest busybody."

Savannah's fingers gripped the edge of the table. Rushing Gibby would do no good. She would tell the story her way, in her own time.

"She said everyone in the club could hear them hollering at each other. Your mama, as you know, had the sweetest disposition. So when Esther told me about the argument, I just figured she was elaborating, as was her way. Then, when the police called me . . ." She swallowed hard. "Your grandfather was out of town, so I had to go over . . ."

"Oh, Aunt Gibby, I didn't know you had to be involved."

"I insisted on seeing them both. Which was stupid. Chief Mosby certainly didn't need an identification. But I just refused to believe it was true." Breath shuddered from her body. "Those are images I'll never get out of my head."

Savannah took both of her hands and squeezed them. She felt terrible for making Gibby recount that time. Was she being selfish, bringing this up when it was most likely just wishful thinking on her grandfather's part?

Gibby cleared her throat and continued, "After the initial shock subsided, Daniel started to question what we had been told. Chief Mosby refused to investigate further, saying the case was closed."

"And he just let it go at that? The letters he wrote Grandmother made it seem that he was threatened in some way."

Gibby sighed. "I don't know anything about that, darlin'. Daniel refused to talk about it anymore. I figured he finally accepted the truth and just didn't want to discuss it."

But he hadn't accepted the truth. The letters she'd read showed that his doubt continued, but something or someone had warned him to let it go. Other than Mosby, had he been threatened by someone else? If so, who? The real killer?

"Thank you, Gibby. I know this was a hard thing to talk about. I'm sorry it brought back bad memories." Savannah stood and leaned over and kissed Gibby's soft, wrinkled cheek. "I've got to go."

"I know what you're thinking, Savannah Rose. It's best to let sleeping dogs lie. Stirring up those old memories won't do anyone any good."

Denying evil in your midst was natural. Gibby was an elderly woman who had lived in Midnight her whole life. Upsetting the equilibrium of what was safe and secure took more than just courage, it took determination.

"Don't worry. I'm good at wheedling the truth out of people without them even realizing it."

Gibby nodded, her relief obvious. While Savannah would do everything she could not to upset her aunt, there was no way she was going to just let this go. The awful and terrible thoughts she'd had about her father for the last eighteen years haunted her. What if he was innocent? Instead of questioning what she had been told, she had accepted that the man she adored didn't exist and was a monster instead.

If Beckett Wilde was innocent and had been murdered, too, she would stop at nothing to discover the real killer. Heaven help anyone who tried to get in her way.

CHAPTER TWENTY-TWO

Three hours later, Savannah was headed back to the house. Exhaustion dimmed her reeling thoughts. She had spent several eye-straining hours reading old newspapers and was no closer to finding the truth. In fact, she thought dismally, she felt as if she was even further from the truth than before.

Midnight Tales, aptly named since it held more gossip than real news, was now a weekly newspaper. Eighteen years ago, it had been printed daily. The library had a copy on microfiche of every edition the newspaper had produced. The murder-suicide had been such big news that the newspaper had actually printed two papers a day for seven days. Every salacious event had been painstakingly detailed. The police chief, the coroner, the maid who'd found her mother's body, and all the people who had heard the argument between Maggie and Beckett at the country club had all been interviewed. Each interview seemed to lead to the same conclusion—that Beckett Wilde had killed his wife in a drunken rage and then committed suicide.

Savannah remembered that her grandfather had stopped his subscription to the newspaper after her parents' deaths, but she hadn't asked why. She had certainly never read the articles until now but could see why they had infuriated Daniel Wilde, especially if he believed his son was innocent. The articles had painted her father as a philanderer and a drunken womanizer. The eyewitness accounts of Beckett's argument with his wife were particularly damning.

There had been shouting. Savannah couldn't discount it since there were so many witnesses. However, her sweet-natured mother losing her temper and making a scene was so out of character. What had set Maggie Wilde off?

Tomorrow she would begin a low-key investigation. As she had promised Aunt Gibby, she would be as subtle as possible. Not only for Gibby's sake but also for her own. Having the town gossips scurrying around with news that Savannah was investigating Beckett's and Maggie's deaths after all these years wasn't something she wanted revealed. Not only because she simply hated being the subject of gossips, but also because she didn't know where this would lead. What if the murderer still lived in Midnight?

Savannah blew out a relieved sigh as she turned onto Wildefire Lane, seeing a hot bubble bath and a glass of wine in her immediate future. She needed the downtime to allow her thoughts to coalesce and to make plans.

Tomorrow her first order of business would be to talk to the former police chief, Harlan Mosby. He wasn't in good health and was in a hospital in Mobile. Had he been involved? Or had he been paid to shut the investigation down? If not, then why had he made those vague threats to her grandfather about taking care of his granddaughters?

Her mind on the myriad avenues she might have to pursue, she was almost at the house before she saw that she had company. Zach's car was parked in the drive and he was sitting in a rocker on the porch, waiting for her.

Should she reveal her suspicions to him? What proof

did she have yet other than the writings of a lonely, bro-kenhearted man? Besides, this thing with Zach was too new. The way they had parted this morning showed just how fragile things were. Introducing something of this magnitude was sure to create problems.

By the time she'd parked and was headed up the walk-way, Savannah knew she would wait until she had more fodder for her suspicions. She shushed the voice inside her head that told her she didn't completely trust him.

Zach watched Savannah approach and tried to gauge her mood. The way he'd walked out on her this morning hadn't exactly been his finest hour. Getting her car serviced and detailed had been in part an apology for stomping out the door like a six-year-old brat. He'd also done it simply because it was in his nature to take care of her. He had missed ten years of that, and if she'd let him, he wanted to make up for it.

The next few minutes might well tell him how his plans were going to go.

She looked good. Maybe a little tired but still so damn beautiful his teeth hurt. He'd done a lot of thinking over the last few hours and hoped like hell that the direction he planned to take would work. Glancing around at his handiwork, he suddenly wondered just how it could. This had to be the lamest way to win a woman's affec-tion since cavemen stopped clubbing their women over the heads and started wooing them instead.

"Hi," Zach said.

Her smile was bright, if a little wary, and Zach took that as a good sign.

"Hi yourself." She gestured at the sack at his feet. "Whatcha got there?"

"A little bribe."

She sat down in the rocker next to him and peeked into the bag. Laughing, she shook her head. "You're the only man I know who would try to bribe a woman with purple hull peas."

Something tightened in his chest as he heard the familiar beautiful sound. He hadn't realized how much he missed the sound of her laughter until she'd come back home. "I remembered how you used to like them. I helped Mrs. Lyman out today . . . she gave me some fresh vegetables from her garden."

Astonishment widened her eyes. "Sour Lyman?"

Zach snorted. "I'd forgotten that was her nickname in school. Were you in her science class?"

"Thankfully no. She retired the year before I could take her class. I remember seeing her in school. She always seemed angry about something."

He couldn't deny that. Delores Lyman had been one of the most reviled teachers in school, seeming to go out of her way to make her students hate her. Zach had taken her class, and despite his working his ass off studying, she'd still almost flunked him. He had thought then and still believed that a lot of her attitude had to do with loneliness. She had no family and few friends. Since he'd come home, he'd made a point of dropping in on her at least once a week to make sure she was okay. And though the elderly woman acted as if it was a huge imposition for him to visit, she always had lemonade and cookies for him. On his lunch break today, he had fixed her leaky faucet. In return, she had offered him fresh peas, okra, squash, and tomatoes.

"The wine's a nice touch." She took the glass of wine he offered her and sipped appreciatively. "Red wine, soft music in the background, and purple hull peas. Chief Tanner, you sure do know the way to a girl's heart."

He hoped to hell that was true. "You don't have to cook them if you don't want to. I just thought it'd be nice to sit out here in the early evening breeze, sip wine, and shell peas."

"I haven't shelled peas since I left home."

She pulled a handful of pea pods from the sack and took the empty bowl he handed her. For a while, the only sounds were Chopin's Nocturne in C Minor, chirping crickets, and the plop of raw peas falling into bowls. His muscles loosened with each second that passed. Maybe this wasn't the most sophisticated way to win a woman's affection, but Savannah had always been different. The tension that had been on her face had eased, replaced by a relaxed serenity.

She broke the silence at last. "How did everything go with Henson and Dayton today? I'm surprised I didn't hear any gossip about their arrests."

"They're already out of jail."

She nodded. "Yeah, I figured. How much was the bond set for?"

"No bond. There weren't any charges."

She stopped shelling and gawked at him. "No charges? You caught them in the act. How could there be no charges?"

From her perspective, he could see where she'd think letting them go was stupid. Yes, he lawfully could have charged them and they might have even served a few months in jail, depending upon which judge drew the case. But Zach saw no purpose in that. The crimes had been against him personally, not anyone else. When Zach had told Henson that a requirement for his release was to call his insurance company and withdraw the claims, he'd been pleased to learn that Henson had never filed any. Maybe the man wasn't as stupid as he looked. Insurance companies took a very grim view of insurance fraud.

"I let them go with a warning. Didn't see a need to take it further."

"That's ridiculous, Zach. After what Henson did to you? And Dayton is an officer of the law. He should be held to a higher standard."

"What Henson did years ago has no bearing on this case. And Dayton's no longer an officer of the law. Both he and Henson know what will happen if anything similar occurs."

She shook her head. "I never thought you'd be such a pacifist."

"I'm a person who doesn't see everything in black or white. These men learned their lesson."

"How can you not want revenge against Henson?"

"Henson means nothing to me, then or now. Would I want to smash his face in? Hell yeah. There was a time when that's all I could think of . . . I even concentrated on getting stronger and trained like a demon with the intent of coming back here and beating the hell out of him."

"What changed your mind?"

"I grew up, Savannah. The man is more than twice my age and has arthritis. I could beat the shit out of him with one hand, but if I did, just who the hell wins? Henson, for making me lower my standards? Me, for being able to knock some old man down who did the same thing to me ten years ago? What's the point? To make myself feel better? Hurting a man who is nothing to me would mean absolutely nothing. I don't see a point in violence for violence's sake."

She was silent for so long, Zach figured she was probably not only questioning his judgment as chief of police but also his manhood. He didn't care a lot what people thought of him, but he did care about Savannah's opinion. Hopefully she would understand someday, even if she didn't agree with his methods.

"What did you tell your deputies about the arrest? Surely that's going to get out."

"I told them that if I heard any talk, I knew exactly who had spread the rumors and they would be fired." He shrugged. "It's over and done with as far as I'm concerned."

"And you really believe Henson and Dayton will keep their noses clean from now on?"

"If they don't, they know I'll be on them like white on rice." Zach leaned forward and caught her gaze. "I'm not a fool, Savannah. I realize that letting them go isn't without risks. But I also believe in redemption."

She held his gaze for a long moment. He knew she heard the double meaning, as he had intended. Did she believe in redemption, too? He sure as hell hoped so.

"So, what are we going to do with all these peas?"

Breath eased from him as he relaxed back against the rocker. Maybe she didn't understand completely, but she wasn't going to challenge him. "I have the makings for a fine Southern dinner in the car. If you want, I'll cook and you can keep me company."

"You want to make dinner here?"

"Yes, if that's okay."

She stood and, holding the bowl of peas in her hand, said, "Then what are we waiting for? I'll start the water for the peas and you go get the rest of your stuff."

Zach stood, too. What he wanted to do was drop everything he had in his hands and fill his hands with her. He wouldn't. He needed to go very slow. Every instinct he had to rush her had to be set aside. This was too important to hurry. He was fighting for his future with the woman he had never stopped loving. Nothing was more important.

Savannah took another sip of her iced tea and watched as Zach finished loading the dishwasher. She had to admit, she could get used to this, sharing cooking responsibilities with a good-looking man and then watching him clean up the kitchen. Silly, but one of her fantasies about Zach used to include this scenario. Most people might laugh at something so mundane, but she'd always been different when it came to the things she wanted. At least until she'd stopped dreaming and fantasizing about anything at all.

She shook off those thoughts. She had learned the hard way that dwelling on them led to even bigger problems. Zach was here now. What the future held, she didn't know, and refused to even speculate on.

They had kept the conversation light during dinner, talking about the mundane or world events. Nothing personal was discussed, for which she was grateful. Though there was a huge part of her that wanted to tell him about the letters and her grandfather's suspicions, she forced herself to stay quiet. Maybe after she talked with Harlan Mosby tomorrow, she would know where to focus her investigation next. Having the current police chief's support would be essential, since she would want to see police and autopsy reports. After her visit with Mosby, she would tell him.

For now, she focused on the fact that a man who had fascinated her from the moment she saw him was standing in her kitchen. And her fascination hadn't lessened. Last night had proven that. She didn't know what she felt for Zach anymore, but the desire was definitely still there.

He pulled out a chair and sat at the table across from her. "How's the packing going?"

The opening was there if she would take it. Telling him about what she'd found in her grandfather's letters was the perfect opportunity to discuss the investigation she had launched.

"I'm still working on Granddad's library. I didn't feel

much like packing today, so I spent a lot of time in the guesthouse."

Slumping down lower in his chair, Zach crossed his muscular arms over his broad chest in a relaxed pose. Savannah was instantly diverted. Memories rushed over her of last night and how he'd carried her upstairs after they'd made love on the stairway. So strong, so very hard. She swallowed.

"Lots of old stuff stored there?"

She jerked back to the present. "What?"

"The guesthouse. Did you find a lot of stuff there you're going to have to get rid of?"

"Not really. Most of that stuff is stored in the attic. There are some antiques and memorabilia that we might donate." She took a breath. "I did find boxes of letters that my grandfather wrote to my grandmother."

His mouth curved into that sweet smile she remembered so well. "Did you read them?"

"Some. There are hundreds, maybe thousands. He wrote her from the time he met her until he died."

"He must have loved her very much." He stood and, holding out his hand, gave her that same sweet smile. "Let's go sit on the screen porch and listen to the crickets."

Unable to resist him or the lure of a quiet, peaceful night, Savannah took his hand and allowed him to pull her to her feet. Tomorrow, after her talk with Mosby, she would go to his office and tell him. It would be better to do that anyway—much more businesslike and professional. Tonight she just wanted to be with Zach, the man.

Out on the porch, Savannah headed to the chairs but Zach pulled her to the swing at the end of the porch. As children, she and her sisters would often all three get on the swing and glide. She remembered more than once that they'd gone too high and one or all of them had been knocked off onto the porch. When she was seven years old, she had fallen off and would have been fine if Bri hadn't fallen on top of her and broken Savannah's arm.

Still holding her hand, Zach began a slow, steady glide. As if they'd been doing this for years, Savannah put her head on his shoulder and closed her eyes. The only sounds were the crickets and frogs, the squeak of the old swing, and the distant bark of a dog.

"Tell me about Savannah. Please."

He had asked her the same question this morning and she had blown him off. Sharing the past ten years with him meant opening up in a way she hadn't allowed herself to open up to anyone. After he'd left, she had closed herself off. With the exception of her sisters, no one knew the real Savannah anymore. Zach had at one time, but he had given that up. Could she allow him back in?

Before she could answer, he sighed and said, "Here I am, asking you to share, and I haven't done much myself, have I?"

Relieved at the reprieve, she answered, "Not a lot."

"Then ask me something . . . anything."

The temptation to ask about other relationships was there but she held off. Not only because she dreaded learning about other women in his life but also because he would expect the same from her. How on earth was she going to explain that in ten years, her relationship history was as barren and dry as the Arizona desert?

Family was a relatively safe topic, at least safer than asking about other relationships, so Savannah started there. "You said that after you left here, you didn't see your mother for a while. How are things between you now?"

"Better, but still strained. Finding out who my real

father was didn't exactly enhance it. I've always felt more like her big brother than her son."

"Is she happy with your stepfather?"

"As happy as I think it's possible for her to be. Leonard still dotes on her and Mom eats that up. As long as he treats her as if she's the most important person on the planet, she seems satisfied."

The one time she had met Francine Adams had been enough for a lifetime. Knowing what he had put up with growing up made Savannah admire Zach even more.

"Did you ever resent having to be the grown-up in the family?"

"Of course I did but I had no other choice. Keeping the family together was priority one for me. I did what I had to do to make that happen. When you have no choices, life can be damn simple—survival and nothing else."

"Are you still close with Josh?"

"Yeah. Maybe even more since we've grown up. He calls me once a week, if he can. Other times, we email each other."

"And the army? You said you liked it."

"After I got used to it, yeah, I liked it. I got the discipline and structure I was looking for and needed. I finally felt as if I was doing something worthwhile."

"Why did you leave?"

He was silent for several seconds and then said, "I was finishing up my second tour in Iraq. Got some shrapnel in one of my legs. When I got out of the hospital, I realized the zest I'd had before was gone. When it came time to sign up again, I just didn't."

She swallowed and asked the one question she didn't want to ask but had to. "And relationships? Girlfriends . . . wives?"

When he shifted, she lifted her head to face him. "I won't lie to you, Savannah. I've had a couple of relationships, but nothing that lasted long and never anything serious. Nothing like I had with you."

She knew she should be happy about that, but for some reason she felt only sadness for them both. If things has worked out the way they had planned, they would have been married for several years, probably would have had at least a couple of kids by now. *Don't go there.*

When he lowered his head and softly kissed her lips, Savannah savored the sensation but couldn't respond. As if he understood, he lifted his mouth from hers and whispered, "It's getting late. I'd better go. I'll call you tomorrow."

Savannah watched him walk away. She wanted to ask him to stay but she felt too vulnerable. Tomorrow she would be stronger, less apt to give way to temptation. She needed to get her head on straight. Last night had been different—they'd satisfied a desire, scratched an itch. But tonight . . . if tonight had shown her anything, it had revealed that Zach was wanting more than just sex. And Savannah honestly didn't know if she had it in her anymore.

She looked out into the backyard and the wilderness beyond. Coming home had become so much more complicated than she had planned. Not only was the man who'd crushed her heart wanting to start up again, she might well have uncovered the truth of a terrible crime. What she learned from Mosby tomorrow could change the course of so many lives forever.

MOBILE, ALABAMA
COUNTY GENERAL HOSPITAL

The beeps and clicks of the machines beside him were distant and faint. It was a sound he'd heard on numerous television shows over the years and one he'd heard when his daddy lay dying.

Harlan Mosby breathed out a shaky, shallow breath. They said it wouldn't be much longer . . . a few days at the most. He tried to be okay with it. Dying wasn't too bad. Pain was as distant as the sound of the machines, hovering but never really penetrating his consciousness. What he felt most was a disappointment in what he'd had. Never had much and was leaving with even less. Had a wife once but she left him after a couple of years and a few too many drunken binges. Be nice if he had a kid or two by his side, but since he'd never cottoned to kids, he hadn't had any. His only relatives were a couple of distant cousins who didn't give a hoot in hell if he lived a hundred years or died yesterday. Which seemed fair since that was pretty much the way he felt about them, too.

Preacher had come by this morning and wanted to know if he wanted forgiveness for anything. As if he'd tell a damn preacher. What he had inside him he'd take to his grave. That's what he had promised, and if nothing else, Harlan Mosby was a man of his word. A small niggle of regret did hound him, though. He had pledged to do the best job he could as Midnight's chief of police and thought he'd done a pretty good job. Kept the riff-raff to a minimum, protected law-abiding citizens, and when a citizen misbehaved, he'd seen them punished—some of them by his own hand. Folks might have looked down on him if they knew some of the things he'd done, but there was no regret in that. *Sometimes you gotta get covered in a little manure if you're gonna watch things grow.*

A small smile twitched at his mouth at the thought. Zach Tanner had learned that lesson all too well. Damned if he hadn't enjoyed that night about as much as he'd ever enjoyed anything. Watching that no-account kid get the shit beat out of him and then get covered in cow shit was still funny after all these years.

The fact that Tanner was now the police chief of Midnight stuck in his craw like a dry chicken bone. If he'd had any money, he would've paid to have someone take care of Zach Tanner once and for all. Trash like that running his town? Maybe it was good he was dying.

No, he had few regrets except maybe when it came to the Wildes. Hell, they'd been a good family . . . a little too highfalutin for his taste, but they'd never done him any harm. The whole thing had bothered him. Yeah, he'd been paid well, but that money hadn't lasted all that long. He hadn't dared ask for more, though, 'cause he didn't trust that he wouldn't be next. The killing of pretty little Maggie Wilde was about as messy as he'd ever seen. Poor woman hadn't had a prayer. And then having to string up Beckett Wilde hadn't been fun, either. Poor bastard had woken right at the last minute and had stared them down, all of them.

Even now, pumped up on morphine to the hilt, he felt a shiver of fear sweep through him as he remembered the burning hatred in the man's eyes. Harlan hoped to hell he didn't have to meet him in the afterlife. He sure as shit wouldn't want to have to tangle with him.

He blew out another shallow breath. Nope, not a whole lot of regrets for sixty-eight years of semi-rough living. Now he was headed to eternal peace, which sounded pretty damn good to him. That is if he didn't believe what that old preacher man had told him about hellfire and eternal damnation. He sure as shit hoped that wasn't true.

The sound of a door squeaking open hit his consciousness. Probably one of those horse-faced nurses checking on him. Seemed like if a man was on his deathbed, they'd have the courtesy to send someone halfway decent-looking to take care of him. Having one of those old biddies being the last face he saw sure as shit didn't help a fellow die peacefully.

Harlan blinked as a shadow came into view. The figure was kind of short and a little on the skinny side. Didn't look like one of the nurses . . . maybe an orderly or some kind of helper. Doctors had stopped coming a few days ago. Guess they figured there was nothing else to be done.

As the dark figure drew closer, Harlan tensed. Something about the shadow seemed familiar. The light flickered on. Harlan gasped. Hell, this was one face he'd gladly spend an eternity never seeing again. Suddenly he wished for one of those horse-faced women to show her face, thinking she might just look pretty damn good right about now.

"What are you doing here?"

Was that weak, shaky voice really his?

"Just checking to see how you're doing."

Coming from someone else, he figured that might be true. For this creature, no way. They'd never been close. The only thing they shared was the big secret. Wary, he answered, "Nice of you but not necessary."

"Oh, but it is necessary. See, one of the Wilde girls is home and delving into old history. Pretty soon she's going to be asking questions. I can't afford for her to come and talk to you."

"I ain't going to say anything. I kept it a secret for eighteen years. There's no reason for me to tell her anything."

"Now that you're dying, your conscience not bothering you?"

He told himself to lie. Even as drugged as he was, he knew not to show any doubts or vulnerabilities. Before he could come up with something, it must have shown in his face.

The cold-blooded killer of Maggie and Beckett Wilde smiled. "That's what I thought."

Out of the corner of his eye, Harlan saw something bright flicker beneath the fluorescent light. Horrified, he watched as a needle was inserted into the IV.

"What . . . what are you doing?"

"Can't take the risk of you being alive if she comes to pay you a visit."

"But . . . I . . . ," Harlan sputtered.

"There, there. It'll all be over soon."

Harlan's finger grappled for the call buzzer. If one of those horse-faced nurses walked in the door, it would be the most beautiful sight in the world. He wasn't ready to die, especially not this way. This was his reward for protecting a secret for eighteen years? Murdered by the killer he had protected? Where was the justice in that?

He watched in bleary-eyed horror as the buzzer was lifted away from his grasp. "Now, now. No sense bothering anybody. These people have better things to do than see to a dying man."

"You bastard," Harlan whispered softly. Darkness began to descend but he could swear he heard soft laughter. Was that his murderer or the devil himself? Or were they one and the same?

Closing his eyes for the last time, Harlan floated away, searching for the peace that came with death. On his last breath, he knew peace was not to be his.

CHAPTER TWENTY-THREE

"Chief Tanner!"

At the sound of a woman's squeal, Zach slammed on his brakes. Seeing Inez Peebles on the sidewalk waving her thin arms to flag him down, he pulled over to the curb and hit the power button to roll down the window of his patrol car. "What's wrong?"

The oldest citizen and biggest gossip in Midnight leaned into the window. "Did you hear the news?"

Backing away slightly from the strong scent of garlic, Zach said, "What news?"

She leaned in closer, her head almost inside the car. Zach had no choice but to hold his breath. The woman was convinced that eating a clove of raw garlic once a day was the key to a lengthy life. Since she was going on ninety and still walked into town four days a week for her card games, he wasn't sure she wasn't right. Didn't make the smell any easier to take, though.

"Harlan Mosby died last night."

He hadn't heard but wasn't surprised by the news. Last time he'd seen the man, Zach had figured it wouldn't be long. Ashen-complexioned and bone-thin, Mosby had looked close to death even then.

"I'm real sorry to hear that."

Inez cackled like a crazed hen. "Now, don't you be lying just 'cause the man's finally gone on to hell. Mosby was a mean old fart and the world's a better place without him."

Not only did Inez have odd eating rituals, she also believed that reaching ninety years of age gave her the license to say what she thought. She rarely spared anyone's feelings.

Since he couldn't deny that Mosby had been a mean old fart, Zach changed the subject. "How's your son getting along?"

Usually the subject of what she called her "no-account, ungrateful son" was a safe bet. She could complain about him for hours. Today she had more interesting things to discuss. "Guess you heard that Savannah Wilde's been digging around for information about her parents' deaths? She was at Faye's Diner at the cracka dawn this morning, asking all sortsa questions. Some folks say that's the real reason she came back home."

A lifetime of not revealing his thoughts kept his face expressionless as he said, "Is that right?"

Her eyes blinked like an ancient owl; she was apparently startled that he hadn't taken the bait. Undeterred, she pressed on. "Reckon she thinks there were some shenanigans going on?"

That was an odd observation. He'd never heard about any doubts that the crime had happened differently. "You were here during that time. What do you think?"

She cackled again. "I think lotsa things, Chief Tanner. Problem is, nobody pays me no mind." Inez stepped back onto the curb. "I gotta get to my bridge game. I like getting there early 'cause that's when I pick up the juiciest news."

Zach pulled away from the curb and continued on his patrol. There should be nothing unusual in Savannah wanting to know more about her parents' deaths. There were any number of reasons she might be curious about the night they died. But when they'd been dating, that was one event she never wanted to discuss. So what had changed?

Her going into Faye's Diner by herself was on the odd side. Had she just woken up hungry and decided to treat herself to a big breakfast, or was there another reason?

He gave himself a mental shake. Inez Peebles had a reputation and a knack for making something out of nothing to stir something up. This was an apparent attempt to do just that.

Besides, ten years makes a huge difference in a person's life. Healing came with the passage of time. Maybe that was the reason Savannah could talk more easily about it now. If she had any suspicions about their deaths, she would have mentioned it to him. Last night would have been the perfect opportunity.

Their evening together had been good but frustrating. There was no one he enjoyed spending time with more than Savannah. Every smile or sigh she gave him made him want her all the more, but he hadn't pursued anything other than those simple kisses when he left. Hell yeah, he'd spent a rough night, hard and aching and wanting her with every breath. He'd known he needed to take it slow, he just hadn't realized how careful he needed to tread. For every step he took forward, Savannah seemed to move further away from him. He had hurt her and asked her forgiveness, but that didn't mean their way would be easy. But never had he been more determined to win.

The radio squawked. "Chief, you there?"

Zach picked up the radio mic, answering, "What's up, Hazel?"

"Got a hysterical call from Gibby Wilcox. Hard to understand what she's saying. Something about somebody being dead over on Wildefire Lane."

His heart stopped and then kicked into overdrive. Clicking on the siren, Zach stomped the accelerator and zoomed through town as if hell itself were racing to consume him. If anything had happened to Savannah, that's exactly what would happen.

MOBILE, ALABAMA
COUNTY GENERAL HOSPITAL

Shocked and unsure of her next move, Savannah sat in her car in the hospital parking lot. Nothing had gone as planned. After spending much of the night tossing and turning, a raging river of questions gushing through her mind, she'd woken before dawn and headed to Faye's Diner.

The early morning crowd at Faye's was always the older residents of Midnight. They were the ones most likely to have been around at the time of her parents' deaths. She had told Gibby she could ask questions without seeming to want to know the answer, and that's what she had intended. Somehow the Fates had worked against her. Maybe it was the humid, overcast day or the thunderous-looking clouds that promised an upcoming torrential rain. Whatever the reason, the diner was almost empty. The only person who could remotely have been around at the time her parents were killed was Faye herself. Not known for her verbose personality, Faye had grunted out a few yeses and nos to her vague leading questions and then walked away.

Savannah had left the diner with no answers to her questions and a slightly queasy stomach from Faye's corned-beef hash special. To make matters worse, the instant she walked out the door, she'd run into Amy Andrews, an old friend from high school. The conversation had only lasted about five minutes, but Savannah felt as if she'd been grilled by a skilled prosecutor. The central theme of Amy's questions had been centered around Savannah's reasons for coming back to Midnight, interspersed with questions about Zach. Wishing for Faye's knack for noncommittal replies, Savannah had kept her answers as vague as possible. Still, when she had finally managed to escape with a promise to call Amy soon, she still felt as though she'd given too much information.

Her day had gone from not so good to rock bottom the moment she'd walked into the hospital and asked to see Mosby. The man had died last night.

Was she being über-paranoid for thinking someone had hurried along his demise? Her job as a prosecutor had taught her to be wary, that coincidences were rare. Yes, they could happen. Mosby had been on his deathbed . . . she'd heard that news even before she had arrived back in Midnight. Still, she wondered. Was it mere coincidence that on the very day she started looking into a possible cover-up surrounding her parents' deaths, the man who had investigated and closed the case on those deaths had died?

The doctor in charge of his case hadn't bothered to hide his amusement when she had questioned him about hospital security. The idea that someone had come in and made sure Mosby died was ludicrous. The man had died of lung cancer and for no other reason. Requesting an autopsy was out of the question. Only hours after he died, Mosby was cremated. He'd had no family; his body had been disposed of in that manner per his wishes.

Other than Aunt Gibby, no one even knew that she suspected anything. And considering how upset Gibby had been, she wouldn't have mentioned it to anyone. Since Mosby had died last night, her vague questions at the diner didn't even come into play.

Savannah tried to push the idea of Mosby's murder from her mind. It was too ridiculous to contemplate. So why couldn't she stop thinking about it?

What now? Did she now go to Zach? What proof did she have yet? Absolutely none, of course. All she had were her grandfather's vague suspicions, her own vaguer doubts, Aunt Gibby's faint memories, and a dead former police chief. She had no doubt that Zach would listen to her concerns, but he couldn't act on anything. Hell, there was nothing to act on. The only way she was going to uncover the truth was to keep digging.

If there was anything to her grandfather's suspicions, someone knew something. They had to. The police and autopsy reports would be helpful, but she wasn't going to get them until she told Zach. Why she was avoiding telling him wasn't something she could clearly define. She knew there was still a distrust, but was it something more? After letting Henson and Clark Dayton go without charging either man, would he perhaps not bother to investigate her suspicions?

She simply had to have more proof. If she gave him irrefutable facts, he'd have no choice but to open up an investigation. But there were two people who needed to know right away. They would be as heavily invested in the truth as Savannah. On top of that, their input and expertise would be invaluable. Pressing speed dial on her cellphone, Savannah placed a call to Samantha.

"Savvy, hey," Sammie said. "I was going to call you later. I wanted to apologize for—"

Savannah cut her off. "I need to talk to both you and Bri together. Can you hang on and let me get her on the line?"

Apparently recognizing the serious edge in her voice, Samantha answered, "Yes. I'll wait."

Savannah put her sister on hold and then hit speed dial for Bri.

Sabrina answered on the first ring. "Hey, Savvy, I'm headed out the door right now. Can I call you back tonight?"

"No, Bri. I've got Sammie on the other line. I need to talk to you both, right now."

"What's wrong?"

"Hold on." Pressing the key to get Sammie's call back, she said, "Okay, both of you there?"

Her sisters answered in unison, "Yes."

"I was in the guesthouse yesterday and found something disturbing."

"What?" Sammie asked.

"Did you know that Granddad wrote letters to Grandmother?"

"Yes," Bri answered. "Remember he said he started them the day they met?"

"Yes, but he apparently didn't stop until he died. I found letters all the way up to the day before he passed away."

"I'm not surprised," Sammie said. "He missed her so much."

"But why is that disturbing?" Bri asked. "As cynical as I am, I think it's sweet."

"That's not the disturbing part." She took a breath. "In the letters, Granddad said he believed that someone else killed Mama and then killed Daddy to make it look like a murder-suicide."

The silence that followed told her that both sisters were as shocked by the news as she had been. Finally Sammie asked hoarsely, "Did he have any proof? What were the reasons for his suspicions?"

"That's the problem. He's really vague about things. Apparently he had doubts that it went down the way they said and started asking questions. I think someone threatened him, or maybe us, if he pursued it."

"Are you sure he wasn't just hoping that was the case?" Bri asked.

"I'm not sure about anything. I talked to Aunt Gibby yesterday. She knew about his suspicions but said he stopped talking about them and she figured he just finally accepted the truth."

"What about the police chief? Have you talked to him?"

"I was going to but he's dead."

"*What?*" Sammie and Bri screeched together.

"He's been sick for a while. It wasn't unexpected."

"Hell, Savannah," Bri said. "We thought you were talking about Zach."

"Good heavens, no. I was talking about Harlan Mosby. I came to the hospital this morning to talk to him and found out he died last night."

"You're thinking someone put him down?"

Savannah winced at Bri's less-than-delicate words but answered, "I don't know. Seems oddly coincidental, but no one knows about my suspicions other than Gibby."

"You think she told someone?"

"I don't know why she would. She got really upset when I was talking about it yesterday, telling me I shouldn't stir up trouble."

"Maybe she told someone she trusted and they told someone, like the real killer."

Savannah had had the same thought, but why would Gibby tell others when she was so concerned that Savannah didn't upset anyone with her questions?

"I spent most of yesterday reading the newspaper accounts. Do you guys remember anyone ever saying that things might not have happened the way we were told?"

"I never heard anything like that," Sammie said.

"Me either," Bri added. "All I ever heard was the bad stuff about Daddy."

Savannah knew exactly what she was talking about. People had come out of the woodwork to share their dislike of Beckett Wilde. Every questionable thing he had done had been built upon and expanded for entertainment of the town gossips.

"What does Zach say?" Sammie asked.

"I haven't told him yet."

"Why not? He could get you all the records on the investigation."

"I want to make sure I have something besides just these vague suspicions."

"What are you going to do?"

"I'm going to start asking around. I went to Faye's Diner this morning but couldn't find a soul to talk to about it. Nesta Kilgore called last night and invited me to dinner next week. She always invites Mama and Daddy's friends. I'll be as vague as I can be and just feel everyone out."

"Why not just ask the Kilgores outright?" Bri said. "They were Mama and Daddy's friends. I'm sure they'd tell you if they knew anything."

"Because I'm going with Zach."

If things hadn't been so serious, Savannah would have laughed at the shocked silence. Though Sammie's shock wouldn't be as great as Bri's. "Anyway, I wanted to tell you two and get your input. Do you think I'm crazy?"

"No," they answered together, and then Bri added, "Daddy doing these horrific things never made sense, but we believed what we were told."

"You guys . . ." Sammie's voice was just above a whisper. "What if Daddy was really innocent? My God . . ."

Sammie didn't need to finish the sentence. If this were true, everything they had believed about their father was wrong. Almost every aspect of their lives had been colored by this one event. What if it had all been a lie?

"Can you fax us copies of the letters?" Sammie asked. "Let us take a look at them?"

"I'll do that as soon as I get home."

"So you and Zach are seeing each other," Bri said.

A lot had happened since she'd talked to Sammie

about kissing Zach. Telling them that she'd done much more than kiss him was out of the question. They'd want to know everything, and right now, she couldn't articulate her feelings. She really wasn't sure what she felt other than this intense need driving her whenever Zach was around.

"Let's just say we've seen each other a few times." She cleared her throat. "He told me what happened . . . why he did what he did."

"Can you tell us?" Sammie asked.

Even to her sisters, she couldn't reveal Zach's pain and humiliation. That was his secret to share with whomever he wanted, not hers. "Let's just say he had a good reason." She sighed raggedly. "And you guys were right. I should have pursued it further."

"You were hurting, Savvy. No one could blame you," Bri said.

"Have you told him what happened?" Sammie asked.

"Not yet."

"You know you're going to have to. Right? Even if this goes nowhere, you've got to tell him."

Savannah swallowed around a sudden lump. "I know. I'm just taking it one day at a time right now."

"You know we've got your back, don't you?" Sammie said.

"Whatever you decide, we're a thousand percent behind you," Bri added.

"Thank you, guys. I love you."

"We love you, too," Sammie said.

"I hate to cut this party short, but I've got a lead to run down ASAP," Bri said.

"Let's talk about this again tomorrow," Savannah said. "That'll give you and Sammie a chance to read the letters and put your thoughts together."

After saying goodbye and disconnecting from her sisters, Savannah dropped her cellphone on the seat beside her but didn't move to start the car. As she stared out the window, her mind whirled with doubts and fears. Was this just a wild-goose chase? Should she ignore her grandfather's letters and let this go?

Loving memories of her mother were always with her, but rarely did she allow her father to enter her mind. Avoiding thoughts of Beckett Wilde was, for Savannah, a matter of self-protection. She had learned to cope with his awful betrayal by simply refusing to acknowledge he had ever existed. And if by chance a stray thought emerged, hatred and bitterness were the only emotions she felt.

But what if he was innocent? What if it had all been a big cover-up? Didn't she owe it to him and to her mother to find out the truth? Didn't she owe it to herself and her sisters? And to her grandfather, who had grieved every day for his son and daughter-in-law? The answer came back a resounding yes. She had no choice—she had to find out the truth. And if it turned out that her father had indeed committed the awful crime, then nothing would be different than it had been. But if he hadn't . . .

Pulling out of the hospital parking lot, Savannah headed back to Midnight. Her grandfather's letters had to have more information than what she had read yesterday. She had rushed out to see Gibby having read only a dozen or so. Her urgency showed her just how upset she had been. Usually she picked through evidence with meticulous concentration. She had a reputation for finding invisible needles in mountainous haystacks. If there were any clues to be found, she would get them.

Which reminded her. *Had* Gibby talked with anyone yesterday about their conversation? Even though Harlan Mosby had been expected to die, she couldn't get it out of her head that his death too conveniently coincided with her investigation.

She pressed a speed-dial key on her cellphone. As soon as Gibby answered, Savannah said, "Hey, Aunt Gibby, it's Savannah. I—"

"Savannah Rose, where in heaven's name are you? I've been trying to reach you all morning."

"You have?" Pulling the phone away from her ear, for the first time she noticed that not only had she put the ringer on silent, she had five missed calls.

The phone back at her ear, she said, "Is something wrong?"

"There certainly is. I went by your house a little while ago and there was a dead possum on your doorstep."

She had left by the side door this morning and hadn't opened the front door. "How sad. Did it crawl up on the porch and die?" She wasn't usually squeamish but the thought of a poor dead animal dying on her front porch wasn't a pleasant one.

"So you haven't talked to Chief Tanner?"

"Zach? No, I haven't. I left for Mobile early this morning."

"Mobile? What for?"

"I wanted to talk to Harlan Mosby."

"But he's dead."

Savannah rolled her eyes. She probably could have saved herself a trip if she had bothered to wait until later. The news of Mosby's death would have reached Midnight quite early. If anyone had been at Faye's this morning, his passing would have been the main topic of conversation.

"I didn't know he'd died until I got to the hospital."

"You need to come on home and soon."

Admittedly, having a dead animal on her doorstep wasn't pleasant, but there was a strange tension to Gibby's voice. "What's wrong?"

"Just come home, honey." The energy and liveliness in Gibby's voice was missing. For the first time in Savannah's memory, Gibby actually sounded like an old woman. Something was definitely up but she was apparently not going to find out till she got home.

"I'm only about half an hour away."

"I'll see you soon. Be careful."

Her aunt's evasiveness was worrisome. Gibby was known for spitting out rapid-fire chatter, and the fact that she didn't want to share what was on her mind was unprecedented.

Savannah checked her voice mail, and sure enough, there were three missed calls from Zach and three abrupt messages.

First: *"Savannah, where the hell are you?"*

Second: *"It's me again. I don't know where you are but call me as soon as you get this message."*

Third: *"I traced your cellphone location. What the hell are you doing in Mobile? Call me, dammit."*

Why was he so angry? She pressed the return-call key; Zach answered before it finished the first ring. "Where the fuck are you?"

She jerked at his obvious fury. "I'm about twenty-five minutes away from Midnight. What on earth is going on?"

The ragged breath he expelled told her more than his angry words that he was way past upset. "There's a dead animal on your doorstep."

"Yes, I know. I just talked to Gibby and she told me about it. Is that why you're so angry?"

"Hell, Savannah. Is that not enough?"

"It probably just got disoriented and came up on the porch by mistake."

"I sincerely doubt that."

"Why?"

"Because, dammit, it's headless."

Her stomach clenched. Okay, that did put a new spin

on things. "Why would someone do something like that?"

"That's what I intend to find out. I'm headed your way."

"There's no need for that. I'll be home in a few minutes."

As if she hadn't spoken, Zach continued, "I'll flash my lights as soon as I see your car. Pull over."

Before she could even answer, he disconnected the call.

Her head shook in disbelief. This day just kept getting more and more bizarre. And now she felt guilty for worrying both Gibby and Zach. Living on her own for so long, she hadn't even considered that not telling anyone where she was going would be a problem. She wasn't usually so thoughtless.

She kept a careful lookout for Zach's car. The very minute she spotted the patrol car, he flashed his lights at her. She watched in her rearview mirror as he made a U-turn in the middle of the road.

Since they were on a two-lane highway, Savannah drove for a few seconds more till she spotted a small clearing. It had apparently once been a roadside picnic area, but all that remained was a rusted old garbage can and a dilapidated picnic table. She pulled to a stop, lowered the driver's-side window, and unbuckled her seat belt. Before she could move, Zach jerked the car door open.

Savannah looked up into his face and froze. Holy crap, his eyes were glittering and his face was almost ashen. "Zach, are you okay?"

Instead of answering, he pulled her out of the car and into his arms. Holding her tight against him, a shudder went through his body.

Savannah was smart enough to keep her mouth shut. Besides, having her body molded to his was pure pleasure. In fact, she was literally melting into his arms, her softness against his hard, muscular frame. Arousal came swiftly . . . and unfortunately at the wrong time.

When his arms finally loosened, she pulled away slightly and said, "What's this all about?"

"If you ever go off without telling anyone where you're going, I'll—"

Her brows raised. "You'll what?"

He shook his head. "Nothing. Just don't do it again. Okay?"

"For the last time, what is wrong?"

"We got a 911 call from your aunt. My dispatcher couldn't get anything out of her other than someone was dead at your house. Then, when I get there and am reassured it's not you, I can't find any trace of you. That's what's wrong."

Cupping his face in her hand, she gently caressed his cheeks, soothing him. "Oh, Zach, I'm so sorry."

He took her hand and held it against his face, then leaned into her and captured her mouth with his. Savannah rose up on her toes and opened, inviting him inside.

Zach groaned as he delved into her sweetness. He'd gone through hell in the last two hours. Seeing her alive and well was as if every wish in the universe had come true. She tasted familiar and wonderful and he never wanted to stop kissing her, holding her.

In the distance, he heard a semitruck headed their way. Regretfully he loosened his arms and stepped back. Savannah looked as dazed as he felt.

"Follow me home."

She nodded slowly and slid back behind the wheel, Zach closed the door and then leaned over into the open window. "Buckle up and drive carefully."

She nodded again and started the engine. Zach jumped into his car, checked for traffic, and then headed back to Midnight. Half his concentration on the car behind him, he grabbed the radio mic and switched it on. "Hazel, you there?"

"I'm here, Chief. Did you find her?"

"Yeah, thanks. She's fine. I'm taking the rest of the day off. Tell Bart Odom he's got patrol and to call me if anything comes up."

Though Hazel's voice was as rough as gravel, he had no trouble hearing the smile in her voice as she said, "Have a good afternoon, Chief."

Switching off the radio, he looked into the rearview mirror and muttered, "I intend to, believe me."

CHAPTER TWENTY-FOUR

Zach glanced in the rearview mirror as he turned onto Beach View Drive. If Savannah hadn't realized they were headed to his house, she knew it now. Not only was his home closer, which meant she could be in his arms sooner, he wanted her to see the place. If she remembered it from years ago, her memories wouldn't be good. The house hadn't been much to look at then. And now, though still small, he'd done a lot of work on it and was proud of how it'd turned out.

He pulled into his driveway and was relieved to see her pull to a stop behind him. As he got out of the patrol car, he watched her face. Yeah, the surprise was there but so was her beautiful smile. She confirmed his thoughts when she stepped out of her car. "Zach, this is amazing. Did you do all of this yourself?"

Despite himself, he couldn't help the warmth her comment gave him. Having grown up in what many people might call a hovel, it felt damn good to be proud of where he now lived, especially since it was the same place.

"I started on it as soon as I came back here. Took me six months to finish."

She came to stand beside him. "You're very good with your hands."

Her low, husky voice made the double entendre even

sexier. He grabbed her hand and pulled her to the house. "Let me refresh your memory of just how good I am."

He turned the key to enter the house, fighting the crazy urge to carry her over the threshold. She'd either think he was insane or it would scare the hell out of her. Resisting the impulse, he just held the door open for her to go inside. The instant the door closed, he grabbed her and swept her into his arms.

Startled, she laughed and said, "But I want to see the house."

"Later."

She didn't argue. Her eyes took on a soft glow as she put her golden head on his shoulder and looked up at him. It took all his resolve not to lay her on the hardwood floor and love her until they were both breathless. Never had she looked more wonderful to him. Since he intended to take his time, a comfortable bed was definitely the way to go.

Turning left, he headed to his bedroom, grateful that his necessity for order included a neat and clean house. His childhood had taught him to do things for himself, and the U.S. Army had reinforced those principles. When he'd gotten up this morning, he'd had no idea he would be spending the afternoon in his bed with Savannah.

He dropped her feet to the floor beside the bed. For just a moment, he took the time to savor that she was actually here, with him. How many torturous nights had he longed for her, never really believing he'd have another chance?

"Zach?" she whispered softly.

Locking his eyes with her, Zach undressed her slowly. In a dim part of his mind, he was surprised at the steadiness of his hands, because everything inside him was at the edge of explosion. After the hell he'd gone through this morning, he was surprised he could function at all.

As he slid the dress from her silky shoulders, she reached up to unbutton his shirt. Zach caught her hands and stopped her. "Not yet."

"Why?"

"Because the instant I get my clothes off, I'm going to be inside you."

Delight brightened her eyes. "Since that's exactly where I want you to be, what's the problem?"

"I've been dreaming of having you here, in my house and in my bed, for days. I want to savor every single moment."

She dropped her hands and Zach rewarded her with a soft quick kiss. "I'll make waiting worth your while."

Her lips curved in amusement. "I'll hold you to that."

Zach lowered his gaze and took in what he had uncovered. A lacy flesh-colored bra covered what he knew was pure perfection, the most beautiful breasts in the universe. Unhooking the front clasp, he pushed the material back and confirmed his memories. Ivory mounds with small rose-colored nipples, her breasts were just the right size for his hands and mouth. Dipping his head, he licked a puckered nipple. Her gasp made him smile. That was a sound he intended to hear a lot in the next few hours.

His tongue swirled around the hardening flesh and then gently bit it, causing another gasp. Unable to wait, Zach wrapped his arms around her, covered her breast with his mouth, and sucked hard, the roaring in his ears almost drowning out her sighs and gasps. Lifting his head, he admired the glistening mound. Leaning forward again, he flicked the tight nipple with his tongue. Her responding gasping sigh was his reward.

"Zach, please," she groaned. "Let me touch you."

The urgent need in her voice almost made him relent, but he had so many more plans for her. Stepping back slightly, he pushed the dress from her hips and swallowed his own gasp. Minuscule panties barely covered her sex. Zach took a deep breath and inhaled the delicious scent of her arousal.

His fingers hooked into the thin band at her hips and pulled the panties down to her knees. "Sit on the bed."

She dropped onto the bed and Zach went to his knees before her. Pulling the whisper-thin material down her long, silky legs, he threw them over his shoulder. She laughed softly and then caught her breath when he pulled her to the edge of the bed and his hands went to her knees, spreading her legs apart.

Zach looked down at the gleaming, moist flesh protected by soft blond curls. Paradise awaited him.

"Do you know how many nights I dreamed of this?" she whispered softly.

Surprised, he looked up at her. "You dreamed of me?"

A sad smile tilted her lips. "So many nights."

His heart clenched. "I promise to make up for every one of those nights."

Something odd flickered in her eyes but she covered it quickly with another soft smile. "Then get to work, mister."

He wasted no time doing her bidding. Using his thumbs to spread the folds of her sex, Zach leaned forward and licked. At her soft gasp of approval, he delved deep, burying his tongue as far inside her as he could go. Plunge, retreat, and then plunge once more, Zach reveled in her taste, her sighs and pleas, and the slender fingers that tangled and pulled at his hair, pressing him deeper into her sex. Seconds later she stiffened as a powerful climax rushed through her. Her release sweet and moist in his mouth made him wish he had enough control to lick her to another orgasm, but he was just barely hanging on now. Still, Zach stayed inside her, using gentle thrusts and small laps of his tongue to ease her back to earth. He continued until her throbbing stopped and her body relaxed. When her hands loosened on his head, he pulled away.

Surging to his feet, he began to unbutton his shirt. Savannah's fingers went to his zipper and he assumed she was going to help him undress. He was only halfway right. Smiling up at him, the burn of desire in her eyes set to the highest flame, she whispered, "My turn."

Her body hot with a fiery need she barely recognized, Savannah unzipped Zach's pants. She had wanted to take it slow and undress him the same way he had undressed her. That wasn't possible anymore. If she didn't get him naked and on the bed with her soon, she wouldn't be responsible for her actions.

With single-minded determination, pleasure and satisfaction her only goals, she opened Zach's pants, revealing steel-gray underwear that barely covered his erection. Impatient, she tugged until both pants and underwear were bunched below his hips. His erection sprang free, the hard length almost smacking her face. Taking advantage, Savannah licked the long, solid steel of him, and then, despite the harsh, urgent sound of his protest, she opened her mouth and took him inside, to her throat.

Zach's hands held her face, at first she thought to push her away, but instead, he weaved his fingers through her hair, giving her the freedom to take as much of him as she wanted. Inexperienced as she was with this kind of lovemaking, the groans and whispers of encouragement coming from above told her she was doing it right. A good thing, because she loved his taste.

"Stop . . . I can't take much more."

Neither could she. As much as she wanted to take him to completion and have him explode in her mouth, she couldn't wait another second to have him deep inside the part of her throbbing to be filled.

She pulled away and scooted to the middle of the bed.

Zach wasted no time pulling off his remaining clothes and then joined her. Before she could bring him to her and inside, she was startled when he pulled her into his arms and held her tight against him as if he never wanted to let her go.

"You okay?"

Breath shuddered through his big body. Not answering, he held her in his steely arms for a few more seconds and then he pulled back slightly to look down at her. The naked emotion on his face astounded her.

Her hand cupped his face. "What's wrong?"

"Not a damn thing," he muttered, and then covered her mouth with his. Plunging deep, his tongue tangled and dueled with hers. Grabbing his shoulders, Savannah held on, loving the fierceness and desperate need she felt in him.

Without taking his mouth from hers, Zach rolled her onto her back and came over her. Savannah wound one leg around his hip, inviting him inside. With one smooth, hard thrust, he was at last a part of her.

Sensation spiraled through him to Savannah, causing them both to climax simultaneously. Face buried against his shoulder, a small squeal erupted from her as a burning, consuming heat, like a thousand tiny suns, exploded within her. Zach stiffened in her arms and she felt his release. Holding him tight, she treasured the trembling of his big body, the groaning breaths, the gasping moans. Most of all, she treasured his whispered words: "Savannah . . . my love."

Zach rolled over, surprised that Savannah was no longer beside him. For a man who'd spent much of his life hearing and reacting to the slightest noise, not hearing Savannah leave the bed should concern him. It didn't. There was no one he trusted more than this woman.

Years ago she'd stolen his heart with her honesty. Nothing had changed.

Raising his head, he spotted her across the room, standing beside the bureau next to the window. Rain bashed against the windowpane. It was abnormally dark for the middle of the day, but Savannah seemed like sunshine. Long, wavy blond hair reached below her shoulders, wild, untamed, and exactly how he loved it. Her skin still held that luminescent glow as if a candle burned within her. The shirt he'd worn earlier hung on her slender frame, landing at mid-thigh and revealing those long, silky legs that had recently been wrapped around him.

Apparently realizing she was being watched, she turned and gave a slow, sexy smile. "I didn't realize you were such a good photographer."

He'd been so focused on admiring her, he hadn't realized that she was looking at the pictures on the bureau. "I never even owned a camera until I went into the army. I traveled to some amazing places and thought I'd just take a few shots here and there. The moment I put the camera in my hand, it was like I'd been missing an appendage."

She picked up one of his favorites—a little Afghan boy, about five years old, holding a ragged teddy bear in one hand and a chocolate bar in the other. Zach had been on foot patrol and had spotted the kid. He'd taken the chocolate out of his backpack and offered it to him. The kid's two front teeth were missing and every soldier who'd witnessed his smile that day had been touched. Zach had snapped the shot and knew he would never consider giving the photograph to anyone else. He'd had more than a few people offer him money for his work. He had never taken photos for money—every picture meant something to him that money couldn't replace.

"That's one of my favorites."

She laughed. "The chocolate bar probably helped with that smile."

He didn't bother to tell her that later that day, the entire village had been wiped out by a tribe of militants who were punishing the villagers for accepting aid from the Americans. Some memories were meant to be buried a thousand miles deep.

"Your house is amazing. I had only seen the outside of it before, but I can tell you did a lot of work on the inside, too. Everything seems fresh and new."

Yeah, he had practically gutted the house. There might've been a few good memories here that he didn't mind remaining, but for the most part, it had been a major catharsis to get rid of everything that reminded him of his childhood.

"After I moved back here, I started up a small construction business. No major building, just renovating. This house was my office, too, so I wanted it to look nice."

"What happened to your business?"

"I turned it over to one of my workers. I still help him out from time to time, but being police chief keeps me plenty busy."

She drew in a deep breath, tightening the material slightly and revealing the sexy, silken body beneath it.

Zach swallowed a groan and patted the pillow beside him, hoping he didn't look or sound too desperate. "Why don't you come back to bed?"

"I was thinking of bringing you something to eat."

At the mention of food, his stomach produced a giant growl reminding him that breakfast had been hours ago. He had skipped lunch because he had been looking for Savannah. "I've got some chicken salad in the fridge."

He was about to throw the sheet off and get out of bed, but she stopped him with "No, stay there. Let me bring it to you."

Other than in the hospital, which he figured didn't count, he'd never been served in bed before. Zach dropped his head back to the pillow. "Now, I could get used to that."

She snorted. "Don't. My kitchen skills have diminished greatly over the years. Having fully prepared food is what I do best." She turned to go out of the room and then stopped, shooting him a sultry smile over her shoulder. "By the way, I'm your dessert."

She disappeared before he could answer back, but his body responded to her words like magic. Arousal surged, tenting the sheet covering him. Zach sighed his contentment. He had her here with him; they'd just made love and would do so again very soon. It was as if his dreams so long in the making were finally coming true.

Where did they go from here? She had a career she loved. Zach had worked hard to attain his position and status here, but it meant nothing without Savannah. How would she feel if he told her he'd move to Nashville if he could be with her? Hell, he still had no idea what he meant to her. There was desire, but was there more? Had she forgiven him for deserting her?

Something else they hadn't yet talked about was the dead animal on her doorstep. Teenage prank or a threat? If it was a threat, who'd made it? Henson and Clark Dayton swore their innocence, and while their level of crimes was at best juvenile and he had absolutely no use for either of them, a dead animal went lower than he thought even they would stoop.

In the midst of searching for Savannah and being convinced someone had taken her, he had called the DA's office in Nashville and talked with her boss. There'd been no more threats made against Savannah. The sentencing for the perp she'd put away would take place next month. Garrison didn't believe the X-Kings had traveled all the way to Midnight to leave a dead animal on her doorstep. Zach hadn't believed it either but felt the need to double-check. And they would remain on his suspect list until he knew the truth. No one was above suspicion. But if not the X-Kings and not Dayton or Henson, then who? And why?

"Lunch is served."

He sat up and smoothed out the bed. "Come join me."

She placed the tray in the middle of the bed and then crawled under the covers with him. Food suddenly no longer seemed an urgent need. He reached for her and she held out her hand to keep him at bay, laughing. "Oh no, we eat our meal and then comes dessert."

He grinned. "I always thought dessert made for a great appetizer."

"Nice try, but I think I'll have more energy if we eat first."

Since he had specific plans that included expending a hell of a lot of energy, Zach picked up a sandwich and took a giant bite. Munching contentedly, he said, "So you don't have the chance to cook often. I remember you were once a damn good cook."

"Either you have a selective memory or you were exceptionally hungry. Most of my stuff was as basic as it comes. Now I don't even have time to cook the basics."

Zach demolished his first sandwich and went back for the second one. "So what's a typical day like for Assistant DA Savannah Wilde?"

Savannah shrugged, uncomfortable with where their discussion was leading. If she told him what her average day was like, he'd soon learn that other than work, her life was about as dull and empty as a hollow drum. She liked it the way it was. Safe and predictable was how she coped. Zach was too inquisitive to just let it go at that. He would want to know why a twenty-eight-year-old woman had almost no social life and the only true friends she had were her two sisters. Explaining that might veer too close to when and how she'd chosen this almost monastic lifestyle. She could not go there now. Both Sammie and Bri had told her she was going to have to tell him the truth at some point. They were right. But at what point? She didn't know. But today wasn't that day.

Aware he was waiting for her reply, she shrugged and said, "I usually get to the office by seven. When I'm in court, I'm usually there from around nine till around four. If I'm not in court, then it's a lot of paperwork, phone calls, some fieldwork." She shrugged again. "You know the drill."

"So what do you do in your downtime?"

"I volunteer at a crisis clinic close to my apartment."

"Do you date much?"

Since her dating life consisted of a handful of blind dates that had been about as exciting as watching paint dry, she shrugged evasively and said, "I'm not seeing anyone special right now."

His eyes held more questions but thankfully he let it go. "Did you get to see your grandfather much after you moved away?"

Feeling safer with this topic, she relaxed and continued eating. "Once a month he would meet the three of us in Mobile."

"Why Mobile?"

"It was close by for him. And he loved the city. I always thought if he'd been younger, he would have moved there after we left home."

"I was real sorry to hear about his passing."

She swallowed around the sudden lump in her throat. "He went quickly and quietly. We'd just seen him the week before, and though he was in his early eighties, he still looked years younger and acted that way, too. It was a shock when Gibby called and told us."

"I wish I'd gotten the chance to say goodbye to him. He was one of the finest men I've ever known."

"He thought a lot of you, too."

"I figured he'd be furious at me for what I did."

He had been furious, much more so than Zach might expect. She'd had to beg him many times not to interfere. If he'd had his way, he would have gone to Fort Benning and literally dragged Zach home.

"He tried to remember . . ." She cleared her throat. "We all tried to remember the good times."

Dropping his half-eaten sandwich on the tray, he took her hand and held it against his mouth. "Do you think you'll ever be able to forgive me?"

"I've already forgiven you, Zach. You explained what happened. That's all in the past." Shoving the tray out of the way, she turned and softly kissed his cheek. "Now, what about that dessert?"

He grabbed her shoulders, pulled her over to straddle him, and growled against her mouth, "Just so you know, I usually ask for second and third helpings on dessert."

Savannah lost herself in the magic, forgetting for just a little while that major issues surrounded them. Sometime soon, they'd have to face them. But for right now . . . for right now, this was all she needed to survive.

CHAPTER TWENTY-FIVE

When he was a kid, if anyone had told Zach that he'd someday have dinner with the mayor of Midnight at his home, he would've asked them what they'd been snorting. It'd never been his dream to hobnob with the elite of this town or any other. He shot a glance at the woman sitting beside him. She was the only elite he'd ever been interested in impressing.

Five days had gone by since the incident with the dead animal on her doorstep. Nothing unusual had happened since then. He was close to thinking that some bored teens had found roadkill somewhere and thought it'd be cool to dump it at someone's door, and it just so happened that person was Savannah. Not that his concern had eased up any. After going through those few hellacious hours when he'd thought something had happened to her, it was going to take a hell of a lot more time for him to stop worrying.

Since that day, he and Savannah had reached a new level in their relationship. They saw each other every day, often had meals together, and spent their nights in each other's arms. Things had progressed much quicker than he ever could have hoped. His feelings for her were a thousand times stronger than they'd been ten years ago. She went into his arms every night as if she belonged there and was more than content to stay there forever. Everything should be perfect. So why the hell wasn't he happy?

Apparently feeling his eyes on her, Savannah twisted in her chair and gave him a smile. Still sweet, still beautiful, but so full of secrets. There was something missing. Something she wouldn't share or wouldn't tell him. It was as if she was holding something back—an emotion, a feeling. He didn't know.

Every time he brought up her life in Nashville, she became evasive. Did she think he'd think less of her if she'd had romantic relationships? It hurt like hell to think of her with another man, but she was a young, beautiful woman. It was only natural for her to have had relationships. Had she been married before, engaged? He wanted to know everything about her and still felt he knew so little.

"You're awfully quiet. Everything okay?"

Zach pulled himself out of his useless introspection. He should be damn happy for what he had right now. A month ago, he figured he'd never even have a chance to be with Savannah again, in any way. This was a hell of a lot better than he deserved.

"I'm fine." And, since he didn't want to discuss how un-fine he was, he changed the subject. "I saw you and Corwin in deep discussion a few minutes ago. He giving you some legal advice?"

He'd meant it as a small joke. Corwin Banks was the most prominent attorney in Midnight, but Zach would bet his last dollar that Savannah was the more knowledgeable when it came to legal issues. She smiled but her eyes remained solemn. Dammit, there it was again. That look of secrecy. Why?

"We were just talking about old times. When my parents were alive."

"They were friends?"

She nodded. "Whenever I come to the Kilgores' for

dinner, Lamont always invites some of my parents' old friends."

"Is that hard for you? Hearing them talk about your parents?"

"It used to be. Not so much anymore."

"Time give you a different perspective?"

"I guess." She shrugged and smiled vaguely. Her voice softened as she asked, "So, your place or mine tonight?"

"Your choice. I'm off tomorrow."

She grinned cheekily. "I was kind of hoping to get you off tonight."

Surprised laughter erupted from him. Learning that Savannah had a wicked, sometimes bawdy sense of humor had been an extra delight. He might have doubts about a lot of things, but when it came to the heat between them, it was hotter than ever.

"What's so funny?" Nesta asked.

Savannah felt a blush to the roots of her hair. She could tease and joke with Zach about things she'd never consider saying to anyone else.

Before Savannah could answer, Nesta giggled. "Never mind. By the look on Savannah's face, I know it was meant for only you two." She beamed at them. "I can't tell you how happy I am to see you two together. I remember when you were both just young'uns and looked at each other like there was no one else in the world. It's so good to see you acting like that again."

Her blush deepened. This thing with Zach was too new and fragile to discuss in public.

"Now I've gone and embarrassed you even more." She looked over her shoulder. "Lamont, get over here and get me out of this hole I'm diggin'."

Savannah laughed and hugged the older woman. "You're fine. This is just kind of new to us, too." She shot an amused look at Zach and was surprised that he wasn't smiling. In fact, he looked downright grim.

Big and burly, Lamont wrapped one arm around his wife, one around Savannah, and grinned down at them both. "What's this? My wife is saying something embarrassing?" He winked at Zach. "When I married Nesta, that was the one thing her daddy warned me about. Her family has a long history of foot-and-mouth disease . . . you know, insert foot into mouth."

"Lamont Lester, that's not true." She paused and then added, "Okay, maybe a little true." Waving her hand at Savannah and Zach, she said, "But don't they look wonderful together?"

Fortunately Lamont was a born politician. "Nesta, I forgot to tell you that the caterer said they were running low on ice."

"What?" Her eyes wide with worry, she quickly excused herself and practically ran toward the kitchen.

Lamont winked again. "That'll keep her occupied for a while." He leaned forward and kissed Savannah on the cheek. "You youngsters enjoy yourselves."

After he left, Savannah took a sip of her wine and shot a glance around. So far, she had talked to Lamont and Nesta, Corwin and DeAnne Banks, Noreen Ingram, and Richard Tatum. She'd been as vague as possible with her questions surrounding the night her parents died, but her discretion would soon have to end. This subtle line of questioning wasn't working.

Tonight she would tell Zach about her grandfather's letters and ask for his help. Yes, she needed to see the police and coroner's reports, but she also hated keeping secrets from him. She only had a little over a month left here in Midnight and wanted to make the most of it. They hadn't talked about the future; Savannah refused to allow herself to think there was one. Optimistic dreams of the future no longer existed in her world. Besides, they lived hundreds of miles apart.

"You about ready to go?"

A chain reaction of sensations swept through her body. Goosebumps zipped up her spine, nipples grew tight and hard, breath increased, and her sex throbbed in anticipated arousal. They'd made love only about four hours ago and she wanted him again. Was ten years of deprivation causing this oversexed reaction? She'd like to think so but she didn't believe that for one moment. No one had ever been able to make her react like Zach. At the mere sound of his deep, sexy voice, she went wet with arousal.

She desperately wanted to say yes. Going home and getting lost in each other sounded like heaven. But there were a few more people she wanted to chat with. "Let's stay for a little while longer."

Again that grim look, but he nodded and said, "I think I saw Cooper Douglas out on the patio. I need to see him about something. I'll catch you later."

He was decidedly upset about something. She shook off her worry and headed to the corner where Kyle Ingram was sitting by himself. Why he came to these parties she couldn't understand. Every time she saw the poor man, he was either alone or had the saddest expression on his face. Noreen, whom she'd talked to earlier, had been her usual sour self, so maybe it made sense he came to parties. Staying at home, alone with his wife, couldn't be fun.

"Hi, Kyle. How are you doing?"

He blinked up at her as if he'd been asleep, and then jumped to his feet. "Savannah, hi. How are you?"

Since one never went anywhere in the South without being prepared to talk about the weather, Savannah started first. "Sweltering in this heat. Must've been close to a hundred today."

"That's what I heard. Sure hope we get more rain soon. That downpour we got the other day got absorbed into the ground like a sponge."

Remembering what she'd been doing during that particular downpour brought a new wave of heat to her body. Great. Zach didn't even need to be near her to turn her on.

Kyle didn't seem to notice her flushed state. The same look he had every time she talked to him came into his eyes . . . some sort of weird adoration. Though the look was disturbing, perhaps if he was distracted, he wouldn't wonder too much about her questions.

"You said you went to school with my mama, didn't you?"

A smile brightened his glum face. "Maggie Mae . . . I used to call her. She was one of my best friends." His face dimmed again. "Until she went off to college."

"You didn't see much of her after that?"

Savannah hadn't thought his face could get any gloomier, but he managed it when he answered, "She met your father."

That he hadn't been a fan of her father's even before her parents' deaths was obvious. Was it jealousy or something more sinister? Then why kill her mother? Why not just kill Beckett Wilde?

"You and my father weren't friends?"

Hatred gleamed so hot in his eyes, Savannah had to force herself not to gasp and step back. The last thing she wanted him to do was shut down or guard his responses.

"Before they got married, I told her that she'd rue the day she married that bastard." His mouth twisted in a sanctimonious purse as he added, "I was right."

For someone who talked almost daily to sadistic, evil people, Savannah was hard to shock or scare. This man had something wrong with him. It wasn't just dissatisfaction with his choices in life or a bad marriage.

Despite her disquiet, she continued with her questions. Hoping to ease the tenseness, she tried a different approach. "How was it that you got into the furniture business?"

"My parents own Ingram's Furnishings."

"How interesting. I didn't make the connection."

Ingram's Furnishings was one of the largest furniture companies in the South. Half the furniture in her apartment came from their store. She made a mental note to give it away when she returned home.

"I talked my daddy into expanding." He straightened his shoulders as he proclaimed proudly, "I opened the first fine-furniture store in Midnight. The other one in town is just mass-produced crap."

"Did you see my mother much after you moved here?"

"She came into the store occasionally."

"What about my father?"

His face closed down and Savannah knew she'd gone too far—interrogating instead of holding a friendly conversation. Before she could figure out a way to get back on track, a soft hand touched her bare arm.

"Excuse me, Savannah Rose," Gibby said. She smiled sweetly at Kyle. "Mind if I steal my niece for a minute?"

Kyle shook his head and backed away. "I was just about to say good night." He gave a small nod to Savannah and said, "Good to see you again."

Savannah watched as Kyle muttered something to Noreen and then they both walked toward the door. When would she ever get a chance to talk to him again?

Turning to her aunt, she smiled, thinking how pretty Gibby looked tonight. "You know, pink really is your color."

Gibby glowed at the compliment but she had something else on her mind. "An idea came to me a few seconds ago that I thought could be significant to your investigation."

Looking around, Savannah winced at the number of people who'd heard that statement. As Gibby grew older, her hearing had become less sharp and her voice had become louder. She took her aunt's elbow and guided her gently toward a more private area a few feet away.

"Now, what was—"

"Gibby, I'm leaving. You coming?"

Hester, Gibby's best friend, stood beside them.

"I'll be there in just a few minutes. I wanted to talk to Savannah a minute."

"I need to get home now. Scooter's medicine was due half an hour ago."

Savannah knew that Scooter was Hester's elderly cat, who, she claimed, was the oldest cat in Alabama. Savannah didn't doubt it, since she swore the cat had been around when she was a little girl.

Gibby sighed. "All right. I'm coming."

"Zach and I can take you home, Gibby."

Instead of answering, Gibby looked at Hester. "Go bring the car around and I'll be on the porch."

Her mission clear, Hester walked away.

"If I don't go with her, she'll pout for a week. Why don't you come by for breakfast in the morning? I froze a delicious breakfast casserole a few months back. We'll have a nice meal and chat."

Since a few months back probably meant she'd frozen the casserole a couple of years ago, Savannah knew indigestion would result. However, it was worth it if Gibby had what she thought was significant information.

"That sounds good. Eight o'clock okay?"

"Perfect."

Savannah leaned down and kissed the soft, creped cheek. "You be careful going home. See you in the morning."

Gibby looked around Savannah. "Zach, you get my girl home at a decent hour, you hear?"

Startled, Savannah turned. Was Zach in the room when Gibby made the statement about her investigation? The glint of fury in his gray eyes answered her question. She had decided to tell him everything tonight. Wrapped in his arms, she had planned to reveal that and possibly more.

Gearing up for what was most likely not going to be the sizzling night of passion and sharing she had been anticipating, she watched Zach charm Gibby and escort her out the door. Savannah went to say her goodbyes to Lamont and Nesta. If Zach's expression was anything to go by, she was not looking forward to the next few minutes.

Hurt and anger were each powerful emotions on their own. Mixed, they could make you say shit you'd regret forever. Which was exactly why Zach hadn't said a word since he'd gotten in the car. Savannah had tried to open up several avenues of conversation, but he hadn't taken the bait. Responding to anything right now would open up a chasm neither of them was prepared to handle. Once his temper was intact, they'd talk. Until then, he'd stay silent.

According to Gibby, Savannah was running an investigation. The conversation he'd had with Inez Peebles the other day took on new meaning. She'd said Savannah was asking questions about her parents. She was investigating what? Their deaths? If so, why? And why now?

He shot a glance over at her. She was staring out the window, her profile as classic and pure as a madonna's. At his request, she'd worn her long hair down, and all during dinner tonight, he'd dreamed about taking her home and burying his hands in those golden tresses as he buried himself inside her. Unless he was totally misjudging the situation, neither of them would be getting that kind of satisfaction tonight.

Pulling into the drive, he got out of the car. She met him in front of the car. "Are you coming in?"

Torn between devouring that sexy, mutinous mouth and just leaving and letting her stew for a while, Zach took another direction. One he should have taken when he first suspected she was keeping secrets. "Yeah, I'm coming in and we're going to talk. You ready to do that?"

"Yes, I was going to tell you tonight anyway."

"Let's go."

They walked side by side to the front door. Zach unlocked the door and held it open for Savannah to enter. The instant he shut the door behind him, she whirled around and said, "I know you're angry, but—"

Zach held up his hand. "Don't even give me the bullshit of saying you were going to tell me tonight. Just tell me."

Issuing an exasperated huff that echoed through the house, she crossed her arms and said, "Fine. Remember I told you I found letters my grandfather wrote to my grandmother?"

When he just stared silently, she continued, "He wrote that he didn't believe my father killed my mother, nor did he think he committed suicide. He believed they were both murdered but it was made to look like a murder-suicide."

"Did he have any proof?"

"As far as I can tell, no, he didn't. Just his suspicions and some vague threats that Mosby made." She turned slightly and said, "Come into the study. I faxed the letters to Sammie and Bri the other day. And I made copies for you, too."

Did she think that was going to make this better? It made sense that she had planned to tell him at some point. She would want to see copies of the police and coroner's reports. He could get those for her, so of course she had to tell him. What he didn't understand was why she hadn't told him immediately.

As he followed her into the large room that had been her grandfather's study, he asked, "When did you find the letters?"

Her shoulders went stiff and he already knew he wasn't going to like her answer. "Last week." She handed him a stack of papers. "I wanted to check things out before I told anyone."

"Anyone being me. Right? Apparently you've told your sisters, your aunt, and how many others?"

"That's all, Zach. I just . . ."

"You just what, Savannah? Have you ever considered that the dead animal on your doorstep might be related to this?"

She shook her head. "That wasn't anything other than a prank. You said so yourself."

"That was before I found out that you might be attracting the attention of a killer."

"A killer is not going to leave a poor dead animal on my doorstep."

"Killers have a tendency to not be completely sane. Don't discount it just because it doesn't seem harmful."

"All right, fine. But—"

Again Zach held out his hand to stop her. "What's your fax number?"

"Why?"

"So I can fax you the police and coroner's reports. I'm assuming that's why you were going to tell me."

"Dammit, Zach, it wasn't like that."

"The number."

Green fire flashed in her eyes as she rattled off the number.

Zach turned to the door. "I'll read over the letters

tonight. It'll take me some time to find the reports, since old records are in the storage room. Tomorrow okay with you?"

"Zach, please. You have to understand. Ever since my parents' deaths, I've hated my father for destroying our family. No one ever mentioned it might not have happened the way we were told. I had to investigate."

"You think I blame you for investigating? That's not my problem and you damn well know it. You've slept by my side for the past week and you kept this from me."

Knowing why she didn't tell him cut deep into his heart. "Look, I've apologized, Savannah. I know I hurt you and I'd give my life to change what I did ten years ago. I can't go back, I can only go forward. You need to make a decision. Either you trust me or you don't."

With that ultimatum, he walked out the door.

CHAPTER TWENTY-SIX

Rain, like small dismal streams, drizzled down the windowpane. From the window of her bedroom, Savannah looked out into the water-drenched backyard. The gloom of the weather couldn't have reflected her mood any better. She hadn't slept all night. Every time she closed her eyes, she saw Zach's face. She had never meant to hurt him.

Even as she had the thought, her conscience snarled a reprimand. How could he not be hurt? Even if he hadn't learned the truth on his own and she had told him first, he would have asked her when she'd read the first letter. Not telling him immediately was a breach of his trust.

She had to come clean about everything. He would be hurt again, but the longer she waited, the worse it would be. Adrenaline-charged panic flooded through her, familiar and unwelcome. She took deep, cleansing breaths, fought for control and won. What remained was a cold lump of dread that settled in her chest. She didn't talk about that time . . . hadn't in years. But what would be worse? The pain of remembering or keeping the truth from Zach? He had every right to know.

A glance at her watch told her she was going to be late if she didn't get a move on. Gibby's house was only a few miles away, but the rain might slow her down. She hurriedly finished dressing and then ran down the staircase. Just as she reached the bottom step, she spotted Zach getting out of his patrol car.

Straightening her shoulders, she composed herself as she went to the door to let him in. She would invite him to come with her to Gibby's. If her aunt had significant information, then Zach needed to hear it, too. And she would apologize again. Knowing she had hurt him was tearing her apart.

She opened the door before he could ring the bell. "I'm glad you're here. I wanted to—"

The grim set of his face barely gave a warning of impending bad news. "I'm here in an official capacity."

"What do you mean?"

"It's Gibby. Someone broke into her house last night." He paused and softened his voice. "I'm sorry, Savannah. She looks to be in bad shape."

The hospital in Midnight was more of a clinic than anything else. Though it had a half dozen beds and three full-time doctors, most people with life-threatening injuries or illnesses were transferred to County General in Mobile. Zach figured that's where Gibby would end up.

The small waiting room was empty with the exception of him and Savannah. The uncomfortable plastic chair squeaked as he shifted his weight. Savannah paced back and forth in front of him. The worry and guilt etched on her face diminished his anger. Seeing Savannah hurting was a hell of a lot worse than anything she could do to him.

The doctors were still working on her aunt. So far, no one had updated them. The extent of her injuries was unknown but Zach had seen her before the ambulance arrived. No one deserved to be beaten like that, least of all a little elderly woman who'd never hurt anyone in her life. Her house had been cordoned off and his deputies were standing guard. As soon as he talked to the doctor, Zach planned to go back to the house and cover every square inch for evidence.

Savannah had been customarily calm until she'd gotten a glimpse of Gibby's battered face through the small window of the emergency room door. Her gasp of distress had slashed at his self-righteous anger, bringing things into perspective. Finding out who'd hurt an elderly woman was his priority, not his bruised ego.

Abruptly stopping her pacing, she stood in front of him and whispered her words like a confession. "This is my fault."

He'd known that was coming. He wasn't about to let Savannah take the blame for the sick bastard who'd done this. "No, it's not. First, we don't even know if this is related to your parents. It could be a burglary gone wrong. She may have surprised the guy when she came in last night."

Silent, she dropped down into the chair beside him. They both knew it wasn't a burglary gone wrong. He'd stayed up most of the night reading through her grandfather's letters. Daniel Wilde had no proof of his suspicions, but the vague references he'd made of threats to Savannah and her sisters if Daniel didn't drop his questions struck a strong chord in Zach's gut.

The letters, the dead animal at Savannah's doorstep, and now Gibby's injuries didn't exactly scream conspiracy and cover-up, but he'd trusted in his instincts too long to ignore them now.

Had Savannah's questions stirred up a hornet's nest? If her parents were indeed murdered, was the killer still out there or was this just someone's fear that the truth would come out?

"And even if this is related to your parents' deaths, the asshole who did this is responsible. You had every right to ask questions if you thought there was a cover-up."

Before she could say it, he added, "Telling me about it wouldn't have prevented what happened to Gibby. There's no way we could have predicted he'd go after her."

The woman beside him swallowed hard and then gave him a heart-wrenchingly sad smile. "Thank you, Zach, for trying to make me feel better. I don't deserve it."

Zach's fists clenched to keep from reaching out to hold her. When she turned away with a soft sob, he said to hell with it and put his hand on her shoulder. "Savannah . . . don't."

"Miss Wilde?"

They went to their feet. Zach's chest tightened when Savannah grabbed for his hand. He squeezed it gently as they waited to hear the news.

The on-call doctor didn't look old enough to be out of high school, much less a full-fledged physician. Looks were deceiving. Zach had dealt with the doctor several times and knew him to be competent.

"Your aunt is going to be fine. She's got some facial lacerations from her fall, a severely bruised nose, a couple of bruised ribs and a sprained wrist. I was afraid of a broken hip, but it's bruised, not fractured. I'd like to keep her here for a couple of days to monitor her."

Savannah slumped against Zach in relief. "Thank you, Doctor. She looked so hurt, I was afraid—"

Frowning, Zach zeroed in on one word. "Fall? Is that what she told you? That she fell?"

"Yes. She regained consciousness a few moments ago. Said she tripped on the carpet at the top of the stairs and that's the last thing she remembered."

Savannah gasped. "I can't believe she's alive. Those steps are so steep. I told her that—"

Zach interrupted. "She said nothing about an intruder?"

"No. We've not pressured her to talk. She's still

groggy and in some pain. You can see her as soon as we get her into a room, but I'd advise against questioning her too much and getting her agitated."

While Savannah asked a few more questions, Zach thought back over what he found when he'd arrived at Gibby's house. The back door had been unlocked, the bed unmade, and she had been wearing a nightgown, indicating she had either been about to get into bed or had possibly even been asleep when the assailant entered. No way in hell did he believe she had tripped on the carpet and fallen. Had she forgotten what happened or was she too afraid to say?

Zach nodded his thanks to the doctor, who walked away with the promise that a nurse would come and get Savannah when Gibby was in a private room.

The relief on Savannah's face said she bought the story of a fall; she hadn't seen Gibby's house.

"She didn't fall, Savannah."

"Are you sure? She said—"

"I don't care what she said. The back door was unlocked and she was either in bed or getting ready for bed when this went down. Don't tell me an eighty-year-old woman is going to leave her back door unlocked and go to bed. Not even in Midnight, Alabama."

"She could have forgotten to lock the door, Zach. Her memory might not—"

"Agreed. However, I've not seen any indication that she has memory problems. Have you?"

"No. You're right. I was just hoping a fall was all it was."

"You and I need to talk. I read through the letters. I need to know what you've learned."

A multitude of emotions whirled through Savannah. She wished she could take a moment and put her thoughts together but knew that would have to come later. If Gibby's injury was in any way related to her investigation of her parents' deaths, there was no time for the slow, methodical thinking she preferred.

"Give me five minutes to see my aunt and then let's go over to her house."

"While you do that, I'm calling a couple of friends of mine, Brody James and Logan Wright. They run a private security company in Mobile. I want Gibby guarded 24/7 and I don't have the manpower to spare."

An ache that had nothing to do with today's events swept through her. Zach, ever the protector and defender—the boy she had fallen in love with still had the same strength and honor as before. Had her hurt blinded her to that fact? Was that why she hadn't told him about the letters from the beginning? Guilt sliced at her conscience with the decisive precision of a machete. He had tried to exonerate her, telling her that this wasn't her fault. She wasn't so sure. If they'd been working together all this time, could Gibby's assault have been prevented?

Savannah pulled her cellphone from her purse. "While you do that, I'm going to call Sammie and Bri. They were coming here this weekend anyway, but they need to know about Gibby."

His expression stoic and grim, Zach nodded and pulled his cellphone from his pocket. Was his serious, businesslike demeanor because he was in chief-of-police mode or something else? Had her selfishness and lack of trust destroyed what she was only now realizing she wanted above all else?

The Wilde house was strangely silent. Zach and Savannah sat at the kitchen table, both lost in their own thoughts.

After a thorough search of the inside and outside of Gibby's house, Zach was convinced of a break-in. The

rain overnight had washed away any telltale prints outside, but a large muddy footprint in the kitchen gave
him an idea of the size of the man. Problem was, there
were a hell of a lot of men in Midnight with a 10½ shoe
size.

Another giveaway had been the back door. The lock
was so damn flimsy, a two-year-old could have broken
in, but the wood surrounding the latch had fresh gouges
and scratches. Someone had jimmied the lock.

Savannah had walked through the house with him
and didn't believe anything had been stolen. Gibby
would have to confirm that, but the house was neat and
seemingly untouched. The television and DVD player in
the living room and laptop computer in the small study
beside the kitchen were out in the open and would've
been easy to carry out. Gibby's purse lay on the hallway
table with her wallet, cash, and credit cards intact. This
had been no burglary.

Brody James was now at the hospital guarding Gibby's room. Had Gibby's attacker meant to kill the elderly woman or just scare the hell out of her? Zach
believed the former. She'd been pushed down an entire
flight of stairs. It was a miracle she wasn't dead. And
when the bastard learned she wasn't dead, would he be
back to finish the job? Brody James would make sure
that didn't happen.

Before they'd left the hospital, he and Savannah had
briefly visited Gibby. Seeing the usually cheerful and
spry woman so beaten up and hurt had infuriated Zach.
Whoever had done this wouldn't get away with it. He'd
make sure of it.

Gibby had been so out of it, she'd barely recognized
Savannah. He hoped like hell she would remember
something when he talked with her again.

He glanced over at Savannah, who looked both worried and furious. While he wanted to reassure her, Zach

held himself back. The blow she'd dealt him last night still stung. He had to push it aside for right now, though. Nothing was more important than learning the truth.

"Okay, let's go over what you know," Zach said.

Her huff of exasperation was reassuring. He hadn't liked seeing the fear and sadness in her eyes. Anger was a much healthier emotion.

"You act as if I've known about this forever, Zach. I found the letters last week. All I've done so far is talk to Gibby, read the newspaper accounts of the events, and ask a few vague questions at Faye's Diner, which was the biggest bust of all. I learned nothing. And I've talked to a few of Mama and Daddy's friends about when they were alive. The one person who I thought could really tell me something was Harlan Mosby. Unfortunately I got to the hospital too late."

"That's why you went to Mobile?"

She grimaced. "That was the main reason but I really did drop a load of stuff off at the Salvation Army."

"So the night before you go to talk to Harlan about his investigation of your parents' deaths, he conveniently dies."

She nodded. "Exactly what I thought. The doctor swore his death was imminent . . . completely expected. He practically laughed in my face when I suggested someone might have killed him."

Zach already knew that Harlan's body had been cremated. Proving that someone had assisted Harlan into going on to the next life would be impossible.

"You said you've talked to your parents' friends. Did you learn anything from them?"

"No. Since I didn't want to arouse anyone's suspicions, I tried to keep my questions more of a conversation than a questioning. Subtlety yielded zero results."

"Since someone tried to kill your aunt, I'd say it did produce one result."

She wilted in front of him like a scorched flower. His remark had been a low blow and he knew it. He'd said it to intentionally hurt her and immediately felt like shit. "I'm sorry, Savannah, I—"

The hurt in her eyes disappeared and was replaced by determination. "Fine. You're right. I screwed up. But here's the thing—why go after Gibby? Why not come after me? I'm the one asking the questions, not her."

"Maybe he thinks she knows something."

She nodded. "Exactly."

The light bulb came on and Zach cursed himself for not thinking of it before. Last night at the dinner party, Gibby had, very loudly, told Savannah she had thought of something she needed to tell her that would aid in her investigation. Anyone in the house could have heard her.

Zach grabbed the notepad she had in front of her. "Name everyone who was there last night and their relationship to your parents."

While she jotted down the names, Zach stood and, without giving it much thought, opened the fridge and took out a pitcher of lemonade. Holding it up, he said, "Want some?"

A small smile curved her lips. "Yes. Thanks."

"What's so amusing?"

"Nothing, really. I just like the way you make yourself at home."

He poured two glasses and set them on the table. "Get used to it."

"What do you mean?"

"I mean that until this is over, I'm living here."

He prepared himself, sure that his blunt statement would get her back up. She surprised the hell out of him when she said, "I like the sound of that."

A gut punch of arousal stole his breath. Damn, he wanted her. Here. Now. On the table, stripped bare, begging for pleasure. Zach downed his beverage in two gulps, hoping the ice-cold drink would diminish the heat. Until they got some things settled between them, that wasn't going to happen.

She slid the notepad across the table. "I can't believe any of them would do this. They all seem so harmless and have been so kind to me."

His eyes scanned the list. "I agree, but you know as well as anyone that looks can be deceiving."

She nodded. "Seems like every few months, I prosecute someone for a heinous crime while everyone else claims shock, saying he seemed like such a nice, quiet guy." Savannah pushed away from the table and stood. "I need to go back and check on Gibby."

"I'll drive you. Maybe she'll be alert enough to talk."

"The doctor said she should be able to come home in a couple of days. I'm thinking about asking her if she wants to stay here."

"I'd let her go home. She'll be more comfortable there. Brody can protect her."

"Sammie and Bri can help out, too. They'll be here tomorrow."

He was surprised Savannah didn't suggest that Sammie or Bri would be protection enough for her, too. Not that it would do any good. Until this case was closed, he would be with her day and night. After that? Zach pushed aside the thought.

Fury swept through Savannah once more as she gazed down at Gibby. The bruises and swelling were more apparent than ever. Her sweet aunt was almost unrecognizable. How could anyone hurt an innocent old lady?

"I promise you, honey, it looks worse than it is," Gibby insisted.

Savannah refused to believe this wasn't her fault. If

she had been more discreet, none of this would have happened. Was this the reason her grandfather had never pursued the truth? A killer in the midst of Midnight seemed ludicrous. Evil wasn't limited to urban areas, she knew; it was just that her hometown had always seemed to stay the same. Now she knew that sameness had been hiding her parents' killer.

"Miss Gibby, you feel up to talking?" Zach asked.

Gibby tried to sit up and then gasped. Savannah was there immediately to stop her and then raised the bed slightly. Zach put another pillow behind her head to help prop her up.

"I'll try my best, Zach, but I can't say I remember much. If I rightly recall, I was getting ready for bed and Samson started meowing real loud. He only does that if something upsets him. I went to pick him up and heard something out in the hallway. I opened the door and didn't see anything, so I stepped out of the bedroom and went to the top of the stairs. I felt someone's hands push me forward. Next thing I knew, I was waking up here in the hospital."

"The doctor said you told him you'd fallen," Zach said.

"Well, I wasn't about to tell him what really happened. What if he mentioned it to someone?"

"Last night at Lamont and Nesta's, you said you had something to tell me. What was it?"

"After your mama and daddy passed, your granddaddy was in a pickle. He was just so worried about you three girls and how this was going to affect you. Lots of people offered to help, some of them even wanted to adopt one of you or all of you, but there was one person who specifically wanted only you, Savannah."

A chill zipped up her spine. Though Savannah and her sisters were identical, the discerning eye could tell them apart. However, even at an early age, people were calling Savannah "Little Maggie" because, except for the wavy hair she'd inherited from her father, she was the spitting image of her mother. She met Zach's eyes and then looked at Gibby again. "Who was it?"

Gibby grimaced. "That's the thing . . . I don't know. Daniel was insulted by all the offers but that was the one that made him uncomfortable."

Revulsion roiled in Savannah's stomach. Someone had wanted her because she looked like her mother. Had that someone had anything to do with Maggie's death?

"Did you notice if Granddad started treating any particular person different than before?"

"Oh, honey, he treated everyone different. Even me." A fleeting expression of hurt appeared on Gibby's battered face. "Guess he didn't trust anyone after that, even family. You and your sisters were his life. He would have done anything to protect you."

Savannah knew that to be true. Her granddad's life had changed dramatically when her parents died. He had stopped socializing with friends and had rarely gone anywhere unless it pertained to his granddaughters. She had often felt guilty about them taking over his life so completely. Now she wondered if he'd closed himself off for a different reason. Because he had no real idea who might have killed her parents, had he suspected everyone? And not knowing who was responsible, had trusted no one?

How she wished she had known these things earlier. If he had shared this secret, maybe they could have discovered the truth together. A fresh wave of grief immobilized her. She had known her granddad had dealt with a lot, she just hadn't known how much.

A large hand grabbed hers and squeezed gently. She looked up into Zach's face and was surprised at the depth of sympathy in his eyes. Longing built up inside her for this wonderful, caring man. She had hurt him with her silence but he was still here for her, offering her his sympathy and support.

Zach held her gaze for a moment, giving her the comfort she so desperately needed. Then, squeezing her hand once more, he turned back to Gibby. "Do you have any suspicions about anyone?"

"I wish I did, Zach. Lord knows there's lots of mean people in this world and this town has its share. Problem is, this person is probably someone we know and would never suspect."

"When you're released, I want you to come stay with me until this is over," Savannah said.

An unusual hardness changed Gibby's expression from that of a badly battered victim to that of an infuriated, determined woman. "I most certainly will not. I've lived in that house more than seventy years. Nobody's going to run me out of it."

"Then Brody, Zach's friend, will stay with you until it's over."

"If you think I'm going to argue about having that sweet young man who's standing outside my room staying in my house, you've got another think coming."

While Zach swallowed what sounded like a snort, Savannah grinned at her aunt. Brody James had probably not been called sweet since he was in diapers. Zach had introduced her to him when they arrived at the hospital. The man was well over six feet tall and more than two hundreds pounds of mostly muscle. A look from his dark brown eyes would make the meanest criminal turn tail and run. But Aunt Gibby had always had a different way of looking at people.

"Do you need anything?"

Gibby shook her head. "Hester, bless her heart, is coming back in a few minutes with some of my things. She's also going to take care of Samson and Oscar for the next few days." Waving her hand at them, she closed her eyes. "You go on now and find out who this terrible person is before he hurts someone else."

Savannah leaned over and kissed Gibby's forehead, feeling an intense affection for the woman who had been in her life for as long as she could remember. They had often laughed at Gibby's antics and tolerated her eccentricities. This incident had brought home to Savannah just how much she loved the older woman. It could have been so much worse.

Zach opened the door for her and they walked out of the room together. Brody was leaning against the wall. Heavily muscled arms were crossed in front of him in a forbidding pose, the vivid tattoos on them making him look all the more fierce.

"Thank you for coming on such short notice and looking out for Gibby. She's very special to me."

Brody gave a nod. "My pleasure, ma'am. She's a real sweet woman."

Savannah held back a laugh. Apparently both Brody and Gibby thought the other was sweet.

"Besides," Brody continued, "Zach only has to ask. He knows Logan and I would do anything for him."

Based on her earlier conversation with Zach, Savannah knew that both Brody and Logan had served with him in the army. She was surprised to see a slight flush of color on Zach's cheeks at Brody's words. There was definitely a story there.

Zach backslapped Brody once again and then they headed outside, back to the patrol car.

Savannah breathed in the hot, humid air of another steamy summer's day in Midnight. Everything seemed peaceful, normal and nonthreatening. The phrase "still waters run deep" aptly fit this town. Who would have guessed that her lazy little hometown held a murderer in its easygoing, laid-back midst?

Suddenly remembering a question she'd meant to ask Zach the moment she saw him this morning, she said, "The police and coroner's reports. Did you have a chance to find them?"

His already grim face went darker. "Yes and no."

She stopped in the middle of the parking lot. "What does that mean?"

"The police report was half-assed . . . barely one page. No photographs of the scene. Two statements from witnesses claiming your father was enraged at the country club. One statement from the bartender at Shorty's Bar saying your father had four bourbons. Two more witness statements from the bar's patrons who said he sat at the bar drinking for a couple of hours and then left."

"No photographs?" Savannah shook her head, appalled at how unprofessional and inept Mosby had been. "What about the coroner's report? There should be a—" She broke off abruptly when he started shaking his head.

"Only one coroner's report—your mother's. Nothing for your daddy."

"That makes no sense. There has to be."

"If there was, it's been lost or was destroyed."

At a loss, she could only stare at him. She would review the police report and coroner's report for her mother's death, but it was the one for her father she had hoped to glean the most information from. That report was the only substantial piece of evidence she would have had to prove that he didn't kill himself. The coroner would have pointed out any other injuries her father had, including defensive wounds. Beckett Wilde would have fought tooth and nail to save not only his life, but also his wife's. The murderer would have had to be as large as or even larger than her father to be able to hang him. And he would have fought with all of his might to prevent that. The report could have revealed so much. Without it, she had nothing.

Unknowingly, she spoke the words out loud. "What am I going to do?"

"Not you, Savannah. We. And what we're going to do is find out who killed your parents."

She took him in then—strong, determined jaw, intelligent eyes, and the honor that had drawn her to him so many years ago. This was a man she could depend on. It shamed her that she had told him she forgave him and trusted him but she so obviously hadn't. But now they had come full circle. The trust was there as it had once been.

She held out her hand to him and blew out a silent relieved sigh when he took it. Giving him a smile of confidence because she truly believed that between the two of them they could conquer anything, she said, "You're right. We are."

CHAPTER TWENTY-SEVEN

Savannah rubbed her throbbing temples as she tried to decipher Mosby's illegible handwriting. What she could make out was a hodgepodge of opinion, not fact. He arrived at the scene, saw her mother's body on the dining room floor. He started looking around, found Beckett hanging from a giant oak tree out back with a note of confession stuffed in his shirt pocket. It supposedly said he killed Maggie and couldn't live with the guilt. So where the hell was the note? Why were there no photographs? No coroner's report for her father? There was absolutely nothing other than a half-page report of Mosby's rambling conjectures.

She dropped the worthless report on the table and sighed. "If nothing else, this report confirms that Mosby was in on the cover-up."

Zach nodded. "Or he did the crime."

That was true. She had never considered Mosby a suspect, only a dishonest officer of the law. "What about the deputies back then? Couldn't we talk—"

She cut off when Zach started shaking his head. "I checked. There were only two and they're both dead."

"Dead how?"

"Car accident and heart attack. Besides, there's no indication that any other law enforcement official was even at the crime scene. Apparently Mosby handled this on his own."

"And the coroner?"

"He's gone, too. He retired and moved to Florida. Died just last year."

She huffed out a breath. Everything led to a dead end. "Okay, so even if Mosby did the killings, he would still have to have help. My dad was a big man. No way could he get him in that tree by himself."

Zach shrugged. "Mosby was a strong man. I had a few run-ins with him and can attest to that. And a motivated man can often do more than what looks possible. His motive to kill your parents is what I can't get my head around."

"I agree. It makes no sense."

"I found out he'd been taking bribes from multiple sources for years. If he didn't do the deed himself, he might've just agreed to a cover-up for the money alone."

Standing, Zach picked up their coffee cups and went to the kitchen counter. "Want more coffee?"

She shook her head and grimaced. "Don't think my stomach can handle more caffeine."

"Which is exactly why you should eat something."

"I'm not hungry."

"You've changed."

"Why do you say that?"

"Stress used to make you eat more. Remember those first few dates we had? I thought I was going to have to pry you away from the table."

Her smile self-deprecating, she said, "If my mouth was full, it meant I couldn't say anything stupid."

He came and sat across the table from her again. "I don't remember you ever saying anything stupid."

She snorted and rolled her eyes. "Then you weren't listening."

"I listened to everything, Savannah," he said quietly.

"I know you did," she said softly. "You were a great listener."

"I still am." He waited a breath and said, "Why didn't you take my calls when I finally got up the guts to get in touch with you?"

Like an extinguished flame, the light disappeared from her face. She shook her head. "Let's not go there right now, Zach."

Would his gut ever stop hurting every time he thought about those days? After finally gathering up the courage to call and apologize and tell her what happened, she had refused to take his calls. He'd been stupid and naïve, believing that was all it would take for her to forgive him. Leaving without an explanation had been the most cowardly thing he'd ever done. And the result had been a broken heart for Savannah and years of remorse and regret for Zach.

"I came to see you in Nashville."

She jerked, clearly startled at his admission. "When?"

"About a year after I tried calling you. I was about to be deployed to Iraq for the first time. I needed to see you . . . I couldn't stop thinking about you. I knew I'd see action . . . might even die. I couldn't live with the thought of never seeing you again and trying to apologize one more time."

"But why . . . what . . . ?"

"Why didn't I follow through?"

"Yes," she whispered.

"I saw you on campus."

Shock . . . and something else flared in her green eyes. "You did?"

His mind went back to that day, remembering it as one of the worst days in his existence. Considering that he'd had some damn bad days, that meant something. She had been sitting on a bench, beneath a tree. Her hair had been pulled away from her face with a barrette, highlighting the incredible purity of her skin. At first he had just stood and looked, thinking she was even more beautiful than she'd been the last time he saw her. Finally the need to be close to her, to touch her, had moved his feet forward. She was reading a book, completely unaware of her surroundings. He'd been about three yards away from her when he'd heard someone shout her name. Zach had stopped in his tracks. She had looked up and waved at the man who came running toward her. The smile of welcome on her face had stolen his breath, but it was watching her go into the guy's arms that had almost brought him to his knees. The man had swung her in the air. Then Zach heard her laugh—it was one of joy and intimacy. He had backed away, disappearing quickly and quietly. That was the day he'd given up hope and let her go for good.

"Zach?"

She was looking at him expectantly, waiting for an answer. He suddenly regretted telling her. What was she supposed to do with that information? He had no right to question whether she was still seeing the guy. He'd given up that right.

Still, he had come this far. "You were sitting under a tree, on a park bench. You wore a blue sundress, tan sandals with a little blue flower on them, and your nails were painted a pale pink color."

"You were that close?"

He nodded, unable to speak as the pain in his gut traveled up to his chest.

"Why, Zach? Why wouldn't you tell me you were there?"

Though full disclosure felt like a knife ripping into his belly, she deserved the truth. "I was about to when a guy called out your name. You smiled at him and went into his arms. You both looked so damn happy." He shrugged. "I knew I was too late."

* * *

Stunned, Savannah sat glued to her chair, barely breathing. Part of her wanted to get up and run, hide from those piercing gray eyes that had always seen through her. Another part wanted to pull him close and hold him next to her heart. He wasn't bothering to hide his pain, the despair he had felt.

What would she have done if she had spotted him that day? Would she have run to him or away? After working so hard to regain her health and sanity, would seeing him have put her back on the edge again? Or would it have healed her completely? She would never know.

She remembered that day and that moment quite well. How odd that Zach had been there to witness it. "He was a friend, Zach. Nothing more. He was flunking one of his classes . . . I helped him prepare for his final. That was the day he learned that he'd passed. He came to thank me. That's all."

The agony in his eyes was her undoing. She walked around the table and, without asking permission, sat in his lap and wrapped her arms around him.

For a moment he was frozen and she wondered if she had done the wrong thing. Then, as if a dam burst, he held her tight against him as he buried his face in her hair. "I am so damn sorry, Savannah. About everything."

Oh God, this hurt. Tears pricked her eyes and her throat closed with shared grief. "Zach . . . I need to tell—"

The radio, attached to Zach's right shoulder, squawked, "Chief Tanner?"

Savannah didn't know whose sigh was the loudest or more ragged, hers or Zach's. His arms loosened with reassuring reluctance and she went to her feet.

"I'm here. What's up?"

"Ethel Mae Hendrix called. Said somebody busted out the windows of her delivery van and wrote something nasty on the side of it. Arthur and Bart are out on calls."

"Okay. I'll head over there now." He stood and said, "I've got to go."

"I know."

Surprising her, he pulled her back into his arms and just held her. Contentment swept through Savannah. She wanted nothing more than to stay like this forever.

Zach pulled away but held on to her shoulders, forcing her to look up at him.

"Look, I know we've done things backward since you came back, but this is something real, Savannah."

Her breath caught in her throat. "I . . ."

"Don't say anything yet. I know we've got a lot of other issues facing us, including finding your parents' killer. When I get back, we'll go over what little evidence we have together and come up with a plan. Okay?"

She nodded mutely.

"Stay here. I don't want you out alone until we catch this bastard."

She nodded again.

His soft kiss felt like a promise and a new beginning. As he stalked out the door, Savannah slumped down into the first available chair. Yes, they did have a killer to catch. With Zach and her sisters working the case, she had no doubt they would be successful. But then what? There were issues he didn't even know about yet. Things that could bring them together or drive a wedge between them that nothing could heal.

Her eyes caught sight of the inept police report. First things first. There was a killer out there who'd not only taken her parents' lives, but had almost taken Gibby's. They had to find him.

Her grandfather's letters were now her only recourse. She had read through the ones immediately following her parents' deaths all the way up to three months after. But had anything happened after that?

When Bri and Sammie arrived, they could read through them all. For now, she would continue reading in hopes she could find something else.

Energized by the thought, Savannah poured herself another glass of iced tea and headed to the guesthouse. If it was the last thing she did, she would find more evidence that would finally bring peace to her and her sisters and justice for her parents.

Warning bells blasted like cannons through Zach's mind as he glared at the middle-aged, gray-haired woman standing at her front door. "What the hell do you mean you didn't call in a report?"

Ethel Mae Hendrix backed up warily, staring at him as if he had two heads. "Just what I said, Chief. I haven't been home all week. In fact, I wasn't supposed to be home until tomorrow but I got done with my business and came back early."

Zach had stopped listening. Grabbing his cellphone from his pocket, he punched in Savannah's number as he ran back to his car. After the fifth ring with no answer, Zach hit the gas and began to pray. He was on the other side of town, which meant it could take up to seven minutes before he reached the Wilde house.

As he continued to call Savannah's cellphone, he grabbed the radio mic. "Hazel, you there?"

"Yeah, I'm here, Chief. What's up?"

"We got any units close to Wildefire Lane?"

"No . . . Something going on?"

"That call you took from Ethel Mae. Can you check the number, see where it came from?"

"Sure. Hold on."

While he waited, he pressed the redial number on his cell and once again it went to voice mail. Where the hell was she? He refused to believe anything had happened to her. Dammit, it was broad daylight and this was Midnight-fucking-Alabama, where everybody and their brother knew what you were doing before you even did it. No way would anyone be stupid enough to try something.

"Chief, can't trace the number. Looks like it might've come from one of those throwaway cellphones."

"But it was definitely a woman who placed the call?"

"Yes, definitely a woman. Sounded like Ethel Mae to me."

Or someone who'd disguised her voice to sound like Ethel Mae. Hell, were they looking at this all wrong? Was Maggie and Beckett Wilde's murderer a woman? How was that possible? It would take an enormous amount of strength to hang an unconscious man. No way would Beckett have been alive and willingly hung himself.

The radio crackled again and Hazel's voice said urgently, "Chief, there's a report of a fire over on Wildefire Lane."

Shit! Pushing ninety on a curvy two-lane road might seem insane, but if anything happened to Savannah, insanity would be the least of his problems.

Savannah lowered the letter she'd been reading and inhaled deeply. Was that smoke? Taking another deep breath confirmed her thoughts. Yes, there was a definite hint of smoke in the air. Someone was probably burning off woods or yard clippings.

She turned back to the letter. This one was dated just months before her grandfather died. His words indicated that the truth continued to haunt him. How she wished he had shared those worries with his family. But even after all that time, he continued to be concerned for his granddaughters' safety.

She sniffed again. Was the smell getting stronger? And why would anyone be burning off woods or yard clippings? Though it had stopped raining, the ground and woods were drenched.

She stood and headed out the bedroom door. The smell was stronger in the hallway. Her heart kicking up a beat, she rushed toward the living room, then jerked to a halt at the entrance. The entire living room and kitchen area were rapidly filling with smoke. The guest-house was on fire?

Holding her breath to keep from inhaling, she ran to the front door. The house was small enough that she could be outside in seconds. She turned the doorknob and pulled. Nothing budged. There was only one lock on the door; it wasn't locked, it was stuck. How?

She told herself not to panic; there were plenty of other ways out of the house. Savannah turned around. Just in the short amount of time she'd been tugging on the door, the smoke had gotten thicker. There was a back door but she'd have to run to the other end of the house, through several smoke-filled rooms, to get to it. Window. She would go out through a window.

In the distance, she heard her cellphone ring. She'd left it lying on the bed. Going back to get it was too dangerous. Her only recourse was to go through a window and then call for help from the main house.

The smoke was so thick, her vision was becoming useless. She dropped to her knees and crawled to the front window. Holding her shirtsleeve in front of her face, she used her fingers to feel around for the lock. Finally she found it and clicked it open, then pushed the window up. Only it wouldn't move. This was ridiculous.

She'd opened this window hundreds of times during the fall and spring. She shoved harder, barely comprehending that wood splintered, cutting the tips of her fingers. A fit of coughing seized her. The smoke was even thicker, obscuring everything. There was another window in the kitchen. She squeezed her stinging eyes tight, appreciating the tears that gave her some relief.

Wait. She could break the window. There was a lamp beside the sofa. She could use it to break the glass and then crawl out. The thought of shredding her legs on the glass was a lot less terrifying than dying of smoke inhalation or burning to death. Unable to see clearly, she stretched her arms out to feel. She knew every square inch of this house; why couldn't she find the lamp? It should be right in front of her.

Time was running out. She'd have to go to the other window. She dropped to her knees again and scurried as fast as she could to the kitchen. When her head hit something solid—the kitchen table—she sobbed in relief. The window was on the other side of the table. Crawling carefully but quickly, she made her way around the table and then stood, arms out in front of her, feeling blindly. Yes, there it was. She felt around for the lock, unlatched it and pushed. Wouldn't budge. Refusing to give up, Savannah turned around and grabbed a kitchen chair. With all of her might, she slammed it against the window. The reverberation rattled her entire body and the chair broke in her hand, but the window didn't crack. Leaded, reinforced glass—a great energy saver but right now she'd give anything if the windows were made of the cheapest material. She could bang on it all day and end up with a bruised or broken hand but no broken glass.

Her heart pounded as fear and dread set in. Someone had set fire to the guesthouse and had blocked all exits. She could hear her breath rasping from her lungs. Dizziness hit her. She dropped to her knees before she fell. Panic tried to overwhelm good sense. She didn't want to die like this. Not when she and Zach had just now found each other again. And her parents' killer? Would he get away with another murder? No!

Savannah forced herself to think. There had to be another way.

The third floor—attic. Yes! Whether her muddled mind imagined the voice or a disembodied voice had actually said the words, she didn't know. But that was her only hope. Tugging her shirt off, she held it in front of her face and, with all the strength she could muster, scurried toward the stairway.

Dark smoke so thick it was like a living entity swirled around her. Seconds became minutes. Then, finally, her knees touched wood. She had reached the stairway.

Her reserves fading fast, Savannah stayed as low as she could and ran instead of crawled up the stairway. If she could make it to the attic, she would crawl out onto the roof and shimmy down the trellis at the back of the house. She hadn't done that in years but it was her only hope.

She made it to the second floor, refused to stop. She told herself that she wasn't hurting; that her lungs weren't aching and her eyes weren't stinging.

She pictured Zach, his beautiful, handsome face. She thought about their future, what they had lost and what they might still have. She thought about Sammie and Bri . . . and Aunt Gibby. Thinking of her loved ones forced energy into her overtaxed body. Forcing her feet to move, she ran toward the staircase that led to the third floor. Seconds later, she practically fell onto the stairs and began to move up. A distant amusement hit her that she was actually sliding up the stairs. It didn't matter how she got there . . . she just had to get there.

Finally in the third-floor hallway, she counted seven

steps to her right. The attic door. Taking a running leap, she slammed into the door, turned the knob, and fell face-first into the room. A distant voice told her to shut the door. With little energy left, she managed to kick her foot out and slam the door shut.

Forcing herself to her feet, she looked around and almost cried. A tidal wave of blackness devoured the air with a voracious appetite eating up all oxygen and replacing it with poison. If the smoke had reached this far up, the house would be engulfed in fire within minutes. Swaying dizzily, she headed toward the other side of the room where the giant window led onto the roof. Whoever had blocked her exit downstairs . . . had they thought to block this one, too?

Lungs screaming for clean, fresh air, she tried to concentrate on taking shallow breaths as she felt for the window. Tears flooded her stinging eyes. Determinedly, Savannah refused to give up. Zach would know by now that something was wrong. She couldn't die now . . . not when they'd just found each other again. She couldn't.

In a small part of her brain, she realized that her thinking was befuddled and hazy. Panic could do that but so could air deprivation. Dear God, was this it? No, she refused to believe this would be the end of her life. The bastard had taken her parents, he would damn well not take her, too.

A sob built in her throat she refused to allow. She needed every bit of her breath to stay conscious. Thankfully the attic was small, only covering the back portion of the house. She could do this, she had to do this. At last, her hands touched resistance again. A wall. Was the window close by? Her hand moved over the rough surface of the wall, searching . . . searching. Sweet Lord, where was the window? On the verge of believing she needed to start over again, she touched glass. The window!

Taking a chance, knowing she only had a few precious seconds before unconsciousness claimed her, she reached for the windowsill. Teeth gritted for strength, she jerked it up. Stuck! No, not possible. She tugged and tugged. Not stuck. Locked. Stupid, stupid . . . Her hand listlessly lifted toward the lock and clicked it open. Then, with the last of her strength, she raised the window. Sweet, fresh air greeted her lungs.

Sobbing and shouting for Zach in her mind, Savannah crawled through the window, vaguely aware of the pain in her knees where the roof scraped her skin. Roaring in her head made her wonder, Was that the sound of fire roaring toward her? Was she about to be consumed?

Her last thought was the vision of a blue sky and the beauty of a peaceful summer's day in Midnight.

"Chief Tanner, you need to get out of here. Now!"

Fear like he'd never known clawed at Zach's heart. His shouts were going unanswered. She was here in the guesthouse, he knew she was. The damn door had been wedged shut . . . she couldn't have escaped. She was still here. "Savannah!"

"Chief, there's not much time left. Get out now!"

Zach ignored the fireman behind him. He had to find her. He'd already been in every room on the first floor. The fire had started in the back of the house, close to the kitchen. The flames were growing heavier. The firemen were working valiantly, but saving the structure might not be possible. But dammit, saving Savannah was.

Racing up the stairs, he continued to yell. As he went from room to room, the small oxygen tank they had loaned him pumped fresh air into his lungs. The goggles protected his eyes, but the smoke was so heavy it was almost impossible to see anything.

Standing at the top of the landing, he lifted the oxygen mask and shouted, "Savannah! Where are you?"

Nothing. Had she gotten out? How? Where? He turned and ran toward the stairway to the third floor. The attic. Maybe she was in the attic. Shouts from the outside stopped him cold. "There she is! At the back . . . the roof!"

Relief gave his feet wings as he raced downstairs, out the door, and to the back of the house. A ladder was being leaned against the building and a fireman was already halfway up. Zach followed him, once again ignoring the shouts for him to stay back. When at last he reached the roof, his heart that had been rejoicing stopped and slammed to the ground. Savannah lay facedown on the roof, unmoving. No, no, no . . . He couldn't be too late.

CHAPTER TWENTY-EIGHT

Agony in her chest woke her. Willing her eyes to open, she realized that they wouldn't cooperate. What was wrong? Where was she? Why did she hurt so much? Panic seized her, causing her breath to labor; more intense pain clutched her chest.

"Shh," a deep, dearly familiar voice whispered. "You're going to be fine. Just breathe slowly."

Zach. She tried to speak, but her mouth wouldn't cooperate. Questions filled her dazed brain. She dug deep, beneath the pain and confusion, searching for reason. Finally it came. Smoke . . . a fire. Someone had tried to kill her . . . had burned down the guesthouse. What about the mansion? Had it burned down, too? Tears seeped from her closed lids, causing them to sting. A sob built in her chest, causing a new agony.

"Savannah, listen to me. You're going to be fine. You inhaled too much smoke and you're on oxygen. Your eyes are fine, too. The doctor has treated them and said your vision won't be compromised. You just need to rest."

Struggling with all her might, she managed a croaking whisper: "The house?"

"The guesthouse is gone. The mansion is untouched."

Relieved and grateful, Savannah at last managed to open her eyes. Zach's red-rimmed eyes and charcoal-blackened face was the most beautiful sight she'd ever seen. "Thank you," she whispered.

A smile lifted his mouth but his eyes remained worried and behind that worry was a simmering rage. The fact that someone had gone to so much trouble and risk astounded her. The killer either believed she knew something or there was evidence he didn't want her to find. The letters . . . oh God, the letters were gone.

"Letters?" she whispered.

"All gone, I'm afraid. I'm sorry, Savannah."

She would deal with that knowledge later. "Aunt . . . Gibby?"

"She's fine. I hadn't planned to tell her until she could see you were all right for herself. Unfortunately Hester got to her first. I assured her you were going to be okay and would be by to see her in a day or so, after you're rested up. I've had to turn half the town away from your door. Everyone is worried about you."

Amazing. With the exception of her family, she'd always felt like such a loner in this town. Having that many people concerned for her gave her a warm feeling until she remembered that one of those people might well be a killer. Had one of them wanted to see her to finish off the job?

She lifted her hand, surprised at how heavy it felt, and tenderly traced the grim lines around his mouth. "Tired?"

Taking her hand in his, he pressed a kiss against her palm. "Scared. So very scared, babe."

Zach never called her an endearment, it had never been his style. The fact that he did now made her wonder. " 'Babe?' " she whispered.

A grin lifted his mouth and finally his eyes smiled, too. " 'Sugar' and 'honey doll' just don't fit the occasion."

Her mouth twitched slightly in a halfhearted attempt

at a smile. Hopefully "honey doll" would never fit the occasion.

His eyes darkened with emotion. "I never want to go through something like that again. We've got to find this fucker before he succeeds in killing someone else."

"Ideas?"

"Yeah. Remember the call I got about Ethel Mae's van?"

She nodded.

"It was a fake call."

She shook her head slowly. No, that didn't make sense . . . did it? "A woman?"

"Yeah."

A woman was doing this? A woman had killed her mother and father? "No . . . sense."

"No, it doesn't make sense, but we'll get to the bottom of it. I checked with Ethel Mae about who knew she would be out of town. Apparently she's gone every year around this time and most everyone knows about it. So that doesn't narrow down our suspects one iota."

"How long . . ." She winced, swallowed, and continued, "Stay . . . here?"

"At least overnight. You were damn lucky. The doctor said you didn't inhale enough smoke to damage your lungs. Brody's partner, Logan Wright, is on his way here from Mobile. He'll alternate with Brody on guarding your aunt. Also, I called Bri and Sammie. They'll be here first thing tomorrow."

A thought stopped her cold. She took a deep breath. Wincing, she spoke as quickly as she could, hoping to minimize the pain in her chest and throat. "A woman hung my father? Not possible. He was six feet tall and weighed close to two hundred pounds."

"She obviously had help. Or maybe a man did this and a woman is helping him for whatever reason."

So the list she had made was still valid. A man and a

woman. A couple? Gruesome and scary, but it made sense. The couples at the party had all been friends with her parents. If one had committed the murder, then the other might have chosen to help. Or it had been a plan between the two of them. Still, what had they hoped to gain by killing her parents? Was it out of spite or envy?

With the attempted murder of Gibby and now Savannah, keeping their investigation a secret was no longer desirable or necessary. Each person on the list of suspects they had devised could be questioned individually. Someone she knew, someone she and her family had trusted for years, had committed the awful crime. And they had made it clear that they would kill again. Desperate people committed desperate acts. If the killers weren't identified soon, what else would they do and who else would be their target?

Savannah woke on a gasp. Bright sunlight, streaming through the sheer drapes at the window, chased away the remnants of a nightmare filled with smoke, fire, and death. She sat up and hissed at the pain. Her entire body felt as though someone had beaten her. Knowing how lucky she was to be alive made that pain bearable, though.

She had been released from the hospital early this morning. Instead of taking her home, Zach had brought her to his house. She hadn't questioned why. Her almost dying yesterday had a major impact on both of them. Seeing the abject terror in Zach's eyes made her want to do whatever she could do to diminish his fear. In turn, Zach was treating her like she was made of spun glass.

After placing her in his bed, he'd lain beside her and held her until she fell back asleep. In his arms, no matter what happened, she felt safe, warm, and cherished. She knew she was loved.

Yesterday she hadn't had the energy to put a coherent

thought to work. Today that had to change. They had to find this maniac before he succeeded in killing someone else. And when this was over, she and Zach were going to have some lengthy alone time.

Losing her grandfather's letters was a blow, as was losing the guesthouse. Sadness still lingered but a welcome and necessary pragmatism was taking over. It was done; there was nothing they could do to save what was lost. The important thing was to dwell on what they had.

She heard them before she saw them. Running steps and then two beautiful women burst into the room at the same time. Bri ran to one side of the bed, Sammie the other.

Sammie had long, straight blond hair that fell past her shoulders, and perfect makeup that, as usual, looked as though it had been professionally applied. Her white sundress was delicately feminine, emphasizing the natural elegance her sister had been born with.

Seemingly just the opposite of her stylish sister, Bri kept her bleached white-blond hair so short it spiked in places. She wore minimal makeup and had on her usual attire—jeans, a white T-shirt, and running shoes.

Both were beautiful, with almost identical features, and yet they were so incredibly different.

Tears pooled in Sammie's eyes as she grabbed Savannah's hand. "My God, Savvy. Are you okay? When Zach called me, I almost freaked out."

Before she could answer, Bri sat on the bed and put her head on Savannah's shoulder. Typical Bri move. When something touched her deeply, she had trouble articulating. After their parents' deaths, she wouldn't talk for over a week.

Savannah smoothed her sister's spiky hair with one hand and squeezed Sammie's hand with her other. "I'm fine. Just still kind of tired."

"Your voice . . . will it be okay?" Sammie asked.

Savannah nodded. "It'll be fine. I just need—"

"To rest. She's not supposed to talk."

Three sets of eyes zoomed to the door where Zach stood. Dressed in faded jeans and a black T-shirt that showed off his broad chest and incredible biceps, he made it hard for Savannah to not salivate. She glanced from one sister to the other and had to swallow a giggle at Bri's and Sammie's slightly glazed looks. This was the first time they'd seen Zach in over ten years and were most likely having a similar reaction to the one she'd had. He had changed from the handsome boy they'd known to a sexy, gorgeous man.

"Sorry, I tried to catch you before you ran into the house." His mouth lifted in a grin. "You two are fast."

"Hello, Zach."

The cool greeting came from Sammie. Bri said nothing. The glazed looks had been replaced with a hostile wariness. This reaction didn't surprise her. They still had no clue why Zach had abandoned her. Though she had told them it was justifiable, until she gave them a better explanation, the hostility would remain.

Zach showed no surprise at this change but his eyes flickered with regret. When he looked at her, his expression softened considerably. "I'll be in my study if you need me." His eyes went cool again as he took in Sammie's and Bri's accusing glares. "Don't let her talk too much."

With those words, he disappeared. Savannah wanted to call him back. As happy as she was to see her sisters, she wanted to soothe Zach. Tell him that her sisters didn't understand.

"Damn, that man looks good." The awe in Bri's words broke the tension. All three women relaxed.

"Have you seen Aunt Gibby?" Savannah asked.

Sammie said, "Not yet. Bri and I arranged to fly into

Mobile around the same time. We rented a car there and drove straight here."

"Is Gibby back home yet?" Bri asked.

Savannah shook her head. "I—"

"Wait." Sammie held up her hand. "You need to rest your voice, which means to find out what's going on, we need to get Zach back in here. First things first, and you don't have to go into detail. Zach's reasons for what he did . . . they were absolutely valid?"

Emotion clutched her heart. That's all her sisters needed—one word from her and there would be no more questions, no more hostility toward Zach. Total faith and trust in each other had been theirs from birth. Nothing could ever change that.

She nodded. Then, because she needed them to know that not only did Zach have her forgiveness, but her feelings for him were stronger than ever, she said, "We're together again."

"Forever?" Bri asked.

Her chest squeezed tight. She didn't know the answer to that but everything within her said she hoped for forever and beyond. "I hope so."

That was good enough for her sisters.

"I'll go get Zach," Sammie said.

As soon as her sister walked out the door, Savannah turned to Bri. "What's wrong with her?"

Bri grimaced and shook her head. "I don't know. I tried to get it out of her on the way here and she wouldn't tell me a damn thing. Just said work had been heavy lately."

Though Sammie was still as beautiful as any cover model, her appearance revealed definite signs of stress. Concern for her sister overrode the pain in Savannah's throat from talking. "She looks like she's lost fifteen pounds and hasn't slept in days."

"I know. As soon as we find the shithead who killed

our parents and tried to kill you and Gibby, we'll get to the bottom of it."

Despite the seriousness, she couldn't help but smile at her sister's summation. Quick, concise, and to the point. That was so Bri.

Sammie reappeared and Zach followed behind her, holding a tray of ice-filled glasses and a pitcher of lemonade. Every time he appeared, her heart did somersaults. Only Zach had ever affected her this way. And thanks to him, she was finally alive again. For ten years she had been in a deep freeze, going through the motions of life without actually living it. Zach had brought her back.

About to thank him for the drinks, she was startled when he leaned over and placed his fingertips against her mouth. "Rest. When you want to say something, use this." For the first time, she noticed that under the tray of drinks was a notepad with an attached pen. Handing them to her, he winked and then proceeded to fill the glasses with lemonade and hand them out.

Relaxing against the pillows, she watched as her sisters sat in the two chairs by the window, leaving Zach to either stand or sit on the bed with Savannah. She was pleased when he grabbed a pillow from the end of the bed, propped it against the headboard, and sat next to her. She scooted closer to him. In an instant, his arm was around her, pulling her even closer. And then, as if it was the most natural thing in the world, she laid her head on his shoulder.

The wide-eyed expression of her sisters made her smile. They might be discussing the murder of her parents, but there was nowhere on earth she'd rather be than right here with three of the most important people in her life.

* * *

Zach released a measured breath, not wanting to disturb the golden head on his shoulder. Having Savannah do that was more than he expected and a hell of a lot more than he deserved. With that one move, she was telling her sisters that she had forgiven him. Earlier their glares could have frozen the balls off a bull. Now that had changed. Though Savannah's opinion was the only one that mattered to him, her endorsement made him feel like he'd won the lottery.

"Okay. So what do we know?" Sammie asked.

"Not a lot," Zach answered. "Since the letters were destroyed, all we have left is a half-assed police report, the knowledge that a woman is involved, and a list of suspects."

"Where's the list?" Bri asked.

Zach took the tablet he'd given Savannah and ripped out a sheet of paper on which he'd listed all the names of the people who'd been at the Kilgores' party. He handed the list to Sabrina, who briefly glanced over it and then gave it to Samantha.

"So there were four couples at the party, plus four other people, and you and Savvy," Samantha said.

"Yeah. Right now they're all under surveillance and have been told not to leave town."

Sabrina snorted. "Bet that went over well."

Zach shrugged. No doubt about it, he hadn't made any friends today. He'd been called a couple of names and lawsuits had been threatened. He didn't give a shit. Someone at that party had killed Maggie and Beckett Wilde and had tried their best to kill Gibby and Savannah. If he had to piss off the entire town or state to get to the truth, that was damn fine with him. Savannah had almost died yesterday. He took that very personally.

"I doubt that I'll be invited to any more of the mayor's barbeques for a while."

"So what's the plan?" Samantha asked.

"We're going to interview each person individually. Both of you have extensive investigative and interviewing skills. Brody James and Logan Wright are army buddies of mine who own a security company in Mobile. Brody is guarding your aunt and Logan is over at the Wilde mansion going over the guesthouse with the arson investigator. Between the five of us, we'll interview them all."

Savannah raised her head and said, "But—"

Zach put his fingers on her soft lips again. Resisting the need to linger and caress her, he said softly, "Use your notepad . . . babe."

She smiled at his endearment; something he had never used until yesterday. Then she jotted quickly, *I can interview, too.*

"Right now you and your voice need to rest."

Before she could write anything else, he added, "One more day and then you can talk to anyone you want. Okay?"

She nodded and settled back against his shoulder again, seemingly satisfied with his answer. He knew that wouldn't last long. Savannah wasn't the type to sit back and let others take charge. She'd throw a fit if he did what he wanted to do, and that was to bundle her and Gibby up and carry them to an undisclosed location. Finding the killer was important; protecting Savannah imperative.

"Where and when do we start?" Bri asked.

"I have the interviews set up at the station starting at four today. If one of you will stay here with Savannah, I'll go with the other one to the station. We can alternate every few hours, today and tomorrow."

He expected an argument, but though she stiffened slightly, she didn't protest. Independent Savannah had suffered a blow yesterday. Zach wanted to kill the bastard for taking away the confidence and self-assurance she'd fought so hard for.

Sabrina stood. "I'll go with you, Zach. Sammie can stay with Savvy for a few hours."

He was surprised when instead of agreeing immediately, Samantha glared briefly at Sabrina and then gave him a strained smile. "Of course I'll stay."

Deciding the sisters had issues only they could resolve, Zach got to his feet. Not caring that her sisters were watching, he leaned down and gave Savannah a lingering kiss on her soft mouth. When he lifted his head, her eyes were gleaming. Unable to resist, he went back for another taste.

Pulling him closer, she weaved her fingers in his hair as she opened her mouth and took the kiss deeper. Zach groaned, wanting nothing more than to lie beside her and lose himself in her beautiful body.

His breathing slightly labored, he lifted his head and said, "You, Savannah Rose Wilde, are a dangerous woman."

A smile of contentment curving her mouth, she released him and lay on the pillow again. "Come back home safely," she whispered.

Knowing if he didn't get out of the room, he would stay longer, Zach straightened and looked around the room. Apparently Samantha and Sabrina had left to give them privacy.

"I'll be back in a few hours. There's food in the fridge if you get hungry. Call me on my cell if you need me for anything. Okay?"

She nodded sleepily and closed her eyes. The doctor had told him she would be drifting in and out of sleep for most of the day. He slipped quietly out of the room and found himself facing two Wilde women with identical looks on their identical faces—determination.

"Okay, Zach, we're willing to take Savvy on faith.

But I swear, if you hurt her again, you'll be answering to someone a lot tougher than she is. Understand?"

The threat came from Sabrina but Samantha nodded her agreement. Stupid, but he almost hugged them both. He'd always admired how the sisters stuck together.

"That's one thing I can promise you both. As long as I'm alive, Savannah will never be hurt again, by me or any other person."

Taking a deep breath, Sabrina gave a nod and said, "Good enough. Now let's go find out who killed our parents."

CHAPTER TWENTY-NINE

Zach knew full well he was breaking protocol by having the three Wilde sisters assist with the interviews. He didn't give a damn. If anyone dared to question him, the sisters' impressive credentials backed up his decision. That the women were highly trained professionals was secondary to him. No one was more invested in getting to the truth.

Noreen and Kyle Ingram were the first to be interviewed. Zach chose to interview Kyle; Sabrina took on Noreen.

Sitting across from the man who'd obviously been in love with Maggie Wilde and had made little effort to hide the fact that he had moved that adoration to Savannah wasn't easy. However, he wanted to get Kyle up close and personal, stare him down and determine if he was a sick, twisted murderer or just a sad, pathetic man.

Hound-dog expression firmly in place, Kyle sat quietly across from him, waiting. He didn't fidget like many people who were being questioned by the police. Zach had seen a suspect's behavior vary from lackadaisical to hysterical. Never had he seen someone like Kyle. The man's sad, defeated air made Zach want to shake him just to get a reaction.

"You know why you're here, Kyle?"

"Yes."

"Look at me," Zach snapped.

Kyle's eye's flickered upward. Zach leaned forward to catch the man's gaze. "Here's the deal. We know Maggie and Beckett Wilde were murdered. We know it was someone they knew. And we know you were obsessed with Maggie Wilde. So, I'm going to ask you outright. Did you kill them?"

Instead of answering directly, his eyes moved away from Zach's stare to focus on the wall. "I loved Maggie Mae. I would never have hurt her."

"But you hated Beckett Wilde."

"She was too good for him."

"What happened that night, Kyle? Did you lose your temper, maybe? Did things get out of hand? Did you go over to see Maggie and Beckett caught you, leaving you no choice but to kill them both?"

His eyes not moving from the wall behind Zach, Kyle answered quietly, "I loved Maggie and I hated Beckett. I didn't kill either of them."

Truth or lie? Zach didn't know. With no polygraph equipment to assist him, he had to go on his gut. Problem was, his gut was being strangely silent on this man. Was it because Kyle seemed to have a sick fascination for Savannah and Zach couldn't see beyond that? Or was there a cold-blooded murderer behind the man's seemingly lifeless demeanor?

"Where were you the night they died?"

"At home . . . with Noreen."

"It was so long ago, how do you know for sure?"

At last, life entered Kyle's eyes. While that should make Zach feel better, since at least the man looked like he had something inside him besides sadness, it didn't.

"If Savannah died today, would you remember eighteen years later what you were doing?"

His chair slammed against the wall behind him as Zach surged to his feet and lunged at Kyle. Grabbing the man's collar, he snarled, "Did you just make a threat against Savannah?"

"Of course I didn't. I'm just explaining that Maggie meant to me what Savannah means to you. The day your life ends, even if you go on living, you never forget."

Okay, that might be a true statement, but Zach had to set the man straight on something. "Let's get one thing clear, Ingram. If you come near Savannah, you'll answer to me. Got it?"

For the first time, Kyle smiled. "I'm glad she's got you to protect her."

Zach dropped his grip on him and backed away. Yeah, maybe he had overreacted. The point Kyle made was a good one, but that didn't take away the concern Zach felt.

"You stay in town . . . don't leave. You hear?"

"Of course. Where am I going to go?"

Right now, with Kyle's creepy words echoing in his ear, Zach wanted to tell him he could go to hell for all he cared. Instead he nodded grimly and watched the man shuffle out the door.

Was Ingram a killer? He was a disturbed individual, of that Zach had no doubt. But did he have it in him to brutally murder two people, one of whom he swore he loved?

Zach didn't know the answer to that but one thing was for sure—Kyle Ingram would be under surveillance until this was over.

After Kyle's bizarre interview, the others were amazingly normal. Even the sour-faced Noreen Ingram claimed to be appalled that both Maggie and Beckett had been murdered. Zach watched a video of the interview and thought Sabrina handled Noreen like a pro. Though the woman made no secret of her bitterness because of Kyle's love for Maggie, there was nothing to indicate that she had been involved in their murders.

Richard and Lisa Tatum's interviews were uninformative but exhausting, with both of them alternately crying and then turning angry for being suspects. This time, Zach took Lisa; Sabrina interviewed Richard. From what he could tell, the Tatums seemed like kind, decent people. Nothing conclusive came from those interviews. Both Richard and Lisa were alibis for each other, saying they'd been in bed by eleven that night. When asked how they knew the exact time from such a long time ago, both of them had the exact same answer: "Because that's our bedtime."

Zach left the station, frustrated and exhausted. The minute he walked into his house and into the bedroom where Savannah lay sleeping, all of that was washed away. Without undressing, he lay down beside her and pulled her close. No matter what happened out in the world, Savannah was his world and all he needed to survive. He fell into a deep, peaceful sleep.

The next round of interviews began again at nine the next morning. Everyone who walked through the doors of the police station seemed to have identical grim and serious expressions.

After almost twelve hours of uninterrupted sleep, Savannah felt renewed and reenergized. When she had woken in Zach's arms this morning, she'd been surprised and concerned that he still had his uniform on . . . she hadn't heard him come in last night. That concern had turned to extreme pleasure when he had gently and thoroughly made love to her. That was the kind of morning wake-up she could definitely get used to. She now felt rested, sated, and ready for whatever the day brought. Hopefully it would bring a killer out of hiding.

Everything ran smoothly, if unenlighteningly, until it came time to question Lamont Kilgore.

"I can't believe you think I had anything to do with your mama and daddy's deaths."

Lamont's accusing, tearful statement was directed at Savannah. Though Zach was conducting the interview and had made her promise to keep her questions to a minimum because of her voice, she felt she had to answer.

"We're just looking for the truth, Lamont." She winced at how raw and strained she still sounded. "I know you loved Mama and Daddy enough to want their killers to come to justice."

Zach gave her a glare of warning to stay quiet before he turned back to Lamont. "How long were you and Beckett friends?"

With one last wounded glance at Savannah, Lamont turned his gaze to Zach. "Almost from birth. My mama and Camille, Beckett's mama, were best friends. Beckett was born just a few months before me, so we grew up together."

"You shared a lot of experiences." Zach smiled slightly, conspiratorially.

Lamont's face lit up as though remembering. "Yeah, we were always trying to one-up each other."

Zach pinned Lamont with a hard stare. "You had quite a few problems when you were younger, didn't you? Got in trouble with the law. Got kicked out of college a couple of times."

Lamont had been a politician too long to be totally caught off guard, but his answer was very un-politician-like. "I was an idiot. Got too big for my britches." He threw Savannah a tight smile. "Your daddy and I saw some rough times back then. We were both hell-raisers. Nothing serious but we did some stupid things."

"You got kicked out of school and Beckett didn't," Zach said. "Bet that pissed you off."

"Best thing to have happened to me."

"Why?"

An expression of joyful amusement swept across his face, and Savannah already knew what he was going to say. "My daddy made me earn my own way for a few months. I was working at a fast-food joint and that's when I met Nesta. She told me I had to straighten up and fly right or she would never see me again. I took her at her word and got my act together."

"And you and Beckett stayed friends through all of this?"

"Absolutely. When I went back to school, I took extra classes to make up for what I had missed. We graduated together . . . were best men at each other's weddings. Our wives became best friends." He glanced down briefly, swallowing hard. "If we'd had children, I figure our kids would have been friends of their girls." His smile was sad as he looked over at Savannah. "We went to your granddaddy after their deaths and asked if we could adopt one of you. Understandably, he refused."

"Which one?" Zach asked.

Lamont blinked in confusion. "Which one what?"

"Which one did you want to adopt?"

"It didn't matter. We loved all the girls equally. If he'd let us, we would have taken all three."

Savannah knew Zach was pursuing this because of Gibby's claim that someone wanted only Savannah because she looked so much like Maggie. At that thought, an idea flashed through her mind. Promising herself to come back to it later, she listened as Zach continued his questions.

"So you stayed friends with Beckett all those years without any kind of disharmony?"

Lamont's brow furrowed as if he was wondering where Zach's questions were leading. She was wondering the same thing, but she held her tongue. Not only because it would undermine his authority in the interview, but she trusted Zach. He had more than proven himself, in competence and integrity. The process had been a long, painful journey, but her trust in Zach was once again all-encompassing and complete. What a joy it was to finally be able to admit that to herself.

Zach could feel Savannah's questioning gaze on him but was relieved that she didn't interrupt. The fact that she didn't gave him encouragement. She was beginning to trust him again. That meant the world to him.

"Disharmony? I'm not sure what you're insinuating, Zach. We might have had our petty disagreements like most friends have, but Beckett remained my best friend until the day he died."

"What about the night of Maggie and Beckett's argument? Seems like you took sides."

Lamont shrugged. "Beckett was behaving like a jackass that night. It was obvious Maggie had had a rough day. Nesta told me that Maggie had cried on and off most of the day. She was emotional and Beckett behaved like an insensitive jerk. Nesta thought I was being too rough on Beckett."

"Why was Mama so emotional?" Savannah's abrupt question didn't surprise him. She would want to know what had upset her mother.

"You girls left for camp that morning. It was the first time she had been without her babies for more than a day since you were born. Saying goodbye had been rough for her. When Beckett did his usual flirtation, it was too much for Maggie. Your daddy was a big flirt but most people, especially your mama, knew it didn't mean nothing. She'd usually roll her eyes and ignore him. I guess that night, with her being so emotional and all, she didn't want to put up with it. And she said so.

"We took her home and left." He leaned into the table and glared hard at Zach. "In case you're wondering, she was alive when we left."

"Nesta said that when you returned home, you and she got into an argument and you stormed out the door. She said you didn't come home till the next morning."

Shame and guilt spread like a dark cloud over Lamont's craggy face. Zach tensed, waiting. Were they about to hear a confession?

Instead of confessing a crime, Lamont went on the defensive. "That doesn't mean I went over and killed my best friend's wife."

"No, but it means you don't have an alibi for your whereabouts."

Lamont's face turned crimson for a moment and then went pale as he whispered, "Nesta doesn't know this . . . I had hoped never to have to tell her." He glanced down at his hands, which Zach noted were twisting nervously on the table. "Nesta and I fought so rarely. I guess . . . She hurt my feelings, I guess. Anyway, I went to a bar and had too much to drink. A few hours later, I woke up . . ." He swallowed hard, his face flushing a deeper red than before. "In another woman's bed."

"And this other woman? Who was she?"

His head jerked up; eyes wide with shame and not a little panic, he stammered, "Th-that's really not important. She isn't around anymore. There's no need to—"

"There's every need. I'll have to contact this woman and verify she was with you."

"Fine." Lamont cleared his throat, looked down at his hands again, and mumbled, "Francine Adams."

Holy hell. How had he not seen this coming? The compassion he could feel coming from Savannah was almost as bad as Lamont's crimson-red face and mumbling apology.

Lamont peeked up at Zach. "I'm real sorry, son. I don't know what came over me."

Zach knew exactly what had come over him. The same thing that had come over half the grown men in Midnight for years. His mother had never discriminated. If a man had money, even a little, then Francine was more than happy to show him a good time. Just because he was married was no concern of hers.

Already knowing Lamont was telling the truth, Zach still warned him. "You know with one phone call I'll find out if you're lying."

"Yes."

Zach stood. "You can leave now. If we need to ask more questions, we'll be sure to call you."

Lamont stood, a plea and an apology in his eyes. "If at all possible, I'd like to keep this between us. Having Nesta know about this, even after all this time, would hurt her deeply."

Zach nodded grimly. "I'll do my best." Hell, the last thing he wanted was Francine's dirty laundry aired out in public again. He'd had enough of that as a kid.

Lamont's sleazy confession didn't shock him. In fact, he was surprised he hadn't been confronted with this before. The reminder to Savannah that he was the son of Midnight's most notorious slut was something he could have done without.

Shoulders slumped like a guilt-ridden man, Lamont

walked out the door. Stupid, but Zach felt bad for him. Would the dirt of his upbringing ever be completely gone?

"Zach," Savannah whispered, "we're not responsible for our parents' sins."

He shot her a wry, twisted grin. "Doesn't stop us from being disgusted or embarrassed by them."

He pulled a cellphone from his pocket and handed it to her. "I picked this up for you this morning. Why don't you go visit with your aunt and then go back to my house and rest?"

Savannah took the phone, then leaned forward and softly kissed his mouth. "I'll see you tonight."

Giving her a solemn nod, he walked out the door, his mind on the unpleasant task in front of him. He had to call his mother and ask her if she remembered sleeping with Lamont Kilgore eighteen years ago. She'd slept with so many, would she even remember?

As soon as Savannah walked in the front door of Gibby's house, she heard the laughter. Her eyes went questioningly to Brody, who was standing guard at the bottom of the stairway.

His face one of amused patience, he shrugged. "Your aunt has an interesting method of recovery. Invite as many visitors as possible and entertain them for as long as she can stay awake."

Aunt Gibby was known for her socials. Almost being murdered wasn't going to stop her. She directed her eyes toward the top of the stairs. "Who's up there?"

Brody pulled a sheet of paper from his shirt pocket. "Hester Shook, Sarah Wills, and Loraine Meadows."

Gibby's bridge club members. "Are they playing bridge?"

"They were last time I checked. I walked out as soon

as they started in on how wonderful their granddaughters and nieces were and why wasn't a nice young man like me married."

Since those were the kinds of questions she would get if she joined them, she said, "Would you tell Aunt Gibby that I came by and I'll call her later?"

"I doubt they'll be here that much longer. Sarah said she had to get home to watch *General Hospital*. It comes on in twenty minutes."

She did her best not to show her amusement. "You're a fan of the soaps?"

He gave her a knowing smile. "Don't laugh till you've seen the show. It's addictive."

She agreed. She'd watched it when she was a teenager. "Okay, I'll stay then. Let me check and see if Deputy Odom wants to come in or needs a cold drink."

As soon as the deputy assured her he was set with a thermos of iced tea, Savannah rushed back inside. Having Brody to herself for a few minutes was the perfect opportunity to find out more about Zach. Who better to ask than a man who'd served with him in the army?

She was happy to see that not only had Brody pulled a chair from the dining room for her to sit on, he had also poured both of them a glass of tea. Gratefully accepting the drink, she settled into her chair and wondered how to approach her questions. She needn't have worried. Brody was much less taciturn than Zach.

Dropping onto the third step of the stairway, Brody took a long swallow of tea and then said, "Zach's a fine man."

"Have you known him a long time?"

"Going on seven years. Logan, Zach, and I served together in Iraq and Afghanistan."

"Funny how you all ended up so close together once you left the service."

"That's no coincidence. I'm from northern Indiana. Logan's from Buffalo, New York. We both hate snow. The way Zach described things in Alabama, from the weather to the beaches to the food . . ." He shrugged. "Hell, there was no way we weren't going to check it out. Once we got here, we decided to stay."

"Do you guys get to see Zach much?"

"Not a lot. An occasional fishing trip. Zach's busy and we've got our hands full with our business."

"What does your agency do?"

"About anything a client wants: bodyguard services, security consultation, missing persons, assistance in investigation of criminal cases, private investigations. We've had to hire two more employees since we got started."

"I'm surprised you were able to come and help us so quickly."

"Zach takes precedence over our clients."

When she had first met Brody, he had said something similar. "Why is that?"

"We owe him our lives. There's nothing we wouldn't do for him."

She settled more comfortably in her seat, anxious to hear more about this part of Zach's past. "Do you mind sharing what happened?"

A cool light entered his eyes. "Why? So you can decide if he's some kind of hero?"

She didn't take offense. He was being protective of his friend. "I already know he's a hero. I just want to know more about him."

Nodding his approval of her answer, he said, "Our team had raided a compound that'd been an al-Qaeda stronghold. We got almost through the entire place without firing a shot. We opened a door, were in the middle of the room when the bullets started flying. There were four shooters. I took a hit in my leg; Logan took one to his chest and another in his arm. Zach took one in his side."

Frozen in her chair, Savannah listened as Brody described the harrowing scene. She had known Zach was wounded in combat—she had seen the scars with her own eyes—but the event became real and terrifying as Brody described in detail how Zach had saved all three of them.

"We managed to get out of the room but the building was surrounded. Logan couldn't run. I couldn't go far or fast. We radioed for help but the rest of our team had gotten caught by another group. We found out later one of our interpreters was an informant. They knew we were coming.

"We both tried to get Zach to leave. Figured that, out of the three of us, he had the best chance to make it out alive. Instead of doing what we told him to do, he circled round and took out two of the shooters. The two others kept firing at me and Logan. We exchanged fire for what seemed like forever. Just when I thought we were done for, here comes Zach back inside. He assessed which one of us was hurt the most—which was Logan. He gave me his ammunition. Then the damn stubborn fool hauled Logan onto his back and carried him out of there."

"And how did you get out?"

A fleeting, haunted look came into his eyes and then gave way to that glint of humor that seemed a part of him. "I figured if Zach made it safely back with Logan, he might send reinforcements back for me or, hell, come back himself."

"But that's not what he did?"

"I was almost out of ammo. No way was I going to just lie there and let the bastards shoot me without trying to run. I managed to crawl to the door and was about to open it when the shooting stopped."

"Why? What happened?"

"Zach. He snuck up on one of the bastards from the back . . . took him out with a knife. Then he shot the last one." He paused for a few seconds, allowing her to absorb the enormity of Zach's heroism.

"So that's why if Zach calls, we come running." Locking eyes with her, he repeated his earlier statement: "He's a fine man, Savannah."

And like a sledgehammer falling from the sky, realization hit her. "You know what happened ten years ago, don't you?"

He grimaced. "Yeah. When you're in a stinking hellhole with death staring you in the face, things that are eating at you can devour you whole. Sometimes you end up sharing those things."

"I wish he had told me earlier."

"You didn't take his calls when he tried."

His tone wasn't accusing but she felt the sting of his words all the same. She and Zach had both made mistakes. He should have contacted her sooner; he should have taken her calls. And she should have pushed aside her pain to take his calls later on. So much wasted time. So much pain that could have been avoided.

"We both messed up."

"And you both have a chance to make it right this time."

Brody was right. They did have the chance. Suddenly she knew she couldn't wait until this case was solved. Finding out who killed her parents was important, but coming clean with Zach couldn't wait any longer.

She went to her feet. "I need to see Zach. Can you tell Aunt Gibby I'll call her later?"

Apparently recognizing that she'd come to some sort of decision, Brody winked and said, "Good luck."

Turning, she ran out the door and to the patrol car.

Telling Zach would be one of the hardest things she'd ever done, but until he knew the truth, they couldn't move on. Now she just had to find the right words that wouldn't hurt him more than he had already been hurt.

CHAPTER THIRTY

Getting a call from Savannah to come to the Wilde mansion wasn't something Zach was expecting. He had liked the idea of her being in his house, in his bed.

When he arrived, he understood why she had moved back home. Not only were her sisters with her, Brody and Logan could have rooms here, too. Savannah, her sisters, and Brody were all sitting in the living room, eating Chinese takeout, when he walked in the door. The instant Savannah spotted him, she jumped from the couch immediately to kiss him hello.

"I didn't intend to stay," she whispered softly. "I just came by for some clothes but Sammie and Bri showed up with dinner, then Brody dropped by. Logan's with Aunt Gibby. We can leave now or go after dinner."

"You don't want to stay here?"

A shy smile, one he hadn't seen since their earliest dates, curved her beautiful mouth. "I like waking up in your bed, beside you."

Heat flashed and arousal came quick and urgent. Despite the fact that he hadn't had anything to eat except a bowl of cereal for breakfast, he wanted nothing more than to grab Savannah and get back to his house immediately. However, knowing she probably hadn't eaten much today, either, he said, "Let's eat here . . . fast."

As if she knew exactly what he was thinking, she

leaned into him and spoke softly, "We'll have dessert at your place."

"Deal."

"I'll fix us a plate. You go wash up."

Despite the desire to rush back, Zach took his time. Today had been filled with shit he could've gone a lifetime without. Calling his mother to verify that she had indeed slept with Lamont Kilgore the night of Maggie's and Beckett's murder had been singularly unpleasant. Either his mother had a good memory of the men she slept with, or, like Savannah said, everyone in Midnight remembered what they were doing the night of the murders. Or hell, maybe Lamont was just that memorable in bed.

Whatever the reason, she had verified that Lamont had been with her until the early morning hours. She had been surprised that Zach hadn't wanted to linger on the phone and chat. The inevitable "When are you coming for a visit?" had been the last straw. Other than Christmas, he did not see Francine. And the only reason he did then was because his brother did his best to come home at Christmas. Josh wasn't always able to give them advance notice of his coming. Many times Zach had arrived only to learn that his brother hadn't been able to make it. Those visits were usually short and awkward.

Finally feeling somewhat clean and refreshed, Zach returned to the living room. Savannah had prepared two plates and placed them side by side on a coffee table. She was sitting on a pillow and patted another one beside her.

Lowering himself down, Zach concentrated on his meal and let the conversation flow around him. Brody and Sammie seemed to be getting along well, exchanging humorous quips. Bri was eating quietly but smiling from time to time. Savannah was doing the same thing he was, focusing on eating as quickly as possible.

His eyes roamed the room. "I watched the taped interviews each of you conducted. Good job." He focused his gaze on Sabrina. "Especially you. You had Noreen Ingram eating our of your hand by the time the interview was over."

Sabrina grinned. "Thanks. Having her bring in an eighteen-year-old calendar to show me exactly what she and Kyle were doing that night was helpful. Me praising her went a long way in making her feel good. I could have done without knowing that they scheduled their sex life on the calendar."

After a few snickers and "ewww"s, Zach said, "Let's discuss any abnormalities and inconsistencies in any of the stories. Anything stand out to anyone?"

Samantha shook her head. "We were talking about that just before you got here. Every person we talked to today had a valid alibi. Apparently the murders have the same memorable significance to them as other major events. They remember what they were doing, who they were with, and where they were when they first heard the news."

"Have we verified the alibis?"

Sabrina shrugged. "As much as we can. When someone tells you they were in bed with their husband or wife eighteen years ago, that's damn hard to verify."

Yeah, that was true. He suddenly felt like a wrung-out dishcloth. "The killer has got to be in this group we're interviewing. Either we're not asking the right questions or somebody's a damn good liar."

"I sat in on all the interviews except the ones you conducted, Zach," Brody said. "These people seemed sincerely disturbed that this was a double murder."

That was the sense he'd gotten, too. "Then who the

hell else could it be? The person who tried to kill Gibby targeted her to prevent the meeting with Savannah."

"Maybe they didn't," Sabrina said. "Maybe she was going to be targeted anyway and it was just coincidence that it happened the same night she made that statement."

Zach shrugged. "Then that means our suspect list has grown to include every person in Midnight who was also a resident eighteen years ago."

His statement put a noticeable damper on the room. Shoulders slumped and sighs were expelled. Finally Brody, in his usual cut-to-the-chase way, said, "An eighteen-year-old half-assed police report, headless roadkill, two attempted murders, and a thousand suspects. Man, you are so screwed."

Silence followed his blunt statement and then laughter exploded, breaking the tension. Even Zach, who was too tired to even consider laughing, managed a smiling acknowledgment. Brody was right—he was screwed. That wouldn't stop him, though. He'd been in difficult places before but none had ever been this important.

"You about finished?"

The soft, sexy voice in his ear caused his thoughts to go into a much more pleasant direction. Zach stood, then held out his hand to help her up. "I'll take our plates to the kitchen. You get your clothes."

"See you soon."

He watched her walk away, admiring the grace and fluidity of her movements, along with the way her jeans molded her perfect ass.

"You're good for her, you know."

Sabrina had approached silently. He had spent almost no time with the sisters since their return, but he had noticed some incredible changes in both Samantha and Sabrina. They were both still beautiful women, but Samantha had a new edgy toughness, which no doubt she'd developed as a homicide detective. However, the change in Sabrina might be the most surprising of all. Oddly, she seemed softer, less damaged than she had years ago. Maybe time and maturity had allowed her to deal with her painful past. Too bad all of this was bringing it home to her again.

"Why do you say I'm good for Savannah?"

"She shines with you. Like she hasn't in ten years." And before he could even begin to appreciate the words, she added a warning: "Don't fuck it up this time. She won't forgive you again."

He gave her a nod of acknowledgment, knowing full well she was right. He'd been given a second chance with the woman he loved. This time, he intended to get it right.

Duffel bag in one hand, hairbrush in the other, Savannah rushed around the room in a frenzied, unorganized manner. A full-blown panic attack was so not sexy. Yes, she wanted to tell Zach the truth. But accepting that and carrying it out were two entirely different things.

The cautious, rational side of her, her usual voice of reason, told her to wait. Not only was Zach exhausted from the events of the past several days, he had a hell of a lot on his plate right now. Adding to it could very well make it worse. The last thing she wanted to do was hurt him again.

Her emotional, impulsive side, which had reemerged only recently, told her he deserved to know everything as soon as possible. Keeping things from the man she loved was wrong, especially this one thing in particular. How on earth did she expect to go forward in their relationship with this hanging over her head? She had to tell him tonight.

Stripping off her jeans and shirt, Savannah searched

for something more fitting for the occasion. What was the appropriate attire to wear when you were going to tell the man you loved news that you knew full well would devastate him? Was she being selfish? Should she keep it to herself? No, he had a right to know.

Clothes flew left and right; her heart rate zoomed. In the midst of a full-on panic attack, she felt strong hands land on her shoulders and turn her around.

"What's wrong?"

Shuddering out a breath, she looked up into the handsome face of the man she had loved forever. Solid, honorable, steady . . . a man she could rely on. Throwing her arms around him, Savannah held him tight. Big, callused hands roamed over her body and Savannah sighed her happiness. Being in Zach's arms made her feel powerful, invincible. She knew he loved her and she loved him. Everything would be fine.

Her pulse rate now high for a different reason, Savannah pulled away and took his hand, leading him to her bed. First they would make love and then they would talk. Before she reached the bed, Zach stopped her and said softly, "Hey, talk to me."

Swallowing hard, she shook her head. "I think I'm just frantic from everything that's happened the last few days."

Drawing her back into his arms, he whispered, "Everything will be okay. I'll make it right, I promise."

She pressed a kiss to the center of his chest. When she heard what sounded like a sigh of longing, she continued to kiss his chest, then moved up his neck, spreading soft kisses as she went. Reaching the solid, square chin she loved so much, she covered it with kisses, too.

Big hands grabbed her head and held her still as his mouth descended. Her kisses had been affectionate and playful. His kiss was thorough, sexy, and serious. She opened for him and the growl from his chest gave her a charge of intense arousal. Standing on her toes, she pressed her softness against his hard body.

As he devoured her mouth, his hands were busy stripping her of her bra and panties. Within seconds she was nude and Zach was pushing her down onto the bed. Her breath heavy with passion, she watched as he quickly dropped his clothing on the floor. When he was finished, Savannah held out her arms to welcome him.

Zach gazed down at the woman lying on the bed, waiting for him. Savannah was every dream he'd ever had. And while he wanted to be inside that sexy body, losing himself in an ecstasy only she could provide, he held back. She'd been through hell the last couple of days. Shadows beneath her eyes told him she needed rest.

"Something wrong?" she whispered.

"Not a damn thing. Just can't get over how beautiful you are or how lucky I am."

"Come down here and I'll let you get even luckier."

Zach lay down beside her and gathered her close, absorbing her soft, silky body into his. She felt fragile and delicate in his arms but he knew there was a thread of steel beneath that delicacy.

A slender hand moved down his stomach, caressing and kneading. Before she could reach her destination, Zach grabbed her hand and held it to his mouth. "Sleep."

"What?"

"You need to rest."

"But I want you inside me."

Breath shuddered from him. He was hanging on by a thread already. Having her tell him exactly what she wanted from him made saying no to her a thousand times harder. He pressed a soft kiss to her mouth. "Let me just hold you."

"But I want—"

Names like "idiot" and "masochist" reverberated through his mind as he rolled her over onto her back and said, "Shh . . . let me take care of you." With those words, Zach proceeded to show with his mouth and his hands just how much he worshipped and adored this woman. Holding her arms above her head, he looked down into the loveliest face in all the world and saw what he thought he'd never see gleaming in her eyes again—love and trust.

He reverently kissed her mouth over and over, then whispered soft kisses across her face and down her slender neck. She groaned and wiggled a little but didn't object to him holding her and loving her without her active participation. This was for both of them.

Trailing openmouthed kisses to each breast, he licked and suckled them gently, then lightly bit one nipple, which brought a gasp and another wiggle of her body. Going lower, he licked and kissed his way down her satin-soft skin, stopping briefly for a quick tongue swirl of her navel. When he saw that she had her legs tightly together, trying to find ease for her arousal, he growled, "Open up, baby."

As he watched her slender legs spread open, he swallowed hard. The trust she was showing him humbled and amazed him. Releasing his hold on her wrists, Zach moved lower on the bed and kneeled between her parted legs. He ground his teeth together, the temptation to plunge deep and give them both relief almost beyond his control. At her soft sigh, he glanced at her face and was reminded of his purpose. Sparking green eyes, hot with desire and love, looked at him beneath her lashes while a smile of pure pleasure curved her luscious lips. This was for Savannah, the most precious and beautiful creature he'd ever known.

Hooking her legs with his forearms, he spread her legs farther apart, dipped his head, and inhaled the sweet musk of her arousal. When she undulated and gasped out, "Zach . . . please," he chuckled but refused to hurry. The anticipation of her taste was a delight in itself. Rushing through anything this fine would be a sin. Nuzzling her softness with his nose, he enjoyed more gasps and groans and then took a long lick as a quick tease. Another sharp gasp came from her. Smiling widely, Zach went for a deeper taste, his tongue thrusting deep within her. Savannah wailed and came quickly against his tongue. Lapping at her, he gave her a few seconds to recover and then began to build the fire again.

Savannah arched up into another fierce orgasm. No matter how much she begged Zach to come inside her, he continued to love her with just his mouth. Three orgasms to his none was so wrong, but she was too weak and felt too wonderful to voice an objection. As he finally moved up and allowed her some rest, she tried again. Reaching for the part of him that she knew needed immediate attention, he once again averted her by grabbing her hand and holding it against his chest.

"Zach . . . why?"

"Because I wanted to show you how special you are to me. Your pleasure is mine."

Her body a languid mass of quivering bliss, Savannah didn't have the energy to argue with a gnat, much less two hundred and ten pounds of determined, sexy masculinity. Snuggling into his arms, she blinked sleepily up at him. "Your turn next time," she whispered.

Pressing a tender kiss to her forehead, he said, "*Our* turn next time. Now sleep for a while."

Feeling cherished and adored, Savannah closed her eyes and drifted. Zach was naked and hot against her body. Every part of him felt hard and unyielding. Never had she felt so comfortable or so safe. Being held in the arms of the man she adored was a dream she never thought she'd be able to realize again. She pushed aside the worry that all was not perfect. For now she would take what she could get. Reality would come soon enough.

CHAPTER THIRTY-ONE

Savannah woke to darkness and the feel of Zach's strong arms holding her close, his hard body warm and enticing against her. His scent was deliciously masculine, with just a hint of the musky aftershave he'd put on this morning. His shallow, even breaths made her smile. She had resisted sleeping but he had been right. They were both exhausted and needed the rest. Relaxed and sated, she closed her eyes on a peaceful sigh of contentment.

She felt the rumble of his voice against his chest as he said huskily, "Guess I'm sleeping over at your house tonight."

She twisted around slightly to squint at the bedside clock. Almost midnight. They'd slept about four hours. Rolling over, she faced him, snuggling deeper into his body. "I don't care where we are as long as I can wake up in your arms."

"Agreed." Though she couldn't see his face, she heard the smile in his voice. "Feel like talking?"

Now? When she felt so relaxed and sated? When all she wanted to do was forget that there were still issues they needed to discuss and one very big secret she'd been keeping? Dread tightened every muscle in her body. "Sure."

Though his arms still held her tight, she sensed his

withdrawal and hesitancy. Even in the dark, she couldn't hide her thoughts and fears from him. "What did you want to talk about?"

Yes, the words were cowardly. She'd winced even as she'd said them. Her conscience sneered at her lack of courage. *Grow a backbone, Savannah!*

His arms loosened around her. "You said you'd forgiven me. Were those just words?"

"Of course not." She propped herself up on an elbow and tried to see him in the dark. "What are you talking about?"

"You're still holding back from me, Savannah. I can sense it."

"Zach, I—"

He swallowed hard. "Do you still not trust me?"

She was hurting him already and she hadn't told him anything. "Of course I trust you. I just need—" Oh God, cutting open her heart and spilling her blood couldn't be more painful than this.

"Dammit, I can't apologize more than I already have." Rolling off the bed, Zach grabbed his jeans, jerked them on, and stalked to the door. "Let me know when you want a real relationship and not just somebody to give you orgasms."

That stung but was nothing she didn't deserve. She'd been putting this off for much too long. Ten years to be exact. This was it . . . now or never. If she didn't tell him now, there was no future. Sitting up in bed, she wrapped her arms around her legs and pressed her forehead against her knees. Raising her head, she took a breath and the painful words were wrenched out of her. "We had a daughter. I named her Maggie Rose . . . after my mama. She lived for three days."

Pale moonlight allowed her to see only the outline of his body seemingly frozen at the door. Pained silence filled the room; even in the darkness, she could feel his anguish.

She heard him swallow hard and then he rasped, "What?"

Now that she'd finally said the words, all energy seeped from her limbs. Slumping back onto the pillow, she continued, "I found out I was pregnant about a month after you left. I was in Nashville, getting ready for my first year at Vandy. That was the only thing that kept me from going crazy worrying about you. When I started getting queasy, I assumed it was from stress. Eventually, when I sat down and allowed myself to think about it, I realized I was pregnant."

The realization hadn't come like a burst of lightning. It had been a gradual knowing . . . maybe her subconscious allowing her to come to terms with the monumental event one step at a time. When finally, at last, she accepted the truth, she had been ridiculously overjoyed. Despite all the hardships that she knew lay ahead, she'd had this tiny, innocent, beautiful being growing inside of her—a piece of Zach no one could take away from her . . . or so she had thought.

"But, the condom . . ."

"Didn't work. Those things are supposed to be like ninety-eight percent effective. I was one of those rare, sad statistics. My first time having sex, practicing safe sex. And I still got pregnant."

She heard him turn away from the door and head back to the bed. His movements were much slower than before—almost as if the weight of his burdens pulled him down. Her heart hurt for him.

The bedside light came on, which thankfully gave only a soft glow. She couldn't face the harsh light right now. Zach sat on the bed, the stark agony in his eyes a reflection of what she had gone through during those dark days.

His voice was so strained, she could barely make out his words. "Is that why you called me?"

"Yes," she whispered. "I knew you didn't want me . . . or at least, that's what I thought. But you had a right to know about the baby."

"And I stupidly and cowardly ignored your calls. My God, how can you even stand to be around me?"

She sat up and grabbed for his hand. "Zach . . . no, it wasn't your fault . . . it wasn't anyone's fault."

The pained anguish in his eyes told her he didn't agree. "What happened?"

"It was a normal pregnancy . . . at least that's what my doctor told me. I started spotting at about thirty-one weeks. She said that often happened and to just stay off my feet. I got through the first semester of college. Granddad came to stay with me." She shook her head as she remembered all that he had done for her. "He amazed me. No judgment or censure. He waited on me hand and foot. I did everything I was supposed to do."

She took a breath and trudged on. "It just wasn't enough. I woke in the middle of the night with a searing pain in my belly. Granddad carried me to the hospital. They told me I was in labor. They assured me that even though she was premature, everything looked fine."

A soft little sob escaped her as she remembered. "Oh, Zach, she was perfect. So incredibly beautiful. I held her in my arms and felt so blessed and happy. I had a part of you that no one could take away from me. On the third day, she just stopped breathing. They rushed her to the NICU, put her on a breathing machine. Nothing they did brought her back. We buried her in a beautiful cemetery right outside of Nashville."

That had been one of the hardest decisions she'd ever made. Rationally she knew she was being silly, but she had wanted her daughter to be placed next to her namesake, Savannah's mother. Her grandfather had convinced her otherwise. No one in Midnight knew about her pregnancy. And though Savannah wasn't ashamed of Maggie Rose, neither did she want all the gossip and spitefulness that would follow if she had brought her daughter back to her hometown to bury.

She forced herself to go on, wanting to get everything said and out in the open at last. "That was a really bad time for me, Zach. When you called me, Maggie had just been gone twelve days. I couldn't talk to you. I could barely talk to anyone. Could barely function." Closing her eyes, she admitted, "God help me, I hated you. I needed to blame someone and you were a convenient target."

At some point, she had overcome her hatred, but unfortunately, something much worse had replaced it.

"I fell into a depression, a hole so dark and deep I didn't think I'd ever come out of it. Couldn't eat or sleep. Poor Granddad was beside himself. I went for counseling and then group therapy. I finally remembered all the things I had to live for, all the people who loved me."

It had been a long, hard road back. College and then law school had helped but most of the credit had to be given to her sisters and grandfather. Without them, she wasn't sure she would have survived.

Zach's silence was stark and chilling. Did he blame her for not trying harder to get in touch with him? Was he angry she hadn't told him sooner?

"I'm so sorry I didn't tell you before." She leaned toward him. "Zach, please." Reaching out, her fingers barely skimmed his shoulders when he twisted away from her and jumped to his feet. The rejection smashed her heart into a million pieces.

* * *

His head shaking in denial, Zach paced around the room in a mindless circle. He thought he'd seen and been through hell before. Nothing compared to this. He'd had a daughter. A precious little girl and she had died before he could see her, hold her in his arms.

And the woman he had abandoned, left pregnant and alone, lay on the bed. Her nonjudgmental acceptance of his treatment of her tore at his gut. She had said she hated him for a while . . . she should still hate him.

All of his life, he had done his best to take care of the people he loved. That had been his driving need for as long as he remembered. A code of honor he'd taken on because he'd known it was the right thing to do. The one time he'd taken the coward's way out, had let his pride get in the way of honor, he had lost more than his self-respect, he'd broken Savannah's heart and denied his daughter a father.

Like a roaring beast in a frenzy of fury, agony ripped at his chest, his throat closed, and tears blurred his vision. A harsh sob erupted from deep within him; a gut-wrenching anguish washed over him, threatening to drown him. He had failed the two people who meant more than life to him. And because of his sheer selfishness, he would never know one of them.

Savannah reached out her hand to him again. "Oh, Zach, no . . . please don't. It wasn't your fault. It wasn't anyone's fault. It just happened."

The emotion he saw on her face, the tears falling from her eyes, the pain he heard in her voice reinforced his self-disgust. He had hurt her once and now, dammit, he was doing it again.

He turned away and stalked out the door. He couldn't talk right now. He had to think, clear his head. What in the hell had he done?

* * *

Oh God, she had known she would hurt him when she told him the truth. She just hadn't realized the depth of that hurt. Guilt sliced through her. She should have told him sooner, in a different way. She should have tried harder to find him. She should have taken his calls. So many should-haves . . . so much regret.

Maybe she shouldn't have told him at all. What good had come from him knowing the truth? The man she adored was hurting and she was responsible.

Grabbing her robe from the end of the bed, Savannah pulled it on and hurried out the door. She couldn't just let him leave like this. He was blaming himself for something that wasn't his fault . . . wasn't anyone's fault. She ran down the landing toward the stairs. The only lights were from the lamps in the foyer below and the light coming from her bedroom. Had everyone gone to bed? Where was Zach? Had he left already? Was she too late?

She was almost to the stairway when a masculine shadow appeared at the other end of the landing, coming from the direction of her parents' room. "Zach?"

He didn't answer. Savannah stayed still, afraid if she went closer he'd walk away from her again. She had to make him understand. "I'm so sorry I didn't tell you before . . . I couldn't. Reliving that time again . . . it brought back so many bad memories." She shook her head rapidly. "No, that's no excuse. I know I should have told you sooner." She took a step closer. "I'm so sorry . . . please forgive me."

"Savannah."

She jerked to a stop, startled that Zach's voice, harsh and urgent, came from behind her and not from the man standing a few feet away.

Who? What . . . Before she could finish the thought, Zach shouted, "Get down!"

Savannah dropped to the floor. Shots were fired; bullets whizzed over her head. Her shocked brain registered multiple gunshots as if bullets were flying everywhere, in every direction. In a distant part of her frozen mind, she knew Zach was shooting at someone. *Please, please, please, let him be okay.*

Seconds later, as if someone had abruptly shoved her into a soundproof room, there was nothing but dead silence. Then the thundering noise of people running and shouting hit her ear. Lights blazed above her. Before she could assimilate all the nuances of the past ten seconds, hands grabbed her and turned her over.

"Savannah . . . baby, are you okay?"

She looked into Zach's worried face and almost sobbed her relief. He was here . . . he was okay. Sitting up, she threw herself into his arms and held on tightly. If she had lost him . . . She shook her head. She didn't even want to finish that thought.

"What the hell happened?"

Her face buried against Zach's naked chest, she didn't have to look up to know that was Brody's voice.

"Someone broke in and tried to kill Savannah."

She raised her head at that. "Me? Are you sure?"

Zach's face was dark, grimmer than she could ever imagine, as he nodded. "He was pointing the gun right at you. I saw his eyes right before I took the shot. He was focused solely on you."

"I don't understand. Why me? There are a whole lot more people on the case now. I don't know more than anyone else. Could he have intended to kill all of us?"

Pulling her to her feet, Zach held on to her as if afraid to let her go. That was perfectly fine with her. She never wanted him to let her go.

"Anyone recognize the shooter?" Brody asked.

Turning, she looked at the body lying a few feet in front of her. Samantha pushed him over onto his back.

The man was thirtyish, balding, medium height and very fit. Even in death, he looked wicked and hardened.

Shaking her head, Savannah answered, "I've never seen him before."

Zach held her away slightly to look down at her. "You're sure you're okay?"

"I'm fine. Just a little shaky."

His hands cupped her face and he reverently and softly kissed her mouth. "I'm so sorry, Savannah. For everything."

She knew he wasn't talking about the events of the last five minutes but what they'd been discussing beforehand. "Don't, Zach. Please. We have to get past that. Okay?"

The smile she so loved brightened his face like a thousand candles. "We've got a lot of things to talk about ... decisions to make."

Despite the fact that someone had just tried to kill her, a wave of happiness swept over her. Her smile as bright as his, she answered, "Yes, we certainly do."

"Hey, Chief," Brody's amused sarcasm broke up the tender moment, "wouldn't want a dead guy to spoil a romantic interlude. Want me to take over for you?"

Laughing at Zach's raised eyebrows and the searing glare he shot Brody, she said, "Go. I'll be fine."

"Okay, but first . . ." He looked left and right and then pulled her into a corner, out of sight from everyone. Lowering his mouth, he kissed her tenderly, passionately, lovingly, and then whispered, "I love you, Savannah Wilde."

Filled with so much emotion she could hardly speak, she said thickly, "And I love you, Zach Tanner. For now. Always. Forever." Caressing his face, she whispered, "Go, do your job. We'll talk later."

The instant his arms dropped and he walked away, she felt alone and bereft. As soon as this was solved, her parents' murderer caught, she wanted to go somewhere alone with Zach—someplace where guns, fires, and bad people existed only in books and movies.

Sabrina and Samantha rushed to her. "Are you okay?"

"I'm fine. Just can't believe all of this is happening."

Sammie shook her head in shared disbelief. "I'm beginning to think Atlanta has nothing on Midnight for mayhem and murder."

A crazy idea sprang into her mind. Blurry and unformed, it seemed too insane to even contemplate. But was it really? She eyed her two sisters speculatively. Would they even consider such a thing?

CHAPTER THIRTY-TWO

Zach ran his fingers through his hair for about the thousandth time in the last two hours. He'd been on the phone all morning. First he'd called Savannah's boss. The man who had tried to kill Savannah was most definitely a hired gun. Had the X-Kings hired a hit man to find Savannah and exact revenge?

The news of a hit man had gotten Reid Garrison's attention in a big way. He hadn't believed the other things that had happened to Savannah, including the fire, had anything to do with the X-Kings, saying that the gang would have been much more direct and brutal if they had wanted to kill Savannah. But hiring a killer to take Savannah out was right up their alley. Reid was now in the process of rounding up the gang members for questioning.

After talking with Savannah's boss, he'd given the Alabama FBI a call. Having used every avenue he had available to him to identify the shooter and coming up empty, he'd hoped, with their resources, they could help. Turned out they'd helped a lot. The shooter was Bobby Tom Benson, former Walker County resident, wanted in several states for a multitude of crimes, including murder. Apparently he was skilled in various areas but his number one occupation was assassin.

There was no doubt that the bastard had targeted Savannah. Zach had been about fifteen feet from the bedroom when he'd heard Savannah walk out. He'd been about to say something when he'd noticed a shadowy movement ahead of her. Thinking it was one of her sisters, he'd waited. When the shadow had walked into a small pocket of light, he'd realized it was a man. He'd known immediately it wasn't Brody or Logan. Not only because the guy had been shorter and more slender than either of them, but Zach had managed to catch a glimpse of his face. The deadly intent had been clear. His eyes had briefly met Zach's before they'd focused solely on Savannah. The gun he'd raised had been pointed directly at her.

The instant Zach learned the shooter's identity, he'd sent the information to Reid Garrison. Armed with that knowledge, if the X-Kings were responsible, hopefully the DA's office could link the gang and Benson together.

But what if the X-Kings had nothing to do with this? Savannah still believed it was related to her parents' murders. If so, why go after her specifically? It made no sense. And if he didn't figure out the truth, it could well cost Savannah her life.

What she had revealed last night still cut into his mind and heart like a dull, rusty saw, tearing and ripping at him. The guilt in knowing how he had let her and their baby daughter down would be something he'd live with for the rest of his life. He'd never have a chance to make it up to Maggie Rose, but he could and would do everything in his power to make it up to her mother. If she would give him the chance.

After all they'd been through, how ludicrous was it that last night was the first time he'd told her he loved her? And she had said she loved him. They finally had a chance to be together the way he'd always wanted. Damned if some sleazebag, murdering son of a bitch would stop them.

Slamming his fist on his desk, he pulled Benson's file toward him again. The FBI had faxed all they had, which actually was fairly extensive. Still, it didn't tell him who had hired him.

It'd been a long shot, but he had even briefly visited with Inez Peebles. When she had informed him of Harlan Mosby's passing, the elderly woman had hinted that she might know something about Beckett's and Maggie Wilde's deaths. He was definitely willing to listen if she had any information. Turned out it had been merely suspicion.

In her garlic-scented words, "I suspected that no-account Mosby of being involved, but nobody paid me no mind."

Zach didn't bother to tell her that it was probably a good thing no one had listened to her. Mosby wouldn't have been above eliminating Inez to protect himself.

The knock on his door was an irritant, but the moment he lifted his head and saw Savannah at the entrance, the distraction was not only welcome but much appreciated.

"Thought we could have lunch together."

Zach strode toward her and grabbed her for a quick kiss. "Want me to order something from Faye's?"

"Not necessary." She held up a small picnic basket. "Let's go to the park."

"No, let's stay here."

"Why?"

"Because I don't want you out in the open until we identify this bastard."

Figuring she would argue, he was surprised when she smiled instead and said, "Then clear off your desk, mister. I'm about to dazzle you with a picnic you'll never forget."

Zach closed the door and locked it. Turning, he gave her grin and said, "This way, we can have dessert, too."

She dropped the basket on his desk and flew into his arms. "Let's have dessert first."

As lunches went, Savannah decided it was the best she'd ever had. An intensely satisfying make-out session had been followed by a delicious lunch prepared by Sabrina, the best cook in the Wilde family. She could definitely get used to this kind of life.

She watched Zach take one last bite of a strawberry, marveling at the peace and happiness she felt. Even though there was some crazed lunatic out there who for some reason wanted her dead, she still felt freer and more content than she had in years.

"Who came with you to the station?"

"Brody dropped me off. I told him I'd call him when I was ready to come home."

"I can take you home."

Spending even an extra five minutes with him sounded good to her. "Something came to me yesterday. I wanted to get your take on it."

"What's that?"

"The way Kyle looks at me . . . Could he be the one who asked my granddad if he could adopt me?" She shook her head. "I know that doesn't mean he killed my parents, but I wondered if that was something we should follow up on, just in case."

"You make a good point. After I take you home, I'll go have another chat with him."

Glad that he had agreed with her assessment, she re-packed the basket while Zach straightened the paper-work on his desk. They were walking toward the door when the phone rang. Grimacing an apology, Zach grabbed it up. "Chief Tanner."

An odd look came across Zach's face and then he said, "I'll tell her." Hanging up the phone, he turned to her with another grimace. "That was Lamont. He called your house and Samantha told him you were here. He wants you to come by his office before you go home."

"Uh-oh. Did he sound angry?"

"Not angry, more like sad."

"I hate that we had to hurt him that way."

"We had no choice."

"I know." She picked up the picnic basket and smiled when Zach pulled it out of her hand. "Will you walk me over there? I promise not to stay more than a few minutes. I just feel like I need to apologize to him."

"I'll drive you over. No open areas until this fucker is caught and behind bars."

Smiling, she caressed his cheek. "I love that you still blush when you say a swearword in front of me."

Turning even redder, he mumbled, "I don't blush."

Laughing, she headed to the door. "Let's go see Lamont. Then you can take me home and make me blush."

Holding her hand, Zach kept Savannah a little behind him as he walked out of the police station. His eyes open for anything unusual, he led her to the patrol car and helped her inside. He ran to the other side, got in, and started up the engine.

"I really don't think anyone's going to try to take a shot at me in broad daylight."

"They tried to kill you in the guesthouse in broad daylight."

She nodded. "Point taken."

He was about to give her another warning about being careful when the radio squawked. "Chief, you there?"

Zach grabbed the mic. "Yeah, I'm here, Hazel."

"I'm patching Bart through."

"Chief." Bart Odom's breathless, excited voice came through the radio. "Something odd's going on over at the Ingrams'."

"Odd how?"

"Looks like they're packing up and leaving."

Shit. Zach shot a look at Savannah, whose eyes reflected his own thoughts. She whispered, "You think they're skipping out, thinking we're onto them?"

"I don't know. But they were told not to leave town." He spoke into the mic. "Keep an eye on them, Bart. If they leave, follow them but don't intercept. I'm on my way."

"Will do," Bart answered.

Zach checked the rearview mirror and started to make a U-turn.

"Wait." Savannah touched his arm. "Where are you going?"

"I'm taking you home."

"But we're right here at Lamont's office."

"I don't want to leave you unprotected."

She picked up the small purse she'd dropped on the floorboard and opened it, showing him her handgun. "I am protected. And I'll call Brody to come pick me up when I'm finished."

He gave her a searching glance. "You're sure?"

She nodded. "Lamont's feelings are already hurt. I hate to turn down an invitation from him."

Zach stopped in front of the mayor's office and got out. Savannah waited for him to open the door for her. Ushering her into the renovated house that had been the mayor's office for as long as Zach could remember, he called out, "Lamont?"

Noting that the receptionist's desk was empty, he went to the private office and knocked on the door. It was opened immediately by a pale, sad-looking version of the Lamont he was used to seeing.

He nodded somberly. "Zach. Savannah. Thanks for coming. This won't take long."

"I need to leave Savannah here with you for a few minutes. A friend of mine will pick her up. We had some trouble last night at the mansion, so don't let her out of your sight. Okay?"

If anything, Lamont went paler. "What kind of trouble?"

"I'll let Savannah explain."

"Then you run along now. I'll watch out for her."

Apparently Savannah had been forgiven, but there had been a definite coolness when Lamont had looked at him. He mentally shrugged. It couldn't be helped. Making enemies of the mayor might not be a good career move, but Savannah's safety trumped his career a million to one. Besides, he wouldn't be police chief once he moved to Nashville.

He looked down at Savannah. "Promise me you won't walk out of the office without Brody."

As if she felt bad about Lamont's cool attitude, she stood on her toes and kissed Zach softly on the mouth. "Cross my heart. See you soon."

Giving an equally cool nod to Lamont, he took one last glance at Savannah and then walked out the door. The sooner he could interview Noreen and Kyle, the sooner he could be back with Savannah. Now the question was, where the hell were the Ingrams headed in such an all-fired hurry? Could they possibly be Maggie and Beckett Wilde's killers?

Savannah waited until Zach walked out the door and then turned to Lamont. "You can't be angry with him. He's only trying to get to the truth."

"I know. It was just so embarrassing to have to go through that interview and admit that, especially to

Zach. I was hoping never to have to revisit my past sins." He waved his hand. "Come on in. Nesta made chocolate chip cookies last night and I think this might be her best batch yet."

Though stuffed from lunch, Savannah knew better than to turn down his offer. Besides, she always had room for chocolate chip cookies.

Sitting in front of his desk, she helped herself to a cookie from the platter Lamont pushed toward her. She bit into the gooey, crispy treat and made appreciative sounds of enjoyment. Poor Lamont seemed so eager to please her, she took another one. He startled her when he suddenly jumped up and said, "Milk. You need milk."

She watched as he went to a small fridge, pulled out a carton of milk, and poured her a large glass.

Knowing she wouldn't be able to finish it all, she merely smiled her thanks and took a sip, then said, "Ice-cold milk and chocolate chip cookies. Doesn't get much better than that."

"Zach said you had some trouble last night. What happened?"

Hoping to keep it as nondramatic as possible, she said, "Someone broke into the mansion with a gun."

Horror crossed his face. "Who? Why? What happened?"

She shrugged. "We're still trying to figure out who and why. Zach had no choice but to shoot him."

His fingers rubbed his forehead as if he had a headache. This new information had obviously distressed him even more. About to reassure him that she was sure they would solve the case soon, she stopped when Lamont sighed heavily and sank deeper into his chair. "I'm going to tell you a story, Savannah. One I never intended to talk about again. But in light of everything that's gone on, I just don't feel like I have a choice. This has just gotten so out of hand."

Not sure where this was going, Savannah settled back into her chair and said cautiously, "Okay."

"You know I loved your mama and daddy like they were my own family."

"And they loved you, too."

"When they were killed, I wanted to die, too. I'd lost my best friend and Nesta lost hers, too. That's why—"

The door burst open behind Savannah. She jerked around, surprised to see Nesta standing at the door. "Sorry to interrupt."

Lamont jumped up from his chair. "Nesta, what are you doing here?"

Her expression one of a long-suffering wife, she sighed heavily. "Cleaning up another one of your messes."

"Nesta, that's not necessary."

Looking as prim and proper as always, Nesta pulled a small gun from her pocket and pointed it at Savannah. "I'm afraid it is, dear."

CHAPTER THIRTY-THREE

Savannah felt as if she'd fallen into a parallel universe where the alter egos of good people lived. Never in a thousand years would she have suspected that Lamont and Nesta had anything to do with her parents' deaths.

She turned to Lamont. "You killed them. But why?"

"Don't be silly, dear," Nesta said. "Lamont couldn't hurt a fly. I did it."

Slender, petite, barely over five feet tall, Nesta Kilgore didn't look strong enough to lift a five-pound sack of flour without help. There was no way she could have committed the murders.

"Nesta, please," Lamont said. "This is all so unnecessary."

Nesta shook her head and threw a pair of handcuffs onto Lamont's desk. "Unfortunately you both have made it very necessary." She nodded at the cuffs. "Handcuff yourself to the arm of the chair, Lamont."

"No, I most certainly will not. Put the gun down, Nesta. This instant."

Cool steel pressed against Savannah's forehead. "You'll never get the bloodstain and brain matter off your desk," Nesta told him. "And I know how you hate a mess."

With a look of profound apology to Savannah, Lamont complied, cuffing both his hands to the arm of the chair. When finished, he looked at his wife again. "Now what?"

Nesta pulled up a chair and sat next to Savannah. Though she was still pointing the weapon at her, at least it wasn't pressed against her head anymore. Releasing a silent breath of relief, Savannah considered her next move. She hadn't had the chance to call Brody, but Zach would be back at some point. She had to figure out how to disarm Nesta before that happened. The thought of Zach walking in with no warning of what was going on chilled her blood. There had to be a way to get Nesta to see reason.

"Before we get started on our chat, let me ask a very important question of you, Savannah. What did you think of my chocolate chip cookies?"

"What?"

"My cookies. Did you like them? I have a very special secret I only share with a few. I mix a box of store-bought cookie mix in with my homemade mix and then add in a little extra brown sugar and of course extra chocolate chips, too."

Speechless, Savannah didn't answer.

Apparently not happy with Savannah's lack of response, Nesta snapped, "I've won awards."

That cookie now threatening to come back up, Savannah managed weakly, "It was delicious."

As if that had been the most important issue on her mind, Nesta settled back in her chair with a satisfied smile. "Good." Then, with scary speed, she switched subjects. "I guess you're wondering how all this took place."

"Nesta, please . . . don't."

"Lamont, if you don't hush up, I'm going to gag you. Now, let me tell the story." She turned back to Savannah. "After all, it's my story to tell."

As if she was lost in the past, her eyes focused on the wall behind Savannah. "It all started so innocent. Your mama and daddy had that fight at the country club and then Beckett just ups and leaves. Poor Maggie was so upset."

She glanced over at Lamont with a sad smile. "We took her home and then we went home. Everything was just fine until Lamont started in about Beckett." Her gaze moved to Savannah. "We had a terrible argument and Lamont stormed out. I just knew he was going to see Maggie." Her gaze shifted back to Lamont's. "I always felt like second best."

"Oh, Nesta honey, you know that's not true." The surprise and pain in Lamont's voice seemed real.

Feeling completely lost, Savannah said, "But why would you feel second best?"

"Because Maggie was Lamont's first love." Nesta's mouth trembled. "He never stopped loving her."

"Nesta, that is most definitely not true. From the minute we met, you know I only had eyes for you."

"You were a good husband, Lamont, I agree. But I still felt that if Maggie hadn't fallen for Beckett, you would have married her instead."

As Lamont shook his head in denial again, Savannah scrambled to make sense of it all. "Mama was your best friend, Nesta. How could you hurt her?"

"You're right, she was. And I adored Maggie. When I went over to the Wilde house, looking for Lamont, I had no intention of hurting anyone. I didn't see Lamont but I decided to go in and talk to Maggie. I know she wasn't encouraging Lamont. She adored your father and never would have cheated. But someone as beautiful as Maggie didn't need to encourage anyone. She attracted men like bees to honey.

"Maggie got angry with me and told me to stop being so paranoid. I guess I was a little too emotional that night, too. I lost my temper, something I rarely do. Next thing I knew, I had a butcher knife in my hand and

Maggie was on the floor, screaming, and there was blood everywhere."

The calm, unemotional confession was the eeriest one Savannah had ever heard. Nesta was as matter-of-fact as if she were giving directions. Savannah remembered the coroner's report. She'd seen classic overkill enough to recognize the pure rage that had ensued during the murder. Eighteen stab wounds to her mother's chest and torso. Nesta's "a little too emotional" had put her in a killing frenzy that night.

Telling herself that she could carry on a conversation with her parents' brutal murderer at gunpoint, Savannah took controlled breaths, searching for and finding the center of calmness that had helped her deal with traumatic events.

"Then what happened?"

"Well, I was horrified, of course. I mean, it's not like I planned it or anything. She just made me so mad." She shook her head and sighed. "Anyway, I knew I was going to need help, so I called Harlan."

"Harlan Mosby, the police chief?"

Nesta nodded. "Few people are aware that we were distantly related. We didn't care for him, of course. He was from the trashy side of the family, but I must admit, he was extremely helpful." She grimaced. "He made me call Lamont. Said he couldn't handle it on his own. I didn't want to. I knew Lamont would be upset with me. Poor man was in a bar, drowning his troubles because of our fight." She gave her husband another loving smile. "After the initial shock wore off, he couldn't have been more supportive."

"And my father?"

"That was unexpected but ended up working out quite well. Our plan had been for me to go home and clean up, then come back and find Maggie dead. It was going to look like a random burglary gone wrong. But then Beckett came home and caught us. I panicked. There was a heavy crystal bowl on the dining room table. I picked it up and smacked Beckett over the head."

She sighed. "Such a shame. Anyway, that's when Harlan came up with the idea. We would make it look like Beckett killed Maggie in a rage and then felt guilty about it all and killed himself."

"So Harlan and Lamont hung my father?"

"No, dear, you keep acting as if Lamont was involved. He wasn't. His only crime was loving Maggie. And though it grieved me to lose my best friend, in some ways, I think Maggie brought it on herself."

"But Lamont was there, wasn't he?"

"I was there," Lamont answered in a hollow, sad voice. "I couldn't do anything but watch. Beckett was unconscious. Harlan strung him up."

"After it was over, we made a pact to never talk about it." Nesta's sweet face went hard. "And we never would have if you hadn't come back home and started prying into things that weren't your concern."

Arguing that the murder of her parents was most definitely her concern would do no good. "And Harlan Mosby? Did you kill him, too?"

Nesta's eyes gleamed with admiration. "Very perceptive of you, Savannah. I'm impressed."

"How did you know I was even suspicious?"

"The library, dear. I volunteer there. When I saw what you had been looking at, reading for hours, I knew you'd somehow figured out all was not what it seemed." She cocked her head. "How did you figure it out, by the way?"

"My grandfather wrote letters to my grandmother. I found them when I started packing. He didn't believe it was a murder-suicide."

"Letters to your grandmother?" Nesta shook her

head. "Well now, that's something I never even considered. What did he say?"

"Just that he didn't believe it was true. What did you and Harlan Mosby do to him?"

"Nothing, of course. Well, almost nothing. A couple of dead animals here and there, some subtle threats from Harlan about you girls. It really took very little effort to keep him quiet."

That was because protecting his granddaughters had been his top priority.

"And Gibby? Why hurt her?"

"I admit, I panicked a bit. I just didn't know what she knew. She'd never mentioned her suspicions to anyone but I couldn't let her talk to you in case she did know something." A proud gleam entered her eyes as she continued, "I thought it was very inspired of me to stuff our gardener's shoes with socks and wear them. They made nice, lovely prints on the tile."

"The dead possum? The fire? The hit man? All your doing?"

"Yes. The possum was roadkill." She grimaced. "So disgusting. But I thought a dead animal might work, since it worked so well with your granddad. I must say, you have much more backbone than Daniel."

"My grandfather was the finest of men. He was protecting us."

"Oh heavens, dear, I didn't mean to imply otherwise." Nesta looked truly concerned that she had offended Savannah. "He was an incredibly fine man and did a wonderful job raising you girls."

"Why me, Nesta? Everyone in town knew we had launched an investigation. Why did you want to kill me specifically?"

"Because you stirred up a hornet's nest, Savannah. Everything has been so wonderful for the past eighteen years. Ask anyone in Midnight and they'll tell you what good people we are." Tears glazed her eyes as she glanced tenderly over at her husband. When she looked back at Savannah, a cold, unemotional woman had replaced the sweet, slightly quirky Nesta she'd known forever. "You deserved to be punished for messing everything up."

"And you did this all on your own?" Savannah shook her head in disbelief. How could a tiny middle-aged woman who didn't look as though she could send back a bad meal at a restaurant be responsible for all that had happened?

"I'm very versatile. Lamont will tell you that."

Savannah turned to Lamont. "Did you know she was doing these things?"

Looking as miserable as any human being she'd ever seen, Lamont shook his head. "I swear I didn't." He looked at his wife. "Nesta, things would have been just fine if you'd left it alone. They had no proof."

"But I didn't know that, Lamont. I had to take care of this. I know I put you in a bad position. I needed to fix things."

How long had Zach been gone? Twenty, twenty-five minutes? He would be back soon. She needed to decide on her plan of action. Lamont wasn't a concern. Not only was he handcuffed to a chair, his expression of sad defeat said it all. Nesta, with the gun and her bizarre, unpredictable behavior, was the worry. So how to defuse the situation and get all of them out alive before Zach came back? The gun in her purse was her backup plan. For now, she wanted to see if she could talk some sense into Nesta.

"So what's your endgame, Nesta?"

She blinked in confusion. "I'm sorry, Savannah. I don't understand that terminology."

"Where do you see this ending? Surely you don't think killing me in Lamont's office will solve the problem."

She laughed in that little-girl way that Savannah had always thought was sweet. Little had she known that it was hiding a cold-blooded murderer. "Of course not, dear. That would be impossible to explain."

"Then what are your plans?"

Instead of answering, Nesta stood and walked over to Lamont. Her face one of loving devotion, she used the hand not holding the gun to caress her husband's face. "You know I've loved you from the moment I met you? That will never change."

"Nesta," Lamont whispered, obviously horrified at what he was seeing as not good news for him. "What are you going to do?"

She turned to Savannah. "After your parents' deaths, Lamont and I made a vow. In honor of our dear friends Maggie and Beckett, we pledged to make a difference. We volunteered, became model citizens. When Lamont was elected mayor, our number one goal was to get a good, decent chief of police in Midnight. Then Zach came home and we knew we'd found our man. Even though he's the product of that floozy Francine Adams and that a no-account Ralph Henson, he turned out to be a fine man. And when you came home, we did our best to bring you back together."

"You know that Ralph Henson is Zach's father?"

Nesta waved the gun in her hand. "Everybody knew that except poor Zach. After what Ralph and Harlan did to that poor boy before he left for the army, they both should've been strung up."

"You know about that, too?"

"But of course. There aren't too many secrets in Midnight."

"And how are you going to keep secret that you murdered me?"

"Another murder-suicide. Poor Lamont was being questioned by Savannah Wilde. Realizing she was onto him, that she suspected he was the murderer of her parents, he killed her in a panic. Then, realizing there was no way he could explain Savannah's death, he took his own life."

"Nesta. No." Lamont's shocked, whispered plea almost made Savannah feel sorry for him. But she had no sympathy left. Nesta might have done the actual deeds but Lamont was guilty of covering it up.

"As soon as the shots are fired, people will come running," Savannah reminded her.

"I'll just run through Lamont's private door over there." She nodded to a small door beside the window. "He had that put in right after he was elected into office. That way, when someone comes to visit that he doesn't want to see, he can leave without hurting anyone's feelings.

"I'll come running in the front door along with everybody else and be properly horrified." She glanced down at Lamont again. "The grief will be real. We've been married almost thirty years, and in all that time, we've never spent a night apart."

Savannah seized on an idea for distraction, hoping like hell it didn't backfire. Nesta still believed her husband had been at a bar, drinking, when she had killed Maggie. "That doesn't mean he's never slept with anyone else, though."

She didn't know who was the most horrified. Lamont's eyes went wide and his face became ghost white. Even though Nesta had already admitted she was going to kill him, he didn't want her to know about his infidelity?

"What are you talking about?" Nesta snapped. "Lamont has always been faithful."

Savannah lowered her right hand. Her purse hung from the arm of her chair. If she could distract Nesta long enough, she could grab it and turn the tables.

"But that's not true, is it, Lamont? Henson's not the only one who slept with the town's floozy." Savannah winced as she said the words.

Nesta whipped around and stared at Lamont. "No, that can't be true. Tell me you did not sleep with that whore!"

Lamont started sputtering excuses as Nesta screeched like a crazed banshee. Savannah acted. Grabbing the gun from her purse, she unlocked the safety and held it steady, pointed directly at Nesta. Thankfully the woman was too busy screaming at Lamont to notice. Now to get the woman to drop the gun before she shot Lamont in her rage.

CHAPTER
THIRTY-FOUR

Zach pulled up in front of Lamont's office. When Bart had called about the Ingrams moving out in a hurry, he'd hoped they'd finally found their killers. Unfortunately, in his eagerness to help, Bart had jumped the gun. What looked like Noreen and Kyle moving out was late spring cleaning. They'd piled both of their cars up with stuff they were taking to the Baptist church for a garage sale.

Still, he'd taken a few minutes to talk with Kyle again and confirmed Savannah's suspicions. Kyle Ingram had indeed been the one to ask if he could adopt Savannah. That churned Zach's guts and he'd taken the opportunity to have another frank, open, one-sided talk with the son of a bitch. Finally, at last, the man got the message. Unless he misinterpreted Kyle's wide-eyed terror, Savannah would never have problems with the man. Taking the time to scare the shit out of Kyle had been well worth Zach's time.

Since he'd only been gone about twenty minutes, Zach figured Savannah was still visiting with Lamont. It was going to take some time to mend the rift in their relationship. He put his hand on the doorknob and then jerked to a halt. He'd trusted his gut his whole life. The one time he hadn't, he'd gotten the hell beaten out of him and it had almost destroyed his and Savannah's lives. That same feeling was hitting him now. Something wasn't right.

He turned and ran around to the back of the building. Lamont's office window faced a small alleyway where he normally parked his car. For some reason, seeing Nesta's car parked beside Lamont's didn't surprise him. He pulled his weapon. Staying low, he ran to the window, then eased his head up to peer inside.

In seconds, Zach took in the bizarre, nightmarish scene. Nesta was waving a gun around the room like a maniac. Tears streamed down her face as she shouted obscenities he hadn't heard since he'd left the army. Lamont was handcuffed to a chair, hunkered down into his seat as if he was trying to disappear. And Savannah had her gun pointed at Nesta. Her hand was steady as a rock and she had the determined look on her face he knew well. She believed she was in control. Only problem was, Nesta had her finger on the trigger. The way she was waving the damn thing, there was no telling what she'd hit when it went off. The instant he had that thought, a bullet zinged from Nesta's gun, embedding itself in the door behind Savannah.

Zach aimed his weapon, focusing on Nesta's hand, which had momentarily stilled. Savannah fired off a shot an instant before he could. Zach watched amazed as Nesta's gun flew across the room. Then the woman grabbed her bleeding hand and dropped down to the floor, howling in pain.

Zach busted through the back door and ran into the office. A pale Savannah was sitting in a chair, her gun in her lap. Nesta was in a corner of the room, holding her bleeding hand, howling and spitting obscenities like a seasoned drill sergeant. Poor Lamont looked to be in the worst shape. He was almost lying in his chair, sobbing like a child.

Striding across the room, he secured Nesta's weapon,

emptying the chamber. He turned to Nesta and hand-cuffed her, ignoring her expletives about his ancestry. Couldn't deny that she was right.

Deciding any threat had been neutralized, he finally allowed himself to focus on Savannah. "Are you okay?"

Pale but incredibly composed, she rose to her feet. "What took you so long?"

Grabbing a crime victim and kissing her soundly was probably against somebody's rules, but damned if Zach cared. Holding her as close as possible, he let his mouth show her how grateful he was to have her safe.

"What's going to happen?"

Lamont's tearful question interrupted them. Savannah pulled away slightly to look over at the man. "How could you hide something like that?"

"I had no choice, Savannah. She was my wife. I had to protect her."

Using the radio mic on his sleeve, Zach called for backup and an ambulance. When Hazel assured him both were on their way, he turned to Savannah and said, "Want to tell me what the hell happened?"

Savannah shuddered out a long shaky breath. She was still too pale for his liking. Pulling her back into his arms, he listened in astonishment as she explained what had happened eighteen years ago. She began with the most startling part of all. "Nesta killed my parents."

Hours later, the three Wilde sisters sat on the carpet in their parents' bedroom. A tray with a bottle of wine and three glasses sat in front of them. It seemed only natural to congregate here. Even after all that had happened today, Savannah felt such relief to be able to think of her father in a warm, loving way again. He had been unjustly judged by everyone, most especially by his daughters.

Savannah poured the wine and handed each of her sisters a glass. Taking a sip from her own glass, she gazed around the room. "I wish so much I could tell him how sorry I am."

Sammie sipped her wine and sighed. "I do, too, but somehow I think he knows."

"I hope so."

She looked over at Bri, who seemed even more pensive than usual. "You okay, Bri?"

Bri shook her head. "I just wish people weren't so fucked up."

"Succinct as always," Sammie said. "Having Nesta and Lamont in jail and clearing Daddy's name is a good day's work."

"I guess." Bri raised her glass and said, "To Mama and Daddy."

Tears glazing her eyes, Savannah clinked glasses with her sisters. "Mama and Daddy . . . the most beautiful couple in the world."

"Speaking of beautiful couples, what's going on with you and Zach?" Sammie asked.

"We haven't really had a chance to talk about the future yet. We're going to be together, I know that. Just not sure where yet."

"What do you want to do?"

She had yet to broach the idea she'd come up with yesterday. After having a long talk with each sister, she knew both of them were dealing with some issues in their personal lives. Sammie had even mentioned she needed a major change in her life. The suggestion Savannah was about to make would definitely qualify.

"I want to start a security agency here in Midnight."

It was the first time she'd said the words out loud. And even to her own ears, they sounded damn good.

"A what?" Sammie asked.

402   ELLA GRACE

Interest sparkling in her eyes, Bri asked, "What do you know about running a security agency?"

"Nothing, but that doesn't mean I can't learn. Brody and Logan would be great resources." She shrugged. "Zach has done a lot for this town. I don't want to see Midnight go back to the way it was. Besides, he loves his job."

"I thought you loved your job, too," Bri said. "You're always working."

"I enjoy parts of it, especially the investigative work. I thought I could bring those skills to a new business . . . if I had some good people working with me who had other important skills."

Savannah waited for a response. She wasn't going to pressure either of them if this wasn't something they were interested in.

"You want us to come back here and work with you," Sammie said.

"Only if you want to."

Sammie's eyes locked with Bri's. "It would be wonderful to be together again."

Bri nodded. "It would be a risky career change, especially for you, Sammie. You just made detective."

Anguish swept over Sammie's face and it took every bit of Savannah's strength not to reach out and comfort her. So far, she knew very little about the things Sammie was struggling with. Her sister had made it clear that she would tell them in due time and that she wanted no sympathy or questions.

"It might be the change I need," Sammie said.

"It could be fun," Bri added.

Happy that they hadn't dismissed the idea out of hand, Savannah said, "Think about it. I don't want to push either of you, but I think we could do some good work together." Raising her glass again, Savannah said, "To the Wilde sisters."

The clink of glasses was a sound of an ending and a beginning, Savannah thought. Closure on a sad, painful past and the beginning of a bright, beautiful future.

Zach entered the bedroom, sure that Savannah would be asleep. It was past two in the morning. Arresting the mayor and his wife for eighteen-year-old crimes, along with all the recent crimes Nesta had been part of, was no small matter. He swore he'd be doing paperwork till Christmas. The only bright spot had been the knowledge that Savannah was at home, safe, and waiting for him. Nothing else mattered but that.

Bone tired and feeling like he hadn't showered in days, Zach started to undress when the small lump in the bed shot up and said, "You're home."

"I figured you'd be asleep."

"And miss you coming home to me? No way."

He dropped his pants to the floor. "I'm grungy. Let me shower and I'll be right back to kiss you hello."

The hot spray of the shower seeped into his bones, easing the tension and washing away the filth of the last few hours. Zach turned to grab the soap and heard the shower door open. When he glanced over his shoulder, his breath caught in his throat. She was magnificent— a golden, slender goddess, naked except for a delicate silver chain at her neck. He blinked the water from his eyes and stared at what was hanging from the chain. Moved beyond words, he touched the delicate ring with a shaking hand.

"I could never throw it away, no matter how hard I tried."

Emotion clogged his throat, making his voice husky. "I can't believe you kept it . . . especially after I broke my promise."

"Maybe I knew that someday you would keep that promise."

"Come here." Pulling her into his arms, Zach held her against him, close to his heart. "I will never break another promise. I love you, Savannah. You're my sunshine when there are only clouds, light when there is only darkness."

She lifted her head and gave him a smile so bright his heart clenched at the brilliance. "I've loved you forever, Zach Tanner."

Lowering his mouth to hers, Zach kissed her, savoring this moment with the woman who'd held his heart from the moment she had called him her hero.

Hours later, replete and so relaxed she could barely move, she rose up on her elbow and looked down at the man of her dreams. Having a second chance with this wonderful, heroic man was more than she could ever have hoped for. She vowed that not a day would go by that she didn't cherish what she had been given.

Someday soon she would take him to their daughter's grave. Maggie Rose would have adored her father and she had no doubt that Zach would have been a wonderful daddy to her. And she had pictures at her apartment, dozens of photographs that she could share with him.

Hopefully, in the not-too-distant future, there would be more babies to hold, love, and cherish.

As if he could read her thoughts, he said softly, "Tell me about Maggie Rose."

She smiled as she remembered the tiny, precious infant she'd been gifted with for only a short time. "She was beautiful, Zach. She had a head full of blond wavy hair, a lot like mine. Her chin was all yours, kind of squarish, very determined. She had my nose. Her eyes were a dark blue, of course, but I swear I saw a hint of gray in them, too."

"I would give anything—"

She pressed her fingers to his mouth. "Shh. I know. And she knows." Wrapping her arms tight around him, she whispered, "I like to think that my parents and grandparents are watching over her now."

His voice thick, he said, "I like that idea, too."

"I have something to tell you."

"What's that?"

"My sisters and I have been talking. I want to start a security agency here in Midnight. I've asked them to consider moving back here and working with me."

He rolled onto his side. Their heads sharing a pillow, their lips almost touching, Zach said softly, "You don't want to go back to Nashville? I was planning to quit my job and find something there. You've worked so hard to achieve what you have. I don't want you to give it up."

"I'm not giving it up . . . I'm just refocusing. I don't have the training that Sammie and Bri have, but I've got the investigative skills and I know the law. I would love to give it a try."

"Years ago, you told me you couldn't wait to leave Midnight."

She smiled. "And like you, I've discovered there are a lot more good things about Midnight than bad. You've already made a difference in this town. I want to stay here with you and make a difference, too."

He reached for her hand, kissed it softly, and held it against his heart. Her fingers spread against his chest, she treasured the reassuring thud of his heartbeat.

"If that's what you want, then that's what I want, too."

"Being with you, building a life together here . . . that's what I want."

"Then that's what you'll have. Anything and everything you wish for, I want to give you."

"You're all I want."

He closed the distance between them and she felt the smile on his lips as he whispered against her mouth, "Then, baby, I'm yours."

EPILOGUE

ONE WEEK LATER

His hands shoved into the pockets of his jeans, Zach stood on the porch, waiting for someone to open the door. He had this planned down to the last detail, except he hadn't counted on his date not showing up. Finally the door opened and Bri said, "What are you doing out here?"

Feeling like an idiot, since they all knew he had a key to the house, he said, "I'm picking Savannah up for our date."

Sabrina grinned and stepped back. "Oh, I didn't get that. Come in. I'm sure Savannah will be down soon."

Entering the house, he stood just inside the door, feeling as nervous and awkward as he had ten years ago on their first date together. And just as it had on that first date, his breath caught in his throat the instant he spotted Savannah coming down the stairs.

He had told her nothing about his plans. Somehow, though, she had recognized the significance, because he could swear she was wearing an exact replica of the dress she'd worn their last night together. Hard to believe she could outshine the beauty she had been that night, but she did. Blond wavy hair flowed over her shoulders like a bright rippling waterfall. Her skin, slightly golden from the sun, glowed with an inner light, and her full lips glistened, making him want to cover them and drown in her taste.

She stood before him and gave him that shy, sweet smile he had dreamed about for years. This night was the culmination of ten years of fantasies.

"You look beautiful."

She whirled around the same way she had that night and said, "Sammie and Bri helped me dress. Just like old times."

Holding out his hand, he pulled her into his arms and whispered against her mouth, "Let's go see what else we can re-create."

Savannah watched Zach's hands on the steering wheel. She remembered looking at his hands on their first date and thinking how strong and capable they seemed. Now they were even more so. Large and thick veined, with a sprinkling of dark hair, those hands spoke of maturity and experience. And they could give the most delicious pleasure.

"Are you hungry?"

"Starving. I've been locked in Granddad's study doing research all day."

"Brody and Logan able to help you?"

She nodded, thinking how Zach's friends had been invaluable. Not only had Brody and Logan offered to send business her way, they had answered innumerable questions.

"I was worried that since we're in a small town, no one would ever hear of the agency. Having Brody and Logan steer business our way will help me get started."

"Have Bri and Sammie made up their minds yet?"

"Not yet. I don't want to rush them. It's a huge deci-sion for them to make. If they come on board, they'll have to go to training in Birmingham for a few weeks."

He shot her an odd glance. "You're not going for training?"

"Not for a while." She shrugged and added, "I'm not sure when Lamont's and Nesta's trial will take place. I've got a call in to the prosecutor's office to see if he has any idea. I know they're really backed up, but whenever it is, I have to be available."

Savannah didn't add that there was another reason she wasn't ready to leave town. For ten years, she had given total focus to her education and career. And while fulfillment in her career was still vitally important to her, she had no problem letting it take a backseat to her personal life. They hadn't had a chance to talk about marriage or the future. When that happened, she refused to be distracted by anything. She had waited too long for this happiness and she wanted to savor every single moment.

"Reid called again."

"To ask you to reconsider?"

She laughed softly. Two days ago, when she had called her boss and told him she was resigning, he had been stunned. He had called today, apparently hoping she had changed her mind. She hadn't and she wouldn't.

"Yes, but I told him 'No way' once again. I think he finally believed me. He also told me that Donny Lee's sentencing got moved up. He was sentenced this morning to forty-five years. And there have been no more threats from the X-Kings. Looks like that's over for good.

"Thank God for that." He caught her gaze and said, "And you're absolutely sure you have no regrets or second thoughts for giving up your career in Nashville?"

"Absolutely, one hundred percent sure. I'm here to stay."

The brilliant smile he shot her made her heart leap with joy. Even though it had been her decision, she

knew Zach had still worried that regret might set in.
But her decision was unequivocal. Midnight was her
home once again. As was Zach.

"I understand that Nesta and Lamont refused to see
you and your sisters."

She nodded as a lump of emotion clogged her throat.
The knowledge that two people she had loved and
trusted all her life had committed such terrible acts cut
her deeply. Sammie and Bri were just as shocked and
hurt. Today they had gone to the jail, hoping to sit down
and have a calm, rational discussion. They had been
turned away.

"I guess I can't blame them. They have no reasonable
excuse for what they did. I'm just sorry my grandfather
isn't here to see justice served. I can't imagine the tor-
ture he went through all those years, knowing a murderer was in his midst but having no clue who it was."

She was surprised when Zach grabbed her hand from
her lap and held it to his mouth. "Hey, no more talk of
sad stuff. This is a special night. Okay?"

Inhaling deeply, she relaxed contentedly against the
car seat. "Deal. Now tell me what this special night en-
tails."

A wicked grin crossed his face, causing her heart rate
to zoom. "It's a surprise."

Zach didn't think he'd been this nervous even on their
first date. So far, she seemed to be having a good time.
The sad, hollow look on her face when they'd been talking about the Kilgores had disappeared.

Savannah's trust issues had taken another serious
blow. Every time she let her guard down and allowed
people into her life and heart, they seemed to let her
down. No wonder she was so wary. Zach was more
than aware that he was hugely responsible for that lack

of trust. And he planned to spend the rest of his life making that up to her.

She settled back into the car seat with a satisfied sigh. "Dinner was delicious. And the violinist was a nice touch. I've never heard 'Sweet Home Alabama' played on a violin."

Since Mickey's Steakhouse no longer existed, he'd opted for a new restaurant out on the bypass. The atmosphere was a little more upscale than Mickey's butcher-block tables and peanut shells on the floor had been. He had to admit, having a violinist walk through the restaurant playing hometown favorites and love songs worked with the atmosphere he'd been hoping to create tonight.

Now for the biggest test of all.

Zach took a breath. "Savannah, do you trust me?"

He sensed no hesitation when she answered, "Absolutely."

"Will you do something for me?"

"Anything."

His chest tight at her unqualified answer, he held up a scarf and said, "The next part of the night is the surprise. Would you wear this until we get there?"

Instead of fear or distrust, he saw only excited curiosity. She turned her back to him and said, "Better make it tight. I don't trust myself not to peek."

Zach placed the scarf over her eyes and tied the knot at the back of her head, careful to not pull her hair. Then, leaning forward, he pressed a soft kiss to her bare shoulder. "I trust you."

"I'm glad," she whispered softly.

Eager to get to the next part of the night, Zach settled her back against the car seat and buckled her seat belt. Then, unable to resist, he softly kissed the sweet curve of her lips, loving the way her mouth smiled beneath his.

With great reluctance, he released her and started the

engine. If he didn't get out of here, they'd end up making out in the restaurant parking lot. His plans included a much more romantic setting and absolutely no on-lookers.

Turning from the parking lot and heading out of town, he glanced over at her and asked, "Are you too full for dessert?"

Her smile became even broader, telling him she knew exactly what he meant. His entire body clenched when she answered softly, "When I'm with you, I'm never too full for dessert."

This was a new and unique experience for her. Not being able to see enhanced her other senses. And oddly, never had she been more aware of Zach's presence. He had always been bigger than life to her, a fantasy come true. But now she sensed his nearness, inhaled the musk of his aftershave, could hear him breathe.

In darkness, her entire environment shifted to sensation and sound. With the increase in her awareness, she was surprised to realize that she was becoming aroused. With each breath, her nipples, always sensitive, rubbed against her bra and dress. Air from the car vents blew a cool breeze against her skin, caressing and soothing. Inside, she was anything but cool, feeling as though a furnace of heat had been ignited. By the time they made it to their destination for the promised "dessert," she would be ravenous.

His question about trust had almost made her cry. There had been fear in his eyes. She wanted to erase that fear. The mistakes of the past, both his and hers, were gone. He had her wholehearted trust and it meant the world to her that she had his.

The car ride was lasting longer than she had anticipated. Though the scarf covered her eyes completely, she kept them closed anyway. Zach was determined to surprise her and she didn't want to do anything that would give her a clue where they were headed.

When the car slowed and the road became bumpy, she fought a smile. She still wouldn't try to peek, but she had a good idea where they would end up. And she couldn't think of a more appropriate place to go.

The car slowed even more and then came to a stop. Her heart thudding in anticipation, she said, "Are we there yet?"

"Almost. Sit tight for a few minutes, okay?"

She nodded and was rewarded with a quick kiss on her mouth. Then she heard him open his car door and get out. Several minutes passed. She could hear him moving around outside the car but had no idea what he was doing.

Five minutes later her door opened and Zach said, "Sorry it took so long."

She felt him unbuckle her seat belt and then he took her hand, pulling her from the car. Before she could comment, her world tilted as he swept her up in his arms and began to carry her. "I don't want you to get your shoes muddy. It rained a couple of nights ago and the ground is still damp."

If he thought she was going to complain about being carried in his arms, he was crazy. She laughed softly and said, "I can already tell I'm going to love this dessert."

Seconds later he lowered her to the ground. She felt something soft beneath her feet and then Zach's hands were behind her head, untying the scarf. Savannah kept her eyes closed until the cloth was completely gone. And then she opened them to a wonderland.

"Oh, Zach," she whispered softly.

Savannah moved in a slow circle, mesmerized and amazed. Zach had turned a small section of Dogwood

Lake into a twinkling paradise. Hundreds of strands of lights had been weaved into the surrounding trees; the lake sparkled as if it held a million fallen stars. Rose petals of every color surrounded the large blanket lying on the ground—a blanket that looked a little worn with age and wonderfully, dearly familiar.

"I wanted to make it as special for you as possible."

Tears blurred her vision and a sob built up in her chest. Swallowing hard, she said huskily, "I can't imagine anything more beautiful. Thank you so much."

Drawing her down onto the blanket, he tenderly removed her shoes. "Remember our last night together, when I made a promise to you that I was yours forever?"

"Yes."

Zach went to one knee and held out a small box. Savannah's heart was in her throat as she watched him open the box to reveal the most beautiful engagement ring imaginable, an oval emerald surrounded by diamonds.

"I failed you before, Savannah. I swear, with everything that's in me, I'll never fail you again. Would you make me the happiest man on earth and give me the extraordinary honor of marrying me?"

Her heart so full she could barely function, Savannah threw herself into Zach's arms and held him tight. "The honor is all mine, Zach Tanner, and yes, I will marry you."

As though he had feared her answer, he released a huge breath. And then, pulling away from her, he looked down into her eyes. "You were my first love, my only love, and you'll be my last. Till the end of time, I'll be yours forever."

Lowering his head, Zach covered her mouth, giving her an exquisitely tender kiss. Then his tongue licked the seam of her mouth, asking entrance. With a groan,

Savannah opened to him, inviting him inside. Her world tilted again as Zach pushed her gently onto the blanket and with infinite gentleness and reverence began to make love to her.

As heat and need took control, desire consumed them both. Wrapped in the arms of her love, the man who had returned her dreams to her and healed her heart, Savannah knew that whatever the future held for them, they would be together. Hand in hand, heart to heart. Forever.

ACKNOWLEDGMENTS

Though I grew up in Alabama and felt uniquely qualified to make this book authentically Southern, I needed assistance in certain areas. I am forever grateful to all those who shared their knowledge, advice, and expertise with me. And, as always, the amazing support of loved ones and friends is greatly appreciated.

With special thanks to:

Jim, for his unconditional love and support, gifts of chocolate when he knows I'm struggling, and lots of laughter.

My mom, sisters, and aunts who show me each day that girls raised in the South are something special.

My precious fur creatures, who shower me with unconditional love. And a special loving thank-you to my little four-legged office manager, Blossom. Heaven became even sweeter the day you left this earth.

My fabulous readers who, when I told them I was writing a new series based in the South, had only one question: When can we read it? Thank you from the bottom of my heart for following me over to this new adventure as Ella Grace.

Anne, Crystal, Jackie, Kara, Kris, Hope, and Shelly for their help and wonderful words of encouragement.

Heather Leonard, for her assistance on prosecuting attorneys and legalese. And a very special gentleman in South Alabama, for patiently answering my many questions on police chiefs, mayors, and small-town politics. Any mistakes are my own.

My editor, Junessa Viloria, for her insight and lovely words of encouragement. And Kim Whalen and Kate Collins, for steering me in this direction. And the many people at Ballantine who made this book possible, including Gina Wachtel, Beth Pearson, Ted Allen, Deb Dwyer, cover artist Craig White, and cover designer Scott Biel.

Turn the page for an exciting preview
of the second book in the Wildefire Series

MIDNIGHT LIES

by Ella Grace

CHAPTER ONE

ATLANTA, GEORGIA
FIVE MONTHS AGO

Charlene Braddock slammed her laptop closed and hurled it across the bedroom. The hard thud as it crashed against the wall gave her no satisfaction or relief. Jealousy and bitterness sizzled and burned like acid inside her. After three years of trying and failing to regain her ex-husband's affections, she was no closer than the day he'd shoved the divorce papers in her face and demanded she sign them or else. Remembering that look in his eyes always made her shiver. He had been furious. Those steely blue eyes of his had blazed with a passion and intensity she had rarely seen. Instead of dissolving their marriage, she had wanted to tear off her clothes and let him work out all that anger and aggression on her body. When Quinn Braddock got worked up, her libido went into overdrive.

Of course, she'd done nothing of the sort, since she wouldn't have received the response she desired. Quinn's control was legendary. Fury might envelope him but it would never consume him. He kept his emotions on a tight leash. Even their final argument before he'd walked out the door for the last time hadn't produced any drama. Sure, there had been full-blown anger, but he'd never let himself get out of control.

Not that Quinn was a cold fish. Oh no, there was definitely passion in him. She had felt and tasted its intensity. Early in their marriage, he had been insatiable. Back then, their apartment had been small and there hadn't been a wall or flat surface where they hadn't screwed like minxes.

His career had ruined them. Long hours of work had left her alone with too much time on her hands. Quinn was a gifted doctor with an excellent reputation. Nice for him, but her life had become tedious. When she had complained about her boredom, Quinn's solution had been for her to find a job or do volunteer work. She had wanted to laugh in his face. She was the wife of a physician—she didn't have to do anything so mundane or common.

That was the day she'd gone out and had her first fling. Getting back at Quinn that way had given her immense satisfaction, so she had continued, discreetly, of course, enjoying the pleasures that illicit relationships could bring. Down-and-dirty sex with a variety of men brought delicious danger to a whole new level. Unfortunately, the satisfaction from each encounter provided only a temporary fix. Charlene had still wanted more. More of what, she didn't know. She had only known she wasn't getting it from Quinn. It became a vicious circle. The more he pulled away from her, the more she had craved his attention, which increased her need to screw around even more.

It was all his fault. She had hoped one day he would understand that and come back to her.

Charlene glared over at the ruined laptop. The local online news report had confirmed what she had longed feared: Quinn had a new woman in his life. One who was, no doubt, giving him everything he wanted in the bedroom.

Memories of some of their happier times went through her mind. Her eyes closed on a shiver of arousal. Vanilla sex with Quinn Braddock was better than the hard and rough stuff she got from all of her other lovers combined.

Still she loved the hard, often brutal sex play. Her newest lover gave dangerous liaisons a whole new meaning. He certainly had no issues with giving her all she could take. Sometimes he gave her much more than she could handle. Last time it had gotten so rough, she'd been almost afraid she wouldn't survive. She had begged him to stop. Not that he had. He had told her his loss of control was because of his desire for her and not because he liked to inflict pain. She didn't care what his reasons were. As long as he provided the pleasure she needed, she would keep him. When that ended, so would their relationship.

But she wanted Quinn back, too. They could be good together again if he would just stop being such a tight-ass.

Charlene cursed the day he'd found her with that weasel Nate Lockhart. Not only had the bastard been a poor substitute for her husband, he'd been ridiculously unimaginative. Every time he did something to her, he'd ask if she liked it. Hell, he should have had enough balls not to care.

It had been a mistake to seduce Nate. Having her husband's friend screwing her brains out had been fun the first couple of times. Quinn wouldn't give her the attention she needed, so it had been another way to get back at him. She'd even gotten off on it when she had been having sex with Quinn, thinking how delicious it was to have him inside her where only hours before his friend had been pumping away.

She hadn't expected Quinn to walk in and find them screwing in Nate's office. It had been her little secret, exciting and dangerous.

Quinn's reaction might have been the most humiliating part of all. He had laughed. Even now, years later, she could hear that abrupt bark of laughter. He had seemed genuinely amused and almost relieved. Dammit to hell, how had it all gone so wrong?

This new woman Quinn was seeing . . . who was she? Of course, Quinn had dated several women since they had divorced. He wasn't a monk. But neither was he one to be caught on camera with a woman unless he wanted to be. Was this the woman who would finally take him away from her forever?

The photograph from the fundraiser had been frustratingly bad. The shot showed Quinn's profile as he looked down at his companion. But even the bad picture made it look as though Charlene's tall, gorgeous ex-husband was enamored of the woman. His half smile, with that sexy, quirky edge, had been for only the female beside him. The photo had just shown the back of the woman. Straight, thick hair fell halfway down her back. She was a blonde. Well, dammit, so was Charlene. And a real one at that. This bitch probably got her color from a bottle. And she was fat and wore frumpy clothes, too.

Charlene blew out a frustrated sigh. Okay, so she wasn't exactly fat, but she was nothing like Charlene, who spent hours each week with a personal trainer, honing her body to slender, hard-bodied perfection.

But at least Charlene was right about the woman's dress. It was definitely not designer-made and was conservative by anyone's standards. With Quinn's talents, he was destined to move up in his career. He had a reputation to maintain. One would think he would be more careful in his selection of dates for high-profile events.

On impulse, Charlene grabbed her cellphone from the nightstand. She couldn't let it go . . . she had to try one more time. They'd had some good times, especially at the beginning. If she could just get him to stop being so uptight. His straight-shooter, Eagle Scout demeanor had been charming at first but had worn thin after a while. Living with such perfection could be damn irritating.

He answered on the first ring, his groggy "Braddock" telling her she'd woken him. She refused to feel any guilt for interrupting what was probably much-needed sleep. This was important, dammit.

"It's me, Quinn. I need to see you."

An explosive sigh came through the phone, making her glad she'd woken him up. The prick!

"What is it this time, Charlene?"

Her eyes roamed around the massive bedroom, trying to come up with some new hook to get him to the house. The necklace draped casually on her dresser caught her eye. She hated the thing. Her taste in jewelry ran toward bold and spectacular. The pearl-and-diamond necklace was a Braddock family heirloom, much too understated and old-fashioned for her. Quinn had given it to her a couple of weeks before they married. She'd never worn it, but when he'd asked for it in their divorce settlement, she had gleefully declined. Just one more twist of the knife. He'd been more pissed about her refusal to return the necklace than he had been about finding her screwing Nate. Yes, he would jump at the chance to get it back.

"I've decided to return the Braddock necklace to you."

"Why? What's the catch?"

Dammit, he didn't even try to hide his suspicion.

"No catch. I hate the thing. But if you don't want it, I'll just—"

"Fine. I'll come by this evening and—"

"No, I'm busy this evening. You need to come right away or I'm selling it to a jewelry store."

The long pause that followed made her wonder if she'd played her hand too forcibly. She had tried to entice him over to the house before and had been successful only a few times. But this was something he really wanted.

"I'll be there within the hour. Meet me at the door with it. I won't come in."

She smiled her satisfaction. *We'll just see about that.*

"Of course, darling. Whatever you say." She ended the call and raced to her closet. She had just the outfit for seducing a reluctant ex-husband back into her bed.

The cellphone in her hand rang. Charlene cursed, sure that Quinn was calling to cancel. She glanced down at the display. Recognizing the number, she sighed, part in relief, part in frustration. Phone to her ear, she opened her closet door as she said, "Darling, how are you?"

"Horny."

Her lovers were usually all about pleasing her. From the beginning, this man had been different. He never sugarcoated what he wanted. Sweet talk and flowers were not his way. And though occasionally he was too crass even for her, the things he did to her in bed made up for his inadequacies. Unfortunately this wasn't a good time for him to be horny and demanding.

"I'm sorry, darling, but I have an appointment in a few minutes. Can you come by tonight?"

"An appointment? With whom?"

Though she resented his nosiness, she hesitated in not telling him. His temper had a volatile edge. A couple of times she'd pissed him off and he'd gone way beyond the pain-filled pleasurable lovemaking she enjoyed and into something intensely scary. The last time that had happened, she'd had to hide the bruises for days.

"My ex-husband is dropping by to discuss our divorce settlement."

"I thought your divorce was settled a long time ago."

"It was, but I kept a piece of jewelry he wanted. I'm redecorating my bedroom and came across it while I was putting things away for the workers to come in."

She winced. Dammit, now she'd probably have to do some kind of decorating just to keep him from asking about it later. If he ever learned she had invited Quinn over to get him into bed . . . She shivered at the thought.

"I'll be there tonight at six. Be ready for me."

A different kind of shiver swept through her. After their first time together, he had set ground rules and expectations. One of those was preparing herself for him. He had given her a list of do's and don'ts, including where to shave, what perfume and makeup to wear, what music to have playing when he walked in the door, and what food he required after their playtime had ended. And always, he wanted her naked.

"I'll be ready," she answered with her most sultry tone.

The line went dead and Charlene dropped the phone on the chair beside her. She only had a few minutes to get ready for Quinn. She withdrew the lace-and-silk black negligee and stripped out of her robe. The anticipation and nervousness of seeing Quinn again made her normally graceful movements stilted. It had been years since they'd slept together. Would he notice that her breasts were larger and perkier? The plastic surgeon had done a marvelous job with them; Quinn had always been a breast man.

After slipping the skimpy gown over the head, she stood in front of the full-length mirror to assess her allure. Damn, she looked good. Though she had just passed her thirty-fifth birthday, she didn't look a day over twenty-five. Her tits and ass were perfect. There was no way in hell Quinn could resist her. So what if she'd slept around? It was past time for him to forget about that.

The doorbell rang. She glanced sharply at her clock. He was way too early. She hurriedly put on the necklace he was coming for and then took one last glance in the mirror. His timing didn't really matter. Even with the too-demure necklace, she looked fabulous.

Running lightly down the stairs, Charlene almost laughed with sheer happiness. Things would work out, she was sure of it. Quinn would be enamored of her again, take her to bed, and do all sorts of delicious things to her. And tonight her lover could take care of any remaining sexual needs she might have. What had begun as a lousy day might well be her best ever. Her nipples tightened in anticipation of the coming events.

She opened the door. "Darling, it's so good—" Stopping abruptly, she stared. "What are you doing here? I told you I had an appointment."

His hazel green eyes gleaming wickedly, he moved forward, giving her no choice but to retreat to the middle of the foyer.

He closed the door behind him and sneered, "Is this the kind of outfit you wear to greet your ex-husband?"

She held back a huff of exasperation. The last thing she needed was for him to be here when Quinn arrived. She should have lied when he had asked her about her appointment.

"I was just about to change into something more appropriate."

"But he is coming over. Right?"

"Quinn? Yes, he'll be here in just a few minutes."

"Then there's not much time, is there?"

"Time for what?"

He came closer. "For this."

Charlene looked down at something gleaming in his hand. "What are you talking? What is that? What—"

A knife thrust toward her. So startled by the attack,

she barely felt the pain in her shoulder. Frozen, she stared up at him in horror.

"No, stop, please . . . Stop!"

The knife struck again. She stumbled backward and turned to run. Too late. Agony in her shoulder and back. This time the pain was intense . . . urgent. Twisting around, Charlene screamed as she raised her hands to fight back, slapping ineffectually as the knife descended again and again. Slashing, ripping, destroying.

Blood was everywhere. He was ruining her beautiful gown. The pain was excruciating . . . unbearable. Why, why, why?

The floor appeared before her, slamming into her face. She lay, panting, too tired to cry, too stunned to speak.

A voice from above whispered silkily: "How about it, *darling*? Was it as good for you as it was for me?"

CHAPTER TWO

"Hey, sleepyhead. Wake up."

Samantha Wilde woke with a smile on her face. That sexy baritone growl did it to her every time. Rolling over onto her back, she blinked sleepily up at the harshly beautiful face of Quinn Braddock—surely the most perfect man on earth. Before she could kiss that perfection and entice him back to bed, her foggy brained registered that he was dressed.

"I thought you weren't going to the hospital until later today."

"That's still the plan. Charlene called and asked me to drop by for a few minutes."

Samantha grimaced in sympathy. She had never met Quinn's ex-wife, but she had heard enough stories about the woman to make her glad she hadn't. Not that Quinn would talk about her. Everything she'd heard had come secondhand. The only thing Quinn had ever said was that he never should have married her. The look on his face when her name came up was enough to keep Samantha from asking more. Quinn was a warm and compassionate man but a cold, hard look entered his eyes at the mention of his ex-wife.

Hiding her yawn behind her hand, Samantha gave a full-body stretch, wincing at her slightly stiff muscles. She had tackled a suspect yesterday when he'd tried to run. Though the perp had gotten the worse part when he had tried to fight her, she still had some aches she needed to work out.

"Still sore?"

Nothing got by this man. She'd once told him that if he ever wanted to leave medicine, he'd make a great cop. "Just a little. A hot shower will help."

"I'll give you a massage tonight."

A shiver of anticipation swept through her. "All over?"

He lowered his mouth over hers and spoke against her lips. "Every soft, silky inch of you will know my touch."

Groaning her anticipation, Samantha wrapped her arms around his broad shoulders and pulled him closer. His mouth moved over hers for several long, satisfying seconds. She uttered a small sound of disappointment when he pulled away from her and stood.

"Gotta go."

Samantha propped herself up on her elbows. "Something wrong at Charlene's house?"

"No." His voice went hard and abrupt.

She wasn't put off by his short answer. She just hated that his day was starting off on such a sour note. Considering the things she'd heard about Charlene, Quinn's relationship with his ex-wife was understandably strained. They'd been divorced for three years now, but Charlene had a tendency to call her former husband often. Samantha had no worries that Quinn would be tempted to go back to her. He might not have much to say about her, but if one read between the lines, his opinion of Charlene was just below that of his regard for slugs.

Hoping to get that hard look off his face, she said, "I'll be working until at least nine tonight. Want to meet for a late dinner somewhere?"

As a new homicide detective, Samantha often had unpredictable hours. Fortunately Quinn's hospital schedule was just as grueling and time-consuming, so he understood about her crazy hours and limited time.

He leaned over and pressed an absent-minded kiss to her forehead. "You'll be too tired to go out. Come over to my place and I'll have something for you."

Another reason she had fallen in love with Quinn Braddock. He loved to spoil her.

Smiling her gratitude, she reached up and caressed his clean-shaven jaw. "I'll bring the wine."

He lowered his head again, moving his lips softly, confidently over hers. Samantha pressed upward, wanting a deeper taste. When he pulled away, her lips pouted her disappointment.

"Be careful. You're half a second away from having this sheet stripped away and me inside you."

A familiar delicious throb began. "Have time for a quickie?"

He glanced at her bedside clock. "You know we never can settle for a quickie. Besides, even a quickie wouldn't work. Aren't you testifying again today?"

He was right on both counts. After their first night together, they had learned that their quickies could last for hours. She wasn't the most knowledgeable when it came to sex, but Quinn's expertise made up for her lack of experience. She couldn't imagine a man pleasing her more, inside or outside the bedroom.

Sighing her regret, she made a promise. "Let's plan for an extended quickie tonight."

"You're on."

Samantha watched in admiration as he went across her bedroom to pick up the car keys he'd left on the dresser. She loved the way he walked. For such a tall, broad-shouldered, muscular man, he moved with amazing agility and grace. She could only imagine that all of his patients, at least the female ones, fell instantly in love with him.

When he turned back, her expression must have revealed her thoughts, because he grinned and said, "Stop looking at my ass and get dressed. Telling the judge what delayed you probably won't win you any points."

So true. This was her second day of testimony, and if there was anything clear about the trial, it was that the judge disliked cops—and female ones in particular.

Before she could respond, he headed to the door, that austere, grim expression back in place. "See you tonight."

She grimaced in sympathy. When compared to meeting with a despised ex-spouse, facing an unfriendly judge didn't sound so bad. "I hope it's not too unpleasant."

"I just hope I can get out of there without strangling her," he muttered, and was out of the apartment almost before Samantha could register his astonishing statement. For Quinn to reveal his hatred was rare. Charlene must have really pissed him off this time.

Samantha dropped her head onto her pillow again. Her granddad would have approved of Quinn's restraint in not discussing other people. Though her hometown of Midnight, Alabama, had been rife with gossipers and busybodies, Daniel Wilde had looked upon gossiping as an evil deed. The fact that the Wilde family had often been the subject of those gossipers hadn't helped.

But her grandfather would have approved of Quinn for other reasons, too. She had often worried that she would never find the right man. She had dated often but had never felt a real connection with anyone. Her sisters, Savannah and Sabrina, had called her a hopeless romantic, insisting that there was no perfect man out there. She had been almost to the point of believing that. Then she'd met Quinn.

Silly, but sometimes she worried that he was too perfect. If perhaps she was seeing only what she wanted to see. When she was a kid, how many times had she looked up at her daddy and thought him to be the most perfect man alive? And what had he done? He had brutally murdered her beautiful mother and then had cowardly taken his own life. That had shaken Samantha's trust to the core and destroyed her innocence.

Then, years later, both of her sisters had thought they'd found their perfect matches, only to learn how wrong they'd been. Why should she have faith in any man at all?

Now Savvy was back in Midnight for a short time to ready the Wilde mansion for sale. And she would most likely have to see the man who had shattered her heart. Life was just too damn unfair sometimes.

Even though Samantha and her sisters understandably had trust issues with men, they'd thankfully had one wonderful example. Daniel Wilde, their grandfather, had epitomized everything honorable and good. If Samantha could find a man half as wonderful as Daniel Wilde had been, she would call herself lucky. And unless she was seriously mistaken, that man was Quinn Braddock.

There was one major fly in her happily-ever-after ointment: Quinn wanted nothing permanent—he had made that clear from the start. Samantha, quite confident in her feminine powers, hadn't been worried when he had made that announcement on their first date. It was the first time any man had ever made that stipulation. Instead of being insulted, she had been amused, almost seeing his warning as a challenge. Weeks later, when she realized she was falling in love with him, she wasn't feeling quite so confident and was most definitely not amused.

After almost four months of dating, their relationship was intense, passionate and more satisfying than anything she'd ever experienced. Even sex was exciting and thrilling. Before Quinn, her sex life had been about as bland as cold grits. She had decided that, for her at least, the idea of sex was much more enjoyable than the actual act. She was good at a lot of things . . . she just wasn't good at that one thing.

Then, the first night she and Quinn made love, she had changed her mind. She had been terrified, worried that she would disappoint him. Quinn had been incredible. Patient and oh so very thorough in his intent to pleasure her. Their lovemaking was everything she had wanted and so much more.

Still, even with the amazing connection they had, Quinn was never wavering in his stance on no commitment. He seemed to enjoy their relationship, laughed with her, talked with her, and made love to her until she was breathless and weak. But there had been no indication that he had changed his mind about anything permanent.

She wasn't giving up on her dreams, though. Beneath the façade of toughness she'd adopted to handle her job as a cop, Samantha was still the romantic her sisters had teased her about. The romance novels she had stashed away in bookshelves and drawers throughout her apartment were testaments to her belief in a forever kind of love. And she was a small-town girl, with traditional values. That meant a wedding, babies, PTA meetings, peewee football, and school plays. She wanted it all. Unfortunately, the man she wanted to share all of that with had firmly denied wanting any of those things.

With an explosive sigh, Samantha sprang from the bed and headed for the shower. Her time was too limited to lie in bed and worry. Besides, staying busy had always been her answer to her troubled thoughts. As a teenager, she'd involved herself in every activity possible. It had made her numerous friends and paved the way for opportunities and honors that many had envied. Little had those people known that all of that had been to stay sane. Cheerleading, homecoming queen, class president, and dance and drama classes had all looked like fun and frivolous activities for a spoiled teenaged girl. That had been fine with her. Few saw beyond the shield she had erected to deal with the crushing pain of her parents' deaths.

She had eventually come to terms with her father's betrayal, but work was still her answer to her worries. Being a homicide detective definitely kept her mind from straying into obsessing over things she couldn't change.

After her shower, she pulled her hair up in a tight, brow-raising bun, applied a minimum of makeup, then stepped into a somber black pantsuit and low-heeled black pumps. She hated that she was dressing for the judge, but she couldn't deny it. Yesterday she'd worn what she had considered a conservative skirt and blouse. The judge had glared at her as if she were wearing a bikini. Hopefully an even primmer outfit would help.

The clock chimed eight times. Grabbing the purse she'd dropped on her dresser, she dashed toward the door. A stomach rumble halfway there reminded her she hadn't eaten. Cursing softly, she detoured into the kitchen, poured a cup of coffee from the pot that Quinn had made, and then looked around for something quick. The overripe banana on the counter or a cold Pop-Tart? Quickly deciding, she shook the foil-wrapped pastry from its box, dropped it into her purse, and headed out the door. Maybe she would call Quinn at lunch and see if he had time to spare. The delightful prospect of seeing him in the middle of the day gave her the boost of energy she needed.

Samantha ran down the stairs, enjoying the heady feeling of being young, healthy and in love with an amazing man, gloriously oblivious to the horror her life was about to become.

* * *

Quinn parked his Audi across the street from Charlene's house. Instead of immediately getting out, he took a few seconds to center his thoughts and push aside his usual revulsion at seeing his ex-wife again. Hell of it was, he wasn't nearly as disgusted with her as he was with himself. He'd made some dumbass mistakes in his life, but marrying Charlene had to be the absolute worst.

An image of Sam came into his mind, instantly soothing him. How he'd fallen so hard, so fast, he would never know. He'd met her at the hospital. She'd been there to interview a shooting victim and he'd been headed home after a grueling night in the ER. They had walked onto the elevator together, along with a couple of other people. Someone had asked for a floor number to be pressed, and he and Sam had reached for the button at the same time. He'd practically smashed her finger and had turned to apologize. Whatever words he'd been about to say were instantly forgotten. Beautiful, brilliant sunshine had invaded his life in an instant.

After his divorce, he had vowed he would never become seriously involved with a woman again—or at least not until he was much older. But now he could definitely see having a long-term relationship with Sam. Not marriage. He was done with marriage. But something deeper than the temporary sexual relationships he'd had since his divorce.

Right now, their hectic schedules prevented them from seeing each other every day. Living together would make it easier on both of them. Waking up beside Sam every morning was something he could definitely get used to.

He wasn't ready to share his feelings with her yet, but he knew it wouldn't be long. And he hoped to hell he wasn't misreading what he'd seen in her eyes. Finally he had found someone he could believe in and trust.

The screech of tires pulled Quinn from his thoughts.

Out of the corner of his eyes, he saw a dark streak, like a vehicle leaving in a hurry. Someone most likely late for work.

Pulling in a deep breath, he got out of the car. This wasn't going to get any easier . . . might as well get this behind him. With quick, determined strides, Quinn headed across the street. Two minutes. That's all the time he would give Charlene. If not for the necklace, he wouldn't even consider coming back here.

He wasn't as stupid as she apparently thought. The necklace was to get him inside her house so she could once again try to seduce him back to her bed. That ploy hadn't worked the dozens or so times she had tried. Would never work. But he did want the damn necklace and was willing to stomach her presence for the two minutes it would take to reject her and get what belonged to him.

Totally focused on the front door, he barely glanced at the massive two-story, light brown brick house Charlene had gotten in the divorce settlement. Purchased eight months before their divorce, the house had never been home to Quinn. Before that, they'd had a perfectly nice condo in the city. Charlene had insisted that decorating her own home would fill her creative void.

A few weeks after they moved in, the unsatisfactory marriage he'd stubbornly been keeping together unraveled further. Quinn had spent most of his nights on the sofa in his study. But one day he'd gone to talk to a friend and had gotten his socks blown off. Seeing Nate and Charlene together on the man's couch had cleared up so many things. Instead of the fury other men might have experienced, Quinn had felt only immense relief. At last, he could let go.

That day might have been the end of his marriage but it was also the day he'd finally started living again.

Quinn rang the doorbell and waited. When there was

no immediate answer, he pounded on the door and was surprised when it squeaked open. Charlene had probably left it open, thinking he'd just come inside. That wasn't going to happen.

Pushing the door open wider, he stayed on the other side and called out, "Charlene, I'm here."

The vile stench of blood attacked his senses immediately and caught him off guard. The stink of violence was a scent he knew all too well. Unlike the hospital, where the smell was almost drowned out by antiseptic cleanliness, this was intense and brutal. The way it smelled in battle. He'd been an army combat medic. The foul odors of carnage and dismemberment were scents you never got used to or forgot.

He pushed the door open further and saw the blood. Then he saw her. Lying on the floor, facedown, blood pooled everywhere. God, there was so much of it.

Training kicked in—Quinn didn't think, he acted. Rushing forward, he dropped to his knees, touched her neck to feel for a pulse. Was that a faint flicker? Holding her neck and head in place, he gently rolled her onto her back and saw immediately why there was so much blood. Her throat had been cut, nicked at the carotid artery. She could bleed out in seconds.

Her eyes flickered open, the light blue depths glazed with pain. There was no recognition in them. Quinn had seen it too often not to know she was mere seconds from death.

"Charlene? Stay with me. You're going to be all right. Try to stay awake."

She opened her mouth to speak but there was only a gurgling sound.

Quinn's hand on her throat stopped some of the bleeding but it was seeping through his fingers. She raised her hand toward his face. Quinn grabbed for it but not before she slashed him with her nails across his face. He jerked back and her hand fell to the floor. One last gurgle emerged from her. Quinn watched as her eyes went still and unfocused in death.

Dammit, if only he'd come a few minutes earlier. The only thing to be done now was to call the police and alert them to a murder. Standing, he put his hand in his pocket for his cellphone. The door behind him slammed against the wall. Quinn whirled around.

"Take your hand from your pocket and put both of them in the air."

A uniformed policeman stood at the door, his gun pointed at Quinn.

Easing his hand out of his pocket, he raised his hands, revealing his phone. "I was just about to call the police. She's dead."

"No shit. Looks like you made sure of that."

The sick feeling in his stomach sunk lower in his gut. "I didn't do this. I tried to save her."

"Yeah, right. Just keep your hands up." The officer glanced over his shoulder at his partner and said, "Cuff him and read him his rights."

Knowing that arguing would do no good, Quinn held his words. As his wrists were cuffed, he took one last look at the sad, horrible end to the woman on the floor. She'd been a pathetic, miserable human being and he'd lost any affection for her long ago, but she hadn't deserved this.

In the backseat of the patrol car, headed to the police station, one thought comforted him. At least he knew who he could call. Sam would figure out what to do about this mess. If there was anyone he could count on, it was Samantha Wilde.